FANTASY: THE B

OTHER BOOKS EDITED BY RICH HORTON

———

Fantasy: The Best of the Year, 2006 Edition
Science Fiction: The Best of the Year, 2006 Edition
Science Fiction: The Best of the Year, 2007 Edition
Space Opera

FANTASY: THE BEST OF THE YEAR

2007 EDITION

Edited by Rich Horton

PRIME BOOKS

FANTASY: THE BEST OF THE YEAR
2007 EDITION

Prime Books
www.prime-books.com

ISBN-10: 0-8095-6298-7
ISBN-13: 978-0-8095-6298-5

TABLE OF CONTENTS

———

THE YEAR IN FANTASY, 2006

Rich Horton

In trying to find a common thread linking the best fantasy stories of 2006 I keep coming back to lyricism. The bulk of these stories strike me as in some sense lyrical: usually beautifully written, and also often about exotic settings—settings that evoke the lyrical from writers. Now is this a real "trend" in fantasy writing, or simply a reflection of my taste? Or put more simply, of course the best stories will tend to be better written, and of course they will tend to have more original settings. Still, that seems to be what has attracted me this year, more then, for example, clever plots or urgent action or profound ideas (though there is some of each of those aspects to be found in here as well).

I note for what it is worth that last year I highlighted an increased frequency of contemporary superhero stories and of fairy tale retellings. There aren't really any such in this book this year (though a few stories have a certain redolence of the fairy tale): but there were certainly some fine examples of each of those subgenres published this year, stories that I strongly considered for inclusion here. (For superhero stories, try for instance Elana Frink's "The Los Angeles Women's Auxiliary Superhero League" and Matthew Johnson's "Heroic Measures," and for a couple of audaciously different fairy tale retellings, I suggest Brian Attebery's "Fairest" and Catherynne M. Valente's "Temnaya and the House of Books.")

Fantasy as a short fiction genre remains a bit more fractured than science fiction. Of the traditional "Big Three" science fiction magazine, only half of *F&SF* is devoted to fantasy in any significant way. The next two magazines in prominence, *Realms of Fantasy* and *Interzone*, are respectively a fantasy and a science fiction magazine. But in the smaller magazines, and online, we see a treasure-trove of fantasy. Two newer magazines, each devoted mostly to a different pole of the fantasy axis, are among the leaders: *Fantasy Magazine* (mostly literary in focus) and *Black Gate* (explicitly focused on adventure fantasy). (Here I must note that I am a contributor of reviews and essays to both of those last mentioned magazines, and *Fantasy Magazine* is published by the same outfit this that publishes this book.)

Many of the very small 'zines that have sprung up in recent years, such as *Lady Churchill's Rosebud Wristlet*, *Flytrap* and *Zahir*, feature a wild mix of stories, but always plenty of fantastical work. The leading online magazine (in my opinion), *Strange Horizons*, features a fairly even mix of fantasy with science fiction. Two prominent new sites, *Jim Baen's Universe* and *Orson Scott Card's Intergalactic Medicine Show*, both feature a healthy mix of the two genres as well. The fairly new British magazine *Postscripts* also publishes stories in a variety of genres (mystery as well as fantasy and science fiction). And *Interzone*'s sister publication, *Black Static*, will be mostly focused on darker fantasy stories.

That's a good quantity of sources of fantasy (and I have hardly scratched the surface). I think this was a good year for fantasy stories in terms of quality—as I hope this book demonstrates. But what about the financial health of the genre? Short fiction remains, I fear, a bit of a stepchild. The major magazines appear to be fairly stable, but not by any means growing. Some of the newcomers are quite promising, but far from stable. *Fantasy Magazine* managed a good total of three issues in 2006, but both *Black Gate* and *Black Static* were missing in action this year, though they should be back in 2007. (*Black Gate*'s publisher and editor John O'Neill has hired Howard Andrew Jones to take some of the load off his editing duties, and *Black Static*, it seems, has been waiting for *Interzone* to get fully on track (which seems to have happened) before it continues.) The online sites are energetic and exciting, but I confess I remain concerned about the economic viability of online short fiction—I'm not sure anyone has yet demonstrated a way to make money that way. And the smaller 'zines are mostly labors of love—and I love them for it, but there is only so much that can be done with their budgets.

What about the stories on hand? I always hope for a mix of established voices and newer voices—and I think we have that here. To begin with some of the more well-known writers: M. Rickert is without question one of the most exciting writers in fantasy today and "Journey into the Kingdom" is my favorite story by her to date: beautifully framed, mysterious, about a young man finding a journal which tells the story of a girl growing up as a lighthouse keeper, and the ghosts she meets—and which then winds out of the frame and twists again and again in getting to the "real" story. Peter Beagle's "Salt Wine" is told by an old sailor, whose voice Beagle captures perfectly. The sailor had a friend, who one day saves a merrow (or merman) from a shark. The merrow gives him a treasure: the recipe for salt wine. Salt wine turns out to be a fabulous drink, and the friend enlists our narrator to help him market this, with at first great success. But there is a dark side, a very surprising one, and the realization of this aspect gives the story a strong moral dimension, turning an absorbing sea story into something darker, something quite beautiful and also heartbreaking. Sometimes I have to make fine distinctions in deciding the genre of a story. Geoff Ryman's "Pol Pot's Beautiful Daughter (Fantasy)," despite some science fictional elements, urged throughout that it was a fantasy: and a powerful one, in which the title young woman in near future Cambodia (who shares the name of Pol Pot's real daughter, but apparently does not much resemble her) is forced to come to terms with her father's legacy, the ghosts he left behind.

Daniel Handler offers "Naturally," a lovely bittersweet story about a ghost and a living woman who have a love affair. (This is also part of his 2006 novel *Adverbs*.) Benjamin Rosenbaum's "A Siege of Cranes" is as harrowing and powerful a story as I saw this year. A peasant in what seems the ancient Middle East comes home to find his village destroyed, his wife and daughter gone. He follows the path of destruction to learn the source of the destruction. The resolution is moving, sad, strongly affecting. This is what fantasy can do at its very best.

Many of the most interesting stories in contemporary fantasy are set in alternate versions of our world, not necessarily explicitly linked, but using some of the geography and history of the real world in interesting altered ways. For example, Greg van Eekhout's "The Osteomancer's Son," set in a different Southern California, ruled by a Hierarch who derives his power from the magic of bones—particularly the bones of fantastical or vanished animals such as the mammoth or the kraken. The whole milieu here is spooky and simply different in a very effective fashion. Another even weirder version of, apparently, California is presented in Ysabeau Wilce's "The Lineaments of Gratified Desire," one of a continuing series of stories set in an over-the-top, exotic, and magickal "Calif," with an over-the-top hero: Hardhands, a sexually-charged aristocrat and rock star of sorts saddled with a five-year-old wife—who is a handful herself.

Quite without meaning to, I managed to select stories for both this volume and the companion science fiction volume that were the authors' first sales. Here we have Matthew Corradi's "Journey to Gantica," a lovely fable about a giant girl who makes a journey to try to find people her own size, and who learns that size is measured in many ways. Other stories by relatively new writers include Matthew Johnson's "Irregular Verbs," about a people so skilled at language that they develop individual languages for the smallest groups, even couples—and particularly about the doomed efforts of a bereaved man to preserve the language he and his wife shared. David J. Schwartz is a fairly new writer who has done a lot of intriguing short work in a wide variety of modes: "The Water-Poet and the Four Seasons" is purely a lyrical look at the life of a man—lyrical enough to call to my mind Wallace Stevens's poem "Sea Surface Full of Clouds." Also, Sarah Totton's "A Fish Story" is a wildly inventive and fun story about a land where fish fly—and where girls, as perhaps everywhere, fall in love with the wrong boys.

Jeffrey Ford's "The Night Whiskey" is spookily offbeat, about a small town where one night a year a few people are privileged to drink the title draft, a distillation of the "deathberry," which allows communication with the dead. The story begins as just odd—almost goofy—but modulates to darkness when one man tries to bring back his lost wife via the whiskey. In Margo Lanagan's "A Fine Magic" a magician plans revenge on two beautiful if rather vain sisters who have rejected his suit. The magic described is lovely and scary—and the results uncompromising. Elise Moser's "Citrine: A Fable" is a strong feminist piece set in a vaguely medieval milieu, in which a beautiful "trophy wife" is freed from her loveless marriage by a painter.

Richard Parks's "Moon Viewing at Shijo Bridge" concerns the retrieval of a lost letter which will vindicate the Empress from accusations of infidelity, and thus cement her son's position as heir. But things aren't quite so simple, and someone is playing a much deeper game. The twisty resolution is both clever and emotionally affecting. "The Original Word for Rain" by Peter Higgins is a moving and bittersweet look at a quiet young man obsessed with learning the original language of Adam—and also obsessed with a pretty librarian.

Fantasy remains, I think, the wellspring of the fictional imagination. In very different ways, "mainstream" fiction, science fiction, and mystery are more constrained—which can be very good, as it promotes rigor (and lack of rigor is one of the besetting sins of bad Fantasy)—but which can also be, simply, a constraint. Here we see stories that succeed without constraints—stories in which the writers are both lyrically and imaginatively free, with wonderful results.

JOURNEY INTO THE KINGDOM

———

M. Rickert

The first painting was of an egg, the pale ovoid produced with faint strokes of pink, blue, and violet to create the illusion of white. After that there were two apples, a pear, an avocado, and finally, an empty plate on a white tablecloth before a window covered with gauzy curtains, a single fly nestled in a fold at the top right corner. The series was titled "Journey into the Kingdom."

On a small table beneath the avocado there was a black binder, an unevenly cut rectangle of white paper with the words "Artist's Statement" in neat, square, hand-written letters taped to the front. Balancing the porcelain cup and saucer with one hand, Alex picked up the binder and took it with him to a small table against the wall toward the back of the coffee shop, where he opened it, thinking it might be interesting to read something besides the newspaper for once, though he almost abandoned the idea when he saw that the page before him was handwritten in the same neat letters as on the cover. But the title intrigued him.

AN IMITATION LIFE

Though I always enjoyed my crayons and watercolors, I was not a particularly artistic child. I produced the usual assortment of stick figures and houses with dripping yellow suns. I was an avid collector of seashells and sea glass and much preferred to be outdoors, throwing stones at seagulls (please, no haranguing from animal rights activists, I have long since outgrown this) or playing with my imaginary friends to sitting quietly in the salt rooms of the keeper's house, making pictures at the big wooden kitchen table while my mother, in her black dress, kneaded bread and sang the old French songs between her duties as lighthouse keeper, watcher over the waves, beacon for the lost, governess of the dead.

The first ghost to come to my mother was my own father who had set out the day previous in the small boat heading to the mainland for supplies such as string and rice, and also bags of soil, which, in years past, we emptied into crevices between the rocks and planted with seeds, a makeshift garden and a "brave attempt," as my father called it, referring to the barren stone we lived on.

We did not expect him for several days so my mother was surprised when he returned in a storm, dripping wet icicles from his mustache and behaving strangely, repeating over and over again, "It is lost, my dear Maggie, the garden is at the bottom of the sea."

My mother fixed him hot tea but he refused it, she begged him to take off the wet clothes and retire with her, to their feather bed piled with quilts, but he said, "Tend the light, don't waste your time with me." So my mother, a worried expression on her face, left our little keeper's house and walked against the gale to the lighthouse, not realizing that she left me with a ghost, melting before the fire into a great puddle, which was all that was left of him upon her return. She searched frantically while I kept pointing at the puddle and insisting it was he. Eventually she tied on her cape and went out into the storm, calling his name. I thought that, surely, I would become orphaned that night.

But my mother lived, though she took to her bed and left me to tend the lamp and receive the news of the discovery of my father's wrecked boat, found on the rocky shoals, still clutching in his frozen hand a bag of soil, which was given to me, and which I brought to my mother though she would not take the offering.

For one so young, my chores were immense. I tended the lamp, and kept our own hearth fire going too. I made broth and tea for my mother, which she only gradually took, and I planted that small bag of soil by the door to our little house, savoring the rich scent, wondering if those who lived with it all the time appreciated its perfume or not.

I did not really expect anything to grow, though I hoped that the seagulls might drop some seeds or the ocean deposit some small thing. I was surprised when, only weeks later, I discovered the tiniest shoots of green, which I told my mother about. She was not impressed. By that point, she would spend part of the day sitting up in bed, mending my father's socks and moaning, "Agatha, whatever are we going to do?" I did not wish to worry her, so I told her lies about women from the mainland coming to help, men taking turns with the light. "But they are so quiet. I never hear anyone."

"No one wants to disturb you," I said. "They whisper and walk on tiptoe."

It was only when I opened the keeper's door so many uncounted weeks later, and saw, spread before me, embedded throughout the rock (even in crevices where I had planted no soil) tiny pink, purple, and white flowers, their stems shuddering in the salty wind, that I insisted my mother get out of bed.

She was resistant at first. But I begged and cajoled, promised her it would be worth her effort. "The fairies have planted flowers for us," I said, this being the only explanation or description I could think of for the infinitesimal blossoms everywhere.

Reluctantly, she followed me through the small living room and kitchen, observing that, "The ladies have done a fairly good job of keeping the place neat." She hesitated before the open door. The bright sun and salty scent of the sea, as well as the loud sound of waves washing all around us, seemed to astound her, but then she squinted, glanced at me, and stepped through the door to observe the miracle of the fairies' flowers.

Never had the rock seen such color, never had it known such bloom! My mother walked out, barefoot, and said, "Forget-me-nots, these are forget-me-nots. But where . . . ?"

I told her that I didn't understand it myself, how I had planted the small bag of soil found clutched in my father's hand but had not really expected it to come to much, and certainly not to all of this, waving my arm over the expanse, the flowers having grown in soilless crevices and cracks, covering our entire little island of stone.

My mother turned to me and said, "These are not from the fairies, they are from him." Then she started crying, a reaction I had not expected and tried to talk her out of, but she said, "No, Agatha, leave me alone."

She stood out there for quite a while, weeping as she walked amongst the flowers. Later, after she came inside and said, "Where are all the helpers today?" I shrugged and avoided more questions by going outside myself, where I discovered scarlet spots amongst the bloom. My mother had been bedridden for so long, her feet had gone soft again. For days she left tiny teardrop shapes of blood in her step, which I surreptitiously wiped up, not wanting to draw any attention to the fact, for fear it would dismay her. She picked several of the forget-me-not blossoms and pressed them between the heavy pages of her book of myths and folklore. Not long after that, a terrible storm blew in, rocking our little house, challenging our resolve, and taking with it all the flowers. Once again our rock was barren. I worried what effect this would have on my mother but she merely sighed, shrugged, and said, "They were beautiful, weren't they, Agatha?"

So passed my childhood: a great deal of solitude, the occasional life-threatening adventure, the drudgery of work, and all around me the great wide sea with its myriad secrets and reasons, the lost we saved, those we didn't. And the ghosts, brought to us by my father, though we never understood clearly his purpose, as they only stood before the fire, dripping and melting like something made of wax, bemoaning what was lost (a fine boat, a lady love, a dream of the sea, a pocketful of jewels, a wife and children, a carving on bone, a song, its lyrics forgotten). We tried to provide what comfort we could, listening, nodding, there was little else we could do, they refused tea or blankets, they seemed only to want to stand by the fire, mourning their death, as my father stood sentry beside them, melting into salty puddles that we mopped up with clean rags, wrung out into the ocean, saying what we fashioned as prayer, or reciting lines of Irish poetry.

Though I know now that this is not a usual childhood, it was usual for me, and it did not veer from this course until my mother's hair had gone quite gray and I was a young woman, when my father brought us a different sort of ghost entirely, a handsome young man, his eyes the same blue-green as summer. His hair was of indeterminate color, wet curls that hung to his shoulders. Dressed simply, like any dead sailor, he carried about him an air of being educated more by art than by water, a suspicion soon confirmed for me when he refused an offering of tea by saying, "No, I will not, cannot drink your liquid offered without first asking for a kiss, ah a kiss is all the liquid I desire, come succor me with your lips."

Naturally, I blushed and, just as naturally, when my mother went to check on the lamp, and my father had melted into a mustached puddle, I kissed him. Though I should have been warned by the icy chill, as certainly I should have been warned by the fact of my own father, a mere puddle at the hearth, it was my first kiss and it did not feel deadly to me at all, not dangerous, not spectral, most certainly not spectral, though I did experience a certain pleasant floating sensation in its wake.

My mother was surprised, upon her return, to find the lad still standing, as vigorous as any living man, beside my father's puddle. We were both surprised that he remained throughout the night, regaling us with stories of the wild sea populated by whales, mermaids, and sharks; mesmerizing us with descriptions of the "bottom of the world" as he called it, embedded with strange purple rocks, pink shells spewing pearls, and the seaweed tendrils of sea witches' hair. We were both surprised that, when the black of night turned to the gray hue of morning, he bowed to each of us (turned fully toward me, so that I could receive his wink), promised he would return, and then left, walking out the door like any regular fellow. So convincing was he that my mother and I opened the door to see where he had gone, scanning the rock and the inky sea before we accepted that, as odd as it seemed, as vigorous his demeanor, he was a ghost most certainly.

"Or something of that nature," said my mother. "Strange that he didn't melt like the others." She squinted at me and I turned away from her before she could see my blush. "We shouldn't have let him keep us up all night," she said. "We aren't dead. We need our sleep."

Sleep? Sleep? I could not sleep, feeling as I did his cool lips on mine, the power of his kiss, as though he breathed out of me some dark aspect that had weighed inside me. I told my mother that she could sleep. I would take care of everything. She protested, but using the past as reassurance (she had long since discovered that I had run the place while she convalesced after my father's death), finally agreed.

I was happy to have her tucked safely in bed. I was happy to know that her curious eyes were closed. I did all the tasks necessary to keep the place in good order. Not even then, in all my girlish giddiness, did I forget the lamp. I am embarrassed to admit, however, it was well past four o'clock before I remembered my father's puddle, which by that time had been much dissipated. I wiped up the small amount of water and wrung him out over the sea, saying only as prayer, "Father, forgive me. Oh, bring him back to me." (Meaning, alas for me, a foolish girl, the boy who kissed me and not my own dear father.)

And that night, he did come back, knocking on the door like any living man, carrying in his wet hands a bouquet of pink coral which he presented to me, and a small white stone, shaped like a star, which he gave to my mother.

"Is there no one else with you?" she asked.

"I'm sorry, there is not," he said.

My mother began to busy herself in the kitchen, leaving the two of us alone. I could hear her in there, moving things about, opening cupboards, sweeping the already swept floor. It was my own carelessness that had caused my father's absence, I was sure of that; had I sponged him up sooner, had I prayed for him more sincerely, and not just for the satisfaction of my own desire, he would be here this night. I felt terrible about this, but then I looked into his eyes, those beautiful sea-colored eyes, and I could not help it, my body thrilled at his look. Is this love? I thought. Will he kiss me twice? When it seemed as if, without even wasting time with words, he was about to do so, leaning toward me with parted lips from which exhaled the scent of salt water, my mother stepped into the room, clearing her throat, holding the broom before her, as if thinking she might use it as a weapon.

"We don't really know anything about you," she said.

To begin with, my name is Ezekiel. My mother was fond of saints and the Bible and such. She died shortly after giving birth to me, her first and only child. I was raised by my father, on the island of Murano. Perhaps you have heard of it? Murano glass? We are famous for it throughout the world. My father, himself, was a talented glassmaker. Anything imagined, he could shape into glass. Glass birds, tiny glass bees, glass seashells, even glass tears (an art he perfected while I was an infant), and what my father knew, he taught to me.

Naturally, I eventually surpassed him in skill. Forgive me, but there is no humble way to say it. At any rate, my father had taught me and encouraged my talent all my life. I did not see when his enthusiasm began to sour. I was excited and pleased at what I could produce. I thought he would feel the same for me as I had felt for him, when, as a child, I sat on the footstool in his studio and applauded each glass wing, each hard teardrop.

Alas, it was not to be. My father grew jealous of me. My own father! At night he snuck into our studio and broke my birds, my little glass cakes. In the morning he pretended dismay and instructed me further on keeping air bubbles out of my work. He did not guess that I knew the dismal truth.

I determined to leave him, to sail away to some other place to make my home. My father begged me to stay, "Whatever will you do? How will you make your way in this world?"

I told him my true intention, not being clever enough to lie. "This is not the only place in the world with fire and sand," I said. "I intend to make glass."

He promised me it would be a death sentence. At the time I took this to be only his confused, fatherly concern. I did not perceive it as a threat.

It is true that the secret to glassmaking was meant to remain on Murano. It is true that the entire populace believed this trade, and only this trade, kept them fed and clothed. Finally, it is true that they passed the law (many years before my father confronted me with it) that anyone who dared attempt to take the secret of glassmaking off the island would suffer the penalty of death. All of this is true.

But what's also true is that I was a prisoner in my own home, tortured by my own father, who pretended to be a humble, kind glassmaker, but who, night after night, broke my creations and then, each morning, denied my accusations, his sweet old face mustached and whiskered, all the expression of dismay and sorrow.

This is madness, I reasoned. How else could I survive? One of us had to leave or die. I chose the gentler course.

We had, in our possession, only a small boat, used for trips that never veered far from shore. Gathering mussels, visiting neighbors, occasionally my father liked to sit in it and smoke a pipe while watching the sun set. He'd light a lantern and come home, smelling of the sea, boil us a pot of soup, a melancholic, completely innocent air about him, only later to sneak about his breaking work.

This small boat is what I took for my voyage across the sea. I also took some fishing supplies, a rope, dried cod he'd stored for winter, a blanket, and several jugs of red wine, given to us by the baker, whose daughter, I do believe, fancied me. For you, who have lived so long on this anchored rock, my folly must be apparent. Was it folly? It was. But what else was I to do? Day after day make my perfect art only to have my father, night after night, destroy it? He would destroy me!

I left in the dark, when the ocean is like ink and the sky is black glass with thousands of air bubbles. Air bubbles, indeed. I breathed my freedom in the salty sea air. I chose stars to follow. Foolishly, I had no clear sense of my passage and had only planned my escape.

Of course, knowing what I do now about the ocean, it is a wonder I survived the first night, much less seven. It was on the eighth morning that I saw the distant sail, and, hopelessly drunk and sunburned, as well as lost, began the desperate task of rowing toward it, another folly as I'm sure you'd agree, understanding how distant the horizon is. Luckily for me, or so I thought, the ship headed in my direction and after a few more days it was close enough that I began to believe in my life again.

Alas, this ship was owned by a rich friend of my father's, a woman who had commissioned him to create a glass castle with a glass garden and glass fountain, tiny glass swans, a glass king and queen, a baby glass princess, and glass trees with golden glass apples, all for the amusement of her granddaughter (who, it must be said, had fingers like sausages and broke half of the figurines before her next birthday). This silly woman was only too happy to let my father use her ship, she was only too pleased to pay the ship's crew, all with the air of helping my father, when, in truth, it simply amused her to be involved in such drama. She said she did it for Murano, but in truth, she did it for the story.

It wasn't until I had been rescued, and hoisted on board, that my father revealed himself to me. He spread his arms wide, all great show for the crew, hugged me and even wept, but convincing as was his act, I knew he intended to destroy me.

These are terrible choices no son should have to make, but that night, as my father slept and the ship rocked its weary way back to Murano where I would likely be hung or possibly sentenced to live with my own enemy, my father, I slit the old man's throat. Though he opened his eyes, I do not believe he saw me, but was already entering the distant kingdom.

You ladies look quite aghast. I cannot blame you. Perhaps I should have chosen my own death instead, but I was a young man, and I wanted to live. Even after everything I had gone through, I wanted life.

Alas, it was not to be. I knew there would be trouble and accusation if my father were found with his throat slit, but none at all if he just disappeared in the night, as so often happens on large ships. Many a traveler has simply fallen overboard, never to be heard from again, and my father had already displayed a lack of seafaring savvy to rival my own.

I wrapped him up in the now-bloody blanket but although he was a small man, the effect was still that of a body, so I realized I would have to bend and fold him into a rucksack. You wince, but do not worry, he was certainly dead by this time.

I will not bore you with the details of my passage, hiding and sneaking with my dismal load. Suffice it to say that it took a while for me to at last be standing shipside, and I thought then that all danger had passed.

Remember, I was already quite weakened by my days adrift, and the matter of taking care of this business with my father had only fatigued me further. Certain that I was finally at the end of my task, I grew careless. He was much heavier than he had ever appeared to be. It took all my strength to hoist the rucksack, and (to get the sad, pitiable truth over with as quickly as possible) when I heaved that rucksack, the cord became entangled on my wrist, and yes, dear ladies, I went over with it, to the bottom of the world. There I remained until your own dear father, your husband, found me and brought me to this place, where, for the first time in my life, I feel safe, and, though I am dead, blessed.

Later, after my mother had tended the lamp while Ezekiel and I shared the kisses that left me breathless, she asked him to leave, saying that I needed my sleep. I protested, of course, but she insisted. I walked my ghost to the door, just as I think any girl would do in a similar situation, and there, for the first time, he kissed me in full view of my mother, not so passionate as those kisses that had preceded it, but effective nonetheless.

But after he was gone, even as I still blushed, my mother spoke in a grim voice, "Don't encourage him, Agatha."

"Why?" I asked, my body trembling with the impact of his affection and my mother's scorn, as though the two emotions met in me and quaked there. "What don't you like about him?"

"He's dead," she said, "there's that for a start."

"What about Daddy? He's dead too, and you've been loving him all this time."

My mother shook her head. "Agatha, it isn't the same thing. Think about what this boy told you tonight. He murdered his own father."

"I can't believe you'd use that against him. You heard what he said. He was just defending himself."

"But, Agatha, it isn't what's said that is always the most telling. Don't you know that? Have I really raised you to be so gullible?"

"I am not gullible. I'm in love."

"I forbid it."

Certainly no three words, spoken by a parent, can do more to solidify love than these. It was no use arguing. What would be the point? She, this woman who had loved no one but a puddle for so long, could never understand what was going through my heart. Without more argument, I went to bed, though I slept fitfully, feeling torn from my life in every way, while my mother stayed up reading, I later surmised, from her book of myths. In the morning I found her sitting at the kitchen table, the great volume before her. She looked up at me with dark circled eyes, then, without salutation, began reading, her voice, ominous.

"There are many kinds of ghosts. There are the ghosts that move things, slam doors and drawers, throw silverware about the house. There are the ghosts (usually of small children) that play in dark corners with spools of thread and frighten family pets. There are the weeping and wailing ghosts. There are the ghosts who know that they are dead, and those who do not. There are tree ghosts, those who spend their afterlife in a particular tree (a clue for such a resident might be bite marks on fallen fruit). There are ghosts trapped forever at the hour of their death (I saw one like this once, in an old movie theater bathroom, hanging from the ceiling). There are melting ghosts (we know about these, don't we?), usually victims of drowning. And there are breath-stealing ghosts. These, sometimes mistaken for the grosser vampire, sustain a sort of half-life by stealing breath from the living. They can be any age, but are usually teenagers and young adults, often at that selfish stage when they died. These ghosts greedily go about sucking the breath out of the living. This can be done by swallowing the lingered breath from unwashed cups, or, most effectively of all, through a kiss. Though these ghosts can often be quite seductively charming, they are some of the most dangerous. Each life has only a certain amount of breath within it and these ghosts are said to steal an infinite amount with each swallow. The effect is such that the ghost, while it never lives again, begins to do a fairly good imitation of life, while its victims (those whose breath it steals) edge ever closer to their own death."

My mother looked up at me triumphantly and I stormed out of the house, only to be confronted with the sea all around me, as desolate as my heart.

That night, when he came, knocking on the door, she did not answer it and forbade me to do so.

"It doesn't matter," I taunted, "he's a ghost. He doesn't need doors."

"No, you're wrong," she said, "he's taken so much of your breath that he's not entirely spectral. He can't move through walls any longer. He needs you, but he doesn't care about you at all, don't you get that, Agatha?"

"Agatha? Are you home? Agatha? Why don't you come? Agatha?"

I couldn't bear it. I began to weep.

"I know this is hard," my mother said, "but it must be done. Listen, his voice is already growing faint. We just have to get through this night."

"What about the lamp?" I said.

"What?"

But she knew what I meant. Her expression betrayed her. "Don't you need to check on the lamp?"

"Agatha? Have I done something wrong?"

My mother stared at the door, and then turned to me, the dark circles under her eyes giving her the look of a beaten woman. "The lamp is fine."

I spun on my heels and went into my small room, slammed the door behind me. My mother, a smart woman, was not used to thinking like a warden. She had forgotten about my window. By the time I hoisted myself down from it, Ezekiel was standing on the rocky shore, surveying the dark ocean before him. He had already lost some of his life-like luster, particularly below his knees where I could almost see through him. "Ezekiel," I said. He turned and I gasped at the change in his visage, the cavernous look of his eyes, the skeletal stretch at his jaw. Seeing my shocked expression, he nodded and spread his arms open, as if to say, yes, this is what has become of me. I ran into those open arms and embraced him, though he creaked like something made of old wood. He bent down, pressing his cold lips against mine until they were no longer cold but burning like a fire.

We spent that night together and I did not mind the shattering wind with its salt bite on my skin, and I did not care when the lamp went out and the sea roiled beneath a black sky, and I did not worry about the dead weeping on the rocky shore, or the lightness I felt as though I were floating beside my lover, and when morning came, revealing the dead all around us, I followed him into the water, I followed him to the bottom of the sea, where he turned to me and said, "What have you done? Are you stupid? Don't you realize? You're no good to me dead!"

So, sadly, like many a daughter, I learned that my mother had been right after all, and when I returned to her, dripping with saltwater and seaweed, tiny fish corpses dropping from my hair, she embraced me. Seeing my state, weeping, she kissed me on the lips, our mouths open. I drank from her, sweet breath, until I was filled and she collapsed to the floor, my mother in her black dress, like a crushed funeral flower.

I had no time for mourning. The lamp had been out for hours. Ships had crashed and men had died. Outside the sun sparkled on the sea. People would be coming soon to find out what had happened.

I took our small boat and rowed away from there. Many hours later, I docked in a seaside town and hitchhiked to another, until eventually I was as far from my home as I could be and still be near my ocean.

I had a difficult time of it for a while. People are generally suspicious of someone with no past and little future. I lived on the street and had to beg for jobs cleaning toilets and scrubbing floors, only through time and reputation working up to my current situation, finally getting my own little apartment, small and dark, so different from when I was the lighthouse keeper's daughter and the ocean was my yard.

One day, after having passed it for months without a thought, I went into the art supply store, and bought a canvas, paint, and two paintbrushes. I paid for it with my tip money, counting it out for the clerk whose expression suggested I was placing turds in her palm instead of pennies. I went home and hammered a nail into the wall, hung the canvas on it, and began to paint. Like many a creative person I seem to have found some solace for the unfortunate happenings of my young life (and death) in art.

I live simply and virginally, never taking breath through a kiss. This is the vow I made, and I have kept it. Yes, some days I am weakened, and tempted to restore my vigor with such an easy solution, but instead I hold the empty cups to my face, I breathe in, I breathe everything, the breath of old men, breath of young, sweet breath, sour breath, breath of lipstick, breath of smoke. It is not, really, a way to live, but this is not, really, a life.

For several seconds after Alex finished reading the remarkable account, his gaze remained transfixed on the page. Finally, he looked up, blinked in the dim coffee shop light, and closed the black binder.

Several baristas stood behind the counter busily jostling around each other with porcelain cups, teapots, bags of beans. One of them, a short girl with red and green hair that spiked around her like some otherworld halo, stood by the sink, stacking dirty plates and cups. When she saw him watching, she smiled. It wasn't a true smile, not that it was mocking, but rather, the girl with the Christmas hair smiled like someone who had either forgotten happiness entirely, or never known it at all. In response, Alex nodded at her, and to his surprise, she came over, carrying a dirty rag and a spray bottle.

"Did you read all of it?" she said as she squirted the table beside him and began to wipe it with the dingy towel.

Alex winced at the unpleasant odor of the cleaning fluid, nodded, and then, seeing that the girl wasn't really paying any attention, said, "Yes." He glanced at the wall where the paintings were hung.

"So what'd you think?"

The girl stood there, grinning that sad grin, right next to him now with her noxious bottle and dirty rag, one hip jutted out in a way he found oddly sexual. He opened his mouth to speak, gestured toward the paintings, and then at the book before him. "I, I have to meet her," he said, tapping the book, "this is remarkable."

"But what do you think about the paintings?"

Once more he glanced at the wall where they hung. He shook his head, "No," he said, "it's this," tapping the book again.

She smiled, a true smile, cocked her head, and put out her hand, "Agatha," she said.

Alex felt like his head was spinning. He shook the girl's hand. It was unexpectedly tiny, like that of a child's, and he gripped it too tightly at first. Glancing at the counter, she pulled out a chair and sat down in front of him.

"I can only talk for a little while. Marnie is the manager today and she's on the rag or something all the time, but she's downstairs right now, checking in an order."

"You," he brushed the binder with the tip of his fingers, as if caressing something holy, "you wrote this?"

She nodded, bowed her head slightly, shrugged, and suddenly earnest, leaned across the table, elbowing his empty cup as she did. "Nobody bothers to read it. I've seen a few people pick it up but you're the first one to read the whole thing."

Alex leaned back, frowning.

She rolled her eyes, which, he noticed, were a lovely shade of lavender, lined darkly in black.

"See, I was trying to do something different. This is the whole point," she jabbed at the book, and he felt immediately protective of it, "I was trying to put a story in a place where people don't usually expect one. Don't you think we've gotten awful complacent in our society about story? Like it all the time has to go a certain way and even be only in certain places. That's what this is all about. The paintings are a foil. But you get that, don't you? Do you know," she leaned so close to him, he could smell her breath, which he thought was strangely sweet, "someone actually offered to buy the fly painting?" Her mouth dropped open, she shook her head and rolled those lovely lavender eyes. "I mean, what the fuck? Doesn't he know it sucks?"

Alex wasn't sure what to do. She seemed to be leaning near to his cup. Leaning over it, Alex realized. He opened his mouth, not having any idea what to say.

Just then another barista, the one who wore scarves all the time and had an imperious air about her, as though she didn't really belong there but was doing research or something, walked past. Agatha glanced at her. "I gotta go." She stood up. "You finished with this?" she asked, touching his cup.

Though he hadn't yet had his free refill, Alex nodded.

"It was nice talking to you," she said. "Just goes to show, doesn't it?"

Alex had no idea what she was talking about. He nodded half-heartedly, hoping comprehension would follow, but when it didn't, he raised his eyebrows at her instead.

She laughed. "I mean you don't look anything like the kind of person who would understand my stuff."

"Well, you don't look much like Agatha," he said.

"But I am Agatha," she murmured as she turned away from him, picking up an empty cup and saucer from a nearby table.

Alex watched her walk to the tiny sink at the end of the counter. She set the cups and saucers down. She rinsed the saucers and placed them in the gray bucket they used for carrying dirty dishes to the back. She reached for a cup, and then looked at him.

He quickly looked down at the black binder, picked it up, pushed his chair in, and headed toward the front of the shop. He stopped to look at the paintings. They were fine, boring, but fine little paintings that had no connection to what he'd read. He didn't linger over them for long. He was almost to the door when she was beside him, saying, "I'll take that." He couldn't even fake innocence. He shrugged and handed her the binder.

"I'm flattered, really," she said. But she didn't try to continue the conversation. She set the book down on the table beneath the painting of the avocado. He watched her pick up an empty cup and bring it toward her face, breathing in the lingered breath that remained. She looked up suddenly, caught him watching, frowned, and turned away.

Alex understood. She wasn't what he'd been expecting either. But when love arrives it doesn't always appear as expected. He couldn't just ignore it. He couldn't pretend it hadn't happened. He walked out of the coffee shop into the afternoon sunshine.

Of course, there were problems, her not being alive for one. But Alex was not a man of prejudice.

He was patient besides. He stood in the art supply store for hours, pretending particular interest in the anatomical hinged figurines of sexless men and women in the front window, before she walked past, her hair glowing like a forest fire.

"Agatha," he called.

She turned, frowned, and continued walking. He had to take little running steps to catch up. "Hi," he said. He saw that she was biting her lower lip. "You just getting off work?"

She stopped walking right in front of the bank, which was closed by then, and squinted up at him.

"Alex," he said. "I was talking to you today at the coffee shop."

"I know who you are."

Her tone was angry. He couldn't understand it. Had he insulted her somehow?

"I don't have Alzheimer's. I remember you."

He nodded. This was harder than he had expected.

"What do you want?" she said.

Her tone was really downright hostile. He shrugged. "I just thought we could, you know, talk."

She shook her head. "Listen, I'm happy that you liked my story."

"I did," he said, nodding, "it was great."

"But what would we talk about? You and me?"

Alex shifted beneath her lavender gaze. He licked his lips. She wasn't even looking at him, but glancing around him and across the street. "I don't care if it does mean I'll die sooner," he said. "I want to give you a kiss."

Her mouth dropped open.

"Is something wrong?"

She turned and ran. She wore one red sneaker and one green. They matched her hair.

As Alex walked back to his car, parked in front of the coffee shop, he tried to talk himself into not feeling so bad about the way things went. He hadn't always been like this. He used to be able to talk to people. Even women. Okay, he had never been suave, he knew that, but he'd been a regular guy. Certainly no one had ever run away from him before. But after Tessie died, people changed. Of course, this made sense, initially. He was in mourning, even if he didn't cry (something the doctor told him not to worry about because one day, probably when he least expected it, the tears would fall). He was obviously in pain. People were very nice. They talked to him in hushed tones. Touched him, gently. Even men tapped him with their fingertips. All this gentle touching had been augmented by vigorous hugs. People either touched him as if he would break, or hugged him as if he had already broken and only the vigor of the embrace kept him intact.

For the longest time there had been all this activity around him. People called, sent chatty e-mails, even handwritten letters, cards with flowers on them and prayers. People brought over casseroles, and bread, Jell-O with fruit in it. (Nobody brought chocolate chip cookies, which he might have actually eaten.)

To Alex's surprise, once Tessie had died, it felt as though a great weight had been lifted from him, but instead of appreciating the feeling, the freedom of being lightened of the burden of his wife's dying body, he felt in danger of floating away or disappearing. Could it be possible, he wondered, that Tessie's body, even when she was mostly bones and barely breath, was all that kept him real? Was it possible that he would have to live like this, held to life by some strange force but never a part of it again? These questions led Alex to the brief period where he'd experimented with becoming a Hare Krishna, shaved his head, dressed in orange robes, and took up dancing in the park. Alex wasn't sure but he thought that was when people started treating him as if he were strange, and even after he grew his hair out and started wearing regular clothes again, people continued to treat him strangely.

And, Alex had to admit, as he inserted his key into the lock of his car, he'd forgotten how to behave. How to be normal, he guessed.

You just don't go read something somebody wrote and decide you love her, he scolded himself as he eased into traffic. You don't just go falling in love with breath-stealing ghosts. People don't do that.

Alex did not go to the coffee shop the next day, or the day after that, but it was the only coffee shop in town, and had the best coffee in the state. They roasted the beans right there. Freshness like that can't be faked.

It was awkward for him to see her behind the counter, over by the dirty cups, of course. But when she looked up at him, he attempted a kind smile, then looked away.

He wasn't there to bother her. He ordered French Roast in a cup to go, even though he hated to drink out of paper, paid for it, dropped the change into the tip jar, and left without any further interaction with her.

He walked to the park, where he sat on a bench and watched a woman with two small boys feed white bread to the ducks. This was illegal because the ducks would eat all the bread offered to them, they had no sense of appetite, or being full, and they would eat until their stomachs exploded. Or something like that. Alex couldn't exactly remember. He was pretty sure it killed them. But Alex couldn't decide what to do. Should he go tell that lady and those two little boys that they were killing the ducks? How would that make them feel, especially as they were now triumphantly shaking out the empty bag, the ducks crowded around them, one of the boys squealing with delight? Maybe he should just tell her, quietly. But she looked so happy. Maybe she'd been having a hard time of it. He saw those mothers on *Oprah*, saying what a hard job it was, and maybe she'd had that kind of morning, even screaming at the kids, and then she got this idea, to take them to the park and feed the ducks and now she felt good about what she'd done and maybe she was thinking that she wasn't such a bad mom after all, and if Alex told her she was killing the ducks, would it stop the ducks from dying or just stop her from feeling happiness? Alex sighed. He couldn't decide what to do. The ducks were happy, the lady was happy, and one of the boys was happy. The other one looked sort of terrified. She picked him up and they walked away together, she, carrying the boy who waved the empty bag like a balloon, the other one skipping after them, a few ducks hobbling behind.

For three days Alex ordered his coffee to go and drank it in the park. On the fourth day, Agatha wasn't anywhere that he could see and he surmised that it was her day off so he sat at his favorite table in the back. But on the fifth day, even though he didn't see her again, and it made sense that she'd have two days off in a row, he ordered his coffee to go and took it to the park. He'd grown to like sitting on the bench watching strolling park visitors, the running children, the dangerously fat ducks.

He had no idea she would be there and he felt himself blush when he saw her coming down the path that passed right in front of him. He stared deeply into his cup and fought the compulsion to run. He couldn't help it, though. Just as the toes of her red and green sneakers came into view he looked up. I'm not going to hurt you, he thought, and then, he smiled, that false smile he'd been practicing on her and, incredibly, she smiled back! Also, falsely, he assumed, but he couldn't blame her for that.

She looked down the path and he followed her gaze, seeing that, though the path around the duck pond was lined with benches every fifty feet or so, all of them were taken. She sighed. "Mind if I sit here?"

He scooted over and she sat down, slowly. He glanced at her profile. She looked worn out, he decided. Her lavender eye flickered toward him, and he looked into his cup again. It made sense that she would be tired, he thought, if she'd been off work for two days, she'd also been going that long without stealing breath from cups. "Want some?" he said, offering his.

She looked startled, pleased, and then, falsely unconcerned. She peered over the edge of his cup, shrugged, and said, "Okay, yeah, sure."

He handed it to her and politely watched the ducks so she could have some semblance of privacy with it. After a while she said thanks and handed it back to him. He nodded and stole a look at her profile again. It pleased him that her color already looked better. His breath had done that!

"Sorry about the other day," she said, "I was just . . . "

They waited together but she didn't finish the sentence.

"It's okay," he said, "I know I'm weird."

"No, you're, well—" she smiled, glanced at him, shrugged. "It isn't that. I like weird people. I'm weird. But, I mean, I'm not dead, okay? You kind of freaked me out with that."

He nodded. "Would you like to go out with me sometime?" Inwardly, he groaned. He couldn't believe he just said that.

"Listen, Alex?"

He nodded. Stop nodding, he told himself. Stop acting like a bobblehead.

"Why don't you tell me a little about yourself?"

So he told her. How he'd been coming to the park lately, watching people overfeed the ducks, wondering if he should tell them what they were doing but they all looked so happy doing it, and the ducks looked happy too, and he wasn't sure anyway, what if he was wrong, what if he told everyone to stop feeding bread to the ducks and it turned out it did them no harm and how would he know? Would they explode like balloons, or would it be more like how it had been when his wife died, a slow painful death, eating her away inside, and how he used to come here, when he was a monk, well, not really a monk, he'd never gotten ordained or anything, but he'd been trying the idea on for a while and how he used to sing and spin in circles and how it felt a lot like what he'd remembered of happiness but he could never be sure because a remembered emotion is like a remembered taste, it's never really there. And then, one day, a real monk came and watched him spinning in circles and singing nonsense, and he just stood and watched Alex, which made him self-conscious because he didn't really know what he was doing, and the monk started laughing, which made Alex stop and the monk said, "Why'd you stop?" And Alex said, "I don't know what I'm doing." And the monk nodded, as if this was a very wise thing to say and this, just this monk with his round bald head and wire-rimmed spectacles, in his simple orange robe (not at all like the orange-dyed sheet Alex was wearing) nodding when Alex said, "I don't know what I'm doing," made Alex cry and he and the monk sat down under that tree, and the monk (whose name was Ron) told him about Kali, the goddess who is both womb and grave. Alex felt like it was the first thing anyone had said to him that made sense since Tessie died and after that he stopped coming to the park, until just recently, and let his hair grow out again and stopped wearing his robe. Before she'd died, he'd been one of the lucky ones, or so he'd thought, because he made a small fortune in a dot com, and actually got out of it before it all went belly up while so many people he knew lost everything but then Tessie came home from her doctor's appointment, not pregnant, but with cancer, and he realized he wasn't lucky at all. They met in high school and were together until she died, at home, practically blind by that time and she made him promise he wouldn't just give up on life. So he began living this sort of half-life, but he wasn't unhappy or depressed, he didn't want her to think that, he just wasn't sure. "I sort of lost confidence in life," he said. "It's like I don't believe in it anymore. Not like suicide, but I mean, like the whole thing, all of it isn't real somehow. Sometimes I feel like it's all a dream, or a long nightmare that I can never wake up from. It's made me odd, I guess."

She bit her lower lip, glanced longingly at his cup.

"Here," Alex said, "I'm done anyway."

She took it and lifted it toward her face, breathing in, he was sure of it, and only after she was finished, drinking the coffee. They sat like that in silence for a while and then they just started talking about everything, just as Alex had hoped they would. She told him how she had grown up living near the ocean, and her father had died young, and then her mother had too, and she had a boyfriend, her first love, who broke her heart, but the story she wrote was just a story, a story about her life, her dream life, the way she felt inside, like he did, as though somehow life was a dream. Even though everyone thought she was a painter (because he was the only one who read it, he was the only one who got it), she was a writer, not a painter, and stories seemed more real to her than life. At a certain point he offered to take the empty cup and throw it in the trash but she said she liked to peel off the wax, and then began doing so. Alex politely ignored the divergent ways she found to continue drinking his breath. He didn't want to embarrass her.

They finally stood up and stretched, walked through the park together and grew quiet, with the awkwardness of new friends. "You want a ride?" he said, pointing at his car.

She declined, which was a disappointment to Alex but he determined not to let it ruin his good mood. He was willing to leave it at that, to accept what had happened between them that afternoon as a moment of grace to be treasured and expect nothing more from it, when she said, "What are you doing next Tuesday?" They made a date, well, not a date, Alex reminded himself, an arrangement, to meet the following Tuesday in the park, which they did, and there followed many wonderful Tuesdays. They did not kiss. They were friends. Of course Alex still loved her. He loved her more. But he didn't bother her with all that and it was in the spirit of friendship that he suggested (after weeks of Tuesdays in the park) that the following Tuesday she come for dinner, "nothing fancy," he promised when he saw the slight hesitation on her face.

But when she said yes, he couldn't help it; he started making big plans for the night.

Naturally, things were awkward when she arrived. He offered to take her sweater, a lumpy looking thing in wild shades of orange, lime green, and purple. He should have just let her throw it across the couch, that would have been the casual non-datelike thing to do, but she handed it to him and then, wiping her hand through her hair, which, by candlelight looked like bloody grass, cased his place with those lavender eyes, deeply shadowed as though she hadn't slept for weeks.

He could see she was freaked out by the candles. He hadn't gone crazy or anything. They were just a couple of small candles, not even purchased from the store in the mall, but bought at the grocery store, unscented. "I like candles," he said, sounding defensive even to his own ears.

She smirked, as if she didn't believe him, and then spun away on the toes of her red sneaker and her green one, and plopped down on the couch. She looked absolutely exhausted. This was not a complete surprise to Alex. It had been a part of his plan, actually, but he felt bad for her just the same.

He kept dinner simple, lasagna, a green salad, chocolate cake for dessert. They didn't eat in the dining room. That would have been too formal. Instead they ate in the living room, she sitting on the couch, and he on the floor, their plates on the coffee table, watching a DVD of *I Love Lucy* episodes, a mutual like they had discovered. (Though her description of watching *I Love Lucy* reruns as a child did not gel with his picture of her in the crooked keeper's house, offering tea to melting ghosts, he didn't linger over the inconsistency.) Alex offered her plenty to drink but he wouldn't let her come into the kitchen, or get anywhere near his cup. He felt bad about this, horrible, in fact, but he tried to stay focused on the bigger picture.

After picking at her cake for a while, Agatha set the plate down, leaned back into the gray throw pillows, and closed her eyes.

Alex watched her. He didn't think about anything, he just watched her. Then he got up very quietly so as not to disturb her and went into the kitchen where he, carefully, quietly opened the drawer in which he had stored the supplies. Coming up from behind, eyeing her red and green hair, he moved quickly. She turned toward him, cursing loudly, her eyes wide and frightened, as he pressed her head to her knees, pulled her arms behind her back (to the accompaniment of a sickening crack, and her scream) pressed the wrists together and wrapped them with the rope. She struggled in spite of her weakened state, her legs flailing, kicking the coffee table. The plate with the chocolate cake flew off it and landed on the beige rug and her screams escalated into a horrible noise, unlike anything Alex had ever heard before. Luckily,

Alex was prepared with the duct tape, which he slapped across her mouth. By that time he was rather exhausted himself. But she stood up and began to run, awkwardly, across the room. It broke his heart to see her this way. He grabbed her from behind. She kicked and squirmed but she was quite a small person and it was easy for him to get her legs tied.

"Is that too tight?" he asked.

She looked at him with wide eyes. As if he were the ghost.

"I don't want you to be uncomfortable."

She shook her head. Tried to speak, but only produced muffled sounds.

"I can take that off," he said, pointing at the duct tape. "But you have to promise me you won't scream. If you scream, I'll just put it on, and I won't take it off again. Though, you should know, ever since Tessie died I have these vivid dreams and nightmares, and I wake up screaming a lot. None of my neighbors has ever done anything about it. Nobody's called the police to report it, and nobody has even asked me if there's a problem. That's how it is amongst the living. Okay?"

She nodded.

He picked at the edge of the tape with his fingertips and when he got a good hold of it, he pulled fast. It made a loud ripping sound. She grunted and gasped, tears falling down her cheeks as she licked her lips.

"I'm really sorry about this," Alex said. "I just couldn't think of another way."

She began to curse, a string of expletives quickly swallowed by her weeping, until finally she managed to ask, "Alex, what are you doing?"

He sighed. "I know it's true, okay? I see the way you are, how tired you get and I know why. I know that you're a breath-stealer. I want you to understand that I know that about you, and I love you and you don't have to keep pretending with me, okay?"

She looked around the room, as if trying to find something to focus on. "Listen, Alex," she said, "Listen to me. I get tired all the time 'cause I'm sick. I didn't want to tell you, after what you told me about your wife. I thought it would be too upsetting for you. That's it. That's why I get tired all the time."

"No," he said, softly, "you're a ghost."

"I am not dead," she said, shaking her head so hard that her tears splashed his face. "I am not dead," she said over and over again, louder and louder until Alex felt forced to tape her mouth shut once more.

"I know you're afraid. Love can be frightening. Do you think I'm not scared? Of course I'm scared. Look what happened with Tessie. I know you're scared, too. You're worried I'll turn out to be like Ezekiel, but I'm not like him, okay? I'm not going to hurt you. And I even finally figured out that you're scared 'cause of what happened with your mom. Of course you are. But you have to understand. That's a risk I'm willing to take. Maybe we'll have one night together or only one hour, or a minute. I don't know. I have good genes, though. My parents, both of them, are still alive, okay? Even my grandmother only died a few years ago. There's a good chance I have a lot, and I mean a lot, of breath in me. But if I don't, don't you see, I'd rather spend a short time with you, than no time at all?"

He couldn't bear it, he couldn't bear the way she looked at him as if he were a monster when he carried her to the couch. "Are you cold?"

She just stared at him.

"Do you want to watch more *I Love Lucy*? Or a movie?"

She wouldn't respond. She could be so stubborn.

He decided on *Annie Hall*. "Do you like Woody Allen?" She just stared at him, her eyes filled with accusation. "It's a love story," he said, turning away from her to insert the DVD. He turned it on for her, then placed the remote control in her lap, which he realized was a stupid thing to do, since her hands were still tied behind her back, and he was fairly certain that, had her mouth not been taped shut, she'd be giving him that slack-jawed look of hers. She wasn't making any of this very easy. He picked the dish up off the floor, and the silverware, bringing them into the kitchen, where he washed them and the pots and pans, put aluminum foil on the leftover lasagna and put it into the refrigerator. After he finished sweeping the floor, he sat and watched the movie with her. He forgot about the sad ending. He always thought of it as a romantic comedy, never remembering the sad end. He turned off the TV and said, "I think it's late enough now. I think we'll be all right." She looked at him quizzically.

First Alex went out to his car and popped the trunk, then he went back inside where he found poor Agatha squirming across the floor. Trying to escape, apparently. He walked past her, got the throw blanket from the couch and laid it on the floor beside her, rolled her into it even as she squirmed and bucked. "Agatha, just try to relax," he said, but she didn't. Stubborn, stubborn, she could be so stubborn.

He threw her over his shoulder. He was not accustomed to carrying much weight and immediately felt the stress, all the way down his back to his knees. He shut the apartment door behind him and didn't worry about locking it. He lived in a safe neighborhood.

When they got to the car, he put her into the trunk, only then taking the blanket away from her beautiful face. "Don't worry, it won't be long," he said as he closed the hood.

He looked through his CDs, trying to choose something she would like, just in case the sound carried into the trunk, but he couldn't figure out what would be appropriate so he finally decided just to drive in silence.

It took about twenty minutes to get to the beach; it was late, and there was little traffic. Still, the ride gave him an opportunity to reflect on what he was doing. By the time he pulled up next to the pier, he had reassured himself that it was the right thing to do, even though it looked like the wrong thing.

He'd made a good choice, deciding on this place. He and Tessie used to park here, and he was amazed that it had apparently remained undiscovered by others seeking dark escape.

When he got out of the car he took a deep breath of the salt air and stood, for a moment, staring at the black waves, listening to their crash and murmur. Then he went around to the back and opened up the trunk. He looked over his shoulder, just to be sure. If someone were to discover him like this, his actions would be misinterpreted. The coast was clear, however. He wanted to carry Agatha in his arms, like a bride. Every time he had pictured it, he had seen it that way, but she was struggling again so he had to throw her over his shoulder where she continued to struggle. Well, she was stubborn, but he was too, that was part of the beauty of it, really. But it made it difficult to walk, and it was windier on the pier, also wet. All in all it was a precarious, unpleasant journey to the end.

He had prepared a little speech but she struggled against him so hard, like a hooked fish, that all he could manage to say was, "I love you," barely focusing on the wild expression in her face, the wild eyes, before he threw her in and she sank, and then bobbed up like a cork, only her head above the black waves, those eyes of hers, locked on his, and they remained that way, as he turned away from the edge of the pier and walked down the long plank, feeling lighter, but not in a good way. He felt those eyes, watching him, in the car as he flipped restlessly from station to station, those eyes, watching him, when he returned home, and saw the clutter of their night together, the burned-down candles, the covers to the *I Love Lucy* and *Annie Hall* DVDs on the floor, her crazy sweater on the dining room table, those eyes, watching him, and suddenly Alex was cold, so cold his teeth were chattering and he was shivering but sweating besides. The black water rolled over those eyes and closed them and he ran to the bathroom and only just made it in time, throwing up everything he'd eaten, collapsing to the floor, weeping, *What have I done? What was I thinking?*

He would have stayed there like that, he determined, until they came for him and carted him away, but after a while he became aware of the foul taste in his mouth. He stood up, rinsed it out, brushed his teeth and tongue, changed out of his clothes, and went to bed, where, after a good deal more crying, and trying to figure out exactly what had happened to his mind, he was amazed to find himself falling into a deep darkness like the water, from which, he expected, he would never rise.

But then he was lying there, with his eyes closed, somewhere between sleep and waking, and he realized he'd been like this for some time. Though he was fairly certain he had fallen asleep, something had woken him. In this half state, he'd been listening to the sound he finally recognized as dripping water. He hated it when he didn't turn the faucet tight. He tried to ignore it, but the dripping persisted. So confused was he that he even thought he felt a splash on his hand and another on his forehead. He opened one eye, then the other.

She stood there, dripping wet, her hair plastered darkly around her face, her eyes smudged black. "I found a sharp rock at the bottom of the world," she said and she raised her arms. He thought she was going to strike him, but instead she showed him the cut rope dangling there.

He nodded. He could not speak.

She cocked her head, smiled, and said, "Okay, you were right. You were right about everything. Got any room in there?"

He nodded. She peeled off the wet T-shirt and let it drop to the floor, revealing her small breasts white as the moon, unbuttoned and unzipped her jeans, wiggling seductively out of the tight wet fabric, taking her panties off at the same time. He saw when she lifted her feet that the rope was no longer around them and she was already transparent below the knees. When she pulled back the covers he smelled the odd odor of saltwater and mud, as if she were both fresh and loamy. He scooted over, but only far enough that when she eased in beside him, he could hold her, wrap her wet cold skin in his arms, knowing that he was offering her everything, everything he had to give, and that she had come to take it.

"You took a big risk back there," she said.

He nodded.

She pressed her lips against his and he felt himself growing lighter, as if all his life he'd been weighed down by this extra breath, and her lips were cold but they grew warmer and warmer and the heat between them created a steam until she burned him and still, they kissed, all the while Alex thinking, I love you, I love you, I love you, until, finally, he could think it no more, his head was as light as his body, lying beside her, hot flesh to hot flesh, the cinder of his mind could no longer make sense of it, and he hoped, as he fell into a black place like no other he'd ever been in before, that this was really happening, that she was really here, and the suffering he'd felt for so long was finally over.

THE WATER-POET
AND THE FOUR SEASONS

David J. Schwartz

Spring stands at the Water-Poet's door in a top hat and tails. He raises a white-gloved hand—the one not holding a white cane—to tip his hat. He asks the Water-Poet to write him a fog sestina, a dozen sudden downpours, and forty-three cool showers for tomorrow.

"Absolutely," says the Water-Poet. He puts precipitation to paper over a repast of pastrami on pumpernickel, and presents the product to Spring the proximate morning.

Spring reads fog so thick it muffles sirens and confounds compasses. "Lovely," he says from somewhere in the gray mist beyond the threshold. "Your payment." He thrusts his top hat out of the fog and pulls out a lumpish, blinking puppy.

The puppy is white with black and brown spots. She has long, floppy ears and a pink tongue. The Water-Poet tries to think of a name. Spot? Floppy? Pinky? He decides on Delta, and once the fog has cleared he takes her for a walk. Sort of. Delta walks two blocks and then sits, exhausted. The Water-Poet carries the puppy to a park and sits with her under an old oak tree. A sudden downpour sends a young woman running for shelter beneath the tree, and she smiles at the puppy and the Water-Poet.

"He's cute," says the young woman. "What's his name?"

"It's a she, actually," says the Water-Poet. "Her name is Delta."

"That's nice," says the young woman, "but I was actually talking to the dog."

By the time Summer, in her bathing cap and swim dress, knocks on the Water-Poet's door, the young woman (whose name turns out to be Hilda) is his wife, and she and Delta are both expecting.

Summer has a list inside a waterproof sleeve. "Three dozen thunderstorms, eleven with tornadoes. Sixteen sun-shower sonnets. Hail the size of robin eggs."

The Water-Poet nods. "What about a freak snowstorm?" he asks.

"Not this year," says Summer.

"A waterspout?"

Summer looks thoughtful. "OK. Make it two." Summer pulls her list out of its sleeve and adds, "Wtrspt.—2" at the bottom. Then she replaces the list, seals the sleeve and wishes the Water-Poet a good day.

"And to you," says the Water-Poet. He molds meters marrying moist melodies to meditations on middle age. The waterspouts flow easily from his pen, and the hail is cathartic, but the thunderstorms are dreary and interminable. When he hands the package over to Summer the next morning he knows it's not his best work.

Summer doesn't seem to notice. She puts up a parasol and reads a sonnet. "Lovely," she says. She hands him an acorn in a plastic bag, and a waterproof sleeve with documentation for the IRS. "Nice doing business with you," she says.

The Water-Poet plants the acorn in his front yard, with a stake beside it so he won't mow it down when he does the lawn. An oak tree sprouts and survives the hail and the three-week drought between a flirtatious sun shower and a cluster of severe storms. By the time Autumn drops by, it is forty feet high and shedding gold leaves.

"I need some cold drizzle," Autumn says as children and puppies run through the doorway past him—out to climb the oak tree, out to go trick-or-treating, out to college. Autumn has a receding hairline and patches on the elbows of his corduroy blazer. He smells like roasted pumpkin seeds.

"Some cold drizzle," he repeats, "a rainy-day epic, six or eight dustings and one late-season blizzard."

"Can we skip the blizzard?" asks the Water-Poet. "No one appreciates blizzards this time of year."

"Blizzards are cool!" says his eight-year-old son, on his way out to collect his BS in Meteorological Science.

Autumn spreads his hands. "I need a blizzard."

Delta steps outside and lies down on the porch. Her coat is almost entirely gray, and she barely lifts her head to acknowledge the succession of her children, grandchildren, and great-grandchildren that trot up to sniff hello.

"Do you need an Indian summer?" the Water-Poet asks. "I could do that."

"You're a Water-Poet," Autumn says.

The Water-Poet throws up his hands. "I need an extra day, then," he says, and he does. In despair he dreams dull, dripping skies defying description. But the next day during their weddings the children bury Delta in leaves until she shrugs herself free and chases them around the yard. The Water-Poet runs with them until his ears hurt, and then he sits on the porch massaging Hilda's feet and composing weather in his head.

"Excellent," Autumn says the next morning, as drizzle darkens the shoulders of his blazer. "Your work shows a real maturity."

The Water-Poet doesn't want to hear that. He longs for the brashness of his early work.

Autumn opens his blazer, and a host of sparrows emerges, flapping their wings and chirping. They settle in a row amid the golden oak leaves and perform selections from The Nutcracker. Hilda and the Water-Poet and their children and Delta and her clan all gather to listen, and when the concert is finished they applaud or howl according to their capabilities. The sparrows bow repeatedly until, at some unknown signal, they ascend simultaneously from their perches and wing their way south. The children kiss their parents and leave with Delta's descendants for cities far away. Hilda and the Water-Poet are left in the big empty house with Delta and the oak tree and a single sparrow, which stays behind and builds a nest in the fruit bowl.

By the time Winter comes around Hilda has passed on, and Delta too. The children are married, in love, or happy, and the Water-Poet lives alone with the sparrow and Alpha, son of Omega, one of Delta's great-great-great-grandchildren.

Winter is a pale woman in a fur coat made from an animal that has never heard of Thinsulate. She wears a puffy fur hat and her hands rest in a fur muff. She tells the Water-Poet that she needs sixty-seven flurries, eight Alberta clippers and a collection of slushy haiku.

"I don't do that anymore," says the Water-Poet. "Not since Hilda died."

"You were contracted for a full year," says Winter. "I can ask the attorneys to explain it to you, if you like."

The Water-Poet is too old to deal with lawyers. "Can I have more time?" he asks.

He doesn't need it. A frenzy of frigidity flows from his fountain pen, framing a life in frost. His lyrics are stark and hopeless and exquisite, bitter and cold and beautiful. Almost, when Winter reads seventeen syllables of traffic-snarling sleet, it seems that her porcelain features will melt and weep. But of course they don't.

"You are a master," she says. She reaches into her coat and pulls out a hardcover book bound with embossed leather. "Your payment."

It is a collection of his water-poems. Once Winter has gone, he sticks it into a pocket of his winter coat and trudges through the wet snow piling up on his front lawn. Alpha follows him to the oak, and the sparrow as well. The sparrow flies up into the high branches and sings a song the Water-Poet cannot put a name to.

He begins to climb. It is difficult at first; he is not as strong as he once was. Alpha is reluctant to follow, and whines at the bottom. The Water-Poet rests after he has climbed fifteen feet or so, and calls to the dog in a gentle voice. "Come on, boy. It's not so bad."

When he stops for another rest at the half-mile mark, Alpha comes running up the trunk and offers his head for scratching. The Water-Poet makes soothing sounds, and the dog bounds away to chase butterflies among the branches and the drifting snow. The voice of the sparrow drifts down from far above, and the Water-Poet resumes climbing.

He climbs through the clouds and sits down in a crotch of the tree. Alpha settles himself at his feet, and the sparrow alights on his shoulder. The Water-Poet takes out the book of his poems and begins to read aloud.

The early poems are ones he has all but forgotten, and they are equal parts pretension and raw emotion. Below him strands of cirrus and stratus swell and spread to cover the earth. He reads on through the works of his middle youth while Alpha dozes and the sparrow provides countermelodies to the cadence of encroaching inundation. Lightning flashes illuminate cumulonimbus from below; wall clouds pile up and begin to spin.

Alpha dreams of a land where he runs with his brothers and sisters and never runs out of breath. Squirrels and other things tease his nostrils with their scents, often near but always just out of reach. When he rolls over, hands scratch his belly and voices speak in soothing tones.

The Water-Poet is too tired to weep, too jaded to be moved by his own poems, but the clouds shed tears for him. They pour themselves out over the world and swell the lakes and streams. Coastlines contract and riverfronts sink beneath the inexhaustible reservoir of sadness in the Water-Poet's heart.

Alpha's dream germinates upon a branch of the oak and swells like a butterfly's cocoon. Inside it lives a young Water-Poet, one whose pain is not large enough to drown the world. The sparrow, overcome with despair, flies into the dream and becomes a multitude of birds which dwell in trees and corduroy blazers and other places hidden to Alpha and his kin.

Alpha's dream grows while the world below shrinks under the Water-Poet's works. Cities blink out from beneath the darkness and inflate the cocoon with parks and fire hydrants and veterinarians with gentle hands. Alpha dreams a man in a top hat and tails who pulls off a white glove and pats him on the head. "Good dog," he says.

The dream becomes a globe with the unhappy man and the sleeping dog at its core; beyond it, the drowned world becomes a reservoir, closed off behind a stone firmament.

The Water-Poet reads the last poem in his collection. His throat is dry, and he shrivels and folds in on himself until he shrinks down to an acorn. Summer plucks him up and seals him in a plastic bag.

Alpha sleeps in darkness until a pale hand strikes a match and lights a fire in a cozy fireplace. Winter takes off her heavy coat, picks up the collection of the Water-Poet's works, and sets it on a shelf next to a thousand similar volumes. Then she pulls a ragged paperback romance from her coat pocket, pets Alpha as he sleeps, and settles down in a leather recliner to wait for her turn to come around again.

POL POT'S BEAUTIFUL DAUGHTER (FANTASY)

Geoff Ryman

In Cambodia people are used to ghosts. Ghosts buy newspapers.

They own property.

A few years ago, spirits owned a house in Phnom Penh, at the Tra Bek end of Monivong Boulevard. Khmer Rouge had murdered the whole family and there was no one left alive to inherit it. People cycled past the building, leaving it boarded up. Sounds of weeping came from inside.

Then a professional inheritor arrived from America. She'd done her research and could claim to be the last surviving relative of no fewer than three families. She immediately sold the house to a Chinese businessman, who turned the ground floor into a photocopying shop.

The copiers began to print pictures of the original owners.

At first, single black and white photos turned up in the copied dossiers of aid workers or government officials. The father of the murdered family had been a lawyer. He stared fiercely out of the photos as if demanding something. In other photocopies, his beautiful daughters forlornly hugged each other. The background was hazy like fog.

One night the owner heard a noise and trundled downstairs to find all five photocopiers printing one picture after another of faces: young college men, old women, parents with a string of babies, or government soldiers in uniform. He pushed the big green off-buttons. Nothing happened.

He pulled out all the plugs, but the machines kept grinding out face after face. Women in beehive hairdos or clever children with glasses

48

looked wistfully out of the photocopies. They seemed to be dreaming of home in the 1960s, when Phnom Penh was the most beautiful city in Southeast Asia.

News spread. People began to visit the shop to identify lost relatives. Women would cry, "That's my mother! I didn't have a photograph!" They would weep and press the flimsy A4 sheets to their breasts. The paper went limp from tears and humidity as if it too were crying.

Soon, a throng began to gather outside the shop every morning to view the latest batch of faces. In desperation, the owner announced that each morning's harvest would be delivered direct to *The Truth*, a magazine of remembrance.

Then one morning he tried to open the house-door to the shop and found it blocked. He went 'round to the front of the building and rolled open the metal shutters.

The shop was packed from floor to ceiling with photocopies. The ground floor had no windows—the room had been filled from the inside. The owner pulled out a sheet of paper and saw himself on the ground, his head beaten in by a hoe. The same image was on every single page.

He buried the photocopiers and sold the house at once. The new owner liked its haunted reputation; it kept people away. The FOR SALE sign was left hanging from the second floor.

In a sense, the house had been bought by another ghost.

This is a completely untrue story about someone who must exist.

Pol Pot's only child, a daughter, was born in 1986. Her name was Sith, and in 2004, she was eighteen-years-old.

Sith liked air conditioning and luxury automobiles. Her hair was dressed in cornrows and she had a spiky piercing above one eye. Her jeans were elaborately slashed and embroidered. Her pink T-shirts bore slogans in English: CARE KOOKY. PINK MOLL.

Sith lived like a woman on Thai television, doing as she pleased in lip-gloss and Sunsilked hair. Nine simple rules helped her avoid all unpleasantness.

1. Never think about the past or politics.

2. Ignore ghosts. They cannot hurt you.

3. Do not go to school. Hire tutors. Don't do homework. It is disturbing.

4. Always be driven everywhere in either the Mercedes or the BMW.

5. Avoid all well-dressed Cambodian boys. They are the sons of the estimated 250,000 new generals created by the regime. Their sons can behave with impunity.

6. Avoid all men with potbellies. They eat too well and therefore must be corrupt.

7. Avoid anyone who drives a Toyota Viva or Honda Dream motorcycle.

8. Don't answer letters or phone calls.

9. Never make any friends.

There was also a tenth rule, but that went without saying.

Rotten fruit rinds and black mud never stained Sith's designer sports shoes. Disabled beggars never asked her for alms. Her life began yesterday, which was effectively the same as today.

Every day, her driver took her to the new Soriya Market. It was almost the only place that Sith went. The color of silver, Soriya rose up in many floors to a round glass dome.

Sith preferred the 142nd Street entrance. Its green awning made everyone look as if they were made of jade. The doorway went directly into the ice-cold jewelry rotunda with its floor of polished black and white stone. The individual stalls were hung with glittering necklaces and earrings.

Sith liked tiny shiny things that had no memory. She hated politics. She refused to listen to the news. Pol Pot's beautiful daughter wished the current leadership would behave decently, like her dad always did. To her.

She remembered the sound of her father's gentle voice. She remembered sitting on his lap in a forest enclosure, being bitten by mosquitoes. Memories of malaria had sunk into her very bones. She now associated forests with nausea, fevers, and pain. A flicker of tree-shade on her skin made her want to throw up and the odor of soil or fallen leaves made her gag. She had never been to Angkor Wat. She read nothing.

Sith shopped. Her driver was paid by the government and always carried an AK-47, but his wife, the housekeeper, had no idea who Sith was. The house was full of swept marble, polished teak furniture, iPods, Xboxes, and plasma screens.

Please remember that every word of this story is a lie. Pol Pot was no doubt a dedicated communist who made no money from ruling Cambodia. Nevertheless, a hefty allowance arrived for Sith every month from an account in Switzerland.

Nothing touched Sith, until she fell in love with the salesman at Hello Phones.

Cambodian readers may know that in 2004 there was no mobile phone shop in Soriya Market. However, there was a branch of Hello Phone Cards that had a round blue sales counter with orange trim. This shop looked like that.

Every day Sith bought or exchanged a mobile phone there. She would sit and flick her hair at the salesman.

His name was Dara, which means Star. Dara knew about deals on call prices, sim cards, and the new phones that showed videos. He could get her any call tone she liked.

Talking to Dara broke none of Sith's rules. He wasn't fat, nor was he well dressed, and far from being a teenager, he was a comfortably mature twenty-four years old.

One day, Dara chuckled and said, "As a friend I advise you, you don't need another mobile phone."

Sith wrinkled her nose. "I don't like this one anymore. It's blue. I want something more feminine. But not frilly. And it should have better sound quality."

"Okay, but you could save your money and buy some more nice clothes."

Pol Pot's beautiful daughter lowered her chin, which she knew made her neck look long and graceful. "Do you like my clothes?"

"Why ask me?"

She shrugged. "I don't know. It's good to check out your look."

Dara nodded. "You look cool. What does your sister say?"

Sith let him know she had no family. "Ah," he said and quickly changed the subject. That was terrific. Secrecy and sympathy in one easy movement.

Sith came back the next day and said that she'd decided that the rose-colored phone was too feminine. Dara laughed aloud and his eyes sparkled. Sith had come late in the morning just so that he could ask this question. "Are you hungry? Do you want to meet for lunch?"

Would he think she was cheap if she said yes? Would he say she was snobby if she said no?

"Just so long as we eat in Soriya Market," she said.

She was torn between BBWorld Burgers and Lucky7. BBWorld was big, round, and just two floors down from the dome. Lucky7 Burgers was part of the Lucky Supermarket, such a good store that a tiny jar of Maxwell House cost US$2.40.

They decided on BBWorld. It was full of light and they could see the town spread out through the wide clean windows. Sith sat in silence.

Pol Pot's daughter had nothing to say unless she was buying something.

Or rather she had only one thing to say, but she must never say it.

Dara did all the talking. He talked about how the guys on the third floor could get him a deal on original copies of *Grand Theft Auto*. He hinted that he could get Sith discounts from Bsfashion, the spotlit modern shop one floor down.

Suddenly he stopped. "You don't need to be afraid of me, you know." He said it in a kindly, grownup voice. "I can see, you're a properly brought up girl. I like that. It's nice."

Sith still couldn't find anything to say. She could only nod. She wanted to run away.

"Would you like to go to K-Four?"

K-Four, the big electronics shop, stocked all the reliable brand names: Hitachi, Sony, Panasonic, Philips, or Denon. It was so expensive that almost nobody shopped there, which is why Sith liked it. A crowd of people stood outside and stared through the window at a huge home entertainment center showing a DVD of *Ice Age*. On the screen, a little animal was being chased by a glacier. It was so beautiful!

Sith finally found something to say. "If I had one of those, I would never need to leave the house."

Dara looked at her sideways and decided to laugh.

The next day Sith told him that all the phones she had were too big. Did he have one that she could wear around her neck like jewelry?

This time they went to Lucky7 Burgers, and sat across from the Revlon counter. They watched boys having their hair layered by Revlon's natural beauty specialists.

Dara told her more about himself. His father had died in the wars. His family now lived in the country. Sith's Coca-Cola suddenly tasted of antimalarial drugs.

"But . . . you don't want to *live* in the country," she said.

"No. I have to live in Phnom Penh to make money. But my folks are good country people. Modest." He smiled, embarrassed.

They'll have hens and a cousin who shimmies up coconut trees. There will be trees all around but no shops anywhere. The earth will smell.

Sith couldn't finish her drink. She sighed and smiled and said abruptly, "I'm sorry. It's been cool. But I have to go." She slunk sideways out of her seat as slowly as molasses.

Walking back into the jewelry rotunda with nothing to do, she realized that Dara would think she didn't like him.

And that made the lower part of her eyes sting.

She went back the next day and didn't even pretend to buy a mobile phone. She told Dara that she'd left so suddenly the day before because she'd remembered a hair appointment.

He said that he could see she took a lot of trouble with her hair. Then he asked her out for a movie that night.

Sith spent all day shopping in K-Four.

They met at six. Dara was so considerate that he didn't even suggest the horror movie. He said he wanted to see *Buffalo Girl Hiding*, a movie about a country girl who lives on a farm. Sith said with great feeling that she would prefer the horror movie.

The cinema on the top floor opened out directly onto the roof of Soriya. Graffiti had been scratched into the green railings. Why would people want to ruin something new and beautiful? Sith put her arm through Dara's and knew that they were now boyfriend and girlfriend.

"Finally," he said.

"Finally what?"

"You've done something."

They leaned on the railings and looked out over other people's apartments. West toward the river was a building with one huge roof terrace. Women met there to gossip. Children were playing toss-the-sandal. From this distance, Sith was enchanted.

"I just love watching the children."

The movie, from Thailand, was about a woman whose face turns blue and spotty and who eats men. The blue woman was yucky, but not as scary as all the badly dubbed voices. The characters sounded possessed. It was though Thai people had been taken over by the spirits of dead Cambodians.

Whenever Sith got scared, she chuckled.

So she sat chuckling with terror. Dara thought she was laughing at a dumb movie and found such intelligence charming. He started to chuckle too. Sith thought he was as frightened as she was. Together in the dark, they took each other's hands.

Outside afterward, the air hung hot even in the dark and 142nd Street smelled of drains. Sith stood on tiptoe to avoid the oily deposits and castoff fishbones.

Dara said, "I will drive you home."

"My driver can take us," said Sith, flipping open her Kermit-the-Frog mobile.

Her black Mercedes Benz edged to a halt, crunching old plastic bottles in the gutter. The seats were upholstered with tan leather and the driver was armed.

Dara's jaw dropped. "Who . . . *who* is your father?"

"He's dead."

Dara shook his head. "Who was he?"

Normally Sith used her mother's family name, but that would not answer this question. Flustered, she tried to think of someone who could be her father. She knew of nobody the right age. She remembered something about a politician who had died. His name came to her and she said it in panic. "My father was Kol Vireakboth." Had she got the name right? "Please don't tell anyone."

Dara covered his eyes. "We—my family, my father—we fought for the KPLA."

Sith had to stop herself asking what the KPLA was.

Kol Vireakboth had led a faction in the civil wars. It fought against the Khmer Rouge, the Vietnamese, the King, and corruption. It wanted a new way for Cambodia. Kol Vireakboth was a Cambodian leader who had never told a lie and or accepted a bribe.

Remember that this is an untrue story.

Dara started to back away from the car. "I don't think we should be doing this. I'm just a villager, really."

"That doesn't matter."

His eyes closed. "I would expect nothing less from the daughter of Kol Vireakboth."

Oh for gosh sake, she just picked the man's name out of the air, she didn't need more problems. "Please!" she said.

Dara sighed. "Okay. I said I would see you home safely. I will." Inside the Mercedes, he stroked the tan leather.

When they arrived, he craned his neck to look up at the building. "Which floor are you on?"

"All of them."

Color drained from his face.

"My driver will take you back," she said to Dara. As the car pulled away, she stood outside the closed garage shutters, waving forlornly.

Then Sith panicked. Who was Kol Vireakboth? She went online and Googled. She had to read about the wars. Her skin started to creep. All those different factions swam in her head: ANS, NADK, KPR, and KPNLF. The very names seemed to come at her spoken by forgotten voices.

Soon she had all she could stand. She printed out Vireakboth's picture and decided to have it framed. In case Dara visited.

Kol Vireakboth had a round face and a fatherly smile. His eyes seemed to slant upward toward his nose, looking full of kindly insight. He'd been killed by a car bomb.

All that night, Sith heard whispering.

In the morning, there was another picture of someone else in the tray of her printer.

A long-faced, buck-toothed woman stared out at her in black and white. Sith noted the victim's fashion lapses. The woman's hair was a mess, all frizzy. She should have had it straightened and put in some nice highlights. The woman's eyes drilled into her.

"Can't touch me," said Sith. She left the photo in the tray. She went to see Dara, right away, no breakfast. His eyes were circled with dark flesh and his blue Hello trousers and shirt were not properly ironed.

"Buy the whole shop," Dara said, looking deranged. "The guys in K-Four just told me some girl in blue jeans walked in yesterday and bought two home theatres. One for the salon, she said, and one for the roof terrace. She paid for both of them in full and had them delivered to the far end of Monivong."

Sith sighed. "I'm sending one back." She hoped that sounded abstemious. "It looked too metallic against my curtains."

Pause.

"She also bought an Aido robot dog for fifteen hundred dollars."

Sith would have preferred that Dara did not know about the dog. It was just a silly toy; it hadn't occured to her that it might cost that much until she saw the bill. "They should not tell everyone about their customers' business or soon they will have no customers."

Dara was looking at her as if thinking: *This is not just a nice sweet girl.*

"I had fun last night," Sith said in a voice as thin as high clouds.

"So did I."

"We don't have to tell anyone about my family. Do we?" Sith was seriously scared of losing him.

"No. But Sith, it's stupid. Your family, my family, we are not equals."

"It doesn't make any difference."

"You lied to me. Your family is not dead. You have famous uncles."

She did indeed—Uncle Ieng Sary, Uncle Khieu Samphan, Uncle Ta Mok. All the Pol Pot clique had been called her uncles. "I didn't know them that well," she said. That was true, too.

What would she do if she couldn't shop in Soriya Market anymore? What would she do without Dara?

She begged. "I am not a strong person. Sometimes I think I am not a person at all. I'm just a space."

Dara looked suddenly mean. "You're just a credit card." Then his face fell. "I'm sorry. That was an unkind thing to say. You are very young for your age and I'm older than you and I should have treated you with more care."

Sith was desperate. "All my money would be very nice."

"I'm not for sale."

He worked in a shop and would be sending money home to a fatherless family; of course he was for sale!

Sith had a small heart, but a big head for thinking. She knew that she had to do this delicately, like picking a flower, or she would spoil the bloom. "Let's . . . let's just go see a movie?"

After all, she was beautiful and well brought up and she knew her eyes were big and round. Her tiny heart was aching.

This time they saw *Tum Teav*, a remake of an old movie from the 1960s. If movies were not nightmares about ghosts, then they tried to preserve the past. *When*, thought Sith, *will they make a movie about Cambodia's future? Tum Teav* was based on a classic tale of a young monk who falls in love with a properly brought up girl but her mother opposes the match. They commit suicide at the end, bringing a curse on their village. Sith sat through it stony-faced. *I am not going to be a dead heroine in a romance.*

Dara offered to drive her home again and that's when Sith found out that he drove a Honda Dream. He proudly presented to her the gleaming motorcycle of fast young men. Sith felt backed into a corner.

She'd already offered to buy him. Showing off her car again might humiliate him.

So she broke rule number seven.

Dara hid her bag in the back and they went soaring down Monivong Boulevard at night, past homeless people, prostitutes, and chefs staggering home after work. It was late in the year, but it started to rain.

Sith loved it, the cool air brushing against her face, the cooler rain clinging to her eyelashes.

She remembered being five-years-old in the forest and dancing in the monsoon. She encircled Dara's waist to stay on the bike and suddenly found her cheek was pressed up against his back. She giggled in fear, not of the rain, but of what she felt.

He dropped her off at home. Inside, everything was dark except for the flickering green light on her printer. In the tray were two new photographs. One was of a child, a little boy, holding up a school prize certificate. The other was a tough, wise-looking old man, with a string of muscle down either side of his ironic, bitter smile. They looked directly at her.

They know who I am.

As she climbed the stairs to her bedroom, she heard someone sobbing, far away, as if the sound came from next door. She touched the walls of the staircase. They shivered slightly, constricting in time to the cries.

In her bedroom she extracted one of her many iPods from the tangle of wires and listened to *System of a Down,* as loud as she could. It helped her sleep. The sound of nu-metal guitars seemed to come roaring out of her own heart.

She was woken up in the sun-drenched morning by the sound of her doorbell many floors down. She heard the housekeeper Jorani call and the door open. Sith hesitated over choice of jeans and top. By the time she got downstairs she found the driver and the housemaid joking with Dara, giving him tea.

Like the sunshine, Dara seemed to disperse ghosts.

"Hi," he said. "It's my day off. I thought we could go on a motorcycle ride to the country."

But not to the country. Couldn't they just spend the day in Soriya? No, said Dara, there's lots of other places to see in Phnom Penh.

He drove her, twisting through back streets. How did the city get so poor? How did it get so dirty?

They went to a new and modern shop for CDs that was run by a record label. Dara knew all the cool new music, most of it influenced by Khmer-Americans returning from Long Beach and Compton: Sdey, Phnom Penh Bad Boys, Khmer Kid.

Sith bought twenty CDs.

They went to the National Museum and saw the beautiful Buddha-like head of King Jayavarman VII. Dara, without thinking, ducked and held up his hands in prayer. They had dinner in a French restaurant with candles and wine, and it was just like in a karaoke video, a boy, a girl, and her money all going out together. They saw the show at Sovanna Phum, and there was a wonderful dance piece with sampled 1940s music from an old French movie, with traditional Khmer choreography.

Sith went home, her heart singing, *Dara, Dara, Dara*.

In the bedroom, a mobile phone began to ring, over and over. *Call 1* said the screen, but gave no name or number, so the person was not on Sith's list of contacts.

She turned off the phone. It kept ringing. That's when she knew for certain.

She hid the phone in a pillow in the spare bedroom and put another pillow on top of it and then closed the door.

All forty-two of her mobile phones started to ring. They rang from inside closets, or from the bathroom where she had forgotten them. They rang from the roof terrace and even from inside a shoe under her bed.

"I am a very stubborn girl!" she shouted at the spirits. "You do not scare me."

She turned up her iPod and finally slept.

As soon as the sun was up, she roused her driver, slumped deep in his hammock.

"Come on, we're going to Soriya Market," she said.

The driver looked up at her dazed, then remembered to smile and lower his head in respect. His face fell when she showed up in the garage with all forty-two of her mobile phones in one black bag.

It was too early for Soriya Market to open. They drove in circles with sunrise blazing directly into their eyes. On the streets, men pushed carts like beasts of burden, or carried cascades of belts into the old Central Market. The old market was domed, art deco, the color of vomit, French. Sith never shopped there.

"Maybe you should go visit your Mom," said the driver. "You know, she loves you. Families are there for when you are in trouble."

Sith's mother lived in Thailand and they never spoke. Her mother's family kept asking for favors: money, introductions, or help with getting a job. Sith didn't speak to them any longer.

"My family is only trouble."

The driver shut up and drove.

Finally Soriya opened. Sith went straight to Dara's shop and dumped all the phones on the blue countertop. "Can you take these back?"

"We only do exchanges. I can give a new phone for an old one." Dara looked thoughtful. "Don't worry. Leave them here with me, I'll go sell them to a guy in the old market, and give you your money tomorrow." He smiled in approval. "This is very sensible."

He passed one phone back, the one with video and email. "This is the best one, keep this."

Dara was so competent. Sith wanted to sink down onto him like a pillow and stay there. She sat in the shop all day, watching him work. One of the guys from the games shop upstairs asked, "Who is this beautiful girl?"

Dara answered proudly, "My girlfriend."

Dara drove her back on the Dream and at the door to her house, he chuckled. "I don't want to go." She pressed a finger against his naughty lips, and smiled and spun back inside from happiness.

She was in the ground-floor garage. She heard something like a rat scuttle. In her bag, the telephone rang. Who were these people to importune her, even if they were dead? She wrenched the mobile phone out of her bag and pushed the green button and put the phone to her ear. She waited. There was a sound like wind.

A child spoke to her, his voice clogged as if he was crying. "They tied my thumbs together."

Sith demanded. "How did you get my number?"

"I'm all alone!"

"Then ring somebody else. Someone in your family."

"All my family are dead. I don't know where I am. My name is . . . "

Sith clicked the phone off. She opened the trunk of the car and tossed the phone inside it. Being telephoned by ghosts was so . . . *unmodern*. How could Cambodia become a number one country if its cell phone network was haunted?

She stormed up into the salon. On top of a table, the $1500, no-mess dog stared at her from out of his packaging. Sith clumped up the stairs onto the roof terrace to sleep as far away as she could from everything in the house.

She woke up in the dark, to hear thumping from downstairs.

The sound was metallic and hollow, as if someone were locked in the car. Sith turned on her iPod. Something was making the sound of the music skip. She fought the tangle of wires, and wrenched out another player, a Xen, but it too skipped, burping the sound of speaking voices into the middle of the music.

Had she heard a ripping sound? She pulled out the earphones, and heard something climbing the stairs.

A sound of light, uneven lolloping. She thought of crippled children. Frost settled over her like a heavy blanket and she could not move.

The robot dog came whirring up onto the terrace. It paused at the top of the stairs, its camera nose pointing at her to see, its useless eyes glowing cherry red.

The robot dog said in a warm, friendly voice, "My name is Phalla. I tried to buy my sister medicine and they killed me for it."

Sith tried to say, "Go away," but her throat wouldn't open.

The dog tilted its head. "No one even knows I'm dead. What will you do for all the people who are not mourned?"

Laughter blurted out of her, and Sith saw it rise up as cold vapor into the air.

"We have no one to invite us to the feast," said the dog.

Sith giggled in terror. "Nothing. I can do nothing!" she said, shaking her head.

"You laugh?" The dog gathered itself and jumped up into the hammock with her. It turned and lifted up its clear plastic tail and laid a genuine turd alongside Sith. Short brown hair was wound up in it, a scalp actually, and a single flat white human tooth smiled out of it.

Sith squawked and overturned both herself and the dog out of the hammock and onto the floor. The dog pushed its nose up against hers and began to sing an old-fashioned children's song about birds.

Something heavy huffed its way up the stairwell toward her. Sith shivered with cold on the floor and could not move. The dog went on singing in a high, sweet voice. A large shadow loomed out over the top of the staircase, and Sith gargled, swallowing laughter, trying to speak.

"There was thumping in the car and no one in it," said the driver.

Sith sagged toward the floor with relief. "The ghosts," she said. "They're back." She thrust herself to her feet. "We're getting out now. Ring the Hilton. Find out if they have rooms."

She kicked the toy dog down the stairs ahead of her. "We're moving now!"

Together they all loaded the car, shaking. Once again, the house was left to ghosts. As they drove, the mobile phone rang over and over inside the trunk.

The new Hilton (which does not exist) rose up by the river across from the Department for Cults and Religious Affairs. Tall and marbled and pristine, it had crystal chandeliers and fountains, and wood and brass handles in the elevators.

In the middle of the night only the Bridal Suite was still available, but it had an extra parental chamber where the driver and his wife could sleep. High on the twenty-first floor, the night sparkled with lights and everything was hushed, as far away from Cambodia as it was possible to get.

Things were quiet after that, for a while.

Every day she and Dara went to movies, or went to a restaurant. They went shopping. She slipped him money and he bought himself a beautiful suit. He said, over a hamburger at Lucky7, "I've told my mother that I've met a girl."

Sith smiled and thought: and I bet you told her that I'm rich.

"I've decided to live in the Hilton," she told him.

Maybe we could live in the Hilton. A pretty smile could hint at that.

The rainy season ended. The last of the monsoons rose up dark gray with a froth of white cloud on top, looking exactly like a giant wave about to break.

Dry cooler air arrived.

After work was over Dara convinced her to go for a walk along the river in front of the Royal Palace. He went to the men's room to change into a new luxury suit and Sith thought: he's beginning to imagine life with all that money.

As they walked along the river, exposed to all those people, Sith shook inside. There were teenage boys everywhere. Some of them were in rags, which was reassuring, but some of them were very well dressed indeed, the sons of Impunity who could do anything. Sith swerved suddenly to avoid even seeing them. But Dara in his new beige suit looked like one of them, and the generals' sons nodded to him with quizzical eyebrows, perhaps wondering who he was.

In front of the palace, a pavilion reached out over the water. Next to it a traditional orchestra bashed and wailed out something old fashioned. Hundreds of people crowded around a tiny wat. Dara shook Sith's wrist and they stood up to see.

People held up bundles of lotus flowers and incense in prayer. They threw the bundles into the wat. Monks immediately shoveled the joss sticks and flowers out of the back.

Behind the wat, children wearing T-shirts and shorts black with filth rooted through the dead flowers, the smoldering incense, and old coconut shells.

Sith asked, "Why do they do that?"

"You are so innocent!" chuckled Dara and shook his head. The evening was blue and gold. Sith had time to think that she did not want to go back to a hotel and that the only place she really felt happy was next to Dara. All around that thought was something dark and tangled.

Dara suggested with affection that they should get married.

It was as if Sith had her answer ready. "No, absolutely not," she said at once. "How can you ask that? There is not even anyone for you to ask! Have you spoken to your family about me? Has your family made any checks about my background?"

Which was what she really wanted to know.

Dara shook his head. "I have explained that you are an orphan, but they are not concerned with that. We are modest people. They will be happy if I am happy."

"Of course they won't be! Of course they will need to do checks."

Sith scowled. She saw her way to sudden advantage. "At least they must consult fortunetellers. They are not fools. I can help them. Ask them the names of the fortunetellers they trust."

Dara smiled shyly. "We have no money."

"I will give them money and you can tell them that you pay."

Dara's eyes searched her face. "I don't want that."

"How will we know if it is a good marriage? And your poor mother, how can you ask her to make a decision like this without information? So. You ask your family for the names of good professionals they trust, and I will pay them, and I will go to Prime Minister Hun Sen's own personal fortuneteller, and we can compare results."

Thus she established again both her propriety and her status.

In an old romance, the parents would not approve of the match and the fortuneteller would say that the marriage was ill-omened. Sith left nothing to romance.

She offered the family's fortunetellers whatever they wanted—a car, a farm—and in return demanded a written copy of their judgment. All of them agreed that the portents for the marriage were especially auspicious.

Then she secured an appointment with the Prime Minister's fortune-teller.

Hun Sen's *Kru Taey* was a lady in a black business suit. She had long fingernails like talons, but they were perfectly manicured and frosted white.

She was the kind of fortuneteller who is possessed by someone else's spirit. She sat at a desk and looked at Sith as unblinking as a fish, both her hands steepled together. After the most basic of hellos, she said. "Dollars only. Twenty-five thousand. I need to buy my son an apartment."

"That's a very high fee," said Sith.

"It's not a fee. It is a consideration for giving you the answer you want. My fee is another twenty-five thousand dollars."

They negotiated. Sith liked the Kru Taey's manner. It confirmed everything Sith believed about life.

The fee was reduced somewhat but not the consideration.

"Payment upfront now," the Kru Taey said. She wouldn't take a check. Like only the very best restaurants she accepted foreign credit cards. Sith's Swiss card worked immediately. It had unlimited credit in case she had to leave the country in a hurry.

The Kru Taey said, "I will tell the boy's family that the marriage will be particularly fortunate."

Sith realized that she had not yet said anything about a boy, his family, or a marriage.

The Kru Taey smiled. "I know you are not interested in your real fortune. But to be kind, I will tell you unpaid that this marriage really is particularly well favored. All the other fortunetellers would have said the same thing without being bribed."

The Kru Taey's eyes glinted in the most unpleasant way. "So you needn't have bought them farms or paid me an extra twenty-five thousand dollars."

She looked down at her perfect fingernails. "You will be very happy indeed. But not before your entire life is overturned."

The back of Sith's arms prickled as if from cold. She should have been angry but she could feel herself smiling. Why?

And why waste politeness on the old witch? Sith turned to go without saying good-bye.

"Oh, and about your other problem," said the woman.

Sith turned back and waited.

"Enemies," said the Kru Taey, "can turn out to be friends."

Sith sighed. "What are you talking about?"

The Kru Taey's smile was as wide as a tiger-trap. "The million people your father killed."

Sith went hard. "Not a million," she said. "Somewhere between two hundred and fifty and five hundred thousand."

"Enough," smiled the Kru Taey. "My father was one of them." She smiled for a moment longer. "I will be sure to tell the Prime Minister that you visited me."

Sith snorted as if in scorn. "I will tell him myself."

But she ran back to her car.

That night, Sith looked down on all the lights like diamonds. She settled onto the giant mattress and turned on her iPod.

Someone started to yell at her. She pulled out the earpieces and jumped to the window. It wouldn't open. She shook it and wrenched its frame until it reluctantly slid an inch and she threw the iPod out of the twenty-first-floor window.

She woke up late the next morning, to hear the sound of the TV. She opened up the double doors into the salon and saw Jorani, pressed against the wall.

"The TV . . . " Jorani said, her eyes wide with terror.

The driver waited by his packed bags. He stood up, looking as mournful as a bloodhound.

On the widescreen TV there was what looked like a pop music karaoke video. Except that the music was very old fashioned. Why would a pop video show a starving man eating raw maize in a field? He glanced over his shoulder in terror as he ate. The glowing sing-along words were the song that the dog had sung at the top of the stairs. The starving man looked up at Sith and corn mash rolled out of his mouth.

"It's all like that," said the driver. "I unplugged the set, but it kept playing on every channel." He sompiahed but looked miserable. "My wife wants to leave."

Sith felt shame. It was miserable and dirty, being infested with ghosts. Of course they would want to go.

"It's okay. I can take taxis," she said.

The driver nodded, and went into the next room and whispered to his wife. With little scurrying sounds, they gathered up their things. They sompiahed, and apologized.

The door clicked almost silently behind them.

It will always be like this, thought Sith. Wherever I go. It would be like this with Dara.

The hotel telephone started to ring. Sith left it ringing. She covered the TV with a blanket, but the terrible, tinny old music kept wheedling and rattling its way out at her, and she sat on the edge of her bed, staring into space.

I'll have to leave Cambodia.

At the market, Dara looked even more cheerful than usual. The fortunetellers had pronounced the marriage as very favorable. His mother had invited Sith home for the Pchum Ben festival.

"We can take the bus tomorrow," he said.

"Does it smell? All those people in one place?"

"It smells of air freshener. Then we take a taxi, and then you will have to walk up the track." Dara suddenly doubled up in laughter. "Oh, it will be good for you."

"Will there be dirt?"

"Everywhere! Oh, your dirty Nikes will earn you much merit!"

But at least, thought Sith, there will be no TV or phones.

Two days later, Sith was walking down a dirt track, ducking tree branches. Dust billowed all over her shoes. Dara walked behind her, chuckling, which meant she thought he was scared, too.

She heard a strange rattling sound. "What's that noise?"

"It's a goat," he said. "My mother bought it for me in April as a present."

A goat. How could they be any more rural? Sith had never seen a goat. She never even imagined that she would.

Dara explained. "I sell them to the Muslims. It is Agricultural Diversification."

There were trees everywhere, shadows crawling across the ground like snakes. Sith felt sick. *One mosquito*, she promised herself, *just one and I will squeal and run away.*

The house was tiny, on thin twisting stilts. She had pictured a big fine country house standing high over the ground on concrete pillars with a sunburst carving in the gable. The kitchen was a hut that sat directly on the ground, no stilts, and it was made of palm-leaf panels and there was no electricity. The strip light in the ceiling was attached to a car battery and they kept a live fire on top of the concrete table to cook. Everything smelled of burnt fish.

Sith loved it.

Inside the hut, the smoke from the fires kept the mosquitoes away. Dara's mother, Mrs. Non Kunthea, greeted her with a smile. That triggered a respectful sompiah from Sith, the prayer-like gesture leaping out of her unbidden. On the platform table was a plastic sack full of dried prawns.

Without thinking, Sith sat on the table and began to pull the salty prawns out of their shells.

Why am I doing this?

Because it's what I did at home.

Sith suddenly remembered the enclosure in the forest, a circular fenced area. Daddy had slept in one house, and the women in another. Sith would talk to the cooks. For something to do, she would chop vegetables or shell prawns. Then Daddy would come to eat and he'd sit on the platform table and she, little Sith, would sit between his knees.

Dara's older brother Yuth came back for lunch. He was pot-bellied and drove a taxi for a living, and he moved in hard jabs like an angry old man. He reached too far for the rice and Sith could smell his armpits.

"You see how we live," Yuth said to Sith. "This is what we get for having the wrong patron. Sihanouk thought we were anti-monarchist. To Hun Sen, we were the enemy. Remember the Work for Money program?"

No.

"They didn't give any of those jobs to us. We might as well have been the Khmer Rouge!"

The past, thought Sith, *why don't they just let it go? Why do they keep boasting about their old wars?*

Mrs. Non Kunthea chuckled with affection. "My eldest son was born angry," she said. "His slogan is 'ten years is not too late for revenge.'"

Yuth started up again. "They treat that old monster Pol Pot better than they treat us. But then, he was an important person. If you go to his stupa in Anlong Veng, you will see that people leave offerings! They ask him for lottery numbers!"

He crumpled his green, soft, old-fashioned hat back onto his head and said, "Nice to meet you, Sith. Dara, she's too high class for the likes of you." But he grinned as he said it. He left, swirling disruption in his wake.

The dishes were gathered. Again without thinking, Sith swept up the plastic tub and carried it to the blackened branches. They rested over puddles where the washing-up water drained.

"You shouldn't work," said Dara's mother. "You are a guest."

"I grew up in a refugee camp," said Sith. After all, it was true.

Dara looked at her with a mix of love, pride, and gratitude for the good fortune of a rich wife who works.

And that was the best Sith could hope for. This family would be fine for her.

In the late afternoon, all four brothers came with their wives for the end of Pchum Ben, when the ghosts of the dead can wander the Earth. People scatter rice on the temple floors to feed their families. Some ghosts have small mouths so special rice is used.

Sith never took part in Pchum Ben. How could she go to the temple and scatter rice for Pol Pot?

The family settled in the kitchen chatting and joking, and it all passed in a blur for Sith. Everyone else had family they could honor. To Sith's surprise one of the uncles suggested that people should write names of the deceased and burn them, to transfer merit. It was nothing to do with Pchum Ben, but a lovely idea, so all the family wrote down names.

Sith sat with her hands jammed under her arms.

Dara's mother asked, "Isn't there a name you want to write, Sith?"

"No," said Sith in a tiny voice. How could she write the name Pol Pot? He was surely roaming the world let loose from hell. "There is no one."

Dara rubbed her hand. "Yes, there is, Sith. A very special name."

"No, there's not."

Dara thought she didn't want them to know her father was Kol Vireakboth. He leant forward and whispered. "I promise. No one will see it."

Sith's breath shook. She took the paper and started to cry.

"Oh," said Dara's mother, stricken with sympathy. "Everyone in this country has a tragedy."

Sith wrote the name Kol Vireakboth.

Dara kept the paper folded and caught Sith's eyes. *You see?* he seemed to say. *I have kept your secret safe.* The paper burned.

Thunder slapped a clear sky about the face. It had been sunny, but now as suddenly as a curtain dropped down over a doorway, rain fell. A wind came from nowhere, tearing away a flap of palm-leaf wall, as if forcing entrance in a fury.

The family whooped and laughed and let the rain drench their shoulders as they stood up to push the wall back down, to keep out the rain.

But Sith knew. Her father's enemy was in the kitchen.

The rain passed; the sun came out. The family chuckled and sat back down around or on the table. They lowered dishes of food and ate, making parcels of rice and fish with their fingers. Sith sat rigidly erect, waiting for misfortune.

What would the spirit of Kol Vireakboth do to Pol Pot's daughter? Would he overturn the table, soiling her with food? Would he send mosquitoes to bite and make her sick? Would he suck away all her good fortune, leaving the marriage blighted, her new family estranged?

Or would a kindly spirit simply wish that the children of all Cambodians could escape, escape the past?

Suddenly, Sith felt at peace. The sunlight and shadows looked new to her and her senses started to work in magic ways.

She smelled a perfume of emotion, sweet and bracing at the same time. The music from a neighbor's cassette player touched her arm gently. Words took the form of sunlight on her skin.

No one is evil, the sunlight said. *But they can be false.*

False, how? Sith asked without speaking, genuinely baffled.

The sunlight smiled with an old man's stained teeth. *You know very well how.*

All the air swelled with the scent of the food, savoring it. The trees sighed with satisfaction.

Life is true. Sith saw steam from the rice curl up into the branches. *Death is false.*

The sunlight stood up to go. It whispered. *Tell him.*

The world faded back to its old self.

That night in a hammock in a room with the other women, Sith suddenly sat bolt upright. Clarity would not let her sleep. She saw that there was no way ahead. She couldn't marry Dara. How could she ask him to marry someone who was harassed by one million dead? How could she explain I am haunted because I am Pol Pot's daughter and I have lied about everything?

The dead would not let her marry; the dead would not let her have joy. So who could Pol Pot's daughter pray to? Where could she go for wisdom?

Loak kru Kol Vireakboth, she said under her breath. *Please show me a way ahead.*

The darkness was sterner than the sunlight.

To be as false as you are, it said, *you first have to lie to yourself.*

What lies had Sith told? She knew the facts. Her father had been the head of a government that tortured and killed hundreds of thousands of people and starved the nation through mismanagement. I know the truth.

I just never think about it.

I've never faced it.

Well, the truth is as dark as I am, and you live in me, the darkness.

She had read books—well, the first chapter of books—and then dropped them as if her fingers were scalded. There was no truth for her in books. The truth ahead of her would be loneliness, dreary adulthood, and penance.

Grow up.

The palm-leaf panels stirred like waiting ghosts.

All through the long bus ride back, she said nothing. Dara went silent too, and hung his head.

In the huge and empty hotel suite, darkness awaited her. She'd had the phone and the TV removed; her footsteps sounded hollow. Jorani and the driver had been her only friends.

The next day she did not go to Soriya Market. She went instead to the torture museum of Tuol Sleng.

A cadre of young motoboys waited outside the hotel in baseball caps and bling. Instead, Sith hailed a sweet-faced older motoboy with a battered, rusty bike.

As they drove she asked him about his family. He lived alone and had no one except for his mother in Kompong Thom.

Outside the gates of Tuol Sleng he said, "This was my old school."

In one wing there were rows of rooms with one iron bed in each with handcuffs and stains on the floor. Photos on the wall showed twisted bodies chained to those same beds as they were found on the day of liberation. In one photograph, a chair was overturned as if in a hurry.

Sith stepped outside and looked instead at a beautiful house over the wall across the street. It was a high white house like her own, with pillars and a roof terrace and bougainvillaea, a modern daughter's house. What do they think when they look out from that roof terrace? How can they live here?

The grass was tended and full of hopping birds. People were painting the shutters of the prison a fresh blue-gray.

In the middle wing, the rooms were galleries of photographed faces. They stared out at her like the faces from her printer. Were some of them the same?

"Who are they?" she found herself asking a Cambodian visitor.

"Their own," the woman replied. "This is where they sent Khmer Rouge cadres who had fallen out of favor. They would not waste such torture on ordinary Cambodians."

Some of the faces were young and beautiful men. Some were children or dignified old women.

The Cambodian lady kept pace with her. Company? Did she guess who Sith was? "They couldn't simply beat party cadres to death. They sent them and their entire families here. The children too, the grandmothers. They had different days of the week for killing children and wives."

An innocent looking man smiled out at the camera as sweetly as her aged motoboy, directly into the camera of his torturers. He seemed to expect kindness from them, and decency. *Comrades*, he seemed to say.

The face in the photograph moved. It smiled more broadly and was about to speak.

Sith's eyes darted away. The next face sucked all her breath away.

It was not a stranger. It was Dara, her Dara, in black shirt and black cap. She gasped and looked back at the lady. Her pinched and solemn face nodded up and down. Was she a ghost too?

Sith reeled outside and hid her face and didn't know if she could go on standing. Tears slid down her face and she wanted to be sick and she turned her back so no one could see.

Then she walked to the motoboy, sitting in a shelter. In complete silence, she got on his bike feeling angry at the place, angry at the government for preserving it, angry at the foreigners who visited it like a tourist attraction, angry at everything.

That is not who we are! That is not what I am!

The motoboy slipped onto his bike, and Sith asked him: What happened to your family? It was a cruel question. He had to smile and look cheerful. His father had run a small shop; they went out into the country and never came back. He lived with his brother in a jeum-room, a refugee camp in Thailand. They came back to fight the Vietnamese and his brother was killed.

She was going to tell the motoboy, drive me back to the Hilton, but she felt ashamed. Of what? Just how far was she going to run?

She asked him to take her to the old house on Monivong Boulevard.

As the motorcycle wove through back streets, dodging red-earth ruts and pedestrians, she felt rage at her father. How dare he involve her in something like that! Sith had lived a small life and had no measure of things so she thought: *it's as if someone tinted my hair and it all fell out. It's as if someone pierced my ears and they got infected and my whole ear rotted away.*

She remembered that she had never felt any compassion for her father. She had been twelve-years-old when he stood trial, old and sick and making such a show of leaning on his stick. Everything he did was a show. She remembered rolling her eyes in constant embarrassment. Oh, he was fine in front of rooms full of adoring students. He could play the *bong thom* with them. They thought he was enlightened. He sounded good, using his false, soft and kindly little voice, as if he was dubbed. He had made Sith recite Verlaine, Rimbaud, and Rilke. He killed thousands for having foreign influences.

I don't know what I did in a previous life to deserve you for a father. But you were not my father in a previous life and you won't be my father in the next. I reject you utterly. I will never burn your name. You can wander hungry out of hell every year for all eternity. I will pray to keep you in hell.

I am not your daughter!

If you were false, I have to be true.

Her old house looked abandoned in the stark afternoon light, closed and innocent. At the doorstep she turned and thrust a fistful of dollars into the motoboy's hand. She couldn't think straight; she couldn't even see straight, her vision blurred.

Back inside, she calmly put down her teddy-bear rucksack and walked upstairs to her office. Aido the robot dog whirred his way toward her. She had broken his back leg kicking him downstairs. He limped, whimpering like a dog, and lowered his head to have it stroked.

To her relief, there was only one picture waiting for her in the tray of the printer.

Kol Vireakboth looked out at her, middle-aged, handsome, worn, wise. Pity and kindness glowed in his eyes.

The land line began to ring.

"*Youl prom,*" she told the ghosts. Agreed.

She picked up the receiver and waited.

A man spoke. "My name was Yin Bora." His voice bubbled up brokenly as if from underwater.

A light blinked in the printer. A photograph slid out quickly. A young student stared out at her looking happy at a family feast. He had a Beatle haircut and a striped shirt.

"That's me," said the voice on the phone. "I played football."

Sith coughed. "What do you want me to do?"

"Write my name," said the ghost.

"Please hold the line," said Sith, in a hypnotized voice. She fumbled for a pen, and then wrote on the photograph *Yin Bora, footballer*. He looked so sweet and happy. "You have no one to mourn you," she realized.

"None of us have anyone left alive to mourn us," said the ghost.

Then there was a terrible sound down the telephone, as if a thousand voices moaned at once.

Sith involuntarily dropped the receiver into place. She listened to her heart thump and thought about what was needed. She fed the printer with the last of her paper. Immediately it began to roll out more photos, and the land line rang again.

She went outside and found the motoboy, waiting patiently for her. She asked him to go and buy two reams of copying paper. At the last moment she added pens and writing paper and matches. He bowed and smiled and bowed again, pleased to have found a patron.

She went back inside, and with just a tremor in her hand picked up the phone.

For the next half hour, she talked to the dead, and found photographs and wrote down names. A woman mourned her children. Sith found photos of them all, and united them, father, mother, three children, uncles, aunts, cousins and grandparents, taping their pictures to her wall. The idea of uniting families appealed. She began to stick the other photos onto her wall.

Someone called from outside and there on her doorstep was the motoboy, balancing paper and pens. "I bought you some soup." The broth came in neatly tied bags and was full of rice and prawns. She thanked him and paid him well and he beamed at her and bowed again and again.

All afternoon, the pictures kept coming. Darkness fell, the phone rang, the names were written, until Sith's hand, which was unused to writing anything, ached.

The doorbell rang, and on the doorstep, the motoboy sompiahed. "Excuse me, Lady, it is very late. I am worried for you. Can I get you dinner?"

Sith had to smile. He sounded motherly in his concern. They are so good at building a relationship with you, until you cannot do without them. In the old days she would have sent him away with a few rude words. Now she sent him away with an order.

And wrote.

And when he came back, the aged motoboy looked so happy. "I bought you fruit as well, Lady," he said, and added, shyly. "You do not need to pay me for that."

Something seemed to bump under Sith, as if she was on a motorcycle, and she heard herself say, "Come inside. Have some food too." The motoboy sompiahed in gratitude and as soon as he entered, the phone stopped ringing. They sat on the floor. He arched his neck and looked around at the walls.

"Are all these people your family?" he asked.

She whispered. "No. They're ghosts who no one mourns."

"Why do they come to you?" His mouth fell open in wonder.

"Because my father was Pol Pot," said Sith, without thinking.

The motoboy sompiahed. "Ah." He chewed and swallowed and arched his head back again. "That must be a terrible thing. Everybody hates you."

Sith had noticed that wherever she sat in the room, the eyes in the photographs were directly on her.

"I haven't done anything," said Sith.

"You're doing something now," said the motoboy. He nodded and stood up, sighing with satisfaction. Life was good with a full stomach and a patron. "If you need me, Lady, I will be outside."

Photo after photo, name after name.

Youk Achariya: touring dancer

Proeung Chhay: school superintendent

Sar Kothida child, aged 7, died of 'swelling disease'

Sar Makara, her mother, nurse

Nath Mittapheap, civil servant, from family of farmers

Chor Monirath: wife of award-winning engineer

Yin Sokunthea: Khmer Rouge commune leader

She looked at the faces and realized. *Dara, I'm doing this for Dara.*

The City around her went quiet and she became aware that it was now very late indeed. Perhaps she should just make sure the motoboy had gone home.

He was still waiting outside.

"It's okay. You can go home. Where do you live?"

He waved cheerfully north. "Oh, on Monivong, like you." He grinned at the absurdity of the comparison.

A new idea took sudden form. Sith said, "Tomorrow, can you come early, with a big feast? Fish and rice and greens and pork: curries and stir-fries and kebabs." She paid him handsomely, and finally asked him his name. His name meant Golden.

"Good night, Sovann."

For the rest of the night she worked quickly like an answering service. This is like a cleaning of the house before a festival, she thought. The voices of the dead became ordinary, familiar. Why are people afraid of the dead? The dead can't hurt you. The dead want what you want: justice.

The wall of faces became a staircase and a garage and a kitchen of faces, all named. She had found Jorani's colored yarn, and linked family members into trees.

She wrote until the electric lights looked discolored, like a headache. She asked the ghosts, "Please can I sleep now?" The phones fell silent and Sith slumped with relief onto the polished marble floor.

She woke up dazed, still on the marble floor. Sunlight flooded the room. The faces in the photographs no longer looked swollen and bruised. Their faces were not accusing or mournful. They smiled down on her. She was among friends.

With a whine, the printer started to print; the phone started to ring. Her doorbell chimed, and there was Sovann, white cardboard boxes piled up on the back of his motorcycle. He wore the same shirt as yesterday, a cheap blue copy of a Lacoste. A seam had parted under the arm. He only has one shirt, Sith realized. She imagined him washing it in a basin every night.

Sith and Sovann moved the big tables to the front windows. Sith took out her expensive tablecloths for the first time, and the bronze platters. The feast was laid out as if at New Year. Sovann had bought more paper and pens. He knew what they were for. "I can help, Lady."

He was old enough to have lived in a country with schools, and he could write in a beautiful, old-fashioned hand. Together he and Sith spelled out the names of the dead and burned them.

"I want to write the names of my family too," he said. He burnt them, weeping.

The delicious vapors rose. The air was full of the sound of breathing in. Loose papers stirred with the breeze. The ash filled the basins, but even after working all day, Sith and the motoboy had only honored half the names.

"Good night, Sovann," she told him.

"You have transferred a lot of merit," said Sovann, but only to be polite.

If I have any merit to transfer, thought Sith.

He left and the printers started, and the phone. She worked all night, and only stopped because the second ream of paper ran out.

The last picture printed was of Kol Vireakboth.

Dara, she promised herself. *Dara next.*

In the morning, she called him. "Can we meet at lunchtime for another walk by the river?"

Sith waited on top of the marble wall and watched an old man fish in the Tonlé Sap river and found that she loved her country. She loved its tough, smiling, uncomplaining people, who had never offered her harm, after all the harm her family had done them. Do you know you have the daughter of the monster sitting here among you?

Suddenly all Sith wanted was to be one of them. The monks in the pavilion, the white-shirted functionaries scurrying somewhere, the lazy bones dangling their legs, the young men who dress like American rappers and sold something dubious, drugs, or sex.

She saw Dara sauntering toward her. He wore his new shirt, and smiled at her but he didn't look relaxed. It had been two days since they'd met. He knew something was wrong, that she had something to tell him. He had bought them lunch in a little cardboard box. Maybe for the last time, thought Sith.

They exchanged greetings, almost like cousins. He sat next to her and smiled and Sith giggled in terror at what she was about to do.

Dara asked, "What's funny?"

She couldn't stop giggling. "Nothing is funny. Nothing." She sighed in order to stop and terror tickled her and she spurted out laughter again. "I lied to you. Kol Vireakboth is not my father. Another politician was my father. Someone you've heard of . . . "

The whole thing was so terrifying and absurd that the laughter squeezed her like a fist and she couldn't talk. She laughed and wept at the same time. Dara stared.

"My father was Saloth Sar. That was his real name." She couldn't make herself say it. She could tell a motoboy, but not Dara? She forced herself onward. "My father was Pol Pot."

Nothing happened.

Sitting next to her, Dara went completely still. People strolled past; boats bobbed on their moorings.

After a time Dara said, "I know what you are doing."

That didn't make sense. "Doing? What do you mean?"

Dara looked sour and angry. "Yeah, yeah, yeah, yeah." He sat, looking away from her. Sith's laughter had finally shuddered to a halt. She sat peering at him, waiting. "I told you my family were modest," he said quietly.

"Your family are lovely!" Sith exclaimed.

His jaw thrust out. "They had questions about you too, you know."

"I don't understand."

He rolled his eyes. He looked back 'round at her. "There are easier ways to break up with someone."

He jerked himself to his feet and strode away with swift determination, leaving her sitting on the wall.

Here on the riverfront, everyone was equal. The teenage boys lounged on the wall; poor mothers herded children; the foreigners walked briskly, trying to look as if they didn't carry moneybelts. Three fat teenage girls nearly swerved into a cripple in a pedal chair and collapsed against each other with raucous laughter.

Sith did not know what to do. She could not move. Despair humbled her, made her hang her head.

I've lost him.

The sunlight seemed to settle next to her, washing up from its reflection on the wake of some passing boat.

No, you haven't.

The river water smelled of kindly concern. The sounds of traffic throbbed with forbearance.

Not yet.

There is no forgiveness in Cambodia. But there are continual miracles of compassion and acceptance.

Sith appreciated for just a moment the miracles. The motoboy buying her soup. She decided to trust herself to the miracles.

Sith talked to the sunlight without making a sound. *Grandfather Vireakboth. Thank you. You have told me all I need to know.*

Sith stood up and from nowhere, the motoboy was there. He drove her to the Hello Phone shop.

Dara would not look at her. He bustled back and forth behind the counter, though there was nothing for him to do. Sith talked to him like a customer. "I want to buy a mobile phone," she said, but he would not answer. "There is someone I need to talk to."

Another customer came in. She was a beautiful daughter too, and he served her, making a great show of being polite. He complimented her on her appearance. "Really, you look cool." The girl looked pleased. Dara's eyes darted in Sith's direction.

Sith waited in the chair. This was home for her now. Dara ignored her. She picked up her phone and dialed his number. He put it to his ear and said, "Go home."

"You are my home," she said.

His thumb jabbed the C button.

She waited. Shadows lengthened.

"We're closing," he said, standing by the door without looking at her.

Shamefaced, Sith ducked away from him, through the door.

Outside Soriya, the motoboy played dice with his fellows. He stood up. "They say I am very lucky to have Pol Pot's daughter as a client."

There was no discretion in Cambodia, either. Everyone will know now, Sith realized.

At home, the piles of printed paper still waited for her. Sith ate the old, cold food. It tasted flat, all its savor sucked away. The phones began to ring. She fell asleep with the receiver propped against her ear.

The next day, Sith went back to Soriya with a box of the printed papers.

She dropped the box onto the blue plastic counter of Hello Phones.

"Because I am Pol Pot's daughter," she told Dara, holding out a sheaf of pictures toward him. "All the unmourned victims of my father are printing their pictures on my printer. Here. Look. These are the pictures of people who lost so many loved ones there is no one to remember them."

She found her cheeks were shaking and that she could not hold the sheaf of paper. It tumbled from her hands, but she stood back, arms folded.

Dara, quiet and solemn, knelt and picked up the papers. He looked at some of the faces. Sith pushed a softly crumpled green card at him. Her family ID card.

He read it. Carefully, with the greatest respect, he put the photographs on the countertop along with the ID card.

"Go home, Sith," he said, but not unkindly.

"I said," she had begun to speak with vehemence but could not continue. "I told you. My home is where you are."

"I believe you," he said, looking at his feet.

"Then . . . " Sith had no words.

"It can never be, Sith," he said. He gathered up the sheaf of photocopying paper. "What will you do with these?"

Something made her say, "What will *you* do with them?"

His face was crossed with puzzlement.

"It's your country, too. What will you do with them? Oh, I know, you're such a poor boy from a poor family, who could expect anything from you? Well, you have your whole family and many people have no one. And you can buy new shirts and some people only have one."

Dara held out both hands and laughed. "Sith?" *You, Sith are accusing* me *of being selfish?*

"You own them, too." Sith pointed to the papers, to the faces. "You think the dead don't try to talk to you, too?"

Their eyes latched. She told him what he could do. "I think you should make an exhibition. I think Hello Phones should sponsor it. You tell them that. You tell them Pol Pot's daughter wishes to make amends and has chosen them. Tell them the dead speak to me on their mobile phones."

She spun on her heel and walked out. She left the photographs with him.

That night she and the motoboy had another feast and burned the last of the unmourned names. There were many thousands.

The next day she went back to Hello Phones.

"I lied about something else," she told Dara. She took out all the reports from the fortunetellers. She told him what Hun Sen's fortuneteller had told her. "The marriage is particularly well favored."

"Is that true?" He looked wistful.

"You should not believe anything I say. Not until I have earned your trust. Go consult the fortunetellers for yourself. This time you pay."

His face went still and his eyes focused somewhere far beneath the floor. Then he looked up, directly into her eyes. "I will do that."

For the first time in her life Sith wanted to laugh for something other than fear. She wanted to laugh for joy.

"Can we go to lunch at Lucky7?" she asked.

"Sure," he said.

All the telephones in the shop, all of them, hundreds all at once began to sing.

A waterfall of trills and warbles and buzzes, snatches of old songs or latest chart hits. Dara stood dumbfounded. Finally he picked one up and held it to his ear.

"It's for you," he said and held out the phone for her.

There was no name or number on the screen.

Congratulations, dear daughter, said a warm kind voice.

"Who is this?" Sith asked. The options were severely limited.

Your new father, said Kol Vireakboth. The sound of wind. *I adopt you.*

A thousand thousand voices said at once, *We adopt you.*

In Cambodia, you share your house with ghosts in the way you share it with dust. You hear the dead shuffling alongside your own footsteps. You can sweep, but the sound does not go away.

On the Tra Bek end of Monivong there is a house whose owner has given it over to ghosts. You can try to close the front door. But the next day you will find it hanging open. Indeed you can try, as the neighbors did, to nail the door shut. It opens again.

By day, there is always a queue of five or six people wanting to go in, or hanging back, out of fear. Outside are offerings of lotus or coconuts with embedded josh sticks.

The walls and floors and ceilings are covered with photographs. The salon, the kitchen, the stairs, the office, the empty bedrooms, are covered with photographs of Chinese-Khmers at weddings, Khmer civil servants on picnics, Chams outside their mosques, Vietnamese holding up prize catches of fish; little boys going to school in shorts; cyclopousse drivers in front of their odd, old-fashioned pedaled vehicles; wives in stalls stirring soup. All of them are happy and joyful, and the background is Phnom Penh when it was the most beautiful city in Southeast Asia.

All the photographs have names written on them in old-fashioned handwriting.

On the table is a printout of thousands of names on slips of paper. Next to the table are matches and basins of ash and water. The implication is plain. Burn the names and transfer merit to the unmourned dead.

Next to that is a small printed sign that says in English HELLO.

Every Pchum Ben, those names are delivered to temples throughout the city. Gold foil is pressed onto each slip of paper, and attached to it is a parcel of sticky rice. At 8 A.M. food is delivered for the monks, steaming rice and fish, along with bolts of new cloth. At 10 A.M. more food is delivered, for the disabled and the poor.

And most mornings a beautiful daughter of Cambodia is seen walking beside the confluence of the Tonlé Sap and Mekong rivers. Like Cambodia, she plainly loves all things modern. She dresses in the latest fashion. Cambodian R&B whispers in her ear. She pauses in front of each new waterfront construction whether built by improvised scaffolding or erected with cranes. She buys noodles from the grumpy vendors with their tiny stoves. She carries a book or sits on the low marble wall to write letters and look at the boats, the monsoon clouds, and the dop-dops. She talks to the reflected sunlight on the river and calls it Father.

THE OSTEOMANCER'S SON

Greg van Eekhout

The bus comes to a stop at Wilshire and Fairfax, just a few blocks from the La Brea Tar Pits. When the doors hiss open, the tar smell washes over me. Thick and ancient, it snakes through my sinuses and settles in the back of my brain like a ghost in the attic.

"Get off or stay on," the driver says, impatient. So I step off into the haunted air.

The walk to Farmer's Market is too short. Not enough time for me to change my mind. For a moment, I wonder if looking at my wallet photo of Miranda would give me some more courage. I know every detail by heart: She's smiling and squinting into the camera, her face sun-dappled and brilliant. The ice cream cone I bought her on her third birthday is a pink smear across her face.

It's easier to think of her that way than to contemplate the handkerchief inside my bowling bag and the small bone contained within its linen folds.

I put my head down and keep walking, entering a maze of stalls and awnings, of narrow paths crowded with bins and baskets and little old ladies with sharp elbows. Shopping carts bark my shins and roll over my toes. Ranchero music and some kind of Southeast Asian pop bounces off my head.

"Hey you got problem?" A man behind the counter beckons with a hooked finger, his face brown and creased like a cinnamon stick. "You got problem, yeah. I can tell. I got just what you need." With a knife, he sweeps bright orange dust into a little paper envelope. It looks that the dehydrated cheese powder that comes with instant macaroni.

"What's that?" I ask.

His smile reveals several gold teeth. "Come from dragon turtle. You see giant dragon turtle wash up in San Diego? You see that on news?"

"I'm not really up on current events." Especially not as regurgitated by state-controlled news organizations.

He nods enthusiastically and edges more powder into the envelope. "This come from San Diego dragon turtle. Wife's younger brother, he lifeguard. He scrape some turtle shell before Hierarch's men confiscate whole carcass."

"What's it for?" I ask, indicating the powder-filled envelope.

"All sorts of stuff. Rheumatism, kidney stones, migraine, epilepsy, bedroom problems . . . All sorts."

"No, thanks," I say as I try to shoulder my way back into the crowd.

"Get you girls," he calls after me. "Make you animal! Guaranteed!"

Dragon turtle can't do any of those things, of course. Not that it's genuine turtle he's selling. I figure it for flour and sulfur, with maybe the tiniest pinch of rhinoceros horn thrown in. You can't even put a street value on the genuine stuff these days.

I know. I've experienced the genuine stuff. It's in my bones.

One Sunday afternoon I found a piece of kraken spine while walking down Santa Monica Beach with Dad. It was a cold day, the sand a sloping plain of gray beneath a slate sky, and we were both underdressed for the weather. But it was Sunday, the one day of the week we had together, and I had wanted to go the beach.

I spotted the spine in the receding foam of the surf. It was just a fragment, like a knitting needle, striped honey and black. I showed it to Dad.

"Good eye," he said, resting his hand on my shoulder. "I don't see many of these outside a locked vault." In his white shirt and gray slacks, he looked like one of the seagulls wheeling overhead. I imagined him spreading his long arms to catch the wind and float to the sky.

I, on the other hand, took after my mom—short and stocky, skin just a shade paler than terra cotta. "Your father is made of air," Mom once told me. "That's why he's so hard to understand; he's not always down here with us. But you and me, kid, you and me are plain as dirt."

Dad held out his hand for the spine. "Kraken live in the deeps," he said. "They hunt for giant squid and sperm whale. Sometimes, in a fight, the spines break off and they wash ashore." He smelled the spine, inhaling so deeply it was almost an act of aggression. "You've found good bone, Daniel. Better than mammoth tusk."

"Really?" John Blackland had never been known to lavish idle praise.

"Better than all the La Brea stuff, in fact. The kraken is even older. Smarter."

I waited while my father's thoughts followed their own silent paths. Then, brightly, he told me to find a shell. "Abalone would be perfect, but I'll take anything from the sea I can use as a crucible."

Within a few minutes I'd located half a mussel shell. We sat on the sand, the shell between us, and Dad cooked the tip of the kraken spine over the flame of his Zippo. Thin tendrils of smoke rose from the spine, smelling of salt and earth and dark, deep mud.

When a single drop of honey-colored fluid oozed from the tip of the spine into the shell, Dad killed the flame. "Okay," he said. "Good. Now, do like me." He lifted the shell to his mouth and lightly touched his tongue to the fluid. I did the same. It burned, but not more than a too-hot mug of cocoa. The oil tasted exactly as it smelled, like something that had come from dark and forgotten places, but also from inside me.

"Quick, now, Daniel. Hold my hand."

For a few moments, the waves crashed ashore and the gulls cried overhead and I shivered in the cold. Then it started. A prickling sensation ran across my skin, raising goose bumps. The tiny hairs on my arms stood at attention. Then, popping in my body, as though my blood were carbonated. It hurt, and I felt it in my lips and eyes, a million pinpricks.

I looked at Dad. His face was a blur. He was actually vibrating, and I realized I was, too, and he smiled at me. "Don't be afraid," he said, his voice shuddering. "Trust me."

I wasn't afraid. Or, rather, the scared part of me was smaller than the part that was thrilled at the power of my father, the power of the kraken, the power inside me.

Lightning struck. Silver-white, cracking bursts.

Pain filled me. I screamed, desperately trying to let some of it out, but there was only more. My body was a sponge for it, with limitless capacity. Pain replaced everything.

When my world finally stilled and my eyes could once again see, Dad and I were surrounded by a moat of liquefied sand. Black, gooey glass smoked and bubbled.

"The kraken is a creature of storms," Dad said. "Now, a part that will always rage inside you. That's the osteomancer's craft: To draw magic from bones, to infuse it into your own." He looked at me a long time, as if to see if I understood.

The pain was over, but the memory of it roiled inside and around me, like smoke from a fire.

Trust me, he'd said.

"Don't tell your mom about this. That kraken spine could have paid for your college education."

Farther back in the recesses of Farmer's Market, closer to the Tar Pits, the smell of asphalt clogs the air. Black ooze seeps through cracks in the alley, and when I walk, my shoes stick to the ground. There's black tar under the pavement. Pockets of gas lurk beneath the sidewalks like jellyfish.

Storage sheds and small warehouses line the alley, guarded by guys, teenagers, just a few years younger than me. They conceal their hands in the pockets of their roomy pants and watch me make my way down a row of cinderblock structures. I stop before a building with a steel roll-down door, and four guards converge on me, forming a diamond with me at the center.

"You must be lost," one says.

They all have eyes the color of coffee ice cream and the same face. Not just similar in appearance, but identical. Maybe they're quadruplets, but more likely they're mirror-spawn. It takes pretty deep magic to create them, but when it comes to the Hierarch and his interests, no expense is ever spared. These guys aren't just rent-a-cop security. These guys are weapons.

"Are these warehouses?" I say, waving vaguely at the buildings around us.

The four share a look and nod in unison.

"Then I think I'm in the right place."

"You'd have been better off lost," says the one behind me. "What's in the bowling bag?"

"A bowling ball."

"What kind?"

"Brunswick." That's the name written on the bag.

"I like to bowl," they all say together. Then, just the one behind me: "Let's take a peek inside."

Two of them unzip the bag, while the other two keep their eyes on me. I reach into my coat pocket and all four get ready to pounce. "Relax," I say, pulling out my leather glasses case. "Just putting on my shades."

Which, really, is all I do.

Frowns form on the faces of the four mirror-spawn. They blink. They work their lips a little. "What are you looking at?" they all ask of each other.

"Nothing," they all decide.

Their diamond formation loosens, and they go back to whatever they were doing before I showed up. I take my bowling bag and continue looking for the right warehouse.

When my first baby tooth fell out I tucked it under my pillow, just as Mom had told me to. The next morning the tooth was gone but I found no coin. Mom and Dad were arguing in the living room. I wanted to go out and see Dad, but not until the fight was over.

I read some comics.

I glued plastic tusks on my Revel Colombian Mammoth model.

With my tongue, I probed the empty socket where my tooth had been.

Finally, the noise in the other room died down, and I heard the front door open and shut. Moments later, a car started and drove away: Dad going back to his apartment.

"From now on," Mom said, standing in the doorway, "when you lose a tooth, put it in an envelope for your father."

"What for?"

She gripped the doorjamb so tight her hand shook. "So he can eat them."

By that age, I already knew Dad worked for the Hierarch—the most powerful osteomancer of all—and I knew that made my father a very important man.

It wasn't until years later, until after the Night of Long Knives, that I knew Dad was a traitor.

This, I found out from Uncle Otis, my father's brother, who took me in after Dad was murdered and Mom defected to Northern California.

I'd left Otis when I turned sixteen and had nearly no contact with him until two weeks ago. I knew he helped out Connie and Miranda with money, dropped in on their little apartment in Boyle Heights to make sure they were okay, but I'd never asked him to do that and I refused to be grateful.

The door jingled as I entered his shop for the first time in seven years.

"You never got tall," he said by way of greeting.

He wasn't alone. On a stool behind a glass display counter of jewelry and cigarette cases and Zippo lighters sat a thin-shouldered man in a sweater the color of wilted lettuce. He gave me a smile with his lipless turtle mouth and took a sip from a Dodgers coffee mug.

"Nice to meet you, Daniel."

I took note of the turtle man's skin, teeth, fingernails. They were by no means healthy colors, but neither were they the deeply embedded telltale brown of a practicing osteomancer. I figured him for a supplier, like Otis.

I should have turned around, gone back home. Trafficking in osteomancy had been a bad idea since the Night of Long Knives—I was surprised Otis hadn't been caught yet—and I always got the feeling the Hierarch's eyes were on me, being the son of John Blackland.

Otis tried to introduce me to the turtle man. "Daniel, this is Mr.—" But the turtle man cut him off with a sharp look. Otis settled on telling me he was a friend of my father's.

I took "friend" as a codeword for former co-conspirator. Dad had been a darling of the Hierarch until he'd decided there was too much power concentrated in the Hierarch's hands, and he hadn't been alone in this belief. Magic wants to be free. But after the Night of Long Knives, what had been the seeds of a revolution had degenerated into merely a black market for osteomantic materials. Now, it was just about skimming a bit off the Hierarch's profit.

I wanted no part of it. Not a sliver. But there was the lure of money and pangs about how little I was doing for Miranda. "Is this a bag job?"

Otis nodded. "The sort of thing you're good at."

I had kept myself out of the family business, but that didn't mean I'd been walking the straight and narrow. Part of the reason I'd left Otis's care was because I felt he wasn't dealing fairly with me when fencing stuff I'd boosted from houses and businesses.

"It's a tricky job, in a place hard to get into and even harder to get out of."

"Government warehouse, I suppose?" Which was tantamount to a suicide mission.

The turtle man looked at me with dark eyes. I recognized that look. In his head, he was stripping me of clothing and skin. He was wondering what my skeleton looked like. "It's not just any government warehouse, Daniel. We're sending you into the Ossuary itself."

The Ossuary. The dragon's greatest treasure trove. The Hierarch's own private stash.

I didn't bother explaining what an impossible task that would be. These guys were veterans. They wouldn't risk exposure in a pointless exercise. But they would risk my life to get their hands on the Hierach's riches.

I, on the other hand, would not. "Thanks, Otis," I said, turning my back and heading for the door. "Don't call me ever again."

I heard the turtle man's coffee cup clank against the glass counter. "You haven't even heard our terms."

"And I'm not going to," I said. "My daughter deserves a living father."

"Daniel, I have something for you." I stopped and watched Otis place a folded handkerchief on the glass counter. The look on his face was infinitely sad as he peeled back the corners of the handkerchief and revealed a small distal phalanx. A finger bone. A child's finger bone, not white, but already turning brown. The bone of a child who has been fed bone. When I was a kid, that's what my bones would have looked like, because even then, Dad was preparing me.

"It belongs to Miranda," the turtle man said. "Do the job or we'll piece her out, bit by bit."

Dad lived in the back of his osteomancer's shop, and that's where I spent most of my time with him during weekend visits. Six years after that afternoon on the beach, I was in his workroom, watching a pair of horn-rimmed glasses bob inside a kettle of boiling oil. The lenses were blanks, but the frames were special, carved from the vertebrae of a Choctaw *sint holo* serpent. I was certain that Dad didn't have legal access to such materials. He'd probably obtained it in one of the back-alley exchanges he'd become increasingly involved with. Things had been different for him, lately. Once one of the Hierarch's chief men, he was more and more on the fringes of things.

Dad stirred the oil with a copper spoon, sniffing the vapors that rose from the pot. He quizzed me: "Any idea what these glasses will do?"

I was bored. Only eight blocks away there was a mall full of video games and CD's to shoplift and girls. I couldn't remember the last time Dad and I had talked about anything other than bones and oils and feathers and powders. Dad's world was full of dead things that stank.

"I have no idea what they do," I said. It was true, but it wasn't what Dad wanted to hear.

He breathed a small sigh. "Smell it, Daniel. You can tell by smell. Smells are ghosts. Let them in and they'll talk to you."

He wouldn't give up until I did as he asked, so, sullenly, I admitted the phantoms. Figuring out what they were trying to tell me was a process requiring the kind of patience and attention I could seldom be bothered to exhibit. I lowered my nose to the kettle.

First, there were my father's tells, not just because he was in the room, but because the kettle contained his magic. There was clean sweat. Old Spice. And tar. Deeply embedded, way down to the marrow of Dad's bones. My father's living ghost. And also something of me. Maybe some of my baby teeth. The smells were all mixed up, and I couldn't tell where he ended and I began.

"What do you think?" Dad whispered, bending close to my ear.

"It's like . . . something I can't hold onto. Like confusion."

Dad straightened. "It's in your bones, now, Daniel. You know how to let the old bones inside you. You only need to listen to them, and they'll tell you how to do whatever you need to do. That's osteomancy. That's deep magic." He gestured at his work counter, littered with jars and vials and little envelopes. "All else is merely recipe."

From outside, the sound of a helicopter rotor pounded the air. The phone rang. Dad went to the front room to answer it, and I stayed behind, eavesdropping on his conversation.

"Not a good time, Otis." Then, his voice dropped. "Yes, I've got something cooking right now."

The sound of the helicopter grew closer, and now it sounded as though there were more than one. I went to the door and saw the look on Dad's face, the way the lines deepened, the haunted shadows of his eyes. "Who else did they get?" he said into the receiver, craning his neck to peer out the living room window. Dad listened to whatever Otis's answer was, his eyes shut tight. When he opened them, he saw me standing in the doorway. "Will you take care of him, Otis? Will you promise me?" There was a pause, and then he put the receiver back in its cradle.

Out on the street, car doors slammed. Dad came over to the work-room doorway and pushed me back inside. "The glasses aren't ready yet," he said. "Wait as long as you can before putting them on. Don't come out till you've heard the thunder. When you walk, make no noise." With that, he shut the door on me.

A few moments later, I heard shouting in the living room, a scuffle. And then cracks of thunder, so close, like bombs detonating in my head. The loudest thing I'd ever heard.

Silence followed, broken by soft footsteps outside the workroom. The doorknob jiggled. Another beat of silence, and something impacted the door. Wood splintered.

I ran to Dad's work counter. The glasses still tumbled inside the boiling oil. With a pair of copper tongs, I lifted out the glasses and put them on, hissing in pain as I burned my fingers and temples and the backs of my ears and the bridge of my nose. My skin blistered, and whatever substance Dad had used to fashion the frames leeched into me.

With another blow the door gave, hanging on one hinge, useless as a broken arm. Half a dozen cops surged in. A gray-haired man in a blue windbreaker, marked with the Hierarch's skull insignia, pushed to the front of the group. I backed up against the workbench. The man in the windbreaker was close enough to touch. He looked at me, right at me, and raised his hand as if to reach out and grab my throat. I remained silent, and he only blinked stupidly in my general direction.

My heart pounding, I forced myself to walk slowly past the cops, who flinched as though brushed by cobwebs. In the living room were four charred bodies. The flesh on their faces and hands bubbled, black and red. The room stank of ozone and meat and kraken.

Dad hadn't managed to get them all. He was on his back. Three cops were cutting the skin off of him with long knives. They'd already flayed his arm, exposing the deep rich brown of his radius and ulna. And they'd peeled his face back to expose his coffee-brown skull.

That night, I ran. Away from Dad's place, away from the rotor blades and searchlights. I ran until I could only walk, walked until I could only stumble, stumbled until I could only crawl. When morning broke, I woke up in wet sand and bathed myself in the cold waves that rolled in on the edge of a winter storm. I will live here, I thought. I will live here on the beach, and I will never take off these glasses, and I will live here as a ghost.

He was already dead, I told myself. When the men cut open Dad to take his bones, he was already dead.

I would keep telling myself that until I could believe it.

The route to the Hierarch's ossuary takes me through a network of tunnels buried so deep beneath the city that, after a while, I can no longer feel the rumble of traffic from Wilshire Boulevard. The stench of tar and magic is almost a solid wall here, the ghosts so thick I can practically scoop them out of the air with my hands. Using the turtle man's collection of lock picks, stolen keys, alarm codes, passwords, and my father's glasses, I eventually find myself at the threshold of the Hierarch's ossuary.

Let's say you're sickeningly wealthy. And let's say what you're rich in is gold, and you want a big room in which to hoard your treasure. What could be more fitting, then, than a room built of solid gold bricks? The Hierarch's ossuary is kind of like that, only it's built of bone. The walls are mammoth femurs stacked end-to-end. The floor, a mosaic of various claws and delicate vertebrae and healing jewels pried from the heads of Peruvian carbuncles. Overhead, mammoth tusks form the domed ceiling. And from the dome hangs a chandelier of unicorn horns, white as snow.

I remind myself to breathe.

Six sentries carry bayonets with basilisk-tooth blades. They exchange uneasy glances as I step deeper into the room. I've been warned by Otis and the turtle man that anyone I encounter this far inside the Hierarch's stronghold will have received advanced training. They will have tasted deep-magic bone.

"Hoss, you okay?" says one of the sentries.

Another shakes his head, looking directly at me. "Nope. Something's creeping me out."

"Yeah, me too. Think we should get the hound in here?"

"Yeah." The sentry reaches for a wall-mounted phone.

I unlace my boot and pry it off. With everything I've got, I chuck it up at the unicorn chandelier. The horns shatter like glass, the sound of children shrieking. I backpedal to avoid the rain of shards.

The sentries look up in horror. They're in charge of protecting a lot of money, and something's just gone dreadfully wrong. They flutter about the mess like maiden aunts over a collapsed soufflé.

I retrieve my boot and make a dash for a passageway into an even larger room.

The entrance of bone was made to impress. This place, large enough to berth an ocean liner, houses yet greater wealth. Floor-to-ceiling shelves occupy most of it, but there are also fully assembled skeletons in chain-link cages: a serpent at least one hundred yards long, a feline body as large as an elephant with a boulder-sized skull. And suspended overhead looms a kraken—flat, shovel-shaped head, tail half the length of a football field, and running down the tail, dozens of spines as long as jousting lances. The stench of its power makes my stomach churn.

There is really only one reason Otis and the turtle man chose me for this job. One thing I can do better than anyone else. There's a scent I'm sensitive to, one I can pick out like a bright white stripe on a black highway. I follow it to a row of towering shelves and bring over a ladder on wheels. I climb. Stacked on the shelves are long cardboard boxes. In front of my face is the one containing my father's bones.

His remains are powerful weapons. I understand why Otis and the turtle man and whoever else is in their cabal wants them.

Most of Dad is missing. Probably sold off. All that's left are some of the small bones of his hands, and some ground powder, just a pinch, in a glass vial. I unzip my bowling bag and dump the remains inside.

A voice from below: "Come down off that ladder, son."

In a linen button-down shirt and tailored black slacks, the Hierarch isn't exactly what I expect, but I recognize his face from coins and postage stamps. He's thin and dark as bones from the tar pits, his fingernails, teeth and eyes saturated with magic.

"Those glasses of yours are very clever," he says, inhaling deeply. "*Sint holo* serpent bones and Deep Rhys herbs. Two sources of invisibility, mixed together, along with your own essence. That's good work. But it's not fooling me, so you might as well come on down now."

I grip the ladder to keep my hands from shaking. I can smell him. His magic is old. "So, you really hang out in your own warehouse? Don't tell me you drive the forklifts."

He smiles indulgently. "No, that takes special training I lack. But when thieves get this far past my defenses, I take personal interest. Now, please, come down."

"Not just yet. I like the view from up here. You have a lot of nice things. Is that really a sphinx?" I wonder if he's noticed my legs shaking.

"Yes. One of only three ever found."

"Where are the other two?"

"I smoked them." And he spits at me. He fires up a dark brown glob that splatters on my cheek. It burns me like acid, hurting so bad, filling me with pain and surprise, that I can't even scream.

A curtain of gray descends over my vision, and I lose balance, falling off the ladder, eight feet down to the concrete floor. I huddle there at the Hierarch's feet, struggling not to give in to the tempting relief of unconsciousness. My cheek burns. And I think I've broken my right arm. But somehow—reflex, dumb luck, who knows?—I've managed to hold onto the bowling bag containing Father's bones. Some of the bones have fallen out. The vial of powder lies shattered, its contents spilled.

I have to get to my feet. I can do this. I can make myself do this. Using my good arm to push myself up, I manage to drive my palm into the tiny shards of glass from the broken vial.

"Are you okay?" the Hierarch asks. I can hear the flesh on my face sizzle.

I try to say "fine," but the word won't come out.

"So, who's that in the bowling bag?"

"John Blackland," I rasp. "He was an osteomancer."

The Hierarch puts his hands in his pockets and bounces on the balls of his feet, as if stretching out his calf muscles. "This entire section of the ossuary is full of osteomancers. It's the osteomancy section. I suppose you're John Blackland's son?"

The Hierarch's spit continues to burn. "Yeah," I gasp. "Daniel Blackland."

It feels like someone's drilling into the cracked bones of my right arm. And my cheek . . . the air hits exposed bone.

The Hierarch squints at the hole in my face as if checking out a door ding on a parked car. "If it's any comfort, you got farther than most. No doubt you've come equipped with some powerful osteo-mantic weapons. But look at me." He holds his brown hands up to-ward my face. "I've smoked, eaten, inhaled, and injected more ancient and secret animals than anyone alive. I'm the *Hierarch*."

"How could I have done this better?" I ask.

"I do make public appearances, you know. You could have tried a car bomb. Or a high-powered rifle. You revenge-obsessed boys have extraordinary passion, but it seems to get in the way of achieving practical goals."

He thinks this is about vengeance, not simple theft. I'm out of courage, and hope, and pretty much everything. But then Dad talks to me. He begins softly, through weak and subtle scents that waft up from his scattered bones: tar, the salt tang of kelp, and a trace of something clean and dark and old from the sea bottom.

That's the osteomancer's craft. To draw magic from bones, to in-fuse it into your own.

My father turned me into a weapon. And while I was off, screwing around, I let inheritors of my father's noble cause turn Miranda into a weapon. I've still got her in my bowling bag. I am a vessel carrying three generations of power. But I'll die before I use my daughter in that way.

Broken arm. Face being eaten away. Glass splinters in my good hand. I put my palm to my ruined cheek. Screaming, I rub residue of my father's ground-up bones into my raw flesh.

Firecrackers pop under my skin.

The Hierarch sees what I've done, and he begins to exude something. A toxic stench, thick as mud, fills my head, more and more until I hear myself shrieking with blind pain.

The Hierarch coughs, and he coughs and coughs, and his eyes never leave mine. His jaw unhinges like a snake's, and brown fluid gushes out of him. Where it hits the floor, concrete liquefies and boils away.

"If there's anything left of you," he says, his voice gargly, "I'll drink it with green tea."

I don't know if I'll live, but I know the Hierarch has lost. Because, overhead, the spines of the kraken skeleton vibrate and sing. And just before the Hierarch unleashes another torrent of magic from inside, the storm I called with Dad strikes. The bolts come down. The bolts come out of me. They come from Dad's bones, soaked with Dad's magic, mixed in my blood. They come from spirits and memories.

When it's over, the Hierarch's charred body melts into a puddle of brown, sizzling fluid.

Ding-dong, dead.

I should just walk out of here. With my glasses, I can get past the guards and get as far from the ossuary as a guy with a broken arm and a ravaged face can get.

But the residue of the Hierarch is thick, powerful magic. There's got to be a sponge and bucket around here somewhere.

We've been driving all day and all night and have been for a few days. Connie rides with Miranda in the back, singing Spanish lullabies, trying to get her to stop crying. I cooked up a salve for her hand, and I don't think it hurts her any longer, but the girl misses the tip of her finger. Of course she does. How could she not? When she's older, maybe I'll give it to her and she can wear it on the end of a necklace.

And once that thought is complete, I want to hit myself. Isn't that the sort of thing Dad might do?

At least once every hour I'm tempted to turn the car around and head back to Los Angeles. There's a fight being waged there between high-ranking ministers and osteomancers, between freelancers and opportunists and twisted idealists like Otis and the turtle man. I shouldn't be tempted to head back and join in, but I am. I'm pretty sure I would prevail. After drinking the Hierarch's remains, I may well be the most powerful osteomancer in all the Californias. Possibly the most powerful on the entire continent. Part of me wants that power. There's something in my bones that craves it.

But then, when the hunger gets too strong, I lean back and get a whiff of Miranda. She carries the taint of magic, a scent much older than she is, and I won't stop driving, till all I can smell is baby powder and shampoo and clean, soft skin.

SALT WINE

———

Peter S. Beagle

All right, then. First off, this ain't a story about some seagoing candytrews dandy Captain Jack, or whatever you want to call him, who falls in love with a mermaid and breaks his troth to a mortal woman to live with his fish-lady under the sea. None of that in this story, I can promise you; and our man's no captain, but a plain blue-eyed sailorman named Henry Lee, AB, who starts out good for nowt much but reefing a sail, holystoning a deck, taking a turn in the crow's-nest, talking his way out of a tight spot, and lending his weight to the turning of a capstan and his voice to the bellowing of a chanty. He drank some, and most often when he drank it ended with him going at it with one or another of his mates. Lost part of an ear that way off Panama, he did, and even got flogged once for pouring grog on the captain. But there was never no harm in Henry Lee, not in them days. Anybody remembers him'll tell you that.

Me name's Ben Hazeltine. I remember Henry Lee, and I'll tell you why.

I met Henry Lee when we was both green hands on the *Mary Brannum,* out of Cardiff, and we stayed messmates on and off, depending. Didn't always ship out together, nowt like that—just seemed to happen so. Any road, come one rainy spring, we was on the beach together, out of work. Too many hands, not enough ships—you get that, some seasons. Captains can take their pick those times, and Henry Lee and I weren't neither one anybody's first pick. Isle of Pines, just south of Cuba—devil of a place to be stranded, I'll tell you. Knew we'd land a berth sooner or later—always had before—only we'd no idea when, and both of us hungry enough to eat a seagull, but too weak to grab one. I'll tell you the God's truth, we'd gotten to where we was looking at bloody starfish and those Portygee man-o'-war jellies and wondering . . . well, there you are, that's how bad it were. I've been in worse spots, but not many.

Now back then, there was mermaids all over the place, like you don't see so much today. Partial to warm waters, they are—the Caribbean, Mediterranean, the Gulf Stream—but I've seen them off the Orkneys, and even off Greenland a time or two, that's a fact. What's *not* a fact is the singing. Combing their hair, yes; they're women, after all, and that's what women do, and how you going to comb your hair out underwater? But I never heard one mermaid sing, not once.

And they ain't all beautiful—stop a clock, some of them would.

Now, what you *didn't* see much of in the old times, and don't hardly be seeing at all these days, was mer*men*. Merrows, some folk call them. Ugly as fried sin, the lot: not a one but's got a runny red nose, nasty straggly hair—red too, mostly, I don't know why—stumpy green teeth sticking up and out every which way, skin like a crocodile's arse. You get a look at one of those, it don't take much to figure why your mermaid takes to hanging around sailors. Put me up against a merrow, happen even *I* start looking decent enough, by and by.

Any road, like I told you, Henry Lee and I was pretty well down to eating our boots—or we would have been if we'd had any. We was stumbling along the beach one morning, guts too empty to growl, looking for someone to beg or borrow from—or maybe just chew up on the spot, either way—when there's a sudden commotion out in the water, and someone screaming for help. Well, I knew it were a merrow straightaway, and so did Henry Lee—you can't ever mistake a merrow's creaky, squawky voice, once you've heard it—and when we ran to look, we saw he had a real reason to scream. Big hammerhead had him cornered against the reef, circling and circling him, the way they do when they're working up to a strike. No, I tell a lie, I misremember—it were a tiger shark, not a hammerhead. Hammer, he swims in big packs, he'll stay out in the deep water, but your tiger, they'll come right in close, right into the shallows. And they'll leave salmon or tuna to go after a merrow. Just how they are.

Now merrows are tough as they're unsightly, you don't never want to be disputing a fish or a female with a merrow. But to a tiger shark, a merrow's a nice bit of Cornish pasty. This one were flapping his arms at the tiger, hitting out with his tail—worst thing he could have done; they'll go for the tail first thing, that's the good part. I says to Henry Lee, I says, "Look sharp, mate—might be summat over for us." Sharks is real slapdash about their meals, and we was *hungry.*

But Henry Lee, he gives me just the one look, with his eyes all big and strange—and then rot me if he ain't off like a pistol shot, diving into the surf and heading straight for the reef and that screaming merrow. Ain't too many sailors can really swim, you know, but Henry Lee, he were a Devon man, and he used to say he swam before he could walk. He had a knife in his belt—won it playing euchre with a Malay pirate—and I could see it glinting between his teeth as he slipped through them waves like a dolphin, which is a shark's mortal enemy, you know. Butt 'em in the side, what they do, in the belly, knock 'em right out of the water. I've seen it done.

That tiger shark never knew Henry Lee were coming till he were on its back, hanging on like a jockey and stabbing everywhere he could reach. Blood enough in the water, I couldn't hardly see anything—I could just hear that merrow, still screeching his ugly head off. Time I caught sight of Henry Lee again, he were halfway back to shore, grinning at me around that bloody knife, and a few fins already slicing in to finish off their mate, ta ever so. I practically dragged Henry Lee out of the water, 'acos of he were bleeding too—shark's hide'll take your own skin off, and his thighs looked like he'd been buggering a hedgehog.

"Barking mad," I told him. "Barking, roaring, *howling* mad! God's frigging *teeth,* you ought to be put somewhere you can't hurt yourself—aye, nor nobody else. What in frigging Jesus' frigging name *possessed* you, you louse-ridden get?"

See, it weren't that we was all such mates back then, me and Henry Lee, it were more that I thought I *knew* him—knew what he'd do when, and what he wouldn't; knew what I could trust him for, and what I'd better see to meself. There's times your life can depend on that kind of knowing—weren't for that, I wouldn't be here, telling this. I says it again, "What the Christ possessed you, Henry bleeding Lee?"

But he'd already got his back to me, looking out toward the reef, water still roiling with the sharks fighting for leftovers. "Where's that merrow gone?" he wanted to know. "He was just there—where's he got to?" He was set to swim right back out there, if I hadn't grabbed him again.

"Panama by now, if he's got the sense of a weevil," says I. "More sense than you, anyway. What kind of bloody idiot risks his life for a bloody merrow?"

"An idiot who knows how a merrow can reward you!" Henry Lee turned back around to face me, and I swear his blue eyes had gone black and wild as the sea off Halifax. "Didn't you never hear about that? You save a merrow's life, he's bound to give you all his treasure, all the plunder he's ever gathered from shipwrecks, sea fights— everything he's got in his cave, it's the rule. He don't have no choice, it's the *rule!*"

I couldn't help it, I were laughing before he got halfway through. "Aye, Henry Lee," I says. "Aye, I've heard that story, and you know where I heard it? At me mam's tit, that's where, and at every tit since, and every mess where I ever put me feet under the table. Pull the other one, chum, that tale's got long white whiskers on it." Wouldn't laugh at him so today, but there you are. I were younger then.

Well, Henry Lee just gave me that look, one more time, and after that he didn't speak no more about merrows and treasures. But he were up all that night—we slept on the beach, y'see, and every time I roused, the fool were pacing the water's edge, this way and that, gaping out into the bloody black, plain waiting for that grateful merrow to show up with his arms full of gold and jewels and I don't know what, all for him, along of being saved from the sharks. *"Rule,"* thinks I. "Rule, me royal pink bum," and went back to sleep.

But there's treasure and there's treasure—depends how you look at it, I reckon. Very next day, Henry Lee found himself a berth aboard a whaler bound home for Boston and short a foremast hand. He tried to get me signed on too, but . . . well, I knew the captain, and the captain remembered me, so that were the end of that. You'd not believe the grudges some of them hold.

Me, I lucked onto a Spanish ship, a week or ten days later—she'd stopped to take on water, and I got talking with the cook, who needed another messboy. I've had better berths, but it got me to Málaga—and after that, one thing led to another, and I didn't see Henry Lee again for six or seven years, must have been, the way it happens with seamen. I thought about him often enough, riding that tiger shark to rescue that merrow who were going to make him rich, and I asked after him any time I met an English hand, or a Yankee, but never a word could anyone tell me—not until I rounded a fruitstall in the marketplace at Velha Goa, and almost ran over him!

How *I* got there's no great matter—I were a cook meself by then, on a wallowing scow of an East Indiaman, and trying to get some greens and fresh fruit into the crew's hardtack diet, if just to sweeten the farts in the fo'c'sle. As for why I were running, with a box of mangoes in me arms . . . well, that don't figure in this story neither, so never you mind.

Henry Lee looked the same as I remembered him—still not shaving more than every three days, I'd warrant, still as blue-eyed an innocent as ever cracked a bos'un's head with a beer bottle. Only change in him I could see, he didn't look like a sailor no more. Hard to explain; he were dressing just the same as ever—singlet, blue canvas pants, same rope-sole shoes, even the very same dirty white cap he always wore—but *summat* was different about him. Might have been the way he walked—he'd lost that little roll we all have, walked like he'd not been to sea in his life. Aye, might have been that.

Well, he give a great whoop to see me, and he grabbed hold of me, mangoes and all, and dragged me off into a dark little Portygee tavern—smelled of dried fish and fried onions, I remember, and cloves under it all. They knew him there—landlord patted his back, kissed him on the cheek, brought us some kind of mulled ale, and left us alone. And Henry Lee sat there with his arms folded and grinned at me, not saying a word, until I finally told him he looked like a blasted old hen, squatting over one solitary egg, and it likely rotten at that. "Talk or be damned to you," I says. "The drink's not good enough to keep me from walking out of this fleapit."

Henry Lee burst out laughing then, and he grabbed both me hands across the table, saying, "Ah, it's just so grand to see you, old Ben, I don't know what to say first, I swear I don't."

"Tell about the money, mate," I says, and didn't he stare *then?* I says, "Your clothes are for shite, right enough, but you're walking like a man with money in every pocket—you talk like your mouth's full of money, and you're scared it'll all spill out if you open your lips too wide. Now, last time I saw you, you hadn't a farthing to bless yourself with, so let's talk about that, hey? That merrow turn up with his life savings, after all?" And *I* laughed, because I'd meant it as a joke. I did.

Henry Lee didn't laugh. He looked startled, and then he leaned so close I could see where he'd lost a side tooth and picked up a scar right by his left eyebrow—made him look younger, somehow, those things did, along with that missing bit of ear—and he dropped his voice almost to a whisper, no matter there wasn't a soul near us. "No," says he, "no, Ben, he did better than that, a deal better than that. He taught me the making of salt wine."

Aye, that's how I looked at him—exactly the way you're eyeing me now. Like I'm barking mad, and Jesus and the saints wouldn't have me. And the way you mumbled, *"Salt wine?"*—I said it just the same as you, tucking me head down like that, getting me legs under me, in case things turned ugly. I did it true. But Henry Lee only sat back and grinned again. "You heard me, Ben," he says. "You heard me clear enough."

"Salt wine," I says, and different this time, slowly. "Salt wine . . . that'd be like pickled beer? Oysters in honey, that kind of thing, is it? How about bloody fried marmalade, then?" Takes me a bit of time to get properly worked up, mind, but foolery will do it. "Whale blubber curry," I says. "Boiled nor'easter."

For answer, Henry Lee reaches into those dirty canvas pants and comes up with a cheap pewter flask, two for sixpence in any chandlery. Doesn't say one word—just hands it to me, folds his hands on the table and waits. I take me time, study the flask—got a naked lady and a six-point buck on one side, and somebody in a flying chariot looks like it's caught fire on the other. I start to say how I don't drink much wine—never did, not Spanish sherry, nor even port, nor none of that Frenchy slop—but Henry Lee flicks one finger to tell me I'm to shut me gob and taste. So that's what I did.

All right, this is the hard part to explain. Nor about merrows, nor neither the part about some bloody fool jumping on the back of a tiger shark—the part about the wine. Because it *were* wine in that flask, and it *were* salty, and right there's where I run aground on a lee shore, trying to make you taste and see summat you never will, if your luck holds. *Salt wine*—not red nor neither white, but gray-green, like the deep sea, and smelling like the sea, filling your head with the sea, but wine all the same. *Salt wine . . . .*

First swallow, I lost meself. I didn't think I were ever coming back.

Weren't nothing like being drunk. I've downed enough rum, enough brandy, dropped off to sleep in enough jolly company and wakened in enough stinking alleys behind enough shebeens to know the difference. This were more . . . this were like I'd fallen overboard from me, from meself, and not a single boat lowered to find me. But it didn't matter none, because *summat* were bearing me up, *summat* were surging under me, big and fast and wild, as it might have been a dolphin between me legs, tearing along through the sea—or the air, might be we were flying, I'd not have known—carrying somebody off to somewhere, and who it was I can't tell you now no more than I could have then. But it weren't me, I'll take me affydavy on that. I weren't there. I weren't anywhere or anybody, and just then that were just where I wanted to be.

Just then . . . Aye, you give me a choice just then, happen I might have chosen . . . But I'd just had that one swallow, after all, so in a bit there I were, me as ever was, back at that tavern table with Henry Lee, and him still grinning like a dog with two tails, and he says to me, "Well, Ben?"

When I can talk, I ask him, "You can make this swill yourself?" and when he nods, "Then I'd say your merrow earned his keep. Not half bad."

"Best *you* ever turned into piss," Henry says. I don't say nowt back, and after a bit, he leans forward, drops his voice way down again, and says, "It's our fortune, Ben. Yours and mine. I'm swearing on my mother's grave."

"If the dollymop's even got one," I says, because of course he don't know who his mam was, no more than I know mine. They just dropped us both and went their mortal ways, good luck to us all. I tell him, "Never mind the swearing, just lay out what you mean by *our fortune*. I didn't save no merrow—fact, I halfway tried to save *you* from trying to save him. He don't owe me nowt, and nor do you." And I'm on me feet and ready to scarper—just grab up those mangoes and walk. Ain't a living soul thinks I've got no pride, but I bloody do.

But Henry Lee's up with me, catching ahold of me arm like an octopus, and he's saying, "No, no, Ben, you don't understand. I need you, you have to help me, sit down and *listen*." And he pulls and pushes me back down, and leans right over me, so close I can see the scar as cuts into his hairline, where the third mate of the *Boston Annie* got him with a marlinspike, happened off the Azores. He says, "I can make it, the salt wine, but I need a partner to market it for me. I've got no head for business—I don't know the first thing about selling. You've got to ship it, travel with it, be my factor. Because I can't do this without you, d'you see, Ben?"

"No, I don't see a frigging thing," I says in his face. "I'm no more a factor than you're a bloody nun. What I am's a seacook, and it's past time I was back aboard me ship, so by your leave—"

Henry Lee's still gripping me arm so it *hurts*, and I can't pry his fingers loose. "Ben, *listen!*" he fair bellows again. "This is Goa, not the City of London—the Indians won't ever deal honestly with a Britisher who doesn't have an army behind him—why should they?—and the Portuguese bankers don't trust me any more than I'd trust a single one of them not to steal the spots off a leopard and come back later for the whiskers. There's a few British financiers, but *they* don't trust anyone who didn't go to Eton or Harrow. Now you're a lot more fly than you ever let on, I've always known that—"

"Too kind," I says, but he don't hear. He goes on, "You're the one who always knew when we were being cheated—by the captain, by the company, by the lady of the house, didn't matter. Any *souk* in the world, any marketplace, I always let you do the bargaining—*always*. You'd haggle forever over a penny, a peseta, a single anna—and you'd get your price every time. Remember? I surely remember."

"Ain't nothing like running a business," I tell him. "What you're talking about is responsibility, and I never been responsible for nowt but the job I were paid to do right. I like it that way, Henry Lee, it suits me. What you're talking about—"

"I'm talking about a *future*, Ben. Spend your whole life going from berth to berth, ship to ship—where are you at the end of it? Another rotting hulk, like all the rest, careened on the beach, and no tide ever coming again to float you off. I'm offering you the security of a decent roof over your head, good meals on your table, and a few teeth left in your mouth to chew them with." He lets go of me then, but his blue eyes don't. He says, "I'd outfit you, I'd pay your way, and I'd give you one-third of the profits—ah, hell, make it forty, forty percent, what do you say? It'll be worth it to me to sleep snug a'nights, knowing my old shipmate's minding the shop and putting the cat out. What do you say, Ben? Will you do it for me?"

I look at him for a good while, not saying nowt. I remember him one time, talking a drunken gang of Yankee sailors out of dropping us into New York harbor for British spies—wound up buying us drinks, they did, which bloody near killed us anyway. And Piraeus—God's teeth, Piraeus—when the fool put the comehither on the right woman at the wrong time, and there we was, locked in a cellar for two days and nights, while her husband and his mates went on and on, just upstairs, about how to slaughter us so we'd remember it. Henry Lee, he finally got them persuaded that I were carrying some sort of horrible disease, rot your cods off, you leave it long enough, make your nose fall into your soup. They pushed the cellar key under the door and was likely in Istanbul, time we got out of that house. Me, I didn't stop feeling me nose for another two days.

So I know what Henry Lee can do, talking, and I sniff all around his words, like a fox who smells the bait and knows the trap's there, somewhere, underneath. I keep telling him, over and over, "Henry Lee, I never been no better than you with figures—I'd likely run you bankrupt inside of a month." Never stops him—he just grins and answers back, "I'm bankrupt already, Ben. I'm not swimming in boodle, like you thought—I've gone and sunk all I own into a thousand cases of salt wine. Nothing more to lose, you see—there's no way you can make anything any the worse. So what do you say now?"

I don't answer, but I up with that naked-lady flask, and I take another swallow. This time I know what's coming, and I set meself for it, but the salt wine catches me up again, lifts me and tosses me like before, same as if I was a ship with me mainmast gone, and the waves doing what they like with me. No, it's not like before—I don't lose Ben Hazeltine, nor I don't forget who I am. What happens, I *find* summat. I find *everything*. I can't rightly stand up proper, 'acos I don't know which way up *is*, and I feel the eyes rocking in me head, and I'm dribbling wine like I've not done since I were a babby . . . but for a minute, two minutes—no more, I couldn't have stood no more— everything in the world makes sense to me. For one minute, I'm the flyest cove in the whole world.

Then it's gone—gone, thank God or Old Horny, either one—and I'm back to old ordinary, and Henry Lee's watching me, not a word, and when I can talk I say, "There's more. I know you, and I know there's more. You want me to come in with you, Henry Lee, you tell me the part you're not telling me. Now."

He don't answer straight off—just keeps looking at me out of those nursery-blue eyes. I decide I'd best help him on a bit, so I say, "Right, then, don't mind if we do talk about merrows. Last time I saw you, you was risking your life for the ugliest one of them ugly buggers, and him having to hand over every farthing he'd got sewn into his underwear, because that's the frigging rule, right? So when did that happen, hey? We never seen him again, far as *I* know."

"He found me," Henry Lee says. "Took him a while, but he caught up with me in Port of Spain. It's important to them, keeping their word, though you wouldn't think so." He keeps cracking his knuckles, the way he always used to do when he weren't sure the captain were swallowing his tale about why we was gone three days in Singapore. "I had it wrong," he says, "that rule thing. I expected he'd come with his whole fortune in his arms, but all the merrow has to bring you is the thing that's most precious to him in the world. The most precious thing in the world to that merrow I saved—I call him Gorblimey, that's as close as I can get to his name—the most precious thing to him was that recipe for salt wine. It's only some of them know how to make it, and they've never given it to a human before. I'm the only one."

Me head's still humming like a honey tree, only it's swarming with the ghosts of all the things I knew for two minutes. Henry Lee goes on, "He couldn't write it down for me—they can't read or write, of course, none of them, I'd never thought about that—so he made me learn it by heart. All that night, over and over, the two of us, me hiding in a lifeboat, him floating in the ship's shadow, over and over and *over,* till I couldn't have remembered my own name. He was so afraid I'd get it wrong."

"How would you know?" I can't help asking him. "Summat like that wine, how could you tell if it *were* wrong, or gone bad?"

Henry Lee bristles up at me, the way he'd have his ears flat back if he was a cat. "I make it exactly the way Gorblimey taught me—*exactly.* There's no chance of any mistake, Gorblimey himself wouldn't know whether I made it or he did. Get that right out of your headpiece, Ben, and just tell me if you'll help me. *Now,*" he growls, mimicking me to the life. He'd land in the brig, anyway once every voyage, imitating the officers.

Now, I'm not blaming nobody, you may lay to that. I'm not even blaming the salt wine, although I could. What I done, I done out of me own chuckleheadedness, not because I was drunk, not because Henry Lee and me'd been shipmates. No, it were the money, and that's the God's truth—just the money. He were right, you can live on a seacook's pay, but that's all you *can* do. Can't retire, and maybe open a little seaside inn—can't marry, can't live nowhere but on a bloody ship . . . no, it's no life, not without the needful, and there's not many can afford to be too choosy how they come by it. I says, "Might do, Henry Lee. Forty percent. Might do. *Might*."

Henry Lee just lit up all at once, one big *wooosh*, like a Guy Fawkes bonfire. "Ah, Ben. Ah, Ben, I knew you'd turn up trumps, old growly truepenny Ben. You won't be sorry, my old mate," and he claps me on the shoulder, near enough knocking me over. "I promise you won't be sorry."

So I left that Indiaman tub looking for another cook, and I signed on right there as Henry Lee's factor—his partner, his first mate, his right hand, whatever you like to call it. Took us a hungry year or so to get our feet under us, being just the two, but the word spread faster than you might have supposed. Aye, that were the thing about that salt wine—there were them as took to it like a Froggie to snails, and another sort couldn't even abide the *look* of it in the bottle. I were with that lot, and likely for the same reason—not 'acos it were nasty, but 'acos it were too good, too *much*, more than a body could thole, like the Scots say. I never touched it again after that second swig, never once, not in all the years I peddled salt wine fast as Henry Lee could make it. Not for cheer, not for sorrow, not even for a wedding toast when Henry Lee married, which I'll get to by and by. Couldn't thole it, that's all, couldn't risk it no more. Third time might eat me up, third time might make me disappear. I stayed faithful to rum and mother's-ruin, and let the rest go, for once in me fool life.

Year and a half, we had buyers wherever ships could sail. London, Liverpool, Marseilles, Hamburg, Amsterdam, Buenos Aires, Athens, New York, Rome, Naples—we did best in seaports, always. I didn't travel everywhere the wine went; we hired folk in time, me and Henry Lee, and we even bought a ship of our own. Weren't no big ship, not so's you'd take notice, but big enough for what we put aboard her, which was the best captain and crew anyone could ask for. That were me doing—Henry Lee wanted to spend more on a fancier ship, but I told him it weren't how many sails that mattered, but the hands on the halyards. And he listened to me, which he mostly did . . . aye, you couldn't never call him stupid, poor sod. I'll say that, anyway.

Used to look out for that merrow, Henry Lee's Gorblimey, times I were keeping the wine company on its way. Not that I'd likely have known him from any other of the ones I'd see now and again, chasing the flying fish or swimming along with the porpoises—even nastier, they looked, in the middle of those creatures—but I'd ponder whiles if he knew what were passing above his head, and what he'd be thinking about it if he did. But Henry Lee never spoke word about merrows nor mermaids, none of all that, not if he could help it. Choused him, whiles, I did, telling him he were afeard Gorblimey'd twig how well we was getting on, and come for his own piece, any day now. That'd rouse him every time, and he'd snap at me like a moray, so I belayed that. Might could be I shouldn't have, but who's to say? Who's to say now?

He'd other matters on his mind by then, what with building himself a slap-up new house on the seafront north of Velha Goa. Palace and a half, it were, to me own lookout, with two floors and two verandas and *four* chimneys—four chimneys, in a country where you might be lighting a fire maybe twice a year. But Henry Lee told me, never mind: didn't the grandest place in that Devon town where he were born have four chimneys, and hadn't he always wanted to live just so in a house just like that one? Couldn't say nowt much to that, could I? Me that used to stare hours into the cat's-meat shop window back home, cause I got it in me head the butcher were me da? He weren't, by the by, but you see?

But I did speak a word or two when Henry Lee up and got wed. Local girl, Julia Caterina and about five other names I disremember, with a couple of *das* in between, like the Portygee nobs do. Pretty enough, she were, with dark brown hair for two or three, brown eyes to crack your heart, and a smile to make a priest give up Lent. Aye, and though she started with nobbut *hello* and *goodbye* and *whiskey-soda* in English, didn't she tackle to it till she shamed me, who never mastered no more than a score of words in her tongue, and not one of them fit for her ears. Good-tempered with it, too—though she fought her parents bare-knuckle and toe to toe, like Figg or Mendoza, until they let her toss over the grandee they'd promised her to, all for the love of a common Jack Tar, that being what he still were in their sight, didn't matter how many Bank of England notes he could wave at them. "She's a lady," I says, "for all she's a Portygee, and you're no more a gentleman than that monkey in your mango tree. Money don't make such as us into gentlemen, Henry Lee. All it does, it makes us rich monkeys. You know that, same as me."

"I'm plain daft over her, Ben," says he, like I'd never spoke at all. "Can't eat, can't sleep, can't do a thing but dream about having her near me all the time. Nothing for it but the altar."

"Speaking of altars," says I, "you'll have to turn Papist, and there's not one of her lot'll ever believe you mean it, no more than I would. And never mind her family—what about her friends, what about that whole world she's been part of since the day she were born? You reckon to sweep her up and away from all that, or try to ease yourself into it and hope they won't twig what you are? Which is it to be, then, hey?"

"I don't know, Ben," says Henry Lee, real quiet. "I don't know anything anymore." He said me name, but he weren't talking to me—maybe to that monkey, maybe to the waves out beyond the seawall. "The one thing I've got a good hold on, when I'm with her, it's like coming home. First time I saw her, it came over me, I've been gone a long time, and now I'm home."

Well, you can't talk sense to nobody in a state like that, so I wished them luck and left them to it. Aye, and I even danced at the wedding, sweating like a hog in a new silk suit, Chinee silk, and kicking the bride's shins with every turn. Danced with the mother-in-law too, with her crying on me shoulder the while, how she'd lost her poor angel forever to this soulless brute of an English *merchant*, which no matter he'd converted, he weren't no real Catholic, nor never would be. I tried to get *her* shins, that one, but she were quick, I'll say that for her.

So there's Henry Lee and his pretty new missus, and him so happy staying home with her, hosting grand gatherings just for folk to look at her, he weren't no use for nowt else, save telling me how happy he were. Oh, he still brewed up the salt wine himself—wouldn't trust me nor no other with the makings—but for the rest of it, I were near enough running the business without him. Took in the orders, paid the accounts, kept the books, supervised the packing and the shipping, every case, every bloody bottle. Even bought us a second ship—found her and bargained for her, paid cash down, all on me own hook. Long way from the Isle of Pines, hey?

Like I say, I didn't make all the voyages. Weren't any degree necessary for me to make none on 'em, tell the truth—and besides I were getting on, and coming to like the land more than I ever thought I would. But I never could shake me taste for the Buenos Aires run. I knew some women there, and a few men too . . . aye, that's a fine town, Buenos. A man could settle in that town, and I were thinking about it then.

So we're three days from landfall, and I'm on deck near sunset, taking the air and keeping a lookout for albatrosses. No finer bird than an albatross, you can keep your eagles. A quiet, quiet evening— wide red sky streaked with a bit of green, fine weather tomorrow. You can hear the gulls' wings, and fish jumping now and then, and the creaking of the strakes, and sometimes even the barrels of salt wine shifting down in the hold. Then I hear footsteps behind me, and I turn and see the bos'un's mate coming up on deck. Can't think of his name right now—a short, wide man, looked like a wine barrel himself, but tough as old boots. Monkey Sucker, that's it, that's what they called him. Because he liked to drink his rum out of a cocoanut, you see. Never see no one doing that, these days.

He weren't looking too hearty, old Monkey Sucker. Red eyes and walking funny, for a start, like his legs didn't belong to him, but I put that down to him nipping at the bung down below. Now I already told you, I never again laid lip to that salt wine from that first day to this, but folk that liked it, why, they'd be waiting on the docks when we landed, ready to unload the cargo themselves right on the spot. And half the crew was the same way, run yourself blind barmy trying to keep them out of the casks. Well, we done the practical, Henry Lee and me: we rigged the hold to keep all but the one barrel under lock and key. That one we left out and easy tapped, and it'd usually last us there and back, wherever we was bound. But this Monkey Sucker . . . no, he weren't just drunk, I saw that on second glance. Not drunk. I wish it *had* been that, for he weren't a bad sort.

"Mr. Hazeltine," he says to me. "Well, Mr. Hazeltine." Kept on saying me name like we'd just met, and he were trying to get a right fix on it. His voice didn't sound proper, neither, but it kept cracking and bleating—like a boy's voice when it's changing, you know. And there were summat bad wrong with his nose and his mouth.

"Monk," I says back, "you best get your arse below decks before the captain claps eyes on you. You look worse than a poxy bumboy on Sunday morning." The light's going fast now, but I can make out that his face is all bad swole up and somehow *twisty*-like, and there's three lines like welts on both sides of his neck. He's got his arms wrapped around himself, holding himself *tight*, the way you'd think he were about to birth four thousand babies at one go, like some fish do it. And he keeps mumbling me name, over and over, but he's not looking at me, not once, he's looking at the rail on the starboard side. Aye, I should have twigged to that straightaway, I know. I didn't, that's all.

Suddenly he says, "Water." Clear as clear, no mistake about it. "Water," and he points over the side. Excited, bobbing on his toes, like a nipper at Brighton. Third time, "*Water*," and at least I were the first to bawl, "Man overboard!" there's that. In the midst of all the noise and garboil, with everyone tumbling on deck to heave to, and the captain yelling at everyone to lower a boat, with the bos'un crazy trying to lower *two*, 'acos he and Monkey Sucker was old mates . . . in the midst of it all, I saw Monkey Sucker in the sea. I *saw* him, understand? He weren't splashing around, waving and screaming for help, and he weren't treading water neither. No, he's trying to swim, calm as can be—only he's trying to swim like a fish, laying himself flat in the water and *wriggling* his legs together, same as if he had a tail, understand? Only he didn't have no tail, and he sank like that, straight down, straight down. They kept that boat out all night, but they never did find him.

We reported the death to the customs people in Buenos Aires, and I sent word to Henry Lee back in Goa. The captain and the mates kept asking the crew about why Monkey Sucker had done it, scragged himself that way—were it the drink got him? Were it over some dockside bint? Did he owe triple interest on some loan to Silas Barker or Icepick Neddie Frey? Couldn't get no answer, not one, that made no sense to them, nor to me neither.

Heading home, every barrel gone, hold full of Argentine wheat for ballast, now it's me turn to chat up the crew, on night watch or in the mess. I go at it like a good 'un, but there's not a soul can tell me anything I don't know.

I were first ashore before dawn at Velha Goa—funny to think of that fine Mandovi River all silted up today, whole place left to the snakes and the kites—and if I didn't run all the way to Henry Lee's house, may I never piss again. Man at the door to let me in, another man to take me hat and offer me a glass. I didn't take it.

I bellow for Henry Lee, and here he comes, rushing downstairs in his shirtsleeves, one shoe off and one on. "Ben, what is it? What's happened? Is it the ship?" Because he never could get used to having two ships of his own—always expected one or t'other to sink or burn, or be taken by the Barbary pirates. I didn't say nowt, just grabbed him by the arm and hauled him off into the room he calls the library. Shut the door, turn around, look into his frighted blue eyes. "It ain't the ship, Henry Lee," I tell him. "It's the hands."

"The hands," he says. "I don't understand."

"And it ain't the hands," I say, "it's the buyers. And it ain't the buyers." I take a breath, wish God'd put a noggin of rum in me fist right now, but there ain't no God. "It's the wine."

Henry Lee shakes his head. He reaches for a bottle on the sideboard, pours himself a drink. Salt wine, it is—I knock it out of his hand, so it splashes on his fancy rug, and now I'm whispering, because if I shout everything comes apart. "It's the wine, Henry Lee. You know it, and now I know."

That about him knowing, that was a guess, and now I'm the one looking away, 'acos of I don't want to find out I'm right. And because it's hard to say the bloody words, either way. "The salt wine," I says. "It frigging well killed a man, this time out, and I'm betting it's done it before."

"No," Henry Lee says. "No, Ben, that's not possible." But I look straight back at him, and I know what he's fighting not to think.

"Maybe he didn't mean no harm, your Gorblimey," I go on. "Maybe he'd no notion what his old precious gift would do to human beings. Maybe it depends on how much of it you drink, or how often." So still in that fine house, I can hear his Julia Caterina turning in the bed upstairs, murmuring into her pillow. I say, "Old Monkey Sucker, he never could keep away from the cask in the hold, maybe that's why . . . why it happened. Maybe if you don't drink too much."

"No," Henry Lee answers me, and his voice is real quiet too. "That wouldn't make sense, Ben. I drink salt wine every day. A lot of it."

He's always got a flask of the creature somewhere about him, true enough, and you won't see him go too long without his drop. But there's no sign of any change, not in his face, nor in his skin, nor his teeth—and that last time Monkey Sucker said "water" I could see his teeth had got all sprawled out-like, couldn't hardly close his mouth. But Henry Lee just went on looking like Henry Lee, except a little bit grayer, a bit wearier, a bit more pulled-down, like, the way quitting the sea will do to you. No merrow borning there, not that I could see.

"Well, then," says I, "it's not the amount of wine. But it *is* the wine. Tell me that's not so, and I'll believe you, Henry Lee. I will."

Because I never knew him lie to me. Might take his time getting around to telling me some things, but he wouldn't never lie outright. But he just shook his head again, and looked down, and he heaved a sigh sounded more like a death rattle. Says, "It could be. It could be. I don't know, Ben."

"You know," I says. "How long?" He don't answer, don't say nowt for a while—he just turns and turns in a little tight circle, this way and that, like a bear at a baiting. Finally he goes on, mumbling now, like

118

he'd as soon I didn't hear. "The Tagus, last year, that time I took Julia Caterina to Lisbon. A man on the riverbank, he just *tumbled* . . . I didn't get a really good look, I couldn't be sure what I was seeing, I swear, Ben." I can't make no sound. Henry Lee grabs me hands, wrings them between his until they hurt. "Ben, it's like you said, maybe Gorblimey didn't know himself—"

I pull me hands free, and for a minute I have to close me eyes, 'acos if I was on a ship I'd be seasick. I hear meself saying, "Maybe he didn't. But we do. We know now."

"No, we don't! It still mightn't be the wine—it could be any number of things." He takes a deep, deep breath, plunges on. "Even if—even if that's so, obviously it's just a few, a very few, not one in a thousand, if even . . . I mean, you don't see it happening everywhere, it's just—it's like the way some folk can't abide shellfish, the way cheese gripes your gut, Ben, every time. It's got to be so with the salt wine."

"Even one," I says. It catches in me throat and comes out a whisper, so I can't tell if he's heard. We stand there, looking at each other, like we're waiting to be introduced. Henry Lee reaches for me hand again, but I step away. Henry Lee starts to say summat, but then he don't. There's blood in me mouth, I can taste it.

"I done bad things, Henry Lee," I says at last. "I know where I'm going when I go, and none to blame but me. I know who's waiting for me there, too—some nights I see their faces all around the room, plain as I now see you. But in me life I never done nothing, *nothing* . . . I got to get out of your house, Henry Lee."

And I'm for the door, because I can't look at him no more. He calls after me—once, twice—and I think he's bound sure to try and drag me back, maybe to gull me into seeing things his way, maybe just not to be alone. But he don't, and I walk on home along the seafront, a deal slower than I came. And when I get there—it were a plain little house, nobbut the one servant, and him not living in, because I can't abide folk around me when I rise—when I got there, I drank meself to sleep with me whole stock of good Christian rum. And in the morning I went to see Henry Lee's lawyer—*our* lawyer—Portygee-Goan, he were, name of Andres Furtado, near enough—and I started working an old fool name of Ben Hazeltine loose from the salt wine business. It took me some while.

Cost me a few bob, too, I don't mind saying. We'd made an agreement long back, Henry Lee and me, that if ever I wanted to sell me forty percent, he'd have to buy me out, will-he, nil-he. But I didn't want no more of that salt wine money—couldn't swallow the notion, no more than I could have swallowed a single mouthful of the stuff ever again after that second time.

So by and by, all what you call the legalities was taken care of, and there was I, on the beach again, in a manner of speaking. But at least I'd saved a bit—wouldn't last forever, but leastways I could bide me time finding other work, and not before the mast, neither. Too old to climb the rigging, too used to proper dining to go back to cooking in burned pots and rusty pannikins in some Grand Banks trawler's galley—aye, and far too fast-set in me ways of doing things to be taking orders from no captain hadn't seen what I've seen in this world. "Best bide ashore awhile, Ben Hazeltine," I says to meself, "and see who might be needing what you yet can do. There'll be someone," I says, "as there always is," and I'd believe it, too, days on end. But I'd been used to a lot of things regular, not only me meals. Henry Lee, he were one of them, him and his bloody salt wine. Not that I'd have gone back working for the fool—over the side meself first, and I can't swim no better than poor old Monkey Sucker. But still.

So when Henry Lee's young wife shows up at me door, all by herself, no husband, no servants, just her parasol and a whole great snowy spill of lace down her front, I asked her in like she were me long-lost baby sister. We weren't close, didn't know each other much past the salon and the dining room, but she were pretty and sweet, and I liked her the best I could. Like I tried to tell Henry Lee, I don't belong in the same room with no lady. Even when it's me own room.

Any road, she come in, and she sat down, and she says, "Mr. Ben, my husband, he miss you very much." Never knew a woman quicker off the mark and to the point than little Mrs. Julia Caterina Five-other-names Lee. I can still see her, sitting in me best company chair, with her little fan and her hands in her lap, and that bit of a smile that she could never quite hide. Henry Lee said it were a nervous thing with her mouth, and that she were shamed by it, but I don't know.

"We're old partners, him and me," I answers her. "We was sailors together when we was young. But I'm done working with him, no point in pretending otherwise. You're wasting your time, ma'am, I have to tell you. He shouldn't ought to have sent you here."

"Oh, he did not sent me," she says quickly. "I come—how is it?—on my ownsome? And no, I do not imagine you to come back for him, I would not ask you such a thing, not for him. But you . . . I think for you this would be good." I gawk at her, and she smiles a real smile now. She says, "You come to us alone—no friend, no woman, never. I think you are lonely."

Not in me life. Nobody in me *life* has ever spoke that word about me. Nobody. Not me, not nobody, never. I can't do nothing but sit there and gawp. She goes on, "He has not many friends either, my Enrique. You, me—maybe one of my brothers, maybe the *abogao*, the lawyer. Not so many, eh?" And she puts out her hands toward me, a little way. Not for me to take them—more like giving me summat. She says, "I do not know what he have done to make you angry. So bad?"

I can't talk—it ain't in me just then, looking at those hands, at her face. I nod, that's all.

No tears, no begging, no trying to talk me round. She just nods herself, and gets up, and I escort her out to where her coachman's waiting. Settling back inside, she holds out one hand, but this time it's formal, it's what nobby Portygee ladies do. I kissed her mother's hand at the wedding, so I've got the trick of it—more like a breath, it is, more like you're smelling a flower. For half a minute, less, we're looking straight into each other's eyes, and I see the sadness. Maybe for Henry Lee, maybe for me—I never did know. Maybe it weren't never there.

But afterwards I couldn't stop thinking about her. I don't mean *her*, not like that, wouldn't have occurred to me. I mean what she said, and the way she looked at me, and her coming to see me by herself, which you won't never see no Portygee lady doing, high nor low. And saying that thing about me being lonely—true or not ain't the point.

It were her *saying* it, and how I felt to hear her. I plain wanted to hear her again, is all.

But I didn't. It would have meant seeing Henry Lee, and I weren't no way up to that. I talked to him in me head every time I saw one or t'other of our ships slipping slow out of the harbor in the morning sun, sails filling and the company pennant snapping atop the mizzenmast. And her hold full of poison. I had time enough on me hands to spend with sailors ashore, and shillings enough to buy another round of what's-your-fancy, and questions enough to keep them talking and me mind unsettled. Because most of them hadn't noticed nothing—no shipmates turning, no buyers swimming out to sea, no changelings whispering to them from the dark water. But there was always a couple, two or even three who'd seen *summat* they'd as soon not have seen, and who'd have to down more than a few jars of the best before they'd speak about it even to each other. Aye, I knew *that* feeling, none better.

They wasn't all off our ships, neither. Velha were still a fair-sized port then, not like it is now, and there was traders and packets and merchantmen in from everywhere, big and small. I were down the harbor pretty regular, any road, sniffing after work—shaming, me age, but there you are—and I talked with whoever'd stay for it, officers and foremast hands alike. Near as I could work it out, Henry Lee were right, in his way—however much of the salt wine were going down however many throats all over the world, couldn't be more than almost nobody affected beyond waking next day with a bad case of the whips and jingles. Like he'd said to me, *just a few, a very few,* and what difference to old Ben Hazeltine? No lookout of mine no more, I were clear out of that whole clamjamfry altogether, and nobody in the world could say I weren't. Not one single soul in the world.

Only I'd been in it, you see. Right up to me whiskers in it, year on year—grown old in it, I had. Call it regret, call it guilt, call it what you like, all I knew was I'd sleep on straw in the workhouse and live on slops and sermons before I'd knock on Henry Lee's door again. Even to have *her* look at me one more time, the way she looked in me house, in me best chair. I've made few promises in me life, and kept less, but

I made that one then, made it to meself. Suppose you could call it a vow, like, if that suits you.

And I kept that one. It weren't easy, whiles, what with me not finding nobbut portering to do, or might be pushing a barrow for a day or two, but I held to that vow right up to the day when one of Henry Lee's men come to say his master were in greatest need of me—put it just like that, "greatest need"—and would I please come right away, *please*. Tell the truth, I mightn't have come for Henry Lee himself, but that servant, trying to be so calm and proper, with his eyes so frantic . . . Goanese Konkany, he were, name of Gopi.

I didn't run there, like I'd last done—didn't even ride in the carriage he'd sent for me. I walked, and I took me own time about it, too, and I thought on just what I'd say, and what he'd do when I said it, and what I'd do then. And before I knew, I were standing on the steps of that fine house, with no butler waiting but Henry Lee himself, with both hands out to drag me inside. "Ben," he keeps saying, "ah, Ben, Ben, Ben." Like Monkey Sucker again, saying *Mr. Hazeltine, Mr. Hazeltine,* over and over.

He looked old, Henry Lee did. Hair gray as stone, all of it—face slumped in like he'd lost all his teeth at once—shoulders bent to break your heart, the way you'd think he'd been stooping in a Welsh coal mine all his life. And the blue eyes of him . . . I only seen such eyes one time before, on a donkey that knew it were dying, and just wanted it over with. All I could think to say were, "You shouldn't never have left the sea, Henry Lee—not never." But I didn't say it.

He turned away and started up that grand long stair up to the second floor and the bedrooms, with his footsteps sounding like clods falling on a coffin. And I followed after, wishing the stair'd never end, but keep us climbing on and on for always, never getting where we had to go, and I wished I'd never left the sea neither.

I smelled it while we was still on the stair. It ain't a *bad* smell, considering: it's cold and clean, like the wind off Newfoundland or when you're just entering the Kattegat, bound for Copenhagen. Aye . . . aye, you could say it's a fishy smell, too, if you care to, which I don't. I'd smelled it before that day, and I've smelled it since, but I don't never smell it without thinking about her, *Señora* Julia Caterina Five-names Lee, Missus Henry Lee. Without seeing her there in the big bed.

He'd drawn every curtain, so you had to stand blind and blinking for a few minutes, till your eyes got used to the dark. She were lying under a down quilt—me wedding gift to the bride, Hindoo lady up in Ponda sewed it for me—but just as we came in she shrugged it off, and you could see her bare as a babby to the waist. Henry Lee, he rushes forward to pull the quilt back up, but she turns her head to look up at him, and he stops where he stands. She makes a queer little sound—hear it outside your window at night, you'd think it were a cat wanting in.

"She can talk still," says Henry Lee, desperate-like, turning to me. "She was talking this morning." I stare into Julia Caterina's pretty brown eyes—huge now, and steady going all greeny-black—and I want to tell Henry Lee, oh, she'll talk all right, no fear. Mermaids *chatter*, believe me—talk both your lugs off, they will, you give them the chance. Mermaids gets lonely.

"She drank so *little*," Henry Lee keeps saying. "She didn't really like any wine, French or Portuguese, or . . . ours. She only drank it to be polite, when we had guests. Because it was our business, after all. She understood about business." I look down at the quilt where it's covering her lower parts, and I look back at Henry Lee, and he shakes his head. "No, not yet," he whispers. *No tail yet,* is what he meant—*she's still got legs*—but he couldn't say it, no more than me. Julia Caterina reaches up for him, and he sits by her on the bed and kisses both her hands. I can just see the half-circle outlines beginning just below her boobies, very faint against the pale skin. *Scales* . . . .

"How long?" Henry Lee asks, looking down into her face, like he's asking her, not me.

"You'd know better than me," I tells him straight. "I only seen one poor sailor, maybe cooked halfway. And no women."

Henry Lee closes his eyes. "I never . . . " I can't hardly hear him. He says, "I never . . . only that one time on the river, in the dark. I never saw."

"Aye, made sure of that didn't you?" I says. "You'll know next time."

He does look at me then, and his mouth makes one silent word—*don't*. After a bit he gets so he can breathe out, "Aren't I being punished enough?"

"Not nearly," I says. But Julia Caterina makes that sound again, and all on a sudden I'm so rotten sorry for her and Henry Lee I can't barely speak words meself. Nowt to do but rest me hand on his shoulder, while he sits there by his wife, and her *turning* under his own hands. Time we leave that sea-smelling room, it's dark outside, same as in.

And I didn't stir out of that house for the next nineteen days. Seems longer to me betimes, remembering—shorter too, other times, short as loving a wall and a barmaid—but nineteen days it were, with all the curtains drawn, every servant long fled, bar Gopi, him who'd come for me. That one, he stayed right along, went on shopping and cooking and sweeping; and if the smell and the closed rooms and us whispering up and down the stair—aye, and the sounds Henry Lee made alone in the night—if it all ever frighted him, he never said. A good man.

Like I figured, she never lost speech. I'd hear them talking hours on end, her and Henry Lee—always in the Portygee, of course, so's I couldn't make out none of it, which was good. Weren't for me to know what Henry Lee was saying to his wife, and her changing into a mermaid along of him getting rich. He tried to tell me some of their talk, but I didn't want to hear it then, and I've forgot it all now—made bleeding sure of *that*. I already know enough as I shouldn't, ta ever so.

Nineteen days. Nineteen mornings rising with me head so full of that sea-smell—stronger every day—I couldn't hardly swallow nowt but maybe porridge, couldn't never drink nowt but water. Nineteen nights lying awake hour on hour in one of the servants' garrets—I put meself there, 'acos I don't dream in them little cubbies the way I do in big echoey rooms such as Henry Lee had for his guests. I don't like dreaming, to this day I don't, and I liked it less then. Never closed me eyes until I had to, in that dark house.

Seventeenth night . . . seventeenth night, I've just finally gotten to sleep when Henry Lee wakes me, shaking me like the house is afire. I come up fighting and cursing—can't help it, always been that way—and I welt him a rouser on the earhole, but he drags me out of the bed and bundles me down to their room with a blanket around me shoulders. I keep pulling away from him, 'acos I know what I'm going to see, but he won't let go. His blue eyes look like he's been crying blood.

He'd covered her with every damp towel and rag in the house, but she'd thrown them all off . . . and there it is, there, laying out on the sheets that Henry Lee changes with his own hands every day, and Gopi takes to the *dhobi-wallah* for washing. There it is.

Everything's gone. Legs, feet, belly, all of it, *everything,* gone as though there'd never been nothing below her waist but that tail, scales flickering and glittering like wet emeralds in the candlelight. Look at it one way, it's a wonderful thing, that tail. It's the longest part of a mermaid or a merrow, and even when it's not moving at all, like hers wasn't just then, I swear you can see it *breathing* by itself, if you stand still and look close. In and out, slow, only a little, but you can see. It's them and it's *not* them, and that's all I'm going to say.

Now and then she'd twitch it a bit, flip the finny end some—getting used to it, like, having a tail. Each time she did that, Henry Lee'd draw his breath sharp, but all he said to me as we stood by the bed, he said, "It's made her more beautiful, Ben, hasn't it?" And it had that. She'd always had a good face, Julia Caterina, but the change had shaped it over, same as it had shaped her body. There was a wildness mixed in with the old sweetness now—mermaids is animals, some ways—and it had turned her, *whetted* her, into summat didn't have no end to how beautiful it could be. I told you early on, they ain't all beautiful, but even the ugly ones . . . see now, people got ends, people got *limits*—mermaids don't. Mermaids got no limits, except the sea.

She said his name, and her voice were different too—higher, yes, but mainly *clearer,* like all the clouds had blown off it. If that voice called for you, even soft, you'd hear it a long way. Henry Lee picked her up in his arms and put his cheek against hers, and she held onto him, and that tail tried to hold him too, bumping hard against his legs. I thought to slip out of there unnoticed, me and me blanket, but then Henry Lee said, quiet-like, "We could . . . I suppose we could put her in the water tonight, couldn't we, Ben?"

Well, I turned round on that fast, telling him, "Not near!" I pointed at the three double lines on both sides of her neck, so faint they were, still barely visible in her skin. "The gill slits ain't opened yet—drop her in a bathtub, she'd likely drown. Happen they might never open, I don't know. I'm telling you straight, I never seen this—I don't *know!*"

She looked at me then, and she smiled a little, but it weren't her smile. I leaned closer, and she said in English, so softly Henry Lee didn't hear, "Unbind my hair."

They don't all have long golden hair, that's just nursery talk. I seen one off Porto Rico had a mane red as sunset clouds, and I seen a fair old lot with thick dark hair like Julia Caterina's. But I never touched none of them before. It weren't me place to touch her neither, and Henry Lee standing by, too, but I done it anyway, like it were the hair asking me to do it, and not her. First twitch, it all come right down over me hands, ripe and heavy and *hot*—hot like I'd spilled cooking oil on meself, the way it clings and keeps burning, and water makes it worse. Truth, for a minute I thought me hands *was* ablaze—seemed like I could *see* them burning like fireships through that black swirly tangle wouldn't let them go. I yelled out then—I ain't shamed none to admit it, I know what I felt—and I snatched me hands right back, and of course there weren't a mark on them. And I looked into her eyes, and they was green and gray and green again, like the salt wine, and she laughed. She knew I were frighted and hurting, and she laughed and laughed.

I thought there were nothing left of her then—all gone, the little Portygee woman who'd sat in me chair and said something nobody else never said to me before. But then the eyes was hers again, all wide with fear and love, and she reached out for Henry Lee like she really were drowning. Aye, that were the worst of it, some way, those last two days, 'acos of one minute she'd be hissing like a cat, did he try to touch her or pet her, flopping away from him, the way you'd have thought he were her worst enemy in the world. Next minute, curled small in his arms, trembling all over, weeping dry-eyed, the way mermaids do, and him singing low to her in Portygee, sounded like nursery rhymes. Never saw him blubbing himself, not one tear.

She didn't stay in the bed much no more, but managed to get around the room using her arms and her tail—practicing-like, you see. Wouldn't eat nothing, no matter Henry Lee cozened her with the freshest fish and crab, mussels just out of the sea. Sometimes at first she'd take a little water, but by and by she'd show her teeth and knock the cup out of his hand. Mermaids don't drink, no more nor fish do.

They don't sleep, neither—not what you'd call sleeping—so there'd be one of us always by her, him or me, for fear she'd do herself a mischief. We wasn't doing much sleeping then ourselves, by then, so often enough we'd find ourselves side by side, not talking, just watching her while she watched the sea through the window and the moon ripened in the trees. The one time we ever did talk about it, he said to me, "You were right, Ben. I haven't been punished nearly enough for what I've done."

"Some get punished too much," I says, "and some not at all. Don't seem to make much difference, near as I can tell."

Henry Lee shakes his head. "You got out the moment you knew we might have harmed even one person. I stayed on. I'll never be quits for this, Ben."

I don't have no answer, except to tell him about a thing I did long ago that I'm still being punished for meself. I'd never told nobody before, and I'm not about to tell you now. I just did it to maybe help Henry Lee a little, which it didn't. He patted me back and squeezed me shoulder a little bit, but he didn't say no more, and nor did I. We sat together and watched Julia Caterina in the moonlight.

Come that nineteenth night, the moon rose full to bursting, big and bright and yellow as day, with one or two red streaks, like an egg gone bad, laying down a wrinkly-gold path you could have walked on to the horizon . . . or swum down, as the case might be. Julia Caterina went wild at the sight, beating at the window the way you'd have thought she were a moth trying to get to the candle. It come to me, she'd waited for this moon the same way the turtles wait to come ashore and lay their eggs in the light—the way those tiny fish

I disremember flood over the beaches at high tide, millions of them, got to get those eggs buried *fast*, before the next wave sweeps them back out to sea. Now it were like the moon were waiting for her, and she knew the way there.

"Not yet," Henry Lee says, desperate-like, "not yet—*they*'ve not . . . " He didn't finish, but I knew he were talking about the pale lines on her neck, darker every day, but still not opened into proper gill slits. But right as he spoke, right then, those same lines swelled and split and flared red, and that sudden, they was there, making her more a fish than the tail ever could, because now she didn't need the land at all, or the air. Aye, now she could stay under water all the time, if she wanted. She were ready for the sea, and she knew it, no more to say.

Henry Lee carried her in his arms all the way down from his grand house—*their* house until two nights ago—to the water's edge, nobody to see nowt, just a couple of fishing boats anchored offshore. A dugout canoe, too, which you still used to see in them days. She wriggled out of his arms there, turning in the air like a cat, and a little wave splashed up in her face as she landed, making her laugh and splash back with her tail. Henry Lee were drenched right off, top to toe, but you could see he didn't know. Julia Caterina—her as had been Julia Caterina—she swam round and round, rolling and diving and admiring all she could do in the water. There's nothing *fits* the sea like a mermaid—not fish, not seals, dolphins, whales, nothing. There in the moonlight, the sea looked happy to be with her.

I can't swim, like I told you—I just waded in a few steps to watch her playing so. All on a sudden—for all the world like she'd heard a call from somewhere—she did a kind of a swirling cartwheel, gave a couple of hard kicks with that tail, and like *that*, she's away, no goodbye, clear of the shore, leaving her own foxfire trail down the middle of that moonlight path. I thought she were gone then, gone forever, and I didn't waste no time in gawping, but turned to see to Henry Lee. He were standing up to his knees in the water, taking his shirt off.

"Henry Lee," I says. "Henry Lee, what the Christ you doing?" He don't even look over at me, but throws the shirt back toward the shore and starts unbuttoning his trews. Bought from the only bespoke gentlemen's tailor in Velha Goa, those pants, still cost you half what you'd pay in Lisbon. Henry Lee just drops them in the water. Goes to work getting rid of his smallclothes, kicking off his soaked shoes, while I'm yapping at him about catching cold, pneumonia. Henry Lee smiles at me. Still got most all his teeth, which even the Portygee nobs can't say they do, most of them. He says, "She'll be lonely out there."

I said summat, must have. I don't recall what it were. Standing there naked, Henry Lee says, "She'll need me, Ben."

"She's got all she needs," I says. "You can't go after her."

"I promised I'd make it up to her," he says. "What I did. But there's no way, Ben, there's no way."

He moves on past me, walking straight ahead, water rising steady. I stumble and scramble in front of him, afeared as I can be, but he's not getting by. "You can't make it up," I tells him. "Some things, you can't ever make up—you live with them, that's all. That's the best you can do." He's taller by a head, but I'm bigger, wider. He's not getting by.

Henry Lee stops walking out toward the deep. Confused-like, shaking his head some, starts to say me name . . . then he looks over me shoulder and his eyes go wide, with the moon in them. "She's there," he whispers, "she came back for me. There, right *there*." And he points, straining on his toes like a nipper sees the Dutch-biscuit man coming down the street.

I turn me head, just for an instant, just to see where he's pointing. *Summat* glimmers in the shadow of the dugout, diving in and out of the moonlight, and maybe it's a dolphin, and maybe it's Henry Lee's wife, turning for one last look at her poor husband who'd driven both of their lives on the rocks. Didn't know then, don't know now. All I'm sure of is, the next minute I'm sitting on me arse in water up to me chin, and Henry Lee's past me and swimming straight for that glimmer—long, raking Devonshire strokes, looking like he could go on forever if he had to. And bright as the night was, I lost sight of him—and her too, *it*, whatever it were—before he'd reached that boat. Bawled for him till me voice went—even tried to go after him in the dugout—but he were gone. They were gone.

His body floated in next afternoon. Gopi found it, sloshing about in the shallows.

Her family turned over every bit of ground around that house of Henry Lee's, looking for where he'd buried her. I'm dead sure they believe to this day that he killed Julia Caterina and then drowned himself, out of remorse or some such. They was polite as pie whenever we met, no matter they couldn't never stand one solitary thing about me—but after she disappeared only times I saw them was at a *feria*, where they'd always cut me dead. I didn't take it personal.

The will left stock and business to the family, but left both ships to me. I sold one of them for enough money to get meself to Buenos Aires, like I'd been wanting, and start up in the freighting trade, convoying everything from pianos to salt beef, rum to birdseed, tea to railroad ties . . . whatever you might want moved from *here* to *there*. Got two young partners do most of the real work these days, but I still go along with a shipment, times, just to play I'm still a foremast hand—plain Able-bodied Seaman, same as Henry Lee. The way it was when we didn't know what he died knowing. What I'll die knowing.

He left me the recipe for salt wine, too. I burned it. I'd wanted to buy up the stock and pour every bottle into the sea—giving it back to the merrows, you could say—but the family wouldn't sell, not to me. Heard they sold it to a German dealer, right after I left Goa, and he took it all home to Berlin with him. Couldn't say, meself.

I seen her a time or two since. Once off the Hebrides—leastways, I'm near about sure it was her—and once in the Bay of Biscay. That time she came right up to the ship, calling to me by name, quiet-like. She hung about most of the night, calling, but I never went to the rail, 'acos I couldn't think of nothing to say.

THE ORIGINAL WORD FOR RAIN

Peter Higgins

When Saul Traherne received a small but useful inheritance following the death of his parents, he took stock of his life. He was twenty-nine, single, and lonely; he loathed his job; and he had no close friends in London. So when the money came, he calculated that he had enough to live on, if he was careful, and he felt free at last to leave the city and join that almost extinct social class, the genteel poor of independent means. Having no taste for material pleasures, he resolved to devote himself to the one real passion of his life, the study of the magical arts, and in particular to the pursuit of his great ambition, recovering the lost original Edenic language of Adam and Eve.

The question of where he should live was resolved a few days after the funeral, in a second-hand bookshop in Clerkenwell, when he came across a footnote in a monograph on the theurgy of Henry Cornelius Agrippa. "*Viscount Thursby of Peignisbright* (Saul read), *a marginal figure on the fringes of the Order of the Golden Dawn, purchased widely across Europe and the Levant between about 1895 and the outbreak of the Great War. Though commonly rooked by unscrupulous dealers, he succeeded in amassing a considerable collection of authentic material, including MSS, incunables, scrying equipment and paraphernalia. He bequeathed his collection, and a substantial fund for its maintenance, to Peignmouth Public Library in furtherance of his noble belief that "the path of return to mankind's rightful place should be made clear for the shopkeeper, the wet-nurse and the labourer in the field*"".

Peignmouth! Saul's parents had taken their annual seaside holidays in Peignmouth when he was a boy, and suddenly in that Clerkenwell shop he was transported back to those long-lost days filled with light and spaciousness and a sense of plenty. He left the bookshop in a daze, and walked the London streets that afternoon in a state of longing and agitation. "It's a message," he thought. " A sign, a calling, not to be ignored. I'm meant to be in Peignmouth." So to Peignmouth he went, where he rented a room in a red-brick terraced house in the hinterland behind the seafront and installed his few belongings.

It was the perfect place for him, small and homely, unchanged in forty years or more, with faded carpets and heavy wooden furniture. There was nothing in it that was new or modern or flimsy. "I can be settled here," he said to himself with quiet satisfaction. He wanted nothing but solitude, and time to pursue his solitary researches. He intended to lead an austere life of study, renunciation and physical discipline. He would be a mendicant scholar, the eremitical neophyte of some obscure religious order. Freed from the need to participate in the compromises and self-distortions that getting money required, he would dedicate himself to the pursuit of luminous, hard-won truth.

Peignmouth Public Library he found to be a grim Victorian building: grey stone walls, steep gabled roofs and lofty mullioned windows that reflected only darkness. Entering the library for the first time, Saul's heart sank when he smelled the familiar library smell of fat and shabby old books and stale raincoats. Any sunshine that might have crept in through the high, dusty windows was flooded out by powerful fluorescent striplights.

There was no sign to direct visitors to the Thursby collection: he had to ask at the counter, and was sent up a narrow staircase that disappeared behind a pillar. Several turns of the staircase and three stiff swing-doors later, he emerged into a long, warm, sleepy room where two or three people were reading under the gaze of an ordinary station-clock.

"Can I help?"

The curator supervising at the desk was a youngish woman, small and slight. Saul beheld waves of strong, pale hair; a blue T-shirt; brown arms; and clever eyes, bright and ocean-green. She blessed him with her smile. "Are you looking for anything in particular?"

"Um, no. I mean, well yes. I just wanted to have a look around, to start with. I'm planning to do some work here, but first, well, I need to . . . you know, get the hang of the place."

She smiled again her beatific smile. "No problem. I'll show you." She left her station to show him how to use the card index, which stuffed several large cabinets—"Thursbury's own classification, a bit idiosyncratic, but you'll get the idea"—and Thursby's massive, privately-printed concordances. All the works he had hoped to find were there, and many more that were new to him, including—Saul was astounded to find—many original manuscripts, and volumes from the authors' own libraries, with their own MS marginalia. Bookshelves ran from floor to ceiling, and alongside the shelves stood row after row of display cases and vitrines containing the other artefacts from Thursby's collection. Here too, Saul found a strange plenty: a Hand of Glory; an ancient baby's caul, mounted on yellowing paper and surrounded by intricate hand-drawn geometry; a collection of divining rods; lengths of black hair tied in a series of complex knots. Against each item was propped an explanatory card, yellowing and densely written in a cramped and backward-sloping hand.

Saul paused before a small, delicate orrery of brass and copper, complete and perfect and simply waiting to be set in motion. The intricate mechanism included an extra planet, represented by a tiny jewel-like sphere of green set to orbit at an extreme angle to the elliptical plane between Venus and Earth. The card read simply: *Fludd's own, shewing Rannalon.*

"Do you want to look at anything more closely?"

"You mean, take them out of the cases? Is that allowed?"

"Sure. You can't take them out of the library, of course. But you can study them here. That's what they're for."

"Oh. Right." He paused a moment. "Uh . . . no. Not just now. Later, maybe."

After that first visit, Saul went to the library every day. Once he had got his bearings and planned out a programme of study for himself, he fell quickly and easily into a regular pattern of life. He would be at the library for opening time and work there all morning, reading and making notes. The afternoons he spent in long, ranging walks, and in the evenings he would return to his room and work again, until he was too tired to think any more, and then he would get into his narrow bed and fall into a heavy, dreamless sleep. He was alone, but he was fulfilled and happy. His collection of notes and sketches grew day by day, gradually taking over and filling his small room.

As he worked on in this way the days lengthened and the pale nights grew shorter week by week. It developed into a hot, bright, dry early summer. The lawns and roadside verges grew dry and yellow. Each day was like the one before: powdery blue skies with scarcely a cloud. The moon took to appearing early in the evenings, silver-white and intangible while the sky was bright with the lingering day, but as the night grew dark, so the moon would turn heavier and buttery, waxing towards the full. Every morning the sun rose earlier, and so did Saul. He found himself waking regularly at five a.m., feeling full of light and air and the currents of life and sleeplessness. He made himself breakfast and sat in the garden drinking tea until the time came when he could leave for his day's work at the library.

But something was threatening to disturb the limpid calm of his monklike life. In those early mornings he found himself thinking less and less about his work in the Collection and more and more about the beatific smile of the curator. Her name was Julia Redgrove, he learned from the helpful notes of advice that she pinned to the reading room walls. He thought about her at his breakfast, and on the way to the library, anticipating his first sight of her that day; and at the library he would look up from his books and watch her, surreptitiously. He got to know the clothes she wore and he watched her body as she moved around the reading room. He found himself wondering about her: where did she live? what did she do in the evenings? And if she did not appear for work as usual, he wondered where she might have gone.

One Sunday morning he came upon her sitting in the window of the café on the esplanade. She was alone, drinking coffee. A pile of newspapers sat on the table at her elbow but she wasn't reading, just looking out of the window. Without stopping to think, Saul went in, picked up a coffee for himself at the counter, and went over.

"Hi," he said. "I don't know if you remember me. From the library."

She looked up and smiled the smile. "Of course I remember. Mr Traherne. The Collection's not exactly overwhelmed with readers."

"Saul," he said. "Can I, um, can I sit down?"

"Sure." She shoved the pile of papers to one side. "I'm Julia."

"I know. I mean, I've seen, I . . . you write your name on all those notices."

She smiled. "So," she said, "what's your special thing, Saul? What are you looking for? In the library?"

"What do you mean?"

"You know. Everyone who comes to the Collection is looking for something, some dream they're following. So what are you looking for?"

"Well . . . " Saul hesitated. He'd never actually talked to anybody about this stuff before. He didn't want to sound . . . strange. But, hell, he thought, she is the Thursby Curator, after all. "Well . . . if you really want to know . . . I'm looking for truth, I suppose. Complete truth." He stopped. Julia looked at him and nodded. "Go on," she said. She seemed interested. Saul hadn't talked to anyone about anything at all for months, not since the funeral, except exchanging a few words with shopkeepers and the like. Now, because he was with Julia and she was listening to him, and seemed to be interested, and seemed to like him, he let go, without really meaning to, and all the bottled-up ideas and images in his head came pouring out.

"When you were young," said Saul, "I mean, really young, when you were a child, did you ever lie on your back and look up at the sky? You know how it looks as if the clouds are fixed in place and the trees are toppling towards you, always toppling but never crashing down? And you lie there and you look up and you feel sort of . . . *complete*. Completely alive. And everything is . . . more vivid. Better. Everything is so *clear*."

"Yes. I know."

"Well, that's it," said Saul. "That's what I want. Not sometimes, but always, all the time, to be that happy."

"But that's poetry," said Julia. "You don't need to look for that in old books of magic."

"No, I don't mean just poetry, not like you mean," he went on. "I mean for real. I think that something went wrong somewhere, a long time ago, and the world got . . . polluted. Like there's dust in the air all the time, soot and smuts, making everything dim and, not *dirty* exactly, but . . . spoilt. Wrong. Disappointing, I suppose. But it doesn't have to be like that. It's only superficial. The dirt is in our head and you can wipe the dirt away." Saul paused, embarrassed. "You think I'm weird, don't you?"

"No, look, sorry, I don't, really. It's interesting. I think about stuff like this too, you know."

"Well . . . what I'm getting at is . . . oh, I don't know where to start, but say . . . everything has its right name, its true name."

"You mean the name Adam gave it," said Julia lightly.

Saul looked at her, full on. An obscure new thing moved inside him, a glimpse of joy. "You know?" he said. "You know? About that?"

"Of course," she said. "Genesis. Adam in the garden of Eden. *'So out of the ground the Lord God formed every beast of the field and every bird of the air, and brought them to the man to see what he would call them; and whatever the man called every living creature, that was its name.'*" She couldn't suppress a grin of triumph when she came up with that. "And the question is," she continued, "what was the language Adam used to name the world as it was being created? Because we were made in God's image and that was God's language too."

"Yes! Yes! That's it!" People were looking. He continued more quietly. "The original language, that names things as they really are, and gives them their full and original meaning. You couldn't lie in that language, you couldn't say what wasn't true, or what was only partly true. If you thought of something by its true name, you'd know it fully and you'd know everything about it. Nothing that mattered would be hidden from you."

"That's wizard language," said Julia. "If you know the hidden name of something, you can control it. And if you say something in the true language, it becomes true. You say 'you're dead' and . . .

bang!" She slapped her hand on the table and flashed her sea-green eyes. "Dead."

"No!" said Saul horrified. "Not that! You *couldn't* do that, you couldn't even *want* to do it. It's the *opposite* of control. It's seeing everything as it really and truly is: everything full of light and air: fire and air, earth, wind: alive with cold fire." Now Julia was looking at him full on. Her face was open and clear and seraphic and full of . . . what? Saul didn't know. "I want to find that original, perfect language again," he continued. "It's been scattered and distorted and forgotten, but it can be found again. Fragments. Echoes. Remembered and handed down unrecognised from generation to generation. That's what I'm looking for. I want to find it and learn it and speak it."

"Blimey," said Julia.

After that first meeting, Saul saw Julia quite often. Sitting in some huddled pub corner, they'd get slightly drunk together and talk about magic and the Collection and the rancorous office politics among what Julia called "the normal staff" at the library. Saul enjoyed these long evenings and looked forward to them, but he was never entirely *sure* about them. What did Julia want from him? What did she *expect*? And what did *he* want?

Every day during that long, dry summer Saul continued to work in the drowsy upstairs room of Peignmouth Public Library, ploughing through book after book, following threads of reference and allusion back through the works of the Renaissance and medieval magi, and then further back before them to their Arabic, Greek and Hebrew forebears. He consulted original manuscripts and he studied the ancient languages in which they were written. As he read ever more widely and deeply, he began to pick up veiled hints and references to other scholars who had followed the same trail before him. And then flashes of insight began to come to him, slowly at first but then ever more frequently. He began to come upon ideas, words and phrases, diagrams, snatches of sound, that would make him physically tremble with excitement. He would note them all down, these shards and fragments, in his notebook.

His first major discovery, the one that put him on the right track, was a single word scribbled on a scrap of brittle yellow paper in one of the display cabinets. The accompanying explanatory card in Thursbury's hand read: "*Shem, retrieved from the mouth of the Prague golem by the Earl of Leicester, 1573.*" The next big step forward was a phrase included in an anonymous marginal correction to Paracelsus' instructions for creating the homunculus. This in turn led him to Roger Bacon's own manuscript of the *Fons Vitae* of Avicebron with an illustration added by a later hand (Bacon's own, in all probability) showing the Sephiroth framed by a beautiful and intricate drawing (or map?) of a labyrinth.

Weeks passed. The summer was turning out to be the hottest and driest on record. It brought out insects in remarkable numbers: butterflies and ladybirds crawled in profusion over the wilting gardens; grasshoppers chirruped in the dry grass, and crane-flies clattered at every window. Spiders, wasps and harvestmen feasted on the profusion, while swallows and martins danced in the high, bright skies, and moth-hunting bats whirred ghostlike in the dusk. Saul would lie in bed on those strange electrified nights, hot and wakeful under just a sheet, with a notebook and pencil on the bedside table so he could scribble down whatever random thoughts came to him. His window stood open, and occasional breezes would enter the room, stirring the yellow curtains, bringing in the cries of seagulls, the brassy summer smells, and rumours of the rolling of dry thunder out at sea. There were flashes of blue lightning, but it never rained.

Throughout that hot dry season, Saul continued to take long solitary walks in the afternoons, when he found that his thoughts returned again and again to Julia; to something she had said; to some small movement she had made; to the memory of the turn of her head. He never spoke to her about it, he barely even acknowledged it to himself, but in his loneliness he was falling in love with her.

However, when he was out on his endless walks, he found it easy enough to put his thoughts of Julia into a box in his head and close the lid. He was serious about his work, and as he walked he would sift through in his mind the phrases, sounds and ideas that he had collected that morning, looking for patterns and connections, keeping alert for the chime of something ringing true, and the answering tremor within himself that told him he had found it. Sometimes as he walked something would stop him dead in his tracks—ivy on a red brick wall; a swift, screaming across the blue sky overhead; a twisted tree-root; a sun-warm stone; the perfect curve of a bay—and he would stare at it and drink it in with all his senses. And then he would start to throw word-fragments at it, sometimes in his mind only, sometimes whispering and sometimes shouting aloud, hurling sound-shapes into the wind. He tried out words and phrases, hand-movements and even broken dance-steps that grew from the strange sediment of his findings and seemed, somehow, right. Then he would stand, stock-still, intent, focused, listening and watching for any response, any answering ring or echo in the world that would tell him he had got it right. But there was nothing. He wasn't discouraged. "I'm like a baby," he told himself, "it's like learning to talk for the first time, all over again. I've got to learn how to make the sounds first. Meaning and understanding will come later. The main thing is to keep trying, and to keep listening. It will come."

Saul's walks tended to carry him out of Peignmouth. He developed a more or less regular route. He would stride away westwards along the coast, past huge Edwardian mansions, with their mock-Tudor frontages, their gothic towers and their gardens bulging with overgrown rhododendron, magnolia and privet. After the mansions came smaller houses, red-brick terraces that gave way to bungalows separated by clipped lawns, parched by the endless summer drought. Then came shabby, weather-beaten shacks and chalets and allotments; and then the dwellings stopped, and the path wound on along the cliff-edge, rising and falling with the contours of the land. Saul walked on, over wind-swept points and through still, warm hollows filled with the sweet coconut-smell of the gorse. The purple sea glimmered far below; linnets and stone-chats flitted beside him; a raven barked; a kestrel pinned itself to the sky against the wind. And Saul sang, every day, his song in Adam's tongue. Every day his voice grew stronger and the song grew fuller, wiser and more complete.

One afternoon in August when the sun was burning and the

sea shimmered, Saul walked further along the cliff-tops than normal. At about four o'clock he was beginning to think about turning
back, when he reached a fingerpost: *Rammas Wood*. The OS map, he
thought, showed a footpath that cut across the neck of the headland
from about here, so he climbed the stone stile between wind-clipped
thorn trees and passed into a still, green world.

Entering the wood was like passing out of time into endlessness,
out of movement into rest. It was warm and quiet and earthy beneath
the leaf-canopy of oak and ash. Saul paused. He felt the heaviness in
the air, the hanging warmth, the watchful presence of the trees. A cat-
spaw of wind stirred the foliage. A pair of fat woodpigeons burst out
of the undergrowth in alarm and clattered clumsily away. Somewhere
out of sight a green woodpecker gave its raucous cry. Saul found that
he was trembling, and he knew beyond all doubting that there and
then, in that moment, suddenly, something had happened, or something had stirred, or something had been found: something hidden
but momentous. He felt completely sure of it. Somewhere and somehow a threshold had been crossed. There was a chance here, now, for
him: an opening.

He sat down on the mossy branch of a fallen oak, shaken and
elated. "This is what I have prepared myself for," he said. "I am ready."
He listened. He heard the wind stirring among the trees, and he felt
. . . movement. He laid his hand along the sun-warm branch and sunk
his fingers into the moss, resting. Woodlice came onto his hand and
explored the gaps between his fingers. A spider stepped delicately up
onto his thumb and began to climb his arm. Caterpillars dropped from
the trees onto his hair. Quietly Saul spoke the true syllable of greeting.
A bird came to a branch above his head, a small whitethroat, and
fixed him with a bright curious gaze. Saul gave the smile of welcome
and felt in return the breeze stirring the feathers on the whitethroat's
back. More birds came. A shrew twittered at him from the leaf-mould.
Saul began to rock gently from side to side, murmuring a slow oak-
song, a rowan-song, a sleeping-owl-song, in tune with the rhythmical
thrumming of the winds in Rammas Wood.

A pressure was building up: an intensity of there-ness and is-ness that could not be sustained. It burst like a berry against the roof of his mouth. Saul spoke. A pulse of heart-sound—Saul-sound, Rammas-sound—exploded outwards in concentric ripples of release, out from the epicentre of Saul, spreading outwards through the woodland in all directions, rippling outwards through fields and rock, touching the sea, touching the cloudless sky. And then it was over. The moment passed. Saul was alone, just Saul, in the ordinary wood. It was as if a cloud had passed in front of the sun, though the ordinary afternoon was as bright and warm as ever.

He felt tired and drained. His legs were trembling, and he wanted to go home. But as he stood up stiffly and turned to go, he saw a face watching him from under the trees: a thin cream face, as small as a child's but not a child's, with dark curly hair and a crow's bright eye, just looking at him, and there was a strong, sour smell of earth in the air. Then the face opened its mouth and leaves came out. A sort of smile, a green smile. And then the face was gone, back into the woods.

Saul ran: back, back, out of the wood and onto the familiar, parched cliff path. The sun was lower on the horizon than he had thought. Running as hard as he dared for fear of pitching himself over the cliff-edge, he headed back towards Peignmouth. As he ran he became aware of a darkening of the air, until he was running through heavy copper light. A dark cloud-mass was rolling up out of the west, sliding across the high, empty blue and closing the sky above Peignmouth. Saul ran on, harder, more desperate, and as he ran he found himself shouting. He shouted rain. The true original word for rain. He called the rain and rain came, warm fat rain, rain-buds splashing open, soft and dark on the hard, dusty ground. A few drops at first, and then many, many: rain came thundering down on the gorse, filling the wet air with sweet earth smells. Saul ran on.

By the time he reached Peignmouth he was soaked to the skin. His clothes were drenched with rain and sweat, he was hot and muddy and breathing hard, and his hair was plastered across his forehead. The rain was streaming down the slate roofs, and the gusting wind was sweeping rain across the roads. The hedges and the garden shrubs were dark and shining. Saul felt as if he were returning to the human world after a long absence. Everything in the rain-drenched street looked fresh and new. As he stood in the rain, gazing across the town that had become his home, he could hardly keep still on his feet, such was the sense of strength welling up inside him. As the rain poured down from the purple sky, he felt an answering torrent of truth and magic rise up within him like a river beginning to flow. He went to find Julia, to speak to her of his triumph and his love.

She was waiting for him in the Fisherman's Arms. She looked slight and bright and together, and her ocean-green eyes flashed with pleasure when she saw him come in.

But she wasn't alone. There was a man with her, a stranger to Saul, tucked in next to her on the bench. Saul went over to them, feeling the confidence and elation draining out of him under the bland, open gaze of the stranger.

"Saul!" said Julia brightly. "This is Richard."

Richard nodded and put out his hand, easy and casual. "Hi, Saul. Nice to meet you." He was wearing a striped shirt, long sleeves buttoned at the wrist. Saul felt painfully aware of his own wet clothes and bedraggled hair. "Saul's the one I've been telling you about, Richard," said Julia. Richard's face registered nothing. "You know. At the library. He's doing this incredibly interesting research."

"Of course," Richard nodded.

Saul turned to Julia. "Sorry I'm late. I was . . . "

"Are you?" said Julia, blithely. "Never mind, sit down. We've got some great news. Richard's got this new job in Paris. He's in banking, did I tell you? It's all terribly high-pressure and he's awfully good at it." Richard smiled placidly and sipped his beer.

"No, I didn't know. That's nice," said Saul.

"And the great thing is," said Julia, "I've got a job there too. At the Bibliotheque Nationale. Second in charge of Renaissance manuscripts. I've been trying for a job like this for years. I can't stay stuck here for ever, can I? And Richard and I will be together." Richard took her hand in his.

"Oh," said Saul. "Well. That *is* great. Congratulations. Look, let me get you both a drink." And he went to the bar, dripping wet, cold and tired.

Late that night he lay alone in his bed in his tiny room, awake and lost. A cool breeze was stirring the curtain and his light was on but he wasn't reading. A moth settled on the lampshade. It had pale mottled wings like lichen on a weathered gravestone. Saul stared at it emptily. In the pattern of its wings he saw inscribed the seven sacred letters. He spoke them quietly one by one as the curtains shifted in the rain-breeze. Beyond the rooftops and the lamp-lit streets, beyond Peignmouth pier, huge slender figures clothed in milky light were rising from the waves and walking towards the shore. Great whales roiled the surface of the waters, and the sky split open and the burning rain began to fall.

THE LINEAMENTS
OF GRATIFIED DESIRE

Ysabeau S. Wilce

> *"Abstinence sows sand all over*
> *The ruddy limbs & flowing hair*
> *But Desire Gratified*
> *Plants fruit of life & beauty there."*
>
> —William Blake

I: Stage Fright

Here is Hardhands up on the stage, and he's cheery cherry, sparking fire, he's as fast as a fox-trotter, stepping high. Sweaty blood dribbles his brow, bloody sweat stipples his torso, and behind him the Vortex buzzsaw whines, its whirling outer edge black enough to cut glass. The razor in his hand flashes like a heliograph as he motions the final Gesture of the invocation. The Eye of the Vortex flutters, but its perimeter remains firmly within the structure of Hardhands' Will and does not expand. He **ululates** a Command, and the Eye begins to open, like a pupil dilating in sunlight, and from its vivid yellowness comes a glimpse of scales and horns, struggling not to be born.

Someone tugs at Hardhands' foot. His concentration wavers. Someone yanks on the hem of his kilt. His concentration wiggles, and the Vortex wobbles slightly like a run-down top. Someone tugs on his kilt-hem, and his concentration collapses completely, and so does the Vortex, sucking into itself like water down a drain. There goes the Working for which Hardhands has been preparing for the last two weeks, and there goes the Tygers of Wrath's new drummer, and there goes their boot-kicking show.

Hardhands throws off the grasp with a hard shake, and looking down, prepares to smite. His lover is shouting upward at him, words that Hardhands can hardly hear, words he hopes he can hardly hear, words he surely did not hear a-right. The interior of the club is toweringly loud, noisy enough to make the ears bleed, but suddenly the thump of his heart, already driven hard by the strength of his magickal invocation, is louder.

Relais, pale as paper, repeats the shout. This time there is no mistaking what he says, much as Hardhands would like to mistake it, much as he would like to hear something else, something sweet and charming, something like: you are the prettiest thing ever born, or the Goddess grants wishes in your name, or they are killing themselves in the streets because the show is sold right out. Alas, Relais is shouting nothing quite so sweet.

"What do you mean you can not find Tiny Doom?" Handhands shouts back. He looks wildly around the congested club, but it's dark and there are so many of them, and most of them have huge big hair and huger bigger boots. A tiny purple girl-child and her stuffy pink pig have no hope in this throng; they'd be trampled under foot in a second. That is exactly what Hardhands had told the Pontifexa earlier that day; no babysitter, he, other business, other pleasures, no time to take care of small children, not on this night of all nights: The Tygers of Wrath's biggest show of the year. Find someone else.

Well, talkers are no good doers, they say, and talking had done no good, all the yapping growling barking howling in the world had not changed the Pontifexa's mind: it's Paimon's night off, darling, and she'll be safe with you, Banastre, I can trust my heir with no one else, my sweet boy, do your teeny grandmamma this small favor and how happy I shall be, and here, kiss-kiss, I must run, I'm late, have a wonderful evening, good luck with the show, be careful with your invocation, cheerie-bye my darling.

And now see:

Hardhands roars: "I told you to keep an eye on her, Relais!"

He had too, he couldn't exactly watch over Tiny Doom (so called because she is the first in stature and the second in fate), while he was invoking the drummer, and with no drummer, there's no show (no show damn it!) and anyway if he's learned anything as the grandson of the Pontifexa of Califa, it's how to delegate.

Relais shouts back garbled defense. His eyes are whirling pie-plates. He doesn't mention that he stopped at the bar on his way to break the news and that there he downed four Choronzon Delights (hold the delight, double the Choronzon) before screwing up the courage to face his lover's ire. He doesn't mention that he can't exactly remember the last time he saw Little Tiny Doom except that he thinks it might have been about the time when she said that she had to visit El Casa de Peepee (oh cute) and he'd taken her as far as the door to the loo, which she had insisted haughtily she could do alone, and then he'd been standing outside, and gotten distracted by Arsinoë Fyrdraaca, who'd sauntered by, wrapped around the most gorgeous angel with rippling red wings, and then they'd gone to get a drink, and then another drink, and then when Relais remembered that Tiny Doom and Pig were still in the potty and pushed his way back through the crush, Tiny Doom and Pig were not still in the potty anymore.

And now, here:

Up until this very second, Hardhands has been feeling dandy as candy about this night: his invocation has been powerful and sublime, the blood in his veins replaced by pure unadulterated Magickal Current, hot and heavy. Up until this very second, if he clapped his hands together, sparks would fly. If he sang a note, the roof would fall. If he tossed his hair, fans would implode. Just from the breeze of the Vortex through his skin, he had known this was going to be a charm of a show, the very pinnacle of bombast and bluster. The crowded club still hums with cold fire charge, the air still sparks, cracking with glints of magick: yoowza. But now all that rich bubbly magick is curdling in his veins, his drummer has slid back to the Abyss, and he could beat someone with a stick. Thanks to an idiot boyfriend and a bothersome five-year-old his evening has just tanked.

Hardhands' perch is lofty. Despite the roiling smoke (cigarillo, incense, and oil), he can look out over the big big hair, and see the club is as packed as a cigar box with hipsters eager to see the show. From the stage Hardhands can see a lot, his vision sharpened by the magick he's been mainlining, and he sees: hipsters, b-boys, gothicks, crimson-clad officers, a magistra with a jaculus on a leash, etc. He does not see a small child or a pink pig or even the tattered remnants of a small child and a pink pig or even, well, he doesn't see them period.

Hardhands sucks in a deep breath and uses what is left of the Invocation still working through his veins to shout: "×◎!"

The syllable is vigorous and combustible, flowering in the darkness like a bruise. The audience erupts into a hollering hooting howl. They think the show is about to start. They are ready and geared. Behind Hardhands, the band also mistakes his intention, and despite the lack of drummer, kicks in with the triumphant blare of a horn, the delirious bounce of the hurdy-gurdy.

"×◎!" This time the shout sparks bright red, a flash of coldfire that brings tears to the eyes of the onlookers. Hardhands raises an authoritative hand towards the band, crashing them into silence. The crowd follows suit and the ensuing quiet is almost as ear-shattering.

"×◎.." This time his words provide no sparkage, and he knows that his Will is fading under his panic. The club is dark. It is full of large people. Outside it is darker still and the streets of South of the Slot are wet and full of dangers. No place for a Tiny Doom and her Pig, oh so edible, to be wandering around, alone. Outside it the worst night of the year to be wandering alone anywhere in the City, particularly if you are short, stout, and toothsome.

"×◎!" This time Hardhands' voice, the voice which has launched a thousand stars, which has impregnated young girls with monsters and kept young men at their wanking until their wrists ache and their members bleed, is scorched and rather squeaky:

"Has anyone seen my wife?"

II: Historical Notes

Here's a bit of background. No ordinary night, tonight, not at all. It's Pirate's Parade and the City of Califa is afire—in some places actually blazing. No fear, tho', bucket brigades are out in force, for the Pontifexa does not wish to lose her capital to revelry. Wetness is stationed around the things that the Pontifexa most particularly requires not to burn: her shrines, Bilskinir House, Arden's Cake-O-Rama, the Califa National Bank. Still, even with these bucket brigades acting as damper, there's fun enough for everyone. The City celebrates many holidays, but surely Pirates' Parade ranks as Biggest and Best.

But why pirates and how a parade? Historians (oh fabulous professional liars) say that it happened thusly: Back in the day, no chain sealed the Bay of Califa off from sea-faring foes and the Califa Gate sprang wide as an opera singer's mouth, a state of affairs good for trade and bad for security. Chain was not all the small city lacked: no guard, no organized militia, no blood thirsty Scorchers regiment to stand against havoc, and no navy. The City was fledgling and disorganized, hardly more than a village, and plump for the picking.

One fine day, Pirates took advantage of Califa's tenderness, and sailed right through her Gate, and docked at the Embarcadero, as scurvy as you please. From door to door they went, demanding tribute or promising wrath, and when they were loaded down with booty they went well satisfied back to their ships to sail away.

But they didn't get far. While the pirates were shaking down the householders, a posse of quiet citizens crept down to the docks and sabotaged the poorly guarded ships. The pirates arrived back at the docks to discover their escape boats sinking, and when suddenly the docks themselves were on fire, and their way off the docks was blocked, and then they were on fire too, and that was it.

Perhaps Califa had no Army, no Navy, no Militia, but she did have citizens with grit and cleverness, and grit and cleverness trump greed and guns every time. Such a clever victory over a pernicious greedy foe is worth remembering, and maybe even repeating, in a fun sort of way, and thus was born a roistering day of remembrance when revelers dressed as pirates gallivant door to door demanding candy booty, and thus Little Tiny Doom has muscled in on Hardhands' evening. With Grandmamma promised to attend an euchre party, and Butler Paimon's night off, who else would take Tiny Doom, (and the resplendently costumed Pig) on candy shakedown? Who but our hero, as soon as his show is over and his head back down to earth, lucky boy?

Well.

The Blue Duck and its hot dank club-y-ness may be the place to be when you are tall and trendy and your hearing is already shot, but for a short kidlet, big hair and loud noises bore, and the cigarillo smoke scratches. Tiny Doom has waited for Pirates' Parade for weeks, dreaming of pink popcorn and sugar squidies, chocolate manikins and jacksnaps, praline pumpkin seeds and ginger bombs: a sackful of sugar guaranteed to keep her sick and speedy for at least a week. She can wait no longer.

Shortness has its advantage; trendy people look up their noses, not down. The potty is filthy and the floor yucky wet; Tiny Doom and Pig slither out the door, right by Relais, so engaged in his conversation with an woman with a boat in her hair that he doesn't even notice the scram. Around elbows, by tall boots, dodging lit cigarettes and drippy drinks held low and cool-like, Tiny Doom and Pig achieve open air without incident and then, sack in hand, set out for the Big Shakedown.

"*Rancy Dancy is no good,*" she sings as she goes, swinging Pig, who is of course, too lazy to walk. "*Chop him up for firewood . . . When he's dead, boil his head and bake it into gingerbread . . .*"

She jumps over a man lying on the pavement, and then into the reddish pool beyond. The water makes a satisfying SPLASH and tho' her hem gets wet, she is sure to hold Pig up high so that he remains dry. He's just getting over a bad cold and has to care for his health, silly Pig he is delicate, and up past his bedtime, besides. Well, it is only once a year.

Down the slick street, Tiny Doom galumphs, Pig swinging along with her. There are shadows ahead of her and shadows behind, but after the shadows of Bilskinir House (which can sometimes be *grabby*) these shadows: so what? There's another puddle ahead, this one dark and still. She pauses before it, and some interior alarum indicates that it would be best to jump over, rather than in. The puddle is wide, spreading across the street like a strange black stain. As she gears up for the leap, a faint rippling begins to mar the mirror-like surface.

"Wah! Wah!" Tiny Doom is short, but she has lift. Holding her skirt in one hand, and with a firm grip upon Pig, she hurtles herself upward and over, like a tiny tea cosy levering aloft. As she springs, something wavery and white snaps out of the stillness, snapping towards her like the crack of a whip. She lands on the other side, and keeps scooting, beyond the arm's reach. Six straggly fingers, like pallid parsnips, waggle angrily at her, but she's well beyond their grip.

"*Tell her, smell her! Kick her down the cellar,*" Tiny Doom taunts, flapping Pig's ears derisively. The scraggly arm falls back, and then another emerges from the water, hoisting up on its elbows, pulling a slow rising bulk behind it: a knobby head, with knobby nose and knobby forehead and a slowly opening mouth that shows razor sharp gums and a pointy black tongue, unrolling like a hose. The tongue has length where the arms did not, and it looks gooey and sticky, just like the salt licorice Grandmamma loves so much. Tiny Doom cares not for salt licorice one bit and neither does Pig, so it seems prudent to punt, and they do, as fast as her chubby legs can carry them, further down the slickery dark street.

III: Irritating Children

Here is Hardhands in the alley behind the club, taking a deep breath of brackish air, which chills but does not calm. Inside, he has left an angry mob, who've have had their hopes dashed rather than their ears blown. The Infernal Engines of Desire (opening act) has come back on stage and is trying valiantly to suck up the slack, but the audience is not particularly pacified. The Blue Duck will be lucky if it doesn't burn. However, that's not our hero's problem; he's got larger fish frying.

He sniffs the air, smelling: the distant salt spray of the ocean; drifting smoke from some bonfire; cheap perfume; his own sweat; horse manure. He closes his eyes and drifts deeper, beyond smell, beyond scent, down down down into a wavery darkness that is threaded with filaments of light which are not really light, but which he knows no other way to describe. The darkness down here is not really darkness either, it's the Magickal Current as his mind can envision it, giving form to the formless, putting the indefinable into definite terms. The Current bears upon its flow a tendril of something familiar, what he qualifies, for lack of a better word, as a taste of obdurate obstinacy and pink plush, fading quickly but unmistakable.

The Current is high tonight, very high. In consequence, the Aeyther is humming, the Aeyther is abuzz; the line between In and Out has narrowed to a width no larger than a hair, and it's an easy step across—but the jump can go either way. Oh this would have been the very big whoo for the gig tonight; musickal magick of the highest order, but it sucks for lost childer out on the streets. South of the Slot is bad enough when the Current is low: a sewer of footpads, dollymops, blisters, mashers, cornhoes, and others is not to be found elsewhere so deep in the City even on an ebb-tide day. Tonight, combine typical holiday mayhem with the rising magickal flood and Goddess knows what will be out, hungry and yummy for some sweet tender kidlet chow. And not even regular run of the mill niblet, but prime grade A best grade royalty. The Pontifexa's heir, it doesn't get more yummy than that—a vampyre could dare sunlight with that bubbly blood zipping through his veins, a ghoul could pass for living after gnawing on that sweet flesh. It makes Hardhands' manly parts shrivel to think upon the explanation to Grandmamma of Tiny Doom's loss and the blame sure to follow.

Hardhands opens his eyes, it's hardly worth wasting the effort of going deep when everything is so close the surface tonight. Behind him, the iron door flips open and Relais flings outward, borne aloft on a giant wave of disapproving noise. The door snaps shut, cutting the sound in a brief echo which quickly dies in the coffin narrow alley-way.

"Did you find her?" Relais asks, holding his fashionable cuffs so they don't trail on the mucky cobblestones. Inside his brain is bouncing with visions of the Pontifexa's reaction if they return home minus Cyrenacia. Actually, what she is going to say is the least of his worries; it is what she might do that really has Relais gagging. He likes his lungs exactly where they are: inside his body, not flapping around outside.

Hardhands turns a white hot look upon his lover and says: "If she gets eaten, Relais, I will eat you."

Relais' father always advised saving for a rainy day and though the sky above is mostly clear, Relais is feeling damp. He will check his bankbook when they get home, and reconsider Sweetie Fyrdraaca's proposition. He's been Hardhands' leman for over a year now: blood sacrifices, coldfire singed clothing, throat tearing invocations, cornmeal gritty sheets, murder. He's had enough. He makes no reply to the threat.

Hardhands demands, not very politely: "Give me my frockcoat."

Said coat, white as snow, richly embroidered in white peonies and with cuffs the size of tablecloths, well, Relais had been given that to guard too, and he now has a vague memory of hanging it over the stall door in the pisser, where hopefully it still dangles, but probably not.

"I'll get it—" Relais fades backward, into the club, and Hardhands lets him go.

For now.

For now, Hardhands takes off his enormous hat, which had remained perched upon his gorgeous head during his invocation via a jeweled spike of a hairpin, and speaks a word into its upturned bowl. A green light pools up, spilling over the hat's capacious brim, staining his hand and the sleeve below with drippy magick. Another commanding word, and the light surges upward and ejects a splashy elemental, fish-tail flapping.

"Eh, boss—I thought you said I had the night off," Alfonso complains. There's lip rouge smeared on his fins and a clutch of cards in his hand. "It's Pirates Parade."

"I changed my mind. That wretched child has given me the slip and I want you to track her."

Alfonso grimaces. Ever since Little Tiny Doom trapped him in a bowl of water and fed him fishy flakes for two days, he's avoided her like fluke-rot.

"Why worry your good luck, boss—"

Hardhands does not have to twist. He only has to look like he is going to twist. Alfonzo zips forward, flippers flapping and Hardhands, after draining his chapeau of Current and slamming it back upon his grape, follows.

IV: Who's There?

Here is The Roaring Gimlet, sitting pretty in her cozy little kitchen, toes toasting on the grate, toast toasting on the tongs, drinking hot ginger beer, feeling happily serene. She's had a fun-dandy evening. Citizens who normally sleep behind chains and steel bolts, dogs a-prowl and guns under their beds, who maybe wouldn't open their doors after dark if their own mothers were lying bleeding on the threshold, these people fling their doors widely and with gay abandon to the threatening cry of "Give us Candy or We'll Give you the Rush."

Any other night, at this time, she'd still be out in the streets, looking for drunken mashers to roll. But tonight, all gates were a-jar and the streets a high tide of drunken louts. Out by nine and back by eleven, with a sack almost too heavy to haul, a goodly load of sugar, and a yummy fun-toy, too. Now she's enjoying her happy afterglow from a night well-done. The noises from the cellar have finally stopped, she's finished the crossword in *The Alta Califa*, and as soon as the kettle blows, she'll fill her hot water bottle and aloft to her snuggly bed, there to dwell the rest of the night away in kip.

Ah, Pirates Parade, best night of the year.

While she's waiting for the water to bubble, she's cleaning the tool from whence comes her name: the bore is clotted with icky stuff and the Gimlet likes her signature clean and sharply shiny. Clean hands, clean house, clean heart, the Gimlet's pappy always said. Above the fireplace, Pappy's flat representation stares down at his progeny, the self-same gimlet clinched in his hand. The Roaring Gimlet is the heir to a fine family tradition and she does love her job.

What's that a-jingling? She glances at the clock swinging over the stove. It's almost midnight. Too late for visitors, and anyway, every-one knows the Roaring Gimlet's home is her castle. Family stays in, people stay out, so Daddy Gimlet always said. Would someone? No, they wouldn't. Not even tonight, they would not.

Jingle jingle.

The cat looks up from her perch on the fender, perturbed.

Heels down, the Gimlet stands aloft, and tucks her shirt back into her skirts, ties her dressing gown tight, bounds up the ladder-like kitchen stairs to the front door. The peephole shows a dimly lit circle of empty cobblestones. Damn it all to leave the fire for nothing. As the Gimlet turns away, the bell dances again, jangling her into a surprised jerk.

The Roaring Gimlet opens the door, slipping the chain, and is greeted with a squirt of flour right in the kisser, and a shrieky command:

"Give us the Candy or We'll give you the Rush!"

The Gimlet coughs away the flour, choler rising, and beholds before her, knee-high, a huge black feathered hat. Under the hat is a pouty pink face, and under the pouty pink face, a fluffy farthingale that resembles in both color and points an artichoke, and under that, purple dance shoes, with criss-crossy ribbands. Riding on the hip of this apparition is a large pink plushy pig, also wearing purple criss-crossy dance shoes, golden laurel leaves perched over floppy piggy ears.

It's the Pig that the Gimlet recognizes first, not the kid. The kid, whose public appearances have been kept to a minimum (the Pontifexa is wary of too much flattery, and as noted, chary of her heir's worth) could be any kid, but there is only one Pig, all Califa knows that, and the kid must follow the Pig, as day follows night, as sun follows rain, as fortune follows the fool.

"Give us the CANDY or we'll GIVE YOU THE RUSH!" A voice to pierce glass, to cut right through the Gimlet's recoil, all the way down to her achy toes. The straw-shooter moves from *present* to *fire*; while Gimlet was gawking, reloading had occurred, and another volley is imminent. She's about to slam shut the door, she cares not to receive flour or to give out yum, but then, door-jamb held halfway in hand, she stops. An idea, formed from an over-abundance of yellow nasty novellas and an under-abundance of good sense, has leapt full-blown from Nowhere to the Somewhere that is the Roaring Gimlet's calculating brain. So much for sugar, so much for swag: here then is a price above rubies, above diamonds, above chocolate, above, well, Above All. What a pretty price a pretty piece could fetch. On such proceeds the Gimlet could while away her elder days in endless sun and fun-toys.

Before the kid can blow again, the Gimlet grins, in her best granny way, flour feathering about her, and says, "Well, now, chickiedee, well now indeed. I've no desire to be rushed, but you are late and the candy is—"

She recoils, but not in time, from another spurt of flour. When she wipes away the flour, she is careful not to wipe away her welcoming grin. "But I have more here in the kitchen, come in, tiny pirate, out of the cold and we shall fill your sack full."

"Huh," says the child, already her husband's Doom and about to become the Roaring Gimlet's, as well. "GIVE ME THE CANDY—"

Patience is a virtue that the Roaring Gimlet is well off without. She peers beyond the kid, down the street. There are people about but they are: drunken people, or burning people, or screaming people, or carousing people, or running people. None of them appear to be observant people, and that's perfecto. The Gimlet reaches and grabs.

"Hey!" says the Kid. The Pig does not protest.

Tiny Doom is stout, and she can dig her heels in, but the Gimlet is stouter and the Gimlet has two hands free, where Tiny Doom has one, and the Pig is too flabby to help. Before Tiny Doom can shoot off her next round of flour, she's yanked and the door is slammed shut behind her, bang!

V. Bad Housekeeping

Here is Hardhands striding down the darkened streets like a colossus, dodging fire, flood, and fighting. He is not upset, oh no indeedy. He's cool and cold and so angry that if he touched tinder it would burst into flames, if he tipped tobacco it would explode cherry red. And there's more than enough ire to go around, which is happy because the list of Hardhands' blame is quite long.

Firstly: the Pontifexa for making him take Cyrenacia with him.

What good is it to be her darling grandson when he's constantly on doodie-detail? Being the only male Haðraaða should be good for: power, mystery, free booze, noli me tangare, first and foremost, the biggest slice of cake. Now being the only male Haðraaða is good for: marrying small torments, kissing the Pontifexa's ass, and being bossed into wife-sitting. He almost got Grandmamma once; perhaps the decision should be revisited.

Secondly: Tiny Doom for not standing still. When he gets her, he's going to paddle her, see if he doesn't. She's got it coming, a long time coming and perhaps a hot hinder will make her think twice about, well, think twice about everything. Didn't he do enough for her already? He married her, to keep her in the family, to keep her out of the hands of her nasty daddy, who otherwise would have the prior claim. Ungrateful kidlet. Perhaps she deserves whatever she gets.

Thirdly: Relais for being such an utter jackass that he can't keep track of a four-year-old. Hardhands has recently come across a receipt for an ointment that allows the wearer to walk through walls. For which, this sigil requires three pounds of human tallow. He's got a few walls he wouldn't mind flitting right through and at last, Relais will be useful.

Fourthly: Paimon. What need has a domicilic denizen for a night off, anyway? He's chained to the physical confines of the House Bilskinir by a sigil stronger than life. He should be taking care of the Heir to the House Bilskinir, not doing whatever the hell he is doing on his night off which he shouldn't be doing anyway because he shouldn't be having a night off and when Hardhands is in charge, he won't, no sieur.

Fifthly: Pig. Ayah, so, well, Pig is a stuffy pink plush toy, and can hardly be blamed for anything, but what the hell, why not? Climb on up, Pig, there's always room for one more!

And ire over all: his ruined invocation, for which he had been purging starving dancing and flogging for the last two week, all in preparation for what would surely be the most stupendous summoning in the history of summoning. It's been a stellar group of daemons that Hardhands has been able to force from the Aeyther before, but this time he had been going for the highest of the high, the loudest of the loud, and the show would have been sure to go down in the annals of musickoly and his name, already famous, would become gigantic in its shadow. Even the Pontifexa was sure to be impressed. And now . . .

The streets are full of distraction but neither Hardhands nor Alfonso are distracted. Tiny Doom's footprints pitty-patter before them, glowing in the gloam like little blue flowers, and they follow, avoiding burning brands, dead horses, drunken warblers, slithering servitors, gushing water pipes, and an impromptu cravat party and, because of their glowering concentration, they are avoided by all the aforementioned, in turn. The pretty blue footprints dance, and leap, from here to there, and there to here, over cobblestone and curb, around corpse and copse, by Cobweb's Palace and Pete's Clown Diner, by Ginger's Gin Goint and Guerrero's Helado, and other blind tigers so blind they are nameless also, dives so low that just walking by will get your knickers wet. The pretty prints don't waver, don't dilly-dally, and then suddenly, they turn towards a door, broad and barred, and they stop.

At the door, Hardhands doesn't bother knocking, and neither does Alfonso, but their methods of entry differ. Alfonso zips through the wooden obstruction as though it is neither wooden nor obstructive. Hardhands places palm down on wood, and via a particularly loud Barbarick exhortation, blows the door right off its hinges. His entry is briefly hesitated by the necessity to chase after his chapeau, having blown off also in the breeze of Barbarick, but once it is firmly stabbed back on his handsome head, onward he goes, young Hardhands, hoping very much that something else will get in his path, because, he can't deny it: exploding things is Fun.

The interior of the house is dark and dull, not that Hardhands is there to critique the décor. Alfonso has zipped ahead of him, cold-fire frothing in his wake. Hardhands follows the bubbly pink vapour, down a narrow hallway, past peeling paneling, and dusty doorways. He careens down creaky stairs, bending head to avoid braining on low ceiling, and into a horrible little kitchen.

He wrinkles his nose. Our young hero is used to a praeterhuman amount of cleanliness, and here there is neither. At Bilskinir House even the light looks as though it's been washed, dried and pressed before hung in the air. In contrast, this pokey little hole looks like the back end of a back end bar after a particularly festive game of Chew the Ear. Smashed crockery and blue willow china crunches under boot, and the furniture is bonfire ready. A faint glow limns the wreckage, the after-reflection of some mighty big magick. The heavy sour smell of blackberries wrinkles in his nose. Coldfire dribbles from the ceiling, whose plaster cherubs and grapes look charred and withered.

Hardhands pokes at a soggy wad of clothes lying in a heap on the disgusting floor. For one testicle shriveling moment he thought that he saw black velvet amongst the sog; he does, but it's a torn shirt, not a puffy hat.

All magickal acts leave a resonance behind, unless the magician takes great pains to hide: Hardhands knows every archon, hierophant, sorceress, bibliomatic, and avatar in the City, but he don't recognize the author of this Working. He catches a drip of coldfire on one long finger and holds it up his lips: salt-sweet-smoky-oddly familiar but not enough to identify.

"Pigface pogo!" says our hero. He has put his foot down in slide and almost gone face down in a smear of glass and black goo—mashy blackberry jam, the source of the sweet stench. Flailing un-heroically he regains his balance, but in doing so grabs at the edge of an over-turned settle. The settle has settled backwards, cock-eyed on its back feet, but Hardhands' leverage rocks it forward again, and, hello, here's the Gimlet—well, parts of her anyway. She is stuck to the bench by a flood of dried blood, and the expression on her face is doleful, and a little bit surprised.

"Pogo pigface on a pigpogopiss! Who the hell is that?"

Alfonzo yanks the answer from the Aethyr. "The Roaring Gimlet, petty roller and barn stamper. You see her picture sometimes in the post office."

"She don't look too roaring to me. What the hell happened to her?"

Alfonzo zips closer, while Hardhands holds his sleeve to his sensitive nose. The stench of metallic blood is warring with the sickening sweet smell of the crushed blackberries, and together a pleasuring perfume they do not make.

"Me, I think she was chewed," Alfonzo announces after close inspection. "By something hungry and mad."

"What kind of something?"

Alfonso shrugs. "Nobody I know, sorry, boss."

As long as Doom is not chewed, Hardhands cares naught for the chewy-ness of others. He uneasily illuminates the fetid shadows with a vivid Barbarick phrase, but thankfully no rag-like wife does he see, tossed aside like a discarded tea-towel, nor red wet stuffy Pig-toy, only bloody jam and magick bespattered walls. He'd never admit it, particularly not to a yappy servitor, but there's a warm feeling of relief in his toes that Cyrenacia and Pig were not snacked upon. But if they were not snacked upon, where the hell are they, oh irritation.

There, in the light of his sigil—sign: two dainty feet stepped in jammy blood, hopped in disgust, and then headed up the back stairs, the shimmer of Bilskinir blue shining faintly through the rusty red. Whatever got the Gimlet did not get his wife and pig, that for sure, that's all he cares about, all he needs to know, and the footprints are fading, too: onward.

At the foot of the stairs, Hardhands poises. A low distant noise drifts out of the floor below, like a bad smell, a rumbly agonized sound that makes his tummy wiggle.

"What is that?"

A wink of Alfonzo's tails and top-hat and here's his answer: "There's some guy locked in the cellar, and he's—he's in a bad way, and I think he needs our help—"

Hardhands is not interested in guys locked in cellars, nor in their bad ways. The footprints are fading, and the Current is still rising, he can feel it jiggling in his veins. Badness is on the loose—is not the Gimlet proof of that?—and Goddess Califa knows what else, and Tiny Doom is alone.

VI: Sugar Sweet

Here is Hardhands, hot on the heels of the pretty blue footsteps skipping along through the riotous streets. Hippy-hop, pitty-pat. The trail takes a turning, into a narrow alley and Hardhands turns with it, leaving the sputtering street lamps behind. Before the night was merely dark: now it's darkdarkdark. He flicks a bit of coldfire from his fingertips, blossoming a ball of luminescence that weirdly lights up the crooked little street, broken cobbles and black narrow walls. The coldfire ball bounces onward, and Hardhands follows. The foot prints are almost gone: in a few more moments they will be gone, for a lesser magician they would be gone already.

And then, a drift of song:

"*Hot corn, hot corn! Buy my hot corn!*
Lovely and sweet, Lovely and Warm!"

Out of the shadow comes a buttery smell, hot and wafting, the jingling of bells, friendly and beckoning: a Hot Corn Dolly, out on the prowl. The perfume is delightful and luscious and it reminds Hardhands that dinner was long since off. But Hardhands does not eat corn (while not fasting, he's on an all meat diet, for to clean his system clear of sugar and other poisons), and when the Hot Corn Dolly wiggles her tray at him, her green ribboned braids dancing, he refuses.

The Corn Dolly is not alone, her sisters stand behind her, and their wide trays, and the echoing wide width of their farthingale skirts, flounced with patchwork, jingling with little bells, form a barricade that Hardhands, the young gentleman, can not push through. The Corn Dolly skirts are wall-to-wall and their ranks are solid and only rudeness will make a breach.

"I cry your pardon, ladies," he says, in feu de joie, ever courteous, for is not the true mark of a gentleman his kindness towards others, particularly his inferiors? "I care not for corn, and I would pass."

"*Buy my hot corn, deliciously sweet,*
Gives joy to the sorrowful and strength to the weak."

The Dolly's voice is luscious, ripe with sweetness. In one small hand she holds an ear of corn, dripping with butter, fragrant with the sharp smell of chile and lime, bursting up from its peeling of husk like a flower, and this she proffers towards him. Hardhands feels a southerly rumble, and suddenly his mouth is full of anticipatory liquid. Dinner was a long long time ago, and he has always loved hot corn, and how can one little ear of corn hurt him? And anyway, don't he deserve some solace? He fumbles in his pocket, but no divas does he slap; he's the Pontifexa's grandson, and not in the habit of paying for his treats.

The Dolly sees his gesture and smiles. Her lips are glistening golden, as yellow as her silky hair, and her teeth, against the glittering, are like little nuggets of white corn.

"*A kiss for the corn, and corn for a kiss,*

One sweet with flavor, the other with bliss" she sings, and the other dollies join in her harmony, the bells on their square skirts jingling. The hot corn glistens like gold, steamy and savory, dripping with yum. A kiss is a small price to pay to sink his teeth into savory. He's paid more for less and he leans forward, puckering.

The dollies press in, wiggling their oily fingers and humming their oily song, enfolding him in the husk of their skirts, their hands, their licking tongues. His southerly rumble is now a wee bit more southerly, and it's not a rumble, it's an avalanche. The corn rubs against his lips, slickery and sweet, spicy and sour. The chili burns his lips, the butter soothes them, he kisses, and then he licks, and then he bites into a bliss of crunch, the squirt of sweetness cutting the heat and the sour. Never has he tasted anything better, and he bites again, eagerly, butter oozing down his chin, dripping onto his shirt. Eager fingers stroke his skin, he's engorged with the sugar-sweetness, so long denied, and now he can't get enough, each niblet exploding bright heat in his mouth, his tongue, his head, he's drowning in the sweetness of it all.

And like a thunder from the Past, he hears ringing in his head the Pontifexa's admonition, oft repeated to a whiny child begging for hot corn, spun sugar, spicy taco or fruit cup, sold on the street, in marvelous array but always denied because: YOU NEVER KNOW WHERE IT'S BEEN. An Admonition drummed into his head with painful frequency, all the other kidlets snacked from the street vendors with reckless abandon, but not the Pontifexa's grandson, whose tum was deemed to delicate for common food and the common bugs it might contain.

Drummed well and hard it would seem, to suddenly recall now, with memorable force, better late than never. Hardhands snaps open eyes and sputters kernels. Suddenly he sees true what the Corn Dollies' powerful glamour have disguised under a patina of butter and spice: musky kernels and musky skin. A fuzz of little black flies encircles them. The silky hair, the silky husks are slick with mold. The little white corn teeth grin mottled blue and green, and corn worms spill in a white wiggly waterfall from gaping mouths.

"Arrgg," says our hero, managing to keep the urp down, heroically. He yanks and flutters, pulls and yanks, but the knobby fingers have him firm, stalk to stalk. He heaves, twisting his shoulders, spinning and ducking: now they have his shirt, but he is free.

"✂︎ ☞ ☜ ◆ ✋ ♪ ✤ ☾!" he bellows, at the top of his magickal lungs. The word explodes from his head with an agonizing aural thud. The Corn Dollies sizzle and shriek, but he doesn't wait around to revel in their popping. Now he's a fleet footed fancy boy, skeddadling as fast as skirts will allow; to hell with heroics, there's no audience about, just get the hell out. He leaves the shrieking behind him, fast on booted heels, and it's a long heaving pause later, when the smell of burned corn no longer lingers on the air, that he stops to catch breath and bearings. His heart, booming with Barbarick exertion, is starting to slow, but his head, still thundering with a sugary rush, feels as though it might implode right there on his shoulders, dwindle down a pinprick of pressure, diamond hard. The sugar pounds in his head, beating his brain into a ploughshare of pain, sharp enough to cut a furrow in his skull.

He leans on a scaly wall and sticks a practiced finger down his gullet. Up heaves corn, and bile, and blackened gunk, and more gunk. The yummy sour-lime-butter taste doesn't have quite the same delicious savor coming up as it did going down, nor is his shuddering now quite so delightful. He spits and heaves, and heaves and spits, and when his inside is empty of everything, including probably most of his internal organs, he feels a wee bit better. Not much, but some. His ears are cold. He puts a quivery hand to his head; his hat is gone.

The chapeau is not the only disappear, Tiny Doom's tiny footprints, too, have faded. Oh for a drink to drive the rest of the stale taste of rotting corn from his tonsils. Oh for a super duper purge to scour the rest of the stale speed of sugar from his system. Oh for a bath, and bed, and deep sweet sleep. He's had a thin escape, and he knows it: the Corn Sirens could have drained him completely, sucked him as a dry as a desert sunset, and Punto Finale for the Pontifexa's grandson. Now it's going to take him weeks of purifications, salt-baths and soda enemas to get back into whack. Irritating. He's also irked at the loss of his shirt; it was brand-new, he'd only worn it once, and the lace on its sleeves had cost him fifty-eight divas in gold. And his hat, bristling with angel feathers, its brim bigger than an apple pancake. He's annoyed at himself, sloppy-sloppy-sloppy.

The coldfire track has sputtered and no amount of Barbarick kindling can spark it alight; it's too late, too gone, too long. Alfonzo, too, is absent of summoning and when Hardhands closes his eyes and clenches his fists to his chest, sucks in deep lungs of air, until the Current bubbles in his veins like the most sparkling of red wines, he knows why: the Current has flowed so high now that even the lowliest servitors can ride it without assistance, is strong enough to avoid constraint and ignore demand. He'd better find the kid soon, with the Current this high, only snackers will now be out, anyone without skill or protection—the snackees—will have long since gone home, or been eaten. Funtime for humans is over, and funtime for Others just begun.

Well, that's fine, Alfonzo is just a garnish, not necessary at all. Is not Tiny Doom his own blood? Does not a shared spark run through their veins? He closes eyes again, and stretches arms outward, palms upward and he concentrates every split second of his Will into a huge vaporous awareness which he flings out over Califa like a net. Far far at the back of his throat, almost a tickle, not quite a taste, he finds the smell he is looking for. It's dwindling, and it's distant, but it's there and it's enough. A tiny thread connecting him to her, blood to blood, heat to heat, heart beat to heart beat, a tiny threat of things to come when Tiny Doom is not so Tiny. He jerks the thread with infinitesimal delicacy. It's thin, but it holds. It's thin, but it can never completely break.

He follows the thread, gently, gently, down darkened alleys, past shuttered facades, and empty stoops. The streets are slick with smashed fruit, but otherwise empty. He hears the sound of distant noises, hooting, hollering, braying mule, a fire bell, but he is alone. The buildings grow sparser, interspaced with empty lots. They look almost like rows of tombstones, and their broken windows show utterly black. The acrid tang of burning sugar tickles his nose, and the sour-salt smell of marshy sea-water; he must be getting closer to the bay's soggy edge. Cobblestones give way to splintery corduroy which gives way to moist dirt, and now the sweep of the starry sky above is unimpeded by building facades; he's almost out of the City, he may be out of the City now, he's never been this far on this road and if he hadn't absolute faith in the Haðraaða family bond, he'd be skeptical that Tiny Doom's chubby little legs had made it this far either.

But they have. He knows it.

Hardhands pauses, cocking his head: a tinge suffuses his skin, a gentle breeze that isn't a breeze at all, but the galvanic buzz of the Current. The sky above is now obscured by wafts of spreading fog, and, bourne distantly upon that breeze, a vague tune. Musick.

Onward, on prickly feet, with the metallic taste of magick growing thicker in the back of his throat. The music is building crescendo, it sounds so friendly and fun, promising popcorn, and candied apples, fried pies. His feet prickle with these promises, and he picks up the pace, buoyed on by the rollicking music, allowing the musick to carry him onward, towards the twinkly lights now beckoning through the heavy mist.

Then the musick is gone, and he blinks, for the road has come to an end as well, a familiar end, although unexpected. Before him looms a giant polychrome monkey head, leering brightly. This head is two stories high, it has flapping ears and wheel-size eyes, and its gaping mouth, opened in a silent howl, is large enough for a gaggle of school children to rush through, screaming their excitement.

Now he knows where he is, where Tiny Doom has led him too, predictable, actually, the most magical of all childhood places: *Woodward's Garden, Fun for All Occasions, Not Occasionally but Always*.

How oft has Hardhands been to Woodward's (in cheerful daylight), and ah the fun he has had there, (in cheerful daylight): The Circular Boat and the Mystery Manor, the Zoo of Pets, and the Whirla-Gig. Pink popcorn and strawberry cake, and Madam Twanky's Fizzy Lick-A-Rice Soda. Ah, Woodward's Garden and the happy smell of sun, sugar, sweat and sizzling meat. But at Woodward's, the fun ends at sundown, as evening's chill begins to rise, the rides begin to shut, the musick fades away and everyone must go, exiting out the Monkey's Other End. Woodward's is not open at night.

But here, tonight, the Monkey's Eyes are open, although his smile is a grimace, less Welcome and more Beware. The Monkey's Eyes roll like red balls in their sockets, and at each turn they display a letter: "F" "U" "N" they spell in flashes of sparky red. Something skitters at our boy's ankles and he jumps: scraps of paper flickering like shredded ghosts. The Monkey's Grin is fixed, glaring, in the dark it does not seem at all like the Gateway to Excitement and Adventure, only Digestion and Despair. Surely even Doom, despite her ravenous adoration of the Circular Boat, would not be tempted to enter the hollow throat just beyond the poised glittering teeth. Despite the promise of the Monkey's Rolling Eyes there is no Fun here.

Or is there? Look again. Daylight, a tiara of letters crowns the Monkey's Head, spelling Woodward's Garden in cheery lights. But not tonight, tonight the tiara is a crown of spikes, whose glittering red letters proclaim a different title: *Madam Rose's Flower Garden*.

Hardhands closes his eyes against the flashes, feeling all the blood in his head blushing downward into his pinchy toes. Madam Rose's Flower Garden! It can not be. Madam Rose's is a myth, a rumour, an innuendo, a whisper. A prayer. The only locale in Califa where entities, it is said, can walk in the Waking World without constraint, can move and do as their Will commands, and not be constrained by the Will of a magician or adept. Such mixing is proscribed, it's an abomination, against all laws of nature, and until this very second, Hardhands thought, mere fiction.

And yet apparently not fiction at all. The idea Tiny Doom in such environs sends Hardhands' scalp a-shivering. This is worse than having her out on the streets. Primo child-flesh, delicious and sweet, and plump full of such energy as would turn the most mild mannered elemental into a rival of Choronzon, the Daemon of Dispersion. Surrounded by islocated elementals and egregores, under no obligation and bound by no sigil, indulging in every depraved whim. Surely the tiresome child did not go forward to her own certain doom.

But his burbling tum, his swimming head, knows she did.

If he were not Banastre Haðraaða, the Grand Duque of Califa, this is the point where'd he'd turn about and go home. First he might sit upon the ground, right here in the dirt, and wallow for a while in discouragement, then he'd rise, dust, and retreat. If he were not himself, but someone else, someone lowly, he might be feeling pretty low.

For a moment, he is not himself, he is cold and tired and hungry and ready for the evening to end. It was fun to be furious, his anger gave him forward motion and will and fire, but now he wants to be home in his downy-soft bed with a yellow nasty newsrag and a jorum of hot wine. If Wish could be made Will in a heart-beat, he'd be lying back on damask pillows, drowning away to happy dreamland.

Before he can indulge in such twaddle, a voice catches his attention.

"Well, now, your grace. Slumming?"

Then does Hardhands notice a stool, and upon the stool a boy sitting, legs dangling, swinging copper-toed button boots back and forth. A pocketknife flashes in his hand; shavings flutter downward. He's tow-headed, and blue-eyed, freckled and tan, and he's wearing a polka-dotted kilt, a redingcote, and a smashed bowler. A smoldering stoogie hangs down from his lips.

"I beg your pardon?"

"Never mind, never mind. Are you here for the auction?"

Hardhands replies regally: "I am looking for a child and a pink pig."

The boy says, brightly, "Oh yes, of course. They passed this way some time ago, in quite a hurry."

Hardhands makes move to go inside, but is halted by the red velvet rope that acts as barrier to the Monkey's mouth.

"Do you have a ticket? It's fifteen divas, all you can eat and three trips to the bar."

Remembering his empty pockets, Hardhands says loftily: "I'm on the List."

The List: Another powerful weapon. If you are on it, all to the good. If not, back to the Icy Arrogance. But when has Hardhands not been on the list? Never! Unthinkable!

"Let me see," says the Boy. He turns out pockets, and thumps his vest, fishes papers, and strings, candy and fish-hooks, bones and lights, a white rat, and a red rubber ball. "I know I had something—Ahah!" This ahah is addressed to his hat, what interior he is excavating and out of which he draws a piece of red foolscap. "Let me see . . . um . . . Virex the Sucker of Souls, Zigurex Avatar of Agony, Valefor Teller of Tales, no, I'm sorry your grace, but you are not on the list. That will be fifteen divas."

"Get out of my way."

Hardhands takes a pushy step forward, only to find that his feet can not come off the ground. The Boy, the Gatekeeper, smells like human but he has powerful praeterhuman push.

"Let me by."

"What's the magick word?"

"☉⌘□◆👁● ꝑ◆♎♏◼♌👁☌&🗡"

This word should blossom like fire in the sultry air, it should spout lava and sparks and smell like burning tar. It should shrink the Boy down to stepping-upon size.

It sparks briefly, like a wet sparkler, and gutters away.

He tries again, this time further up the Barbarick alphabet, heavier on the results.

"☉⌘□◆👁● ☜✗👁□◆♏."

This word should suck all the light out of the world , leaving a blackness so utter that it will leave the Boy gasping for enough breath to scream.

It casts a tiny shadow, like a gothick's smile, and then brightens.

"Great accent," says the Boy. He is grinning sympathetically, which enrages Hardhands even more, because he is the Pontifexa's grandson and there's nothing to be sorry about for THAT. "But not magickal enough.

Hardhands is flummoxed, this is a first, never before has his magick been stifled, tamped, failed to light. Barbarick is tricky, it is true. In the right mouth the right Barbarick word will explode the Boy into tiny bits of bouncing ectoplasm, or shatter the air as though it were made of ice, or turn the moon into a tulip. The right word in the wrong mouth, a mouth that stops when it should glottal or clicks when it should clack, could turn his tummy into a hat, roll back time, or turn his blood to fire. But, said right or said wrong, Barbarick never does nothing. His tummy is, again, tingling.

The Boy is now picking his teeth with the tip of his knife. "I give you a hint. The most magickal word of them all."

What more magick than ✠✠✠✠ or ⌀⌀⌀⌀⌀? Is there a more magickal word that Hardhands has never heard of? He's an adept of the sixth order, he's peeked into the Abyss, surely there is no Super Special Magickal Word hidden from him yet—he furrows his pure white brow into unflattering wrinkles, and then, a tiny whiny little voice in his head says: *what's the magick word, Bwannie, what's the magick word?*

"Please." Hardhands says. "Let me pass, please."

"With pleasure," the Boy says, "But I must warn you. There are ordeals."

"No ordeal can be worse than listening to you."

"One might think so," the boy says, "You have borne my rudeness so kindly, your grace, that I hate to ask you for one last favour, but I fear I must."

Hardhands glares at the boy, who smiles sheepishly.

"Your boots, your grace. Madama doesn't care for footwear on her clean carpets. I shall give you a ticket, and give your boots a polish and they'll be nice and shiny for you, when you leave."

Hardhands does not want to relinquish his heels, which may only add an actual half an inch in height, but are marvelous when it comes to mental stature, who can not help but swagger in red-topped jackboots, champagne shiny and supple as night?

He sighs, bending. The grass below is cool against our hero's hot feet, once liberated happily from the pinchy pointy boots (ah vanity, thy name is only sixteen years old) but he'd trade the comfort, in a second, for height.

He hops and kicks, sending one boot flying at the kid (who catches it easily) and the other off into the darkness.

"Mucho gusto. Have a swell time, your grace."

Hardhands stiffens his spine with arrogance and steps into the Monkey's Mouth.

VII. Time's Trick

Motion moves in the darkness around him, a glint of silver, to one side, then the other, then in front of him: he jumps. Then he realizes that the form ahead of him is familiar: his own reflection. He steps forward, and the Hardhands before him resolves into a Hardhands behind him, while those to other side, move with him, keeping pace. For a second he hesitates, thinking to run into mirror, but an outstretched arm feels only empty air, and he steps once, again, then again, more confidently. His reflection has disappeared; ahead is only darkness.

So he continues on, contained with a hollow square of his own reflections, which makes him feel a bit more cheerful, for what can be more reassuring but an entire phalanx of your own beautiful self? Sure, he looks a bit tattered: bare chest, sticky hair, blurred eyeliner, but it's a sexy tattered, bruised and battered, and slightly forlorn. He could start a new style with this look: *After the Deluge*, it could be called, or, *A Rough Night*.

Of course Woodwards' has a hall of mirrors too, a horrifying place where the glasses stretch your silver-self until you look like an emaciated crane, or squash you down, round as a beetle. These mirrors continue, as he continues, to show only his perfect self, disheveled, but still perfect. He laughs, a sound which, pinned in on all sides as it is, quickly dies. If this is the Boy's idea of an Ordeal, he's picked the wrong man. Hardhands has always loved mirrors, so much so that he has them all over his apartments: on his walls, on his ceilings, even, in his Conjuring Closet, on the floor. He's never met a reflection of himself he didn't love, didn't cherish, cheered up by the sight of his own beauty—what a lovely young man, how blissful to be me!

He halts and fumbles in his kilt-pocket for his favorite lip rouge (*Death in Bloom*, a sort-of blackish pink) and reapplies. Checks his teeth for color, and blots on the back of his hand. Smoothes one eyebrow with his finger-tip, and arranges a strand of hair so it is more fetchingly askew—then leans in, closer. A deep line furrows behind his eyes, a line where he's had no line before, and there, at his temple, is that a strand of gray amidst the silver? His groping fingers feel only smoothness on his brow, he smiles and the line vanishes, he grips the offending hair and yanks: in his grasp it is as pearly as ever. A trick of the poor light then, and on he goes, but sneaking glances to his left and right, not from admiration, but from concern.

As he goes, he keeps peeking sideways and at each glance, he quickly looks away again, alarmed. Has he always slumped so badly? He squares his shoulders, and peeks again. His hinder, it's huge, like he's got a caboose under his kilt, and his chin, it's as weak as custard. No, it must just be a trick of the light, his hinder is high and firm, and his chin as hard and curved as granite, he's overstressed and overwrought and he still has all that sugar in his system. His gaze doggedly forward, he continued down the silver funnel, picks up his feet, eager, perhaps for the first time ever, to get away from a mirror.

The urge to glance is getting bigger and bigger, and Hardhands has, before, always vanquished temptation by yielding to it, he looks again, this time to his right. There, he is as lovely as ever, silly silly. He grins confidently at himself, that's much better. He looks behind him and sees, in another mirror, his own back looking further beyond, but he can't see what he's looking at or why.

Back to the slog, and the left is still bugging him, he's seeing flashes out of the corner of his eye, and he just can't help it, he must look: his eyes, they are sunken like marbles into his face, hollow as a sugar skull, his skin tightly pulled, painted with garish red cheekbones. Blackened lips pull back from grayish teeth—his pearly white teeth!—He chatters those pearly whites together, his bite is firm and hard. He looks to the right and sees himself, as he should be.

Now he knows, don't look to the left, keep to the right and keep focused, the left is a mirage, the right is reality. The left side is a horrible joke and the right side is true, but even as he, increasing his steps to almost a run (will this damn hallway never end?), the Voice of Vanity in his head is questioning that assertion. Perhaps the right side is the horrible joke, and the left side the truth, perhaps he has been blind to his own flaws, perhaps—

This time: he is transfixed at the image which stares back, as astonished as he is: he's an absolute wreck. His hair is still and brittle, hanging about his knobby shoulders like salted sea grass. His ice blue eyes look cloudy, and the thick black lines drawn about them serve onto to sink them deeper into his skull. Scars streak lividly across his cheeks. Sunken chest and tattoos faded into blue and green smudges, illegible on slack skin. He's too horrified to seek reassurance in the mirror now behind him, he's transposed on the horror before him: the horror of his own inevitable wreckage and decay. The longer he stares the more hideous he becomes. The image blurs for a moment, and then blood blooms in his hair, and dribbles from his gaping lips, his shoulders are scratched and smudged with black, his eyes starting from his skull. He is surrounded by swirling snow, flecks of which sputter on his eyelashes, steam as they touch his skin. The shaft of an arrow protrudes from his throat.

"Oh how bliss to me," the Death's Head croaks, each word a bubble of blood.

With a shout, Hardhands raises his right fist and punches. His fist meets the glass with a nauseous jolt of pain that rings all the way down to his toes. The glass bows under his blow but doesn't crack. He hits again, his corpse reels back, clutching itself with claw-like hands.

The mirror refracts into a thousand diamond shards, and Hardhands throws up his other arm to ward off glass and blood. When he drops his shield, the mirrors and their Awful Reflection are gone.

He stands on the top of stairs, looking out over a tumultuous vista: there's a stage with feathered denizens dancing the hootchy-coo. Behind the hootchie-coochers, a band plays a ferocious double-time waltz. Couples slide and twist and turn to the musick, their feet flickering so quickly they spark. The scene is much like the scene he left behind at the Blue Duck, only instead of great big hair, there are great big horns, instead of sweeping skirts there are sweeping wings, instead of smoke there is coldfire. The musick is loud enough to liquefy his skull, he can barely think over its howling sweep.

The throng below whirls about in confusion—denizens, demons, egregores, servitors—was that a Bilskinir-Blue Bulk he saw over there at the bar, tusks a-gleaming, Butler Paimon on his damn night-off? No matter even if it is Paimon, no holler for help from Hardhands, oh no. Paimon would have to help him out, of course, but Paimon would tell the Pontifexa for sure, for Paimon, in addition to being the Butler of Bilskinir, is a suck-up. No thanks, our hero is doing just fine on his own.

A grip pulls at Hardhands' soft hand, he looks down into the wizened grinning face of a monkey. Hardhands tries to yank from the grasp, the monkey has pretty good pull, which he puts into gear with a yank, that our hero has little choice but to follow. A bright red cap shaped like a flower pot is affixed to Sieur Simian's head by a golden cord, and he's surprisingly good at the upright; his free hand waves a path through the crowd, pulling Hardhands behind like a toy.

The dancers slide away from the monkey's push, letting Hardhands and his guide through their gliding. By the band, by the fiddler, who is sawing away at his fiddle as though each note was a gasp of air and he a suffocating man, his hair flying with sweat, his face burning with concentration. Towards a flow of red velvet obscuring a doorway, and through the doorway into sudden hush, the cessation of the slithering music leaving sudden silence in Hardhands' head.

Now he stands on a small landing, overlooking a crowded room.

The Great Big Horns and Very Long Claws and etc. are alert to something sitting upon a dais at the far end of the room. Hardhands follows their attention and goes cold all the way to his bones

Upon the dais is a table. Upon the table is a cage. Within the cage: Tiny Doom.

VIII. Cash & Carry

The bidding has already started. A hideous figure our hero recognizes as Zigurex the Avatar of Agony is flipping it out with a dæmon whose melty visage and dribbly hair Hardhands does not know. Their paddles are popping up and down, in furious volley to the furious patter of the auctioneer:

" . . . unspoiled untouched pure one hundred percent kid-flesh plump and juicy tender and sweet highest grade possible never been spanked whacked or locked in a closet for fifty days with no juice no crackers no light fed on honey dew and chocolate sauce . . . "

(Utter lie, Tiny Doom is in a cheesy noodle phase and if it's not noodles and it's not orange then she ain't gonna eat it, no matter the dire threat.) Tiny Doom is barking, frolicking about the cage happily, she's the center of attention, she's up past her bedtime and she's a *puppy*. It's fun!

The auctioneer is small, delicate and apparently human, although Hardhands is willing to bet that she's probably none of these at all, and she has the patter down: "Oh she's darling oh she's bright she'll fit on your mantel, she'll sleep on your dog-bed, she's compact and cute now, and ah the blood you can breed from her when she's older. What an investment, sell her now, sell her later, you're sure to repay your payment a thousand times over and a free Pig as garnish can you beat the deal—and see how bright she does bleed."

The minion hovering above the cage displays a long length of silver tipped finger and then flicks downward. Tiny Doom yelps, and the rest of the patter is lost in Hardhands' roar as he leaps forward, pushing spectators aside: "THAT IS MY WIFE!"

His leap is blocked by bouncers, who thrust him backwards, but not far. Ensues: rumpus, with much switching and swearing and magickal sparkage. Hardhands may have Words of Power, and a fairly Heavy Fist for one so fastidious but the bouncers have Sigils of Impenetrableness or at least Hides of Steel, and one of them has three arms, and suction cups besides.

"THAT IS MY WIFE!" Hardhands protests again, now pinned. "I demand that you release her to me."

"It's careless to let such a tempting small morsel wander the streets alone, your grace." Madam Rose cocks her head, her stiff wire headdress jingling, and the bouncers release Hardhands.

He pats his hair; despite the melee, still massively piled, thanks to Paimon's terrifically sticky hair pomade. The suction cups have left little burning circles on his chest and his bare toes feel a bit tingly from connecting square with someone's tombstone-hard teeth, but at least he solaces in the fact that one of the bouncers is dripping whitish ooze from puffy lips and the other won't be breeding children anytime soon; just as hard a kick, but much more squishy. The rooms a wreck, too, smashed chairs, crumpled paper, spilled popcorn, oh dear, too bad.

"She's my wife to be, as good as is my wife, and I want her back." He makes movement towards the cage, which is now terribly quiet, but the bouncers still bar the way.

Zigurex upsteps himself, then, looming over Hardhands who now wishes he had been more insistent about the boots: "Come along with the bidding; it's not all night, you see, the tide is rising and the magick will soon sail."

The other dæmon, who is both squishy and scaly, bubbles his opinion, as well. At least Hardhands assumes it is his opinion, impossible to understand his blubbering, some obscure dialect of Barbarick, or maybe just a very bad accent, anyway who cares what he has to say anyway, not Hardhands, not at all.

"There is no bidding, she's not for sale, she belongs to me, and Pig, too, and we are leaving," he says.

"Do you bid?" Madam Rose asks.

"No I do not bid. I do not have to bid. She is my wife."

"One hundred fifty!" Zigurex says, last-ditch.

The Fishy Thing counters the offer with a saliva spray glug.

"He offers two hundred," says Madam Rose, "What do you offer?"

"Two hundred!" says Hardhands, outraged. "I've paid two hundred for a pot of lip rouge. She's worth a thousand if she's worth a diva—"

Which is exactly of course the entirely wrong thing to say but his outrage has gotten the better of his judgment, which was already impaired by the outrage of being manhandled like a commoner to begin with, and which also might not have been the best even before then.

Madam Rose smiles. Her lips are sparkly pink and her teeth are sparkly black. "One thousand divas, then, for her return! Cash only. Good night good night and come again!"

She claps her hands, and the bouncers start to press the disappointed bidders into removing.

"Now look here—" says Hardhands. "You can't expect me to buy my own wife, and even if you could expect me to buy my own wife, I won't. I insist that you hand her over right this very second and impede me no longer."

"Is that so?" Madam Rose purrs. The other bidders retreat easily, perhaps they have a sense of where this is all going and decide its wise to get out of the way whilst there is still a way to get out of. Even Sieur Squishy and Zigurex go, although not without several smoldering backways looks on the part of the Avatar of Agony, obviously a sore loser. Madam Rose sits herself down upon a velvet covered chair, and waves Hardhands to do the same, but he does not. A majordomo has uprighted the brazier and repaired the smoldering damage, decanted tea into a brass teapot and set upon a round brass tray. Madam Rose drops sugar cubes into two small glasses and pours over: spicy cinnamon, tangy orange.

Hardhands ignores the tea; peers into the cage to access damage.

"Pig has a tummy ache, and wants to go home, Bwannie." The fat little lip is trembling and despite himself, Hardhands is overwhelmed by the tide of adorableness, that he should, being a first rate magician and poet, be inoculated against. She is so like her mother, oh his darling sister, sometimes it makes him want to cry.

He retreats into gruff. "Ayah, so well, Pig should not have had so much candy. And nor should Pig have wandered off alone."

"He is bad," agrees Doom. "Very bad."

"Sit tight and do not cry. We will go home soon. Ayah?

"Ayah." She sniffs, but holds the snuffle, little soldier.

Madam Rose offers Hardhands a seat, which he does not sit upon, and a glass, which he waves away, remembering anew the Pontifexa's advice, and also not trusting Madam's sparkle grin. He's heard of the dives where they slide sleep into your drink; you gulp down happily and wake up six hours later minus all you hold dear and a splitting headache, as well. Or worse still, gin-joints that sucker you into one little sip, and then you have such a craving that you must have more and more, but no matter how much you have, it shall never be enough. He'll stay dry and alert, thank you.

"I have no time for niceties, or social grace," he says, "I will take my wife and pig, and leave."

"One thousand divas is not so great a sum to the Pontifexa's grandson," Madam Rose observes. "And it's only right that I should recoup some of my losses—look here, I shall have to redecorate, and fashionable taste, as your grace knows, is not cheap."

"I doubt there is enough money in the world to buy you good taste, madama, and why should I pay for something that is mine?"

"Now who owns who, really? *She* is the Heir to the House Haðraaða, and one day she'll be Pontifexa. *You* are just the boy who does. By rights all of us, including you, belong to her, in loyalty and in love. I do wish you would sit, your grace." Madam Rose pats the pillow beside her, which again he ignores.

This statement sets off a twinge of rankle because it is true. He answers loftily, " We are all the Pontifexa's obedient servants, and are happy to bend ourselves to her Will, and her Will in the matter of her Heir is clear. I doubt that she would be pleased to know of the situations of this night."

Madam Rose sets her red cup down. An ursine-headed minion offers her a chocolate, gently balanced between two pointy bear-claws. She opens red lips, black teeth, long red throat and swallows the chocolate without a chew.

"I doubt," she says, "that the Pontifexa shall be pleased at tonight's situation at all. I do wish you would sit, your grace. I feel so small, and you so tall, so high above. And do sample, your grace. I assure you that my candy has no extra spice to it, just wholesome goodness you will find delicious. You have my word upon it."

Hardhands sits, and takes the chocolate he is offered. He's already on the train bound for Purgelandia, he might as well make the journey worth the destination. The Minion twinkles azure bear eyes at him. Bears don't exactly have the right facial arrangement to smirk, but this bear is making a fine attempt, and Hardhands thinks what a fine rug Sieur Oso would make, stretched out before a peaceful fire. In the warmth of his mouth, the chocolate explodes into glorious peppery chocolate yum. For a second he closes his eyes against the delicious darkness, all his senses receding into sensation of pure bliss dancing on his tongue.

"It is good chocolate, is it not?" Madam Rose asks. "Some say such chocolate should be reserved for royalty and the Goddess. But we do enjoy it, no?"

"What do you want?" Hardhands asks, and they both know that he doesn't just mean for Tiny Doom.

"Putting aside, for the moment, the thousand divas, I want nothing more to be of aid to you, your grace, to be your humble servant. It is not what I may want from you but what you can want from me."

"That I have told you."

"Just that?"

In the cage, Tiny Doom is silent and staring, she may be a screamer, but she does, thankfully, know when to keep her trap shut.

"I can offer you no other assistance? Think on it, your grace. You are an adept, and you traffic with denizens of the deep, through the force of your Will. I am not an adept, I also have traffic with those same denizens."

The second chocolate tangs his tongue with the sour-sweet brightness of lime. "Contrary to all laws of Goddess and nature," he says thickly, when the brilliant flavour has receded enough to allow speech. "Your traffic is obscene. It is not the same."

"I didn't say it was the same, I said we might compliment each other, rather than compete. Do you not get tired of your position, your grace? You are so close, and yet so far. The Pontifexa's brightest boy, but does she respect you? Does she trust you? This little girl, is she not the hitch in your git-along, the sand in your shoe? Leave her with me, and she'll never muss your hair again, or wrinkle your cravat."

"I don't recall inviting you to comment upon my personal matters," says Hardhands, a la prince. "And I don't recall offering you my friendship either."

"I cry your pardon, your grace. I only offer my thoughts in the hope—"

He's tired of the game now, if he had the thousand divas he'd fork them over, just to be quit of the entire situation, it was fun, it was cool, it's not fun it's not cool, he's bored, the sugar is drilling a spike through his forehead and he's done.

"I'll write you a draft, and you'll take it, and we shall leave, and that's the end of the situation." Hardhands says loftily.

Madam Rose sighs, and sips her tea. Another sigh, another sip.

"I'm sorry, your grace, but if you can not pay, then I must declare your bid null, and reopen the auction. Please understand my position. It is, and has always been, the policy of this House to operate on a cash basis; I'm sure you understand why—taxes, a necessary evil, but perhaps more evil than necessary," Madam Rose smiles at him, and sips again before going on. "My reputation rests upon my policies, and that I apply them equally to all. Duque of Califa or the lowliest servitor, all are equal within my walls. So you see, if I allow you license I have refused others, how shall it appear then?"

"Smart," answers our hero. "Prudent. Wise."

Madam Rose laughs. "Would that others might consider my actions in that light, but I doubt their charity. No, I'm sorry, your grace. I have worked hard for my name. I can not give it up, not for you or for anyone."

She puts her tea glass down and clicks her tongue, a sharp snap that brings Sieur Bear to her side. "The Duque has decided to withdraw his bid; please inform Zigurex that his bid is accepted and he may come and claim his prize."

Hardhands looks at Doom in her cage, her wet little face peers through the bars. She smiles at him, she's scared but she has confidence that Bwannie will save her, Bwannie loves her. Bwannie has a sense of déjà vu; hasn't he been here before, why is it his fate to always give in to her, little monster? Tiny Doom, indeed.

"What do you want?" he repeats.

"Well," Madam Rose says brightly. "Now that you mention it. The Pontifexina is prime, oh that's true, but I know one more so. More mature, more valuable, more ready."

Now it's Hardhands' turn to sigh, which he does, and sip, wetting parched throat, now not caring if the drink be drugged, or not. "You'll let her go? Return her safe and sound?"

"Of course, your grace. You have my word on it."

"Not a hair on her head or a drop from her veins or a tear from her eye? Not a scab, or nail, or any part that might be later used against her? Completely whole? Untouched, unsmudged, no tricks?"

"As you say."

Hardhands puts his glass down, pretending resignation. "All right then. You have a deal."

Of course he don't really give in, but he's assessed that perhaps its better to get Doom out of the way. He can play rough enough if it's only his own skin involved, but why take the change of her collateral damage? When she's out of the way, he calculates, and Madam Rose's guard is down, then we'll see, oh yes, we'll see.

Madam Rose's shell-white hand goes up to her lips, shading them briefly behind two slender fingers. Then the fingers flip down and flick a shard of spinning coldfire towards him. Hardhands recoils, but too late. The airy kiss zings through the air like an arrow of outrageous fortune and smacks him right in the middle of Death in Bloom. The kiss feels like a kick to the head, and our hero and his chair flip backwards, the floor rising to meet his fall, but not softly. The impact sends his bones jarring inside his flesh, and the jarring is his only movement for the sigil has left him shocked and paralyzed.

He can't cry out, he can't flinch, he can only let the pain flood down his palate and into his brain, in which internal shouting and swearing is making up for external silence. He can't close his eyes either, but he closes his outside vision and brings into inside focus the bright sharp words of a sigil that should suck all the energy from Madam Rose's sigil, blow it into a powderpuff of oblivion.

The sigil burns bright in Hardhands' eyes, but it is also trapped and can not get free. It sparks and wheels, and he desperately tries to tamp it out, dumping colder, blacker sigils on top its flare, trying to fling it outward and away, but it's stuck firmly inside his solar plexus, he can fling it nowhere. It's caught in his craw like a fish bone, and he's choking but he can't choke because he can not move. The sigil's force billows through him: it is twisting his entrails into knots, his bones into bows, it's flooding him with a fire so bright that it's black, with a fire so cold that it burns and burns and burns, his brain boils and then: nothing.

IX. Thy Baited Hook

Here is Hardhands, returning to the Waking World. His blood is mud within his veins, he can barely suck air through stifled lungs and there's a droning in his ears, no not droning, humming, Tiny Doom:

"Kick her bite her that's the way I'll spite her! Kick her bite her that's the way I'll spite her! Kick her bite her that's the way I'll spite her!"

The view aloft is raven-headed angels, with ebony black wings swooping loops of brocade across a golden ceiling. Then the view aloft is blocked by Tiny Doom's face; she still has the sugar mustache, and her kohl has blurred, cocooning her blue eyes in smoky blackness. Her hat is gone.

"Don't worry, Bwannie," she pats his stiff face with a sticky hand, "Pig will save us."

His brain heaves but the rest of him remains still. The frame of his body has never before been so confining. Diligent practice has made stepping his mind from his flesh an easy accomplishment, are there not times when a magician's Will needs independence from his blood and bones? But never before has he been stuck, nor run up against someone's else sigils as harder and more impenetrable has his own. Lying in the cage of his own flesh he is feeling helpless, and tiny, and it's a sucky feeling, not at all suited to his stature of Pontifexa's grandson, first rate magician and—

"I will bite you," says Doom.

"I doubt that," is the gritty answer, a deep rumble: "My skin is thick as steel and your teeth will break."

"Ha! I am a shark and I will bite you."

"Not if I bite you first, little lovely, nip your sweet tiny fingers, crunch crunch each one, oh so delicious, what a snack. Come here, little morsel."

The weight of Tiny Doom suddenly eases off his chest, but not without kicking and gripping, holding on to him in a vice-like grip, oww, her fingers dig like nails into his leg but to no avail. Tiny Doom is wrenched off of him, and in the process he's wrenched side-ways, now he's got a nice view of the grassy floor, a broken teapot, and, just on the edge, someone's feet. The feet are shod in garish two-tone boots: magenta upper and orange toe-cap. Tiny Doom screams like a rabbit, high and horrible.

"You'll bruise her," says a voice from above the feet. "And then the Pontifexa will be chuffed."

"I shall not hurt her one jot if she's a good girl, but she should shut her trap, a headache I am getting."

Good for her, Tiny Doom does not shut her trap, she opens her trap wider and shoots the moon, with a piercing squeal that stabs into Hardhands' unprotected ears like an awl, slicing all the way down to the center of his brain. With a smack, the shriek abruptly stops.

Two pretty little bare feet drift into Hardhands' view. "Stop it you two. She must be returned in perfect condition, an' I get my deposit back. It's only the boy that the Pontifexa wants rid of; the girl is still her heir. Leave her alone, or I shall feed you both into my shredder. Chop chop. The guests are waiting and he must be prepared."

"She squirms," complains the Minion.

Madam Rose, sternly: "You, little madam, stop squirming. You had fun being a puppy, and cupcakes besides, and soon you shall be going home to your sweet little bed. How sad Grandmamma and Paimon shall be if I must give them a bad report of your behavior."

Sniffle, sniff. "But I want Bwannie."

"Never you mind Bwannie for now, here have a Choco-Sniff, and here's one for Pig, too."

Sniff, sniffle. "Pig don't like Choco-Sniffs."

Hardhands kicks, but it's like kicking air, he can feel the movement in his mind, but his limbs stay stiff and locked. And then his mind recoils: What did Madam Rose say about the Pontifexa? Did he hear a-right? Deposit? Report?

"Here then is a jacksnap for Pig. Be a good girl, eat your candy and then you shall kiss Bwannie good-bye."

Whine: "I want to go with Bwannie!"

"Now, now," Madam Rose's cheery tone tingles with irritation, but she's making a good show of not annoying Tiny Doom into another session of shrieking. "Now, Bwannie must stay here, and you must go home—do not start up with the whining again, it's hardly fitting for the Pontifexa's heir to cry like a baby, now is it? Here, have another Choco-Sniff."

Then more harshly, "You two, get the child ready to be returned and the boy prepared. I shall be right back."

The pretty feet float from Hardhands' view and a grasp attaches to Hardhands' ankle. Though his internal struggle is mighty, externally he puts up no fuss at all. Flipped over by rough hands, he sees above him the sharp face of a Sylph, pointy eyes, pointy nose, pointy chin. Hands are fumbling at his kilt buckles; obscurely he notices that the Sylph has really marvelous hair, it's the color of fresh caramel and it smells, Hardhands notices, as the Sylph bends over to nip at his neck, like new-mown grass. A tiny jolt of pretty pain, and warm wetness dribbles down his neck.

"Ahhh . . . " the Sylph sighs, "You should taste this, first rate knock-back."

"Madama said be nice."

"I am being nice, as nice as pie, as nice as he is. Nice and sweet," The Sylph licks at Hardhands' neck again; its tongue is scrape-y, like a cat's, and it hurts in a strangely satisfying way. "Sweet sweet darling boy. He is going to bring our garden joy. What a deal she has made. Give the girl, but keep the boy, he's useful to us, even if she don't want him anymore. A good trick he'll turn for Madama. Bright boy."

Hardhands is hoisted aloft, demon claws at his ankles and his wrists, slinging him like a side of beef on the way to the barbeque pit. His eyes are slitted open, his head dangling downward, he can see only a narrow slice of floor bobbing by. A carpet patterned with entwined snakes, battered black and red tiles, white marble veined with gold. He's watching all this, with part of attention, but mainly he's running over and over again what Madam Rose had said about the Pontifexa. Was it possible to be true? Did Grandmamma set him up? Sell him out? Was this all a smokescreen to get him out of her hair, away from her treasure? He can not believe it, he will not believe it, it can not be true.

Rough movement drops Hardhands onto the cold floor, and metal clenches his ankles. The bracelets bit into his flesh as he is hoisted aloft, and all the blood rushes to his head in a explosion of pressure. For a second, even his slit of sight goes black, but then, just as suddenly, he finds he can open his eyes all the way. He rolls eyeballs upward, and seeing retreating minion backs. He rolls eyes downward and sees polished marble floor and the tangled drape of his own hair, Paimon's pomade having finally given up. The gryves are burning bright pain into his ankles, and he's swaying slightly from some invisible airflow, but the movement is kind of soothingly and his back feels nice and stretched out. If it weren't for being the immobilization, and obvious bait, hanging upside could be kind of fun.

Our hero tries to wiggle, but can't, tries to jiggle but is still stuck. He doesn't dare try another sigil and risk blowing his brains out, and without the use of his muscles he can not gymnastic himself free. He closes his internal eyes, slips his consciousness into darkness, and concentrates. His Will pushes and pushes against the pressure that keeps him contained, focuses into a single point that must burn through. After a second, a minute, an eternity, all bodily sensation—the burn of the gyres, the stretch of his back, the pressure of his bladder, the breeze on his face—slips away, and his Will floats alone on the Current.

Away from the strictures of his body, Hardhands' consciousness can take any form that he cares to mold it to, or form at all, a spark of himself drifting on the Currents of Elsewhere. But such is his fondness for his own form, even Elsewhere, that when he steps lightly from the flesh hanging like a side of beef, he coalesces into a representation of himself, in every way identical to his corporeal form, although with lip rouge that will not smudge, and spectacularly elevated hair.

On Elsewhere feet, Hardhands' fetch turns to face its meaty shell, and is rather pleased with the view; even dangling upside down, he looks pretty darn good. Elsewhere, the sigil that has caged Hardhands' motion is clearly visible as a pulsating net of green and gold, interwoven at the intercises with splotches of pink. A Coarctation Sigil, under normal circumstances no stronger than pie, but given magnitude by the height of the Current, and Hardhands' starchy condition. The fetch, however, is not limited by starch, and the Current just feeds its strength. Dismantling the constraint is the work of a matter of seconds, and after the fetch slides back into its shell, it's a mere bagatelle to contort himself down and free.

Casting free of the gyres with a splashy Barbarick command, Hardhands rubs his ankles, and then stands on tingly feet. Now that he has the leisure to inspect the furnishings, he sees there are no furnishings to inspect because the room, while sumptuously paneled in gorgeous tiger-eye maple, is empty other than a curvy red velvet chase. The only ornamentations are the jingly chains dangling from the ceiling. The floor is bare stone, cold beneath his bare feet. And now, he notices that the flooring directly under the dangle is dark and stained, with something that he suspects is a combination of blood, sweat and tears.

Places to go and praterhuman entities to fry, no time to linger to discover the truth of his suspicions. Hardhands turns to make his exit through the sole door, only to find that the door is gone, and in its place, a roiling black Vortex, as black and sharp as the Vortex that he himself had cut out of the Aeyther, only hours before. He is pushed back by the force of the Vortex, which is spiraling outward, not inward, thus indicating that Something is coming, rather than trying to make him go.

The edges of the Vortex glow hot-black, the wind that the Vortex is creating burns his skin; he shields his eyes with his hand, and tries to stand upright, but his tingly feet can not hold against the force, and he falls. The Vortex widens, like a surprised eye, and a slit of light appears pupil-like in its darkness. The pupil widens, becomes a pupae, a cocoon, a shell, an acorn, an egg, growing larger and larger and larger until it fills the room with unbelievable brightness, with a scorching heat that is hotter than the sun, bright enough to burn through Hardhands' shielding hand. Hardhands feels his skin pucker, his eyes shrivel, his hair start to smolder, and then just as he is sure he is about to burst into flames, the light shatters like an eggshell, and Something has arrived.

Recently, Hardhands' Invocations have grown quite bold, and, after some bitter tooth and nails, he's pulled a few large fish into his circle. But those are as like to This as a fragment of beer bottle is to a faceted diamond. He knows, from the top of his pulsating head to the tips of his quivering toes that this is no servitor, no denizen, no elemental. Nothing this spectacular can be called, corralled or compelled. This apparition can not be nothing but the highest of the high, the blessed of the blessed: the Goddess Califa herself.

How to describe what Hardhands sees? Words are too simple, they can not do justice to Her infinite complexity, she's Everything and Nothing, both fractured and whole. His impressions are blurred and confused, but here's a try. Her hair is ruffled black feathers, it is slickery green snakes, it is as fluffy and lofty as frosting. Her eyes— one, two, three, four, maybe five—are as round and polished as green apples, are long tapered crimson slits, they are as flat white as sugar. She's as narrow as nightfall, She's as round as winter, She's as tall as moonrise, She's shorter than love. Her feet do not crush the little flowers, She is divine, She is fantastic.

She simply is.

Hardhands has found his footing only to lose it again, falling to his knees before her, her fresh red smile as strong as a kick to the head, to the heart. Hardhands is smitten, no not smitten, he's smote, from the tingly tingly top of his reeling head to the very tippy tip of his tingling toes. He's freezing and burning, he's alive, he's dying, he's dead. He's hypmooootized. He gapes at the Goddess, slack-jawed and tight-handed, wanting nothing more than to reach out and grasp at her perfection, bury himself in the ruffle of her feathers. Surely a touch of Her hand would spark such fire in him that he would catch alight and perish in a blaze of exquisite agony but it would be worth it, oh it would be worth very cinder.

The Goddess's mouth opens, with a flicker of a velvet tongue and the glitter of a double row of white teeth. The Barbarick that flow from Her mouth in a sparkly ribband is a crisp and sweet as a summer wine, it slithers over Hardhands' flushed skin, sliding into his mouth, his eyes, his ears, and filling him with a dark sweet rumble.

"Georgiana's toy," the Goddess purrs. He didn't see Her move but now She is poured over the chaise like silk, and the bear-head minion is offering bowls of snacks, ice cream sundaes, and magazines. "Chewable and sweet, ah lovely darling yum."

Hardhands has forgotten Georgiana, he's forgotten Tiny Doom, he's forgotten Madam Rose, he's forgotten himself, he's forgotten his exquisite manners—no not entirely, even the Goddess's splendor can not expunge good breeding. He toddles up onto sweaty feet, and sweeps the floor with his curtsy.

"I am your obedient servant, your grace," he croaks.

The Goddess undulates a languid finger and he finds himself following Her beckon, not that he needs to be beckoned, he can barely hold himself aloof, wants nothing more than to throw himself forward and be swallowed alive. The Goddess spreads Her wings, Her arms, Her legs, and he falls into Her embrace, the prickle of the feathers closing over his bare skin, electric and hot.

X. Doom Acts

Here is Tiny Doom howling like a banshee, a high pitched shriek that usually results in immediate attention to whatever need she is screaming for: more pudding, longer story, hotter bath, bubbles. The Minion whose arm she is slung under must be pitch deaf because her shrieks have not the slightest impact upon him. He continues galumphing along, whistling slightly, or perhaps that is just the breeze of his going, which is a rapid clip.

She tries teeth, her fall-back weapon and always effective, even on Paimon whose blue skin is surprisingly delicate. The Minion's hide is as chewy as rubber and it tastes like salt licorice. Spitting and coughing, Tiny Doom gives up on the bite. Kicking has no effect other than to bruise her toes and her arms are too pinned for hitting, and, down the stairs they go, bump bump, Bwannie getting further and further away. Pig is jolting behind them, she's got a grip on one dangly ear, but that's all, and his bottom is hitting each downward stump, but he's too soft to thump.

An outside observer might think that Doom is wailing for more candy, or perhaps is just over-tired and up past her bedtime. Madam Rose certainly thought that her commotion was based in over-tiredness, plus a surfeit of sugar, and the Bouncer thinks its based in spoiled-ness, plus a surfeit of sugar, but they are both wrong. Sugar is Doom's drug of choice, she's not allowed it officially, but unofficially she has her ways (she knows exactly in what drawer the Pontifexa's secretary keeps his stash of Crumbly Crem-O;s and Jiffy-Ju's, and if that drawer is empty, Relais can be relied upon to have a box of bon-bons hidden from Hardhands in the bottom of his wardrobe), and so her system can tolerate massive quantities of the stuff before hyper-activity and urpyness sets in.

No. She is wailing because every night, at tuck-in time, after the Pontifexa has kissed her, and kissed Pig and together they have said their prayers, then Paimon sits on the edge of Tiny Doom's big white frilly bed and tells her a story. It's a different story every night, Paimon's supply of fabulosity being apparently endless, but always with the same basic theme:

Kid is told what To Do.

Kid does Not Do what Kid is told To Do.

Kid gets into Bad Trouble with various Monsters.

Kid gets Eaten.

The End, yes you may have one more drink of water, and then no more excuses and it's lights out, and to sleep. Now.

Tiny Doom loves these stories, whose Directives and Troubles are always endlessly inventively different, but which always turn out the same way: with a Giant Monstrous Burp. She knows that Paimon's little yarns are for fun only, that Kids do not really get eaten when they do not do what they are told, for she does not do what she is told all the time, and she's never been eaten. Of course, no one would dare eat her anyway, she's the Heir to the Pontifexa, and has Paimon and Pig besides. Paimon's stories are just stories, made to deliciously shiver her skin, so that afterwards she lies in the haze of the nightlight, cuddled tight to Pig's squishiness, and knows that she is safe.

But now, tonight, she's seen the gleam in Madam Rose's eye and seen the look she gave her minions and Tiny Doom knew instantly that Bwannie is in Big Trouble. This is not bedtime, there is no Paimon, and no nightlight, and no drink of water. This is all true Big Trouble and Tiny Doom knows exactly where Big Trouble ends. Now she is scared, for Bwannie and for herself, and even for Pig, who would make a perfect squishy demon dessert.

Thus, shrieking.

"BWWWWWWWWWWWWANNNNIE!" Doom cries, "BWA-AANIE!"

They jump the last step, Tiny Doom jolting bony hip, oww, and then round a corner. Doom sucks in the last useless shriek. Her top half is hanging half over the servitor's shoulder and her dangling down head is starting to feel tight, plus the shrieking has left her breathless, so for a few seconds she gulps in air. Gulping, her nose running yucky yuck. She wiggles, whispers, and lets go of Pig.

He plops down onto the dirty floor, hinder up and snout down, and then they round another corner and he's gone.

She lifts her head, twisting her neck, and there's the hairy interior of a pointy ear.

She shouts: "HEY MINION!"

"I ain't listening," says the Minion. "You can shout all you want, but I ain't listening. Madam told me not to listen and I ain't."

"I GOTTA PEE."

"You gotta wait," the Minion says, "You be home soon and then you can pee in your own pot. And you ain't gotta shout in my ear. You make my brain hurt, you loudness little bit, you."

"I GOTTA PEE NOW!" Doom, still shouting, anyway, just in case there are noises behind them. "I'M GONNA PEE NOW!"

The Minion stops and shifts Tiny Doom around like a sack full of flour, and breathes into her face. "You don't pee on me, loudness."

Like Paimon, the Minion has tusks and pointy teeth but Paimon's tucks are polished white and his teeth sparkle like sunlight, and his breath smells always of cloves. The Minion's tusks are rubbed and worn, his teeth yucky yellow and he's got bits of someone caught between them.

Doom wrinkles her nose and holds her breath and says in a whine: "I can't help it, I have to go, my hot chocolate is all done." Her feet are dangling and she tries to turn the wiggle into a kick, but she can't quite reach the Minion's soft bits, and her purple slippers wiggle at empty air.

"You pee on me and I snack you up, nasty baby." The minion crunches spiny fangs together, clashing sparks. "Delish!"

"You don't dare!" says Tiny Doom stoutly. "I am the Pontifexina and my grandmamma would have your knobby hide if you munch me!!"

"An' I care, little princess, if you piss me wet, I munch you dry—"

"⌒ ⬅ℯᵞ◗×⌒◗×" whispers Tiny Doom and spits. She's got a good wad going, and it hits the Minion right on the snout.

The Minion howls and drops her. She lands on stingy sleepy feet, falls over, and then scrambles up, stamping. The Minion is also stamping, and holding his hairy hands to his face; under his clawing fingers smoke is steaming. He careens this way and that, Doom dodging around his staggers, and then she scoots by him, and back the way they had just come.

Tiny Doom runs as fast as her fat little legs will run, her heart pounding because she is now in Big Trouble, and she knows if the Minion quits dancing and starts chasing, she's going to be Eaten too. The hot word she spit burned her tongue and that hurts too, and where's Pig? She goes around another corner, thinking she'll see the stairs that they came down, but she doesn't, she sees another long hallway. She turns around to go back, and then the Minion blunders towards her, his face a melt-y mess, and she reverses, speedily.

"*I dance around in a ring and suppose and the secret sits in the middle and knows.*" She sings very quietly to herself as she runs.

Carpet silent under her feet; a brief glimpse of another running Doom reflected off a glass curio cabinet; by a closed door, the knob turns but the door will not open. She can feel the wind of closing in beating against her back, but she keeps going. The demon is shouting mean things at her, but she keeps going.

"*You dance around in a ring and suppose and the secret sits in the middle and knows.*"

A door opens and a were-flamingo trips out, stretching its long-neck out; Doom dodges around its spindly legs, ignoring yelps. Ahead, more stairs, and there she aims, having no other options, can't go back and there's no where to go sideways.

At the top of the stairs, Doom pauses and finally looks behind. The Minion has wiped most of his melt off, livid red flares burn in his eye sockets and he looks pretty mad. The were-flamingo has halted him, and they are wrangling, flapping wings against flapping ears. The minion is bigger but the were-flamingo has a sharp beak—rapid fire pecking at the minion's head. The minion punches one humongous fist and down the flamingo goes, in a flutter of pink feathers.

"I SNACK YOU, SPITTY BABY!" the Minion howls and other things too mean for Doom to hear.

"*We dance around in a ring and suppose and the secret sits in the middle and knows.*"

Doom hoists herself up on the banister, squeezing her tummy

against the rail. The banister on the Stairs of Infinite Demonstration, Bilskinir's main staircase, is fully sixty feet long. Many is the time that Doom has swooped down its super-polished length, flying miles through the air, at the end to be received by Paimon's perfect catch. This rail is much shorter, and there's no Paimon waiting, but here we go!

She flings her legs over, and slides off. Down she goes, lickety-split, bumping over splinters, but still getting up a pretty good whoosh. Here comes the demon, waving angry arms, he's too big to slide, so he galumphs down the stairs, clumpty clump, getting closer. Doom hits the end of the banister and soars onward another five feet or so, then ooph, hits the ground, owww. She bounces back upward, and darts through the foyer and into the mudroom beyond, pulling open her pockets as she goes.

Chocosniffs and jacksnaps skitter across the parquet floor, rattling and rolling. Sugarbunnies and beady-eyes, jimjoos and honeybuttons scatter like shot. Good bye crappy candy, good bye yummy candy, good-bye.

"I DANCE AROUND A RING AND SUPPOSE AND THE SECRET SITS IN THE MIDDLE AND KNOWS."

Ahead, a big red door, well barred and bolted, but surely leading Out. The bottom bolt snaps back under her tiny fingers, but the chains are too high and tippy-toe, hopping, jumping will not reach them. The Demon is down the stairs, he's still shouting and steaming, and the smell of charred flesh is stinky indeed.

A wall rack hangs by the door, and from coats and cloaks dangle like discarded skins; Doom dives into the folds of cloth and becomes very small and silent. She's a good hider, Tiny Doom, she's learned against the best (Paimon).

Her heart pounds thunder in her ears, and she swallows her panting. When Paimon makes discovery (*if* he makes discovery), it means only bath-time, or mushy peas, or toe-nail clipping. If the demon finds her, Pontifexina or not, it's snicky snack time for sure. She really did have to potty too, pretty bad. She crosses her ankles and jiggles her feet, holding.

In the other room, out of sight, comes yelling, shouting, roaring and then a heavy thud that seems to shake the very walls. The thud reverberates and then fades away.

Silence.

Stillness.

Tiny Doom peeks between the folds. Through the archway she sees rolling candy and part of a sprawled bulk. Then the bulk heaves, hooves kicking. The demon's lungs have re-inflated and he lets out a mighty horrible roar—the nastiest swear word that Tiny Doom has ever heard. Doom, who had poked her head all the way out for a better view, yanks back, just in time. The Word, roiling like mercury, howls by her, trailing sparks and smelling of shit.

A second roar is gulped off in mid-growl, and turns into a shriek, which is then muffled in thumping and slurping, ripping, and chomping. Doom peeks again: the demon's legs are writhing, wiggling, and kicking. A thick stain spreads through the archway, gooey and green. Tiny Doom wiggles her way out of the velvet and runs happily towards the slurping sound.

XI. Desire Gratified

Inside the Goddess's embrace, Hardhands is dying, he's crying, he's screaming with pleasure, with joy, crying his broken heart out. He's womb-enclosed, hot and smothering, and reduced to his pure essence. He has collapsed to a single piercing pulsing point of pleasure. He has lost himself, but he has found everything else.

And then his ecstasy is interrupted by another piercing sensation: pain. Not the exquisite pain of a well placed needle, or perfectly laid lash, but an ugly pain that gnaws into his pleasurable non-existence in an urgent painful way. He wiggles, tossing, but the pain will not go away, it only gnaws deeper, and with each razor nibble it slices away at his ecstasy. And as he is torn away from the Goddess's pleasure, he is forced back into himself, and the wiggly body-bound part of himself realizes that the Goddess is sucking him out of life. The love-torn spirit part of him does not care. He struggles, trying to dive down deeper into the bottomless divine love, but that gnawing pain is tethering him to the Waking World, and he can't kick it free.

Then the Goddess's attention lifts from him, like a blanket torn away. He lies on the ground, the stones slick and cold against his bare skin. The echo of his loss pounds in his head, farrier-like, stunning him. A shrill noise pierces his agony, cuts through the thunder, a familiar high pitched whine:

"Ya! Ya! Ya!"

His eyes are filled with sand; it takes a moment of effort before his nerveless hands can find his face, and knuckle his vision clear. Immediately he sees: Tiny Doom, dancing with the bear-headed Minion. Sieur Oso is doing the Mazorca, a dance which requires a great deal of jumping and stamping, and he's got the perfect boots to make the noise, each one as big as horse's head. Tiny Doom is doing the Ronde-loo, weaving round and round Sieur Oso her circular motion too sick-making for Hardhands to follow.

Then he realizes: no, they are not dancing, Sieur Oso is trying to squash Tiny Doom like a bug, and she, rather than run like a sensible child, is actually taunting him on. Oh Haðraaða!

Dimly Tiny Doom's husband sparks the thought that perhaps he should help her, and he's trying to figure out where his feet are, so as to arise to this duty, when his attention is caught by a whirl, not a whirl, a Vortex the likes of which he has never before seen, a Vortex as black as ink, but streaked hot pink, and furious furious. Though he can see nothing but the cutting blur of the spin, he can feel the force of the fight within; the Goddess is battling it out with something, something strong enough to give her a run for her divas, something tenacious and tough.

"Bwannie! Bwannie!" cries Doom. She is still spinning, and the Minion is starting to look tuckered, his stomps not so stompy anymore, and his jeers turned to huffy puffs. Foam is dribbling from his muzzle, like whipped cream.

Hardhands ignores Tiny Doom.

"Αϖαυντ!" Hardhands grates, trying to through a Word of encouragement into the mix, to come to his darling's aid. The Word is a strong one, even his weakened state, but it bounces off the Vortex, harmless, spurned, just as he has been spurned. The Goddess cares nothing for his Hardhands' love, for his desire, he chokes back tears, and staggers to his feet, determined to help somehow, even if he must cast himself into the fire to do so.

Before he can do anything so drastic, there is the enormous sound of suction sucking in. For a split second, Hardhands feels himself go as flat as paper, his lungs suck against his chest, his bones slap into ribbands, his flesh becomes as thin as jerky. The Current pops like a cork, the world re-inflates and Hardhands is round and substantial again, although now truly bereft. The Goddess is gone.

The Vortex has blushed pink now, and its spin is slowing, slower, slower, until it is no longer a Vortex, but a little pink blur, balanced on pointy toes, ears flopping—what the hell? Pig?

He has gone insane, or blind, or both? In one dainty pirouette Pig has soared across the room and latched himself to the Minion's scraggly throat. Suddenly invigorated, Sieur Oso does a pirouette of his own, upward, gurgling.

"What is going on—!" Madam Rose's voice raises high above the mayhem-noises, then it chokes. She has stalled in the doorway, more minions peering from behind her safety. Tiny Doom has now attached to Sieur Oso's hairy ankle and her grip—hands and teeth—are not dislodged by his antic kicking, though whether the minion is now dancing because Tiny Doom is gnawing on his ankle or because his throat is a massive chewy-mess, it's hard to say. Pig disengages from Sieur Oso and leaps to Madam Rose, who clutches him to her bosom in a maternal way, but jerkily, as though she wants less of his love, not more. Her other slaveys have scarpered, and now that the Goddess is gone, Hardhands sees no particular reason to linger either.

He flings one very hard Barbarick word edgewise at the antic bear. Sieur Oso jerks upward, and his surprised head sails backwards, tears through the tent wall, and is gone. Coldfire founts up from the stump his neck, sizzling and sparky. Hardhands grabs Tiny Doom away from the minion's forward fall, and she grasps onto him monkey-wise, clinging to his shoulders.

"PIG!" she screams, "PIG!"

Madam Rose manages to disentangle Pig, and flings him towards Hardhands and Tiny Doom. Pig sails through the air, his ears like wings, and hits Hardhands' chest with a soggy thud and then tumbles downward. Madam Rose staggers, she is clutching her throat, her hair has fallen down, drippy red. Above her, the tent ceiling is flickering with tendrils of coldfire, it pours down around her like fireworks falling from the sky, sheathing her bones in glittering flickering flesh. The coldfire has spread to the ceiling now, scorching the raven angels, and the whole place is going to go: coldfire doesn't burn like non-magickal fire, but it is hungry and does consume, and Hardhands has had enough consumption for tonight. Hefting Tiny Doom up higher on his shoulder, he turns about to retreat (run away).

"PIG! PIG!" Tiny Doom beats at his head as he ducks under the now flickering threshold, "PIG!"

The coldfire has raced across the roof beyond him and the ante-chamber before him is a heaving weaving maelstrom of magick, the Current bubbling and sucking, oh it's a shame to let such yummy power go to waste, but now is perhaps not the time to further test his control. Madam Rose staggers out of the flames, the very air around her is bubbling and cracking, spitting Abyss through cracks in the Current, black tendrils that coil and smoke.

Tiny Doom, still screaming: "PIG!"

Hardhands jumps and weaves through the tentacles of flame, flinging banishings as he goes, and the tendrils snap away. He's not going to stop for Pig, Pig is on his own, Hardhands can feel the Current boiling, in a moment there will be too much magick for the space to contain, there is going to be a giant implosion and he's had enough implosions for one night, too. Through the dining room they run, scattering cheese platters, waiters, cocktails and conservationists, crunching crackers underfoot, knocking down a minion—there—open veranda doors, and beyond those doors, the sparkle of hurdy-gurdy lights. Doom clinging to his head like a pinchy hat, he leaps over the bar, through breaking bottles and scattered ice, and through the doors, into blessed cool air.

The sky above turns sheet white, and the ground shifts beneath his feet in a sudden bass roll. He sits down hard in the springy grass, lungs gasping. Tiny Doom collapses from his grasp and rolls like a little barrel across the springy turf. The stars wink back in, as though a veil has been drawn back, and suddenly Hardhands is limp with exhaustion. The Current is gone. And so, he realizes, when he turns his tired head and looks backwards is Madam Rose's.

Well, good riddance, good bye, adios, farewell. From the space where Madam Rose's used to be, Pig tippy-dances, pirouetting towards Doom, who receives him with happy cries of joy.

Hardhands lies on the grass and stars upward at the starry sky, and he moves his head back and forth, drums his feet upon the ground, wiggles his fingers just because he can. He feels drained and empty, and sore as hell. The grass is crispy cool beneath his bare sweaty back, and he could just lie there forever. Behind the relief of freedom, however, there's a sour sour taste.

He was set up. The whole evening was nothing but a gag. His grandmother, his darling sweet grandmother whom he did not kill out of love, respect and honour, whom he pulled back from the brink of assassination because he held her so dear, his grandmamma sold him to Madam Rose.

Him, Hardhands, sold him!

The Pontifexa has played them masterfully: Relais' incompetence, Tiny Doom's greed, Madam Rose's cunning, and his own sense of duty and loyalty. He'd gone blindly in to save Tiny Doom and she was the bait and he the stupid stupid prey, all along.

He, Hardhands, expendable!

"Bwannie—get up! Pig wants to go home!"

For a second our hero is wracked with sorrow, he takes a deep breath that judders his bones, and closes his eyes. The darkness is sparked with stars, flares of light caused by the pressure of holding the tears back. But under the surface of his sorrow, he feels an immense longing, longing not for the Pontifexa, or hot water, or for Relais' comforting embrace, or even for waffles. Compared to this longing, the rest of his feelings—anger, sorrow, guilt, love—are nothing. He should be already plotting his revenge, his pay-back, his turn-about-is-fair-play, but instead he is alive with thoughts of sweeping black wings, and spiraling hair, and the unutterable blissful agony of Desire.

"Pig wants a waffle, Bwannie! And I must potty, I gotta potty now!"

Hardhands opens his eyes to a dangly pink snout. Pig's eyes are small black beads, and his cotton stitched mouth is a bit red around the edges, as though he's smeared his lipstick. He smells of salty-iron blood and the peachy whiff of stale coldfire.

"Would you please get Pig out of my face?" he says wearily. The mystery of Pig is beyond him right now; he'll consider that further, later.

Tiny Doom pokes him. She is jiggling and bobbing, with her free hand tightly pressed. She has desires ungratified of her own; her bladder may be full, but her candy sack is empty. "Pig wants you to get up. He says Get Up Now, Banastre!"

Hardhands, thinking of desire gratified, gets up.

JOURNEY TO GANTICA

———

Matthew Corradi

Adelia decided one day that the Dell in the Hills was too small for her. She had grown five-span over the last year, making her taller than the tallest Miller and stronger than the strongest Iron-Weaver, both of whom had battled giants during the Fell Winters in the longer days of their youth. Since size and strength are truly reflections of inner heart, the Dell Folk openly praised Adelia's skill with axe and anvil and sword. But secretly they laughed when she could no longer sleep in her goose-down bed, or fit her legs under the dinner table, or even stand up straight in her own mother's kitchen. Such is the bloom of jealousy in small hearts, and that is how Adelia knew that it was time to say goodbye.

Perhaps Adelia didn't really mind that much, for she had always aspired to become a giant-slayer, a champion for the smallest of people and destroyer of monsters laying waste to villages. She dreamed of wearing a cape made of a giant's woven hair and strapping her sword on with a belt made of a giant's leathery skin. With such size and strength there was no more noble service to the Land than that of giant-slayer. And no greater glory.

Adelia said goodbye to her mother, who was the only person who didn't want to see Adelia leave. Adelia's mother was a small woman of the glens from Downland, a weaver by trade, and her small size was her source of motivation, for she took pride in the pain it gave her. But it broke her heart that her daughter could not understand that pain, much less share in it. When Adelia left, so, too, did her mother's hope that Adelia would ever come to discover the strength and dignity found in the heart of a small woman.

Now, it happens that a giant hadn't been seen among the Dell Folk for many seasons, so Adelia traveled Upland, among the other various Folk, and everywhere she went she asked, "Where is a giant that I may slay?" And the Folk told her that the giants all dwelt farther Upland, in the realm of Gantica, and rarely came Downland these days. So farther Upland she ventured in search of Gantica, and she skirted the Lakes of Sorrow, where the Lonely Giant had shed tears to fill all the valleys and the dales. She crossed the twin rivers Fantis and Gantis, made by the long meandering wagon wheels of the Lost Giant. And she cautiously skirted the Burial Hills, where many a Wicked Giant had been killed in the Fell Winters, their massive bodies turned to dirt and stone after years in sun and rain.

The day came in the land of the Plains Folk that berries and nuts were hardly enough to quell the rumble in Adelia's stomach. She met a poor farmer who gave her a meal of mutton and ale in return for help in fencing his ox stables. The farmer, unfortunately, had seen no giants that she might slay. Farther Upland she plowed another farmer's fields in return for a week's worth of venison. Then she helped dig a well for the farmer's son. In a month she had raised several barns and thatched several cabins, and by the end of summer Adelia had helped harvest many fields of brittle-corn and pig-wheat and golden-eared fur-flax.

All the Plains Folk that Adelia helped were small, and they seemed smaller with each passing day. But since small Folk were not so good at helping themselves Adelia took pride in bartering her size and strength to aid them in their daily tasks. And with all this work Adelia herself continued to grow in size, until she stood nearly as tall as one Folk standing on the shoulders of another, and her popularity in the Land grew, and her reputation spread before her.

For the Mountain Folk Adelia helped quarry granite and mine copperstone; for the Wood Folk Adelia helped fell trees and mill them into lumber; for the River Folk Adelia helped dam rapids and sculpt ship-slips out of riverbanks. In each part of the Land Adelia asked,

"Where is a giant I may slay?" And the Folk told her there were no giants here to slay, for they all dwelt farther Upland, in the realm of Gantica, and rarely came Downland these days. But in the meantime there were plenty of bridges to build and roads to clear.

The days passed and Adelia grew, and the Folk of the Land praised her strength and size. But now behind her back they also grumbled about how much fruit she ate and griped about how much cotton it took to make clothes big enough to fit her, and sometimes they found it easier and cheaper to get ten men to do what Adelia could do herself. The farther Upland she ventured the less friendly the Folk became, until the Fen Folk refused her passage across their border bogs, and the Prairie Folk ran from the fields and shut themselves deep underground in their burrowed homes.

Adelia didn't quite understand this change until one morning she awoke from sleep in a quiet glade to a small cry of challenge, and found a tiny woman perched on her chest, sword raised in defiance. "Upon the bones of my fallen ancestors," the little woman proclaimed, "today shall be your last day in the Land, foul beast of Gantica! Prepare to meet the vengeance that shall seal thy doom!" And the woman brought her sword down, but it barely put a dimple in Adelia's shirt. Adelia picked the girl up and held the little figure up to her face, and Adelia realized in horror that this woman thought *she* was a giant, and was trying to *kill* her.

This shocked Adelia, and leaving the little woman far behind Adelia ran and ran—Upland, as far as she could. Suddenly she no longer cared about vengeance or fame or size or strength, and certain horrible questions would not leave her alone: was she, Adelia, really a giant? Was this what it meant to be a giant, alone and hunted in the far reaches of the Land?

Adelia was now afraid to approach any of the Small Folk, perhaps in fear of persecution, perhaps in fear of what truths they might reveal. She dared not return home to the Dell, not with her source of pride now suddenly her source of shame. In fact, if she were truly a giant then perhaps Gantica was the only place she would ever find answers to her questions. So Upland she reluctantly continued, homesick and confused, her destination somehow still the same, if not her motivation.

It was in this sparsely populated realm that Adelia finally met her first giant. Or perhaps it was more accurate to say *another* giant, though Adelia was not yet comfortable thinking of herself that way. This giant sat hunched over a small instrument, a fiddle, and wiped tears from the corners of his eyes.

"Why are you so sad?" Adelia asked.

The giant replied, "The fiddle was my life, and now . . . ." He tried to draw the bow across the strings, but his fingers were too large, and the only sound was a weak scraping of wood on wood. Adelia took the pieces from him, and though she could barely handle them properly herself, she managed a few pure notes that brought a smile to the Fiddle Giant's eyes. When the sweet sounds faded, Adelia asked the giant if he came from Gantica, but he said he did not, and only knew that it existed somewhere farther Upland.

It was not long before Adelia encountered the Family Giant, who had a wife and two children, but could no longer live with them, not because he was too big, but because his mere presence brought threats and jealousy and prejudice to them from smaller Folk. It gave the Family Giant pleasure to tell Adelia of his wife and children, and so Adelia listened for a time to the love and pride in his voice, and she somehow felt him lucky to have such a family to miss. Before leaving, Adelia asked of Gantica, but the Family Giant only knew that it existed farther Upland, and he could tell her nothing more.

Next she met the Drunken Giant, trapped in sobriety, all skin and bones, who could never again sip enough ale to deliver himself into that realm of uncaring bliss. He, too, denied any knowledge of Gantica, and Adelia in turn had nothing to offer that would ease his pain, and so she left him to his misery. Adelia encountered many other giants in this realm of the Land: the Brooding Giant, the Callous Giant, the Pious Giant. All, like her, were unwilling victims of unwanted size, but none, it turned out, knew much of Gantica.

The sorrows of these giants at first weighed heavily upon Adelia's hopes, but then her gloom turned to resolve, and she determined not to let such suffering become her final fate. Adelia hired the services of a dwarf manager, for it was well known that small-statured dwarves were manipulative and greedy, and hence good at exploiting entrepreneurial opportunities such as giants.

This particular dwarf manager knew from experience that when money and power is involved, social institutions are more prone to overlooking the stereotypes of size than are rigid-minded individuals. So, with the dwarf perched upon her shoulder Adelia came to the part of the Land full of City Folk. There, the sneaky mayors and sly councilmen all marveled in appreciation when she looked them in the eye as they stood on the third story of the town hall. For these people Adelia happily leveled old slums, raised new high-occupancy dwellings, and boosted municipal pride (not to mention the mayor's approval ratings). All of this she did in between carrying produce home for elderly ladies, corralling panicked ponies, and putting out kitchen fires.

For a while the City Folk followed Adelia and praised each great feat, and Adelia once again grew larger. She became a legend to the City Folk, a marvel of physical achievement, and their worship filled her soul. But then a strange thing happened: Adelia found that dwarf managers take a large percentage of profits, and she herself really earned little more each night than a small (for her) dinner and a list from her manager of tasks to complete the following day. Even worse, she discovered that familiarity breeds apathy, for as the novelty of Adelia's size wore off the City Folk grew tired of donating entire wagons full of melons and squash just to feed her. When the worship subsided, the melons and squash did little to fill her stomach, and even less to fill her soul.

Gradually Adelia's duties shifted to ferrying councilmen and public officers across town, then to delivering eviction notices and collecting taxes, and tracking down criminals, from petty thieves on the lam to tenants late on the rent for their high-occupancy dwellings. After that, the City Folk were noticeably less friendly all around.

In these days Adelia also found it difficult to attain comfort.

Sleeping on the hard ground of the central plaza every day left her tired, and the only place for her to bathe was the river, yet it was difficult to find a bit of privacy there at any hour. There was no slab of soap big enough to cleanse her, no towel big enough to dry off with, no fire big enough to warm her bones on the cold autumn nights. Amidst so many people she felt very lonely.

Then one day the smoldering coals of pettiness burst into flame between Adelia's city and its neighbor, and the respective mayors declared war for reasons miniscule or unfounded, or lost in hypocrisy. The mayor ordered Adelia to dam the River Fantis to cut off the other city's water supply, and to hurl boulders over the outer wall, and to use the battering ram to break down the enemy's central gates.

Adelia no longer cared about the hollow praise of small-minded and small-hearted Folk, and declined to act. But the mayor brought out her contract and explained that she was legally bound to carry out any action deemed necessary for the safety of the city, and such action now included said hostility. Adelia's dwarf manager admitted that such a clause was in the fine print, but Adelia had never read the fine print, for the contract was the size of her thumb, and she could no longer read scrolls or books or binding contracts, and even to hear people clearly she had to bend over. (This gave her a constant back-ache, of course, but there was never anyone big enough to rub it for her.)

In the end, Adelia left, for none of the City Folk, even as a collective whole, could do much about it. As she strode away, they jeered and threw melons and squash and called her names that reminded her sadly of the cruel whispers she had heard in the days before she left the Dell in the Hills. The jealousy and bigotry of Small Folk, it seemed, was not confined by geography nor governed by civility.

Adelia found the Land beyond the cities to be a brutal territory in which jealousy and bigotry were mere vices. Burdened by her lingering shame, Adelia did things she later could not, or would not, remember. There were wars here, and giants in armor leading armies across smoking battle plains. There were terrible games of strength and wit and chance: giants against animals, giants against criminals, giants against giants. There was gambling and swindling and treachery from giants and men and dwarves alike. Adelia learned that the best way to find a shirt that fits a giant is to steal one from another giant. She also learned that two giants are still stronger than one, and in the end only a giant's strength of will could match a giant's strength of muscle.

Through all of this Adelia listened for word of Gantica, but still, news was always the same: *Upland*. And so Upland she drifted, until gradually the games disappeared, and the battles, and the men, and the dwarves, and even the other giants, and eventually Adelia entered lands filled only with poppy-covered meadows and pine-scented woods. And though the shame of the past did not leave, at least it subsided into memory.

It was not long before Adelia noticed everything around her growing larger—not individually, but as a whole. Day by day the trees around her grew taller, until she could no longer see over them, and so, too, did the meadows and hills and rivers and rocks. Soon everything around her grew to just the right size for her comfort. A single melon filled her stomach, a single brook cleansed her body, and a single tree gave her shade.

Perhaps she had finally found Gantica, where the Land was large enough for giants to live in comfort. But the world did not stop growing. Soon bushes were the size of trees, rocks the size of boulders, and flowers towered far over her head. And farther Upland it took her hours just to walk around pebbles and weave her way under common blades of grass. On a whim Adelia crawled into the center of a dandelion puff, allowing the wind to carry her where it would. When the dandelion fell apart Adelia found herself stranded in an endless forest, and she despaired at her sudden insignificance. But then her misery and bitterness faded, and she decided to embrace this new opportunity: she would abandon the deceitful ways of men and dwarves and giants for the simple life of the animals.

To do that she would have to learn their language.

First Adelia learned the tongue of the ladybugs, who were friendly creatures, but more importantly, patient teachers. From there she learned to speak with the wood slugs, who had nothing better to do anyway than strike up long conversations, and then the moths, and the butterflies and ants and beetles. Animals, she discovered, loved to talk. Not only that, animals were also bluntly honest: subtlety was not a strong point, and sarcasm was forever lost upon them.

In this part of the Land, where even the insects were larger than Adelia, she bartered information in return for food and shelter, but mostly for protection: the vole would protect her from the asp in return for word of the fox's current appetite; the asp would protect her from the fox in return for the location of the vole's latest burrow; and the fox would protect her from the vole in return for a description of the asp's current sleeping habits. Along the way Adelia came to know that voles were really cantankerous creatures at heart, and foxes overly mischievous, and asps often lazy. But such qualities were not to be criticized, for that was the nature of each animal, and judgment was a concept that had yet to muddle their view of the Land.

At first Adelia admired this honesty among animals, and she wondered why it was lacking in the human Folk she had met. Then gradually she came to realize that honesty wasn't necessarily the same as sympathy, or compassion. And in truth, Adelia often felt a little ashamed, peddling the wants of this creature against the desires of that creature, most of which came down to the hope of a tasty meal at the expense of the other. So maybe the animals weren't so different from the Folk after all, or perhaps the Folk weren't so different from the animals, just better at disguising their hunger. Either way, the animals cared little about the painful things she had seen and done in days gone by, and this helped her soul to mend.

Then one day in her wanderings Adelia came to the realm of the Mushroom Folk. These were a small, humble people of her own size who took her in and made her one of their own. She did not mention her past to them, and to her relief they did not ask. Their kindness surprised Adelia, for what had she ever seen from Small Folk but jealousy and treachery and lies? Then again, in this part of the Land, Adelia herself was a Small Folk, and small was a relative thing now anyway, and that all left her more than a little confused.

Life with the Mushroom Folk was not easy. Survival is hard work, after all, even collectively. But the Mushroom Folk taught her how to build a home from a toadstool stalk, and grow crops of terraced truffles, and carve portabella boats to ride the brooks and streams surrounding the village. To her surprise, Adelia was very glad to have human companionship once again, not to mention a fresh start. In return for all this, Adelia helped raise latticed covers above the village and erect thick walls of bramble and thistle, all to keep out foxes, voles, and asps. Adelia often lamented the fact that in days past, when she had been much larger, she could have done in an hour what it took the village of the Mushroom Folk an entire season to do. But when that season was done and Adelia was tired as she had never been before in her life, somehow the work was also more satisfying than anything she had ever done before in her life.

After that season of living in mushrooms Adelia grew restless, and thanking the Mushroom Folk for their kindness she resumed her journey Upland. She borrowed the services of a silver-back hummingbird (for silver-back hummingbirds are always wistful and restless, and only need a simple excuse to dash off on adventures) and she traveled for many days, living at times with the Willow Folk, and then the Brittle-Corn Folk, then the Sunflower Folk. When she eventually came to the Turnip Folk, who lived in a giant garden, she paused and wondered: in whose garden did these Folk live? The Farmer's garden, they answered, pointing to the giant-sized farmhouse beyond the garden.

Here Adelia set free the silver-back hummingbird, and though the Turnip Folk warned her to stay away from the house, she cautiously approached it anyway. Was this a part of Gantica? Were these giants of the farmhouse the true giants of the fabled realm? If they were, what good would it do her now that she was once again smaller than a giant's thumb? She had no answers, but needed to find out.

The Turnip Folk were right, of course: she should have stayed away. For the Farmer's little boy (a freckle-faced, tousled red-head who really wasn't so little) promptly caught her in a cup. After running her through the farmhouse with shouts of glee he stuck her in a small cage of wire mesh, and there she sat for several days, occasionally fed a shred of lettuce or a moldy carrot. The Farmer's boy often checked on her, and clapped his hands, until eventually the Farmer took the boy and Adelia in the cage to the nearest village. Together they sold her to an old man with long white hair and tiny eyes lost behind oversized spectacles. Adelia's lasting impression of the Farmer's boy was the huge grin that spread across his face when the Farmer dropped half the sale price of ten pennies into his eager hands.

The old man who bought her had no name, at least as far as Adelia ever knew. He was just called the Maker, and what he made were clocks. In his dark, dusty shop sat hundreds of time-pieces, maybe even thousands, from tiny tin pocket-watches to masterful iron-wood grandfather clocks. The Maker put Adelia to work cleaning and repairing the clocks, for what better way to build and maintain such tiny parts than with a tiny person? Adelia learned to mesh pinions and set balance wheels and calibrate gear trains. After a while she became an expert at wrestling mainsprings back into alignment, and honing pendulum weights and calculating gear reductions.

She thought at first it would be easy to escape the shop, especially with so many dark corners, but she hadn't counted on the cat. No matter where she went within the shop, the tabby shadowed her, watching and guarding, seemingly never sleeping. They talked on occasion, when the tabby was bored, and it made a point of telling her she was lucky to work for the Maker, who was too consumed by his craft ever to bother making life difficult for her. Other Small Folk had it worse off, forced to run secret messages across town on the backs of rats, or to scurry around under floorboards to spy for deceitful politicians, or jealous wives of deceitful politicians, or distrustful lovers of jealous wives of deceitful politicians.

This was little comfort to Adelia, who felt every bit a slave in the Maker's shop, and eventually concluded that this village of giants certainly was not Gantica. As the days passed and she cleaned or repaired the clocks, she would sometimes detect the scent of freshly chopped pepper-wood, or the musk of a man's sweat, or the fragrance of dried rose petals. Other times Adelia heard the ringing of hammer on anvil, or the bray of a horse, or even felt the humidity of the ocean seep out from the inside of a clock escapement. And then one day she found she could hear voices from the clocks, as if she were eavesdropping, and she heard many things common and polite, and sometimes she also heard things secret and personal, like whispers of passion or promises of love. But she also heard things sinister and dark, cries of pain and whimpers of misery, and plots born of jealousy, greed and regret.

Cleaning and maintaining the clocks then became daunting to Adelia. As she crawled inside each she felt as if she were crawling inside a person, and though some were pleasant, many were not. She learned to avoid the clocks that were broken, for out of them came the smell of decay and dirt and worms. Then one day Adelia recognized the voice in one of the clocks as a mayor of the City Folk. In another clock she recognized the voice of the Fiddle Giant, and in still another the voice of the Family Giant. In others she heard the voices of the Mountain Folk, and the Mushroom Folk, and even the Farmer and the Farmer's little boy.

After that Adelia took extra care with the clocks, for she knew they were more than just clocks, and the Maker was more than just a clocksmith. She was also tempted then—tempted as she had never been tempted before—to spend less effort with some of the clocks she did not care for, perhaps to clean the pinions poorly, or mis-align the gears slightly. Now that she was small she had a power like no giant ever had, for she knew what happened when the clocks stopped working. But in the end she could not bring herself to act that way. Maybe she was too afraid, or too weak. Or maybe the vision of someone else standing over *her* clock left a cold uncertainty in her stomach.

Some time later Adelia stumbled across a small, unassuming pocket-watch in the back of the shop, and from it came the scent of fresh spun wool in dye, the click of a loom shuttle, and the sound of a woman singing. There was loneliness in that voice, and tears came to Adelia's eyes, for she realized the same loneliness had been in that voice the day Adelia had left the Dell in the Hills. Adelia had simply not recognized it then, or chose to ignore it. Now Adelia missed her mother greatly and wanted more than anything to return home to tell her so. But the teeth on the gears were wearing down, and though she gave the watch extra special attention and the finest of care, Adelia knew it was running slow.

One night, Adelia put the pocket-watch on her back and carried it to the Maker's workbench, and when he came in the next morning and sat down she said to him, "Sir, what can be done for this piece?"

From behind his dirty, chipped spectacles the Maker said, "I work with simple gears and springs, my dear. This time-piece requires something else for repair, something beyond my power."

Adelia lowered her head.

"But not," he added, "beyond your power."

The Maker gave a soft whistle over ancient gums and tangled beard, and in through the morning light flew the same silver-back hummingbird that had carried Adelia from the Mushroom Folk to the Sunflower Folk and beyond. It alighted on the workbench next to Adelia with a nervous flit.

"Go," the Maker said. "Go Upland, and do not be afraid of a judgment tempered by humility."

Adelia was surprised, but she did not hesitate, and so left the Maker and his shop, and rode on the back of the hummingbird out of the village, Upland once again. She had not gone far when the world around her began to shrink. The hummingbird struggled to stay aloft, as it, too, shrank, and Adelia became too heavy for it. Adelia then set it free and continued on foot, wandering for days, until finally she began to doubt the Maker's words, or to think that she had misunderstood his meaning. The Land turned to desert, and then to marsh, and then to swamp, all the while growing smaller until one day the trees and rivers and animals and the Land itself were just the right size for her.

When the swamps became rolling hills she came to a village where all the Folk poured forth to greet her with shouts of surprise and welcome. The Iron-Weaver said, "Was your vision always cast so far Upland that you do not recognize your own Folk?" And then it dawned on her that these were the Dell Folk, and this was the Dell in the Hills, though how she had returned home by only venturing Upland, she could not understand.

When Adelia's mother rose from the bench behind her loom and saw Adelia walking up the pathway, she knew her daughter had grown. In Adelia's bearing was a trace of the Land, a strength not of gears and springs, nor even of flesh and bone, but rather of spirit and will. Adelia in turn saw her mother's eyes brighten and her breath quicken, and finally she dared believe the Maker had been right.

Adelia entered her mother's kitchen without having to duck her head, she ate dinner at her mother's table without scraping her knees, and that night Adelia slept comfortably in the goose-down bed of her childhood. Whether in her journey the Land had changed around her, or she had changed within the Land, Adelia did not know.

Adelia realized there would never be a return to the childhood she had left. She even wondered if she could stay in the Dell at all, for it would be difficult to follow the Maker's advice here, where the past whispers of jealousy among the Dell Folk had not been forgotten (by either side). And yet that night, after dreaming of mainsprings as large as mountains and pendulums swinging far and wide on the Upland horizon, Adelia finally decided that here, in her mother's house, was the best place to try.

IRREGULAR VERBS

Matthew Johnson

apiluar: to let a fire burn out
gelas: to treat something with care
pikanau: to cut oneself with a fishhook

It is a well-known fact that there are no people more gifted at language than those of the Salutean Isles. Saluteans live in small villages on a thousand small, densely populated islands; isolated but never alone, their languages change constantly, and new ones are born all the time. A Salutean's family has a language unintelligible to their neighbours, his old friends a jargon impenetrable to anyone outside their circle. Two Saluteans sharing shelter from the rain will, by the time it lets up, have developed a new dialect with its own vocabulary and grammar, with tenses such as "when the ground is dry enough to walk on" and "before I was entirely wet."

It was in just such circumstances that Sendiri Ang had met his wife, Kesepi, and in such circumstances that he lost her. An afternoon spent in a palm-tree shadow is enough for two people to fall in love, a few moments enough time to die when at sea. Eighteen monsoons had passed in between, enough time for the two of them to develop a language of such depth and complexity that no third person could ever learn it, so utterly their own that it was itself an island, without ties to any its neighbours.

For the ten days of his mourning Sendiri had stayed on the private floor of his house, listening to the fading echoes of his wife's voice. On the eleventh day he descended to the public floor. That was the longest time thought to be safe: any more away from the great conversation, the hour in the evening in which all Saluteans join in maintaining their one common language, ran the risk of leaving a person stranded, isolated by changes in dialect.

His friend Teman was waiting for him, feeding new coals for the brazier to replace those that had burned cold. It was just like Teman, Sendiri thought, to think of a little thing like that, and for a moment the sight of his old friend cheered him a little.

"Apa kabar?" Teman said.

Sendiri just stared, at first not recognizing the words in Grand Salutean. "How should I be?" he asked after a moment. "I'm here, and she's not." As soon as he spoke he regretted it, gave thanks that it was in Teman's nature to chew his words thoroughly before spitting them out.

"That's true," Teman said mildly.

Wincing, Sendiri sat on the reed mat next to his friend. "I'm sorry," he said. "Thank you for coming here, and for the coals. I've gotten very tired of cold rice."

Teman smiled, clearly relieved at Sendiri's change of mood. "It's hard, I know—coming back down. Rejoining the rest of the world."

Sendiri shook his head. "Ten days, to mourn someone who— someone—it just isn't enough."

"A lifetime isn't enough," Teman said, smiling sadly. "But it's all we have."

That night Sendiri realized he had forgotten a word. He had been dozing, half-asleep, the smell of the squid curing in the thatch above reminding him of his and Kesepi's last fishing trip together, when suddenly he could not remember the word for the moment, at the end of the long season before the goatfish run, when you think you will die if you have another bite of dried fish. He couldn't remember which of them had coined it, one of a hundred thousand words they shared, but he knew that it was gone.

That's ridiculous, he thought. *It's just nibbling the line* . . . He ran through syllables in his mind, trying to catch a memory that slipped and dodged around him, but it was no use: the hook was empty. He shook briefly, reaching out instinctively across the hammock for the warmth that had once reassured him.

Sendiri cast his mind back, remembering conversations they had had, testing the memory like a tongue probing a loose tooth. *Mana adalah jaring*—What was that word? Suddenly gaps were appearing in his memories. Where there was a Grand Salutean equivalent, the word from that language slipped in; things for which that language had no words were simply gone. Most frustrating, some were words he knew he had remembered that morning. So far only one in a hundred, perhaps, was gone, but more were joining them.

He had never really thought of a language disappearing before. When his mother had died, he and his father preserved their family language, and when his father had died other people, relatives and neighbours had known enough of it to keep it alive in his mind. Kesepi's family, though, had been from another village, not witness to their life together, and they had had no children to carry their language on. When it faded from his mind it would be as if it had never been. As if she had never been.

Sendiri sat up, watched the holes in the thatch for the first hint of dawn, cursing the darkness. He would need light for what he had to do, and every moment that passed was his enemy.

Saluteans, on the whole, are not much for writing things down. Their languages are too fluid and mercurial to be caught on paper; only Grand Salutean has a written form, introduced by missionaries of the Southerner to spread his words to the isles and used by village headmen and island chiefs to record debts and proclamations. Sendiri, whose father-in-law had been a headman, knew how to read and write, and like most islanders knew how to dry and prepare squid ink to sell to foreigners. Though his and Kesepi's language was as alike to Grand Salutean as a ray is to a monkey he bent its letters to his purposes, torturing and teasing the characters until they could record the sounds that would never be spoken again. He began opening the bundles of cold rice which friends and relatives had left as mourning-gifts, to write on their banana-leaf wrapping.

Frantically he wrote word after word, pausing only to mix more ink when the bowl was dry. After some hours the house shook, but he did not look up from his work; only when he heard the ladder up to the private floor creaking did he pause, put down the straightened fishhook he'd been using as a quill.

"Sendiri?" Teman's voice called from halfway up. Friends though they were, the private floor was inviolate without an invitation.

"What is it?" Sendiri asked.

"The conversation," Teman said.

Sendiri exhaled sharply, set his work aside carefully. Had it been that long already? The great conversation was held an hour before dusk—he had not even noticed the shadows creeping across the floor. "Just a moment," he said, his joints complaining as he stood.

He heard Teman climbing back down the ladder, waited until he felt the house sway as his friend's feet hit the floor below before heading down himself. Teman waited until he had reached the floor, then the two wordlessly passed along the way to the broad walkway that joined his house to the rest of the village. Below, the receding tide had exposed the mud into which the village's posts were sunk, and the afternoon sun had left it stinking; everywhere nets were hanging to dry, their sharp salty smell burning Sendiri's nose.

At the public walkway all the villagers were stretched out in the line that made up the great conversation. All voices were speaking in Grand Salutean—in most cases, the only time they would speak it that day. Teman's uncle Paman, the headman, moved up and down the line, making small talk and ensuring everyone used the correct form, without words or constructions from other dialects creeping in. All Saluteans know that their gift for languages could easily be a curse: without a common tongue, the separate islands of their speech would drift inexorably apart.

Sendiri joined in the conversation gamely, the words tasting flat and oily in his mouth. What, after all, could Grand Salutean express? Village business, fishing advice, weather talk. Teman had returned to his assigned place in the line, so Sendiri made small talk with his neighbours, two nattering old women, Kiri on one side and Kanan on the other; meaningless prattle of rotting walkway boards and late fish-runs. Finally the sunlight reddened, the walkway fell into shadow, and he could go home. The conversation was over.

Freed, he ran back to his house, felt the mangrove poles that supported it sway as he shot up the ladder. He sat down, spat in the inkbowl to moisten it, picked up his quill and—what had he been about to write? He scanned the leaf he had left on the floor, hoping to find some clue in what he had written before, saw no connections in the list of words he had been writing. Searching his mind for the words he had inventoried that morning, he found even more were gone. It was more than him simply forgetting them, he realized: the language was eroding, an atoll being washed away by the ocean of Grand Salutean. He would have to forego the conversation, then, until the language was preserved. He laughed. What would be lost? No poetry had ever been written in Grand Salutean. It was a deliberately simple language, shorn of all subtlety, a language of nothing but nouns and verbs; no genders, no tenses but now and not-now, no pronouns but I and not-I. It would do him no harm not to use it for a few days.

————

keluarga: to move to a new village
ngantuk: to call out in one's sleep
lunak: to search for something without finding it

As the night went on, though, he started to wonder just how long it would have to be. Even with all the words he had lost, he wondered if he could ever write down what was left. He had enough fish oil to burn his lamp for a night, maybe two; more urgently, he was nearly out of banana leaves to write on. Squinting, he made the letters as small as the tip of the hook would allow, and began jotting apostrophes to separate words instead of spaces. Earlier, when he had devised his system of writing, he had not thought about space. Now he cursed his decision to use combinations of letters to represent sounds that did not exist in Grand Salutean, rather than inventing new characters. He was netted now, though. A dictionary had to be consistent, or it was useless; this much he had learned from Grand Salutean.

He kept writing, pushing himself to make the letters smaller and smaller. Hunched over the banana leaf on the floor, his arm held tightly to keep his strokes small, Sendiri's forearm jerked, scratching a line across the floorboard. He swore, drew the quill back to throw it across the room in anger, when he saw that the ink had dried on the wood without smudging. Of course, he thought; what else would be a suitable record of the language he and Kesepi had shared than the other thing that was theirs alone, their house? Excited, he raised his arms to stretch his back, dipped the quill in the ink bowl, and began writing along the edge of the wall. He worked his way inward as dawn came, and the daylight hours passed; worked in silence as Teman once again came up the ladder, called his name, called again, and finally left. His quill scratched against the floorboards as he followed an inward spiral towards the center of the room, always trying to increase his pace, to write words down faster than they could be washed away by his mind's tide.

Thunder made him look up. It was dark again: lightning flashed through the holes in the thatch, illuminating the room for a moment. Focused on his work, he had not noticed the smell of rain in the air, the sound as it fell on the roof. Now, in the lightning's flare, he could see puddles sitting on the floor, smudging and washing away most of what he had written. He froze for a moment, rigid with anger; then, too tired even to rage, Sendiri fell to the floor and let himself sleep.

Asleep, he saw himself sitting with Kesepi in their boat, leaning against the palm-stem gunwales on a calm sea. She was speaking, but the words made no sense, and he knew that he had at last forgotten their language entirely. He opened his mouth to speak, then noticed something resting in his hand: looking down, he saw that it was the book he had been writing, containing every word the two of them had ever spoken. Flipping through the book, he tried to speak, to say one of the things he wished he had said, but all he could do was string words together. Kesepi, now in a boat of her own, began to drift away. Sendiri called to her, but the words he read from the dictionary had no emotion, and no reaction registered on her face. Even in its perfect state, he realized, the book was just a record, a dead thing without the soul of the language.

He woke from fevered dreams to see Teman sitting on the mat nearby, a bowl of water at his side. His friend rose to his knees and held out the bowl. "Have some of this," Teman said. "I think you've had a fever."

"Thank you," Sendiri croaked, then took a drink. He felt a sharp pain as he sat up; the hook he had been using as a quill had stuck in his side, leaving a black inkspot when he plucked it out. "Why are you—"

"You've missed two conversations," Teman said, "and you were moaning last night, loud enough your neighbours could hear. The talk is . . . "

Sendiri nodded. He knew what the talk would be. Sometimes when a person dies, they take the souls of those they love with them to the sea floor; what's left is just a hantu, a dead, empty shell. To see or even talk to a hantu is dangerous, itself an omen of death.

"Maybe I'm not alive," Sendiri said. "All that's worth saving is fading away."

Teman frowned, gestured around at the smudged marks on the floor. "Is that what this was all about?"

"It's useless, I realize that now," Sendiri said. "Even if I had all the words, it would be no more alive than a dried fish." He rubbed the spot where the hook had jabbed him with his thumb. The inkmark was still there, just under his skin. "It needs to live . . . "

Teman waited for his friend to continue, rose to his feet when he did not. "Well—I shouldn't even be up here. I hope you'll forgive me." He moved to the top step of the ladder, began climbing down.

"No—wait," Sendiri said. "You have to help me. Help me keep her alive."

"But you said—"

"No, please. I have an idea. Help me."

Teman paused at the top of the ladder. "Sendiri—you have to let go. I know how you feel, but *you have to let go.*"

Sendiri picked up the hook he had been using as a quill, held it up to show to Teman. "Please. Just stay—help me."

"You have to come out for the conversation. Today."

"One day. That's all."

Teman took a breath, nodded. "All right," he said.

———

hadapi: to awake to one's lover's face
cinta: to love truly
mencintai: to love for the last time

At the end of the day, as the shadows reached over the main walkway, Sendiri rejoined the conversation. Many people turned to look, not only because of his absence but because of the black marks that had appeared on his face, arms and legs. Those nearby saw that the marks were letters pricked out under his skin, forming words that meant nothing even to those that could read Grand Salutean. Only he and Teman knew that the words, in fact, covered his whole body, arranged so that their location and position would represent the grammar of the language he and Kesepi had shared: the oldest root words along the spine, verbs on the muscles, every inch of skin recalling the meaning and inflexion of a word.

Despite the small commotion he was causing, Sendiri paid the inkmarks little mind. The Saluteans have no mirrors or steel, and their sea is too dark to ever show a clear reflection, so he would never see most of the words Teman had scribed on his skin. That was not important, though. All that mattered was that they would not fade away. That they were, still, a living language.

A FISH STORY

Sarah Totton

In the Vale of Brecon where the fishermen hunt their game amid deep and succulent cloud, where the yaks are pink, and where the maidens are all beautiful (with some exceptions) lived the grand old dowager, Lydia Batterfly.

Lydia Batterfly's greatest regret in life was her niece, Dagmar. Dagmar was neither inclined toward the practice of womanly etiquette, nor suffiently attractive to be forgiven her disinclinations. Despite attendance at finishing school for two full years, she stubbornly refused to act like a lady. Worse, was her tendency to make a spectacle of herself over the most inappropriate things, most recently and deplorably, "that awful tower boy," as the dowager Batterfly referred to him.

"I don't know why you bother with him," said the dowager.

"His name is Henry," said Dagmar, "and I bother because he is *superb.*"

"Not by *our* standards," said Lydia, by which she meant the standards of any sensible woman of good breeding and taste.

Henry, the bell tower boy was nearly seventeen with limbs as long as a spider monkey's and hair so short it barely colored his scalp. He went about town in simple white clothes, displaying no familial colors—the shameful apparel of a bastard. Henry's job was to climb the tower and play the fish until their echoes rang from the valley walls. There were five fish in the tower, caught from the Sonorous River, in the days when fish swam in rivers, by one Martidel Bayliss, the greatest fisherman in Brecon history. His enormous catches had been bronzed for posterity and hung in the tower where they were twice daily made to clatter amongst themselves in a semblance of music. Henry, the current bell tower boy, was recognized as one of the better practitioners of the art of fish-clattering. Dagmar had been in love with him from the moment she'd first seen him, trousers rolled up to his knees in the Friday Bog with a frog clutched in his fist, squeezing it just hard enough to make its eyes protrude.

The greatest disappointment in Dagmar's life was that Henry did not appear to be likewise infatuated with her. She ascribed this, given her deceptively unremarkable appearance, to his simply not having noticed her. She set about to remedy this.

On the eve of the coldest night of the year, just after the last murmur of the fish jangles had died away, Dagmar stationed herself below the tower looking up at the fish chamber fifty feet above. In her hands, she held her uncle's bangy-wurdle, salvaged from the dowager Batterfly's lumber room. Bangy-wurdles were the instruments of the insane, the bizarrely eccentric and the lower classes of society. No one of good breeding would even admit to owning one. The instrument produced a music often described as "a din of iniquity."

Practicing in secret, Dagmar had spent the summer learning to master the instrument. She reasoned it thusly: a piano was too difficult to drag to the town square, and a clarinet didn't allow for singing. And sing she did. She sang a song she had composed for her love, amidst daydreams of his froggy hands, his simian limbs and his days at play among the shining fish. At the close of the second verse, as she launched into the chorus, she saw a white face thrust out from the tower window.

"What's that fuss?" said Henry. "Are you ill?"

She finished the chorus and shouted up to him, "A song professing my love for you, dear Henry. Sit back and enjoy while I serenade you." And she continued to play what was later described by the town wag as, "the musical equivalent of a cat caught under a pram wheel."

Despite several pleas from around the square for Dagmar to hold her peace, she played on, singing of Henry's attributes.

"My what?" Henry shouted. "What are you saying?"

"Your glorious shining fingers," she shouted back.

There were some hoots of laughter from one of the nearby houses.

"Clear off," said Henry. "People will hear you."

"You are the most desirable man in the Vale of Brecon, and I am not going to stop until everyone knows it." Dagmar continued to play. She had not quite finished her fourth turn through the chorus when Henry, desperate to shut her up, emptied a water pail out of the tower window. The air was so cold that the cascade had nearly crystallized by the time it broke over Dagmar's head. Dagmar squeaked in shock and almost dropped the bangy-wurdle on the cobblestones.

"Now go home!" said Henry. And he banged the tower shutters closed.

Dagmar took a few moments to collect her wits, shaking the beads of ice from her coat and brushing them from the bangy-wurdle. Her hair was now frozen into points.

Lydia Batterfly's house abutted the square, and Dagmar retreated to it. There was no point in further stating her suit if Henry had closed the window. Unfortunately, as soon as she tried to open the front door, her wet hand froze fast to the metal knob. Try as she might, she could not get it free. Her shouts for assistance were met with answering shouts to shut up. Eventually, though, they drew her fondest friend Eora, the duchess' daughter, from the house next door. Eora was of that sensible type who are really quite wonderful in a pinch, though they tend to be dull and full of advice for living a good life at other times. On this occasion, Eora, who'd watched the entire spectacle from her bedroom window, came prepared carrying a bowl full of hot water from the kettle. The bowl had contained some exotic fruits which were now dumped over her mother's oak dining table. Eora proceeded to pour the steaming contents of the bowl over Dagmar's hand in an attempt to loosen it from the doorknob. The major difficulty being to stop herself laughing so hard that she dropped it.

"Yes, all right, all right," said Dagmar peeling her hand from the door handle. "It isn't funny. I mean, you have no idea what love does to a person. You'll see."

Though really, Dagmar thought, Eora was the sort of person who would fall in love—or something respectably close to it—with a suitable gentleman approved by her mother the duchess, and they would be wed in a ghastly ceremony in which Dagmar would be forced to attend in some abominable dress. Dagmar loathed dresses.

Word gets about in small places, and it wasn't long before Eora's mother, the Duchess, was informing Lydia Batterfly of what Dagmar had been up to while she had been out of town.

"She's sending me back to finishing school," said Dagmar to Eora that afternoon.

"Not again! That's what . . . The fourth time? What are you going to do?"

"Third, and I think she's going to find that Madame Loge will have nothing to do with me. She doesn't like to be reminded of her failings. They're so few and far between. As to what I'm going to do, I've thought of another plan."

"Plan?"

"To win Henry."

Eora stared at Dagmar and said nothing. Perhaps it was a tactful omission of words. When at last she spoke, she said, "What are you going to do?"

"Come with me and see," said Dagmar. She led the way down the center of the street, down the narrower alleyways of Brecon town, to Tyrone's Fishing Tackle Emporium.

"What on Earth?" Eora muttered.

Dagmar went inside and accosted the shop's proprietor. "I would like your best and strongest rod, please."

"Yes, madam," said the proprietor. "We have a variety of—"

"The longest one you've got."

"Oh," said the merchant, and he led her to the window of the shop from which he pulled a small brass cylinder.

"That doesn't look very large, man," said Dagmar.

"If you would come outside." The merchant stepped out into the street and proceeded to extend the rod. The mechanism was a telescopic one. The merchant pulled each joint out, lengthening it until it stretched the entire length of the alley and protruded out over the High Street sidewalk. Curious onlookers peered at it warily and walked around it.

"Well?" said the merchant.

"I suppose if that's the longest one you've got, it will have to do," said Dagmar. "How much is it?"

"Oh, madam, workmanship like this . . . This is a one-of-a-kind, made on the Gwyntog Coast and designed after the one used by Martidel Bayliss who once fished with it in the ocean. It is the most beautiful piece of wo—"

"I'm amazed you're willing to part with it."

"I could be coerced," said the merchant. "But it would take a king's ransom."

"Far be it from me to part a man from his beloved rod. We'll look elsewhere, thanks."

"You will not find a larger or better rod in the entire Vale of Brecon."

"That's as may be, but I haven't got a king to ransom."

"Perhaps we could negotiate."

A price was settled, though the merchant claimed he would go bankrupt, and Dagmar claimed she would have no dowry. "Though without this, there would be no need for a dowry."

"Why, Dagmar?" said Eora. "What are you going to do?"

"I," said Dagmar, "am going to catch the Barbary Fish, and then—"

"You're out of your mind!" said the merchant. "You?! The best fisherman in the history of Brecon spent his entire career trying, and even he couldn't catch the Barbary Fish."

"Please," said Dagmar. "You interrupted me. As I was saying. I am going to catch the Barbary Fish and present him to Henry the tower boy as a token of my love."

"Dagmar . . . " said Eora.

"I know," said Dagmar. "I'll need bait."

Dagmar strode off waving her rod, now telescoped down to a more manageable twelve inches. Eora was forced to run to keep up with her. Dagmar led her to the fishing grounds at Leechfield. The day was gloriously clear, and there were several fishermen sprawled amid the long grasses, eyes following the spiderfloss of their fishing lines which disappeared into the sky, ending at their lures glinting from colorful balloons. High above them, the braver fishermen rode in baskets beneath larger balloons, harpoons held at the ready, sighting along the Vale for the cloud-wisps of fish-spoor.

Dagmar made straight for the oldest and raggedest of the veteran fishermen at Leechfield and without preamble, said, "If you were to try for the Barbary Fish, where would you set your line and how would you bait your hook?"

The man looked at Dagmar and snorted. "Five miles of golden spiderfloss, four of silver. And for a lure, the blue-stained glass from the window of Epiphany. And everyone knows the Barbary Fish frequents the hills at Devil's End."

"You've never tried to catch him yourself?"

"I'm not mad."

"Well then, thank you, sir," said Dagmar.

That night, someone broke the Epiphany window. It was later determined that a stone had been thrown through it. Three days after this Dagmar's aunt found the family tapestry bundled up in the cupboard under the stairs. Half of it had been unravelled, and the gold and silver threads had all been pulled out. None of the servants would own up to doing it.

Shortly afterwards, Dagmar became suddenly attentive at her macramé and crochet lessons. Madam Loge began to entertain cautious hopes for her reform.

Ten days later, Dagmar appeared dripping wet at Eora's door. "You'll have to help me," said Dagmar. She led her friend to Leechfield where a gathering of fishermen were ringed around the convex, glittering side of an enormous fish.

"Is that the Barbary—"

"Well, no, actually," said Dagmar. "But it's quite a respectable one, I think. It dragged me across Leechfield and all along the Sonorous River. Do you see this?" Dagmar proudly displayed a missing tooth.

"Came out when I hit the Bridge. No one warned me it might take me up. Anyway, it dropped me in the sea and I suppose it expected me to let go, but I wasn't going to give it the satisfaction. I worried it about a bit, then it seemed to tire, enough that I could wind it in close enough to start biffing and kicking it. It got the message and went to ground here. Which was lucky, as I didn't fancy landing in the quarry."

"What are you going to do with it?" said Eora.

"Have it bronzed, of course. It's easily bigger than any of the ones in the tower now."

Eora's eyes grew wide, but she didn't comment. The look of fanatical determination in Dagmar's eyes stilled her tongue.

Henry, as it happened, was neither pleased, nor impressed when Dagmar, accompanied by a parade of dancing acrobats and men in military costume, presented the bronzed fish to him at the door of the tower.

"That won't fit up the steps," he said.

"We'll hoist it from outside," said Dagmar. "This is a gift to you, a token of my esteem."

"Look," said Henry. He glanced at the acrobats somersaulting crosswise in front of him and lowered his voice. "Stop doing this."

"Doing what?"

"Giving me things, publicly declaring your feelings for me."

"Martidel Bayliss didn't stop trying to catch the Barbary fish and look at him."

"Right, but he never caught it, though, did he?" said Henry.

"No, but he spent his *entire life* trying. Isn't that utterly marvelous? That is dedication, Henry, as I am dedicated in my love for you."

"But I don't love you. I don't even like you. What you're doing . . . It's embarrassing me. It's insulting. Stop it."

Dagmar's face fell, and her brow furrowed in thought. "Very well." She bowed. "But take the fish."

"So, you have seen sense at last," said Eora as they sipped wine in the conservatory.

Dagmar shrugged. "If you mean have I given up, then no. Not at all."

"But he ordered you to leave him alone."

"Ah, yes. And that is because I have not done enough to earn his love. I have not sacrificed enough, I have not suffered enough."

"And you think he has not suffered enough either." Eora sighed. "This is fatuous. It's senseless."

"No. Senseless is in the country of Giving Up. What is the purpose of living if I can't pursue him? If I stopped, it would mean I didn't really love him. And I do."

"He says he doesn't love you."

"If he really believes that . . . "

"Yes?" Eora leaned closer.

" . . . then I haven't been trying hard enough."

Exasperated, Eora proclaimed, "A woman pursuing a man is a scandal. I think you are doing it to mortify your aunt Lydia."

"I am doing it for the glory," said Dagmar. "A glory most women are afraid to taste."

For a few weeks nothing new transpired, except that Dagmar began to pay rapt attention to her art instructor. Then one morning, a large mural was found covering the front of Dagmar's house. It depicted a man, endowed with yak-like proportions, strutting atop an enormous tower from which a golden fish hung.

The next day, Henry of the bell tower asked the swineherd's daughter to marry him.

"Now, even you must admit defeat," said Eora.

"Not at all," said Dagmar. "This girl, what do you know about her?"

"She's very beautiful."

"Ah," said Dagmar, "But did she earn her beauty, or did she happen upon it by way of the womb? What has she done to be *worthy* of Henry?"

"Well, nothing," said Eora, "except I suppose that he likes her. And perhaps she was patient enough to let him make up his own mind about that, and doesn't wake him at midnight singing his praises, or drop uninvited fish and acrobats in his lap."

"No," said Dagmar. "It can't be that simple. If he truly believes he loves her, then it's because I haven't tried hard enough."

Eora happened to meet Henry in Evelyn Street the next afternoon. They greeted each other cordially, if cautiously, like two people who share an embarrassing complaint.

"It won't work," said Eora. "I mean, if that's why you've done it."

"What?"

"Proposing to another girl. In fact, I think you've spurred her on to try even harder to win you."

"Tell her from me that she can go to hell," Henry muttered. "Tell her I'll send her there myself if she doesn't stop it." He stalked off.

Eora went off to do as he asked, but at the door to Dagmar's house, she stopped. Her hand, lifted to tap on the door, dropped to her side, and she regarded it pensively. What was the use talking to Dagmar? She wouldn't listen to reason.

A few days later, Dagmar was sitting on the bank of the Sonorous River, working out a plot to stop Henry's wedding.

She was planning the speech she would make when the minister asked if there were any objections to the wedding. Of course there were. Anyone could see that Henry had become engaged solely to annoy her and not because he loved this other girl.

Dagmar was deep in thought writing her speech when a shadow fell across the parchment. She looked up, but instead of an obtrusive cloud, she saw a man looming over her.

"You're in my light," said Dagmar. "Move off."

"*You* are my light," said the man.

Dagmar, whose head had bowed to the task of writing almost before the words were out of her mouth looked up suddenly. "What?"

"Lady, for whose sake alone I breathe, listen while I tell you that I adore you."

It was the fisherman from Leechfield. The old, ragged man who'd told her about baiting hooks.

"You're cracked!" said Dagmar. "You're twice my age for a start. And anyway, in case you hadn't noticed, and you must be deaf, mad and stupid if you haven't, I'm in love with Henry the tower boy."

"Henry is engaged to the swineherd's daughter."

"That's what he thinks," said Dagmar, standing up and brushing the heads of grasses from her cloak.

"He is betrothed," said the fisherman. "Whereas I am not. We are better suited to each other." He began to follow Dagmar as she made her way back to the square.

"Don't you have fish to catch?" said Dagmar.

"None more beautiful than you, and none more sly and worthy than you." As they walked, the fisherman's voice rose so that people in the square turned to watch them.

"Look," said Dagmar, rounding on him, "Look here, back off. I've told you to go. Everyone knows where my heart belongs."

The fisherman fell to his knees. "Most glorious girl, listen to me while I declare my love for you in front of these people, for no one could be more worthy of a fisherman's love than the woman who tried for the Barbary Fish."

"Yes, yes, all right. Everyone knows I didn't get him, but thanks for bringing it to their attention. Now clear off."

The fisherman grabbed hold of the hem of Dagmar's cloak so that she had to jerk it free. She turned and stalked off.

The fisherman followed her, tossing glass-glazed fish scales over her head. "A tribute," he said.

Someone nearby sniggered. Dagmar had to make an undignified run to her house, slamming and bolting the door behind her.

"It isn't funny, Eora," said Dagmar. She had to raise her voice to be heard over the wailing coming from below the window as the Leechfield fisherman serenaded her.

"I think it's romantic," said Eora. "Why don't you consider him?"

"Look, Eora, there are two kinds of people in the world. The Pursuers and the Pursued. And the Pursuers neither like nor wish to be pursued. It is an insult to their nature."

"I heard that Henry proposed to the swineherd's daughter," said Eora. "She didn't pursue him at all."

Dagmar frowned. "Do you know, that man is singing off-key? I didn't sing off-key when I serenaded Henry . . . did I?"

Eora shrugged. "I couldn't really tell over Henry's shouting at you to shut up."

"And at least I composed an original song," said Dagmar. "This raving nit is borrowing an old chestnut and trotting it out like it's the latest thing. He's doing a poor job of it all around." Dagmar shot to her feet and marched to the bathroom, filled a tub with the coldest water she could manage and wrestled it back to the window. She tipped the water out of the window onto the singing fisherman.

"Hmmm," she said. "Perhaps I ought to learn from my own mishaps."

Eora brightened. "Yes!"

Then Dagmar picked up the potted plant next to the window and tipped out over the ledge as well. "Yes, the water makes the soil stick quite well," she said, peering down. "It *does* pay to learn from one's mistakes."

The next day in church, the Leechfield fisherman presented Dagmar with a garland of the finest cerise yak's hair. Yak's hair garlands were considered *de rigueur* at the time. Dagmar stood up in the pew and shouted, "Stop! I cannot think of anything more annoying, more aggravating, more infuriating than your pursuit of me when I have clearly told you that I am not interested. You are an ass. An ass' ass, and your attention to me is insulting." As she said this, her eyes happened upon Henry who was standing by the door to the tower, about to ring his fish to signify the end of the service.

Dagmar's cheeks turned a shade reminiscent of the most fashionable yak's hair, and she walked out.

Henry married the swineherd's daughter without incident and

they lived in comfortable married squabblehood, his wife being un-encumbered with the notion that she had married a perfect man.

Dagmar failed finishing school in spectacular fashion for the third time and finished up a merry spinster, living on the outskirts of town. On fine days, she can sometimes be seen using her famous brass rod. She has yet to catch the Barbary Fish.

The Leechfield fisherman moved to the City where he bought a suite of rooms in one of the city towers from which the trawling was more rewarding than from his former, cheaper lodgings in a down-to-earth bungalow. It was an expensive purchase, but affordable to one who has benefited from the dowry of a duchess' daughter.

The fish served at Eora's wedding fed six hundred people.

THE NIGHT WHISKEY

Jeffrey Ford

All summer long, on Wednesday and Friday evenings after my job at the gas station, I practiced with old man Witzer looking over my shoulder. When I'd send a dummy toppling perfectly onto the pile of mattresses in the bed of his pick-up, he'd wheeze like it was his last breath (I think he was laughing), and pat me on the back, but when they fell awkwardly or hit the metal side of the truck bed or went really awry and ended sprawled on the ground, he'd spit tobacco and say either one of two things—"That there's a cracked melon" or "Get me a wet-vac." He was a patient teacher, never rushed, never raising his voice or showing the least exasperation in the face of my errors. After we'd felled the last of the eight dummies we'd earlier placed in the lower branches of the trees on the edge of town, he'd open a little cooler he kept in the cab of his truck and fetch a beer for himself and one for me. "You did good today, boy" he'd say, no matter if I did or not, and we'd sit in the truck with the windows open, pretty much in silence, and watch the fire flies signal in the gathering dark.

As the old man had said, "There's an art to dropping drunks." The main tools of the trade were a set of three long bamboo poles—a ten-foot, a fifteen-foot, and a twenty- foot. They had rubber balls attached at one end that were wrapped in chamois cloth and tied tight with a leather lanyard. These poles were called "prods." Choosing the right prod, considering how high the branches were that the drunk had nestled upon, was crucial. Too short a one would cause you to go on tip toes and lose accuracy, while the excess length of too long a one would get in the way and throw you off balance. The first step was always to take a few minutes and carefully assess the situation. You had to ask yourself, "How might this body fall if I were to prod the shoulders first or the back or the left leg?" The old man had taught me that generally there was a kind of physics to it but that sometimes intuition had to override logic. "Don't think of them as falling but think of them as flying," said Witzer, and only when I was actually out there under the trees and trying to hit the mark in the center of the pick-up bed did I know what he meant. "You ultimately want them to fall, turn in the air, and land flat on the back," he'd told me. "That's a ten pointer." There were other important aspects of the job as well. The positioning of the truck was crucial as was the manner with which you woke them after they had safely landed. Calling them back by shouting in their ears would leave them dazed for a week, but, as the natives had done, breaking a thin twig a few inches from the ear worked like a charm—a gentle reminder that life was waiting to be lived.

When his long time fellow harvester, Mr. Bo Elliott, passed on, the town council had left it to Witzer to find a replacement. It had been his determination to pick someone young, and so he came to the high school and carefully observed each of us fifteen students in the graduating class. It was a wonder he could see anything through the thick, scratched lenses of his glasses and those perpetually squinted eyes, but after long deliberation, which involved the rubbing of his stubbled chin and the scratching of his fallow scalp, he singled me out for the honor. An honor it was too as he'd told me, "You know that because you don't get paid anything for it." He assured me that I had the talent hidden inside of me, that he'd seen it like an aura of pink light, and that he'd help me develop it over the summer. To be an apprentice in the Drunk Harvest was a kind of exalted position for one as young as me, and it brought me some special credit with my friends and neighbors, because it meant that I was being initiated into an ancient tradition that went back further than the time when our ancestors settled that remote piece of country. My father beamed with pride, my mother got teary eyed, my girlfriend, Darlene, let me get to third base and part way home.

Our town was one of those places you pass but never stop in while on vacation to some National Park; out in the sticks, up in the mountains—places where the population is rendered in three figures on a board by the side of the road; the first numeral no more than a four and the last with a hand painted slash through it and replaced with one of lesser value beneath. The people there were pretty much like people everywhere only the remoteness of the locale had insulated us against the relentless tide of change and the judgment of the wider world. We had radios and televisions and telephones, and as these things came in, what they brought us lured a few of our number away. But for those who stayed in Gatchfield progress moved like a tortoise dragging a ball and chain. The old ways hung on with more tenacity than Relletta Clome, who was 110 years old and had died and been revived by doctor Kvench eight times in ten years. We had our little ways and customs that were like the exotic beasts of Tasmania, isolated in their evolution to become completely singular. The strangest of these traditions was the Drunk Harvest.

The Harvest centered on an odd little berry that, as far as I know, grows nowhere else in the world. The natives had called it *vachimi atatsi*, but because of its shiny black hue and the nature of its growth, the settlers had renamed it the deathberry. It didn't grow in the meadows or swamps as do blueberries and blackberries, no, this berry grew only out of the partially decayed carcasses of animals left to lie where they'd fallen. If you were out hunting in the woods and you came across say, a dead deer, which had not been touched by coyotes or wolves, you could be certain that that deceased creature would eventually sprout a small hedge from its rotted gut before autumn and that the long thin branches would be thick with juicy black berries. The predators knew somehow that these fallen beasts had the seeds of the berry bush within them, because although it went against their nature not to devour a fallen creature, they wouldn't go near these particular carcasses. It wasn't just wild creatures either, even livestock fallen dead in the field and left untouched could be counted on to serve as host for this parasitic plant. Instances of this weren't common but I'd seen it first-hand a couple of times in my youth—a rotting body, head maybe already turning to skull, and out of the belly like a green explosion, this wild spray of long thin branches tipped with atoms of black like tiny marbles, bobbing in the breeze. It was a frightening sight to behold for the first time, and as I overheard Lester Bildab, a man who foraged for the deathberry, tell my father once, "No matter how many times I see it, I still get a little chill in the backbone."

Lester and his son, a dim witted boy in my class at school, Lester II, would go out at the start of each August across the fields and through the woods and swamps searching for fallen creatures hosting the hideous flora. Bildab had learned from his father about gathering the fruit, as Bildab's father had learned from his father, and so on all the way back to the settlers and the natives from whom *they'd* learned. You can't eat the berries; they'll make you violently ill. But you can ferment them and make a drink, like a thick black brandy that had come to be called *Night Whiskey* and supposedly had the sweetest taste on earth. I didn't know the process, as only a select few did, but from berry to glass I knew it took about a month. Lester and his son would gather them and usually come up with three good size grocery sacs full. Then they'd take them over to The Blind Ghost Bar and Grill and sell them to Mr. and Mrs. Bocean, who knew the process for making the liquor and kept the recipe in a little safe with a combination lock. That recipe was given to our forefathers as a gift by the natives, who, two years after giving it, with no provocation and having gotten along peacefully with the settlers, vanished without a trace, leaving behind an empty village on an island out in the swamp . . . or so the story goes.

The celebration that involved this drink took place at The Blind Ghost on the last Saturday night in September. It was usually for adults only, and so the first chance I ever got to witness it was the year I was made an apprentice to old man Witzer. The only two younger people at the event that year were me and Lester II. Bildab's boy had been attending since he was ten, and some speculated that having witnessed the thing and been around the berries so long was what had turned him simple, but I knew young Lester in school before that and he was no ball of fire then either. Of the adults that participated, only eight actually partook of the Night Whiskey. Reed and Samantha Bocean took turns each year, one joining in the drinking while the other watched the bar, and then there were seven others, picked by lottery, who got to taste the sweetest thing on earth. Sheriff Jolle did the honors picking the names of the winners from a hat at the event and was barred from participating by a town ordinance that went way back. Those who didn't drink the Night Whiskey drank conventional alcohol, and there were local musicians there and dancing. From the snatches of conversation about the celebrations that adults would let slip out, I'd had an idea it was a raucous time.

This native drink, black as a crow wing and slow to pour as cough syrup, had some strange properties. A year's batch was enough to fill only half of an old quart gin bottle that Samantha Ocean had tricked out with a hand-made label showing a deer skull with berries for eyes, and so it was portioned out sparingly. Each participant got no more than about three quarters of a shot glass of it, but that was enough. Even with just these few sips it was wildly intoxicating, so that the drinkers became immediately drunk, their inebriation growing as the night went on although they'd finish off their allotted pittance within the first hour of the celebration. "Blind drunk," was the phrase used to describe how the drinkers of it would end the night. Then came the weird part, for usually around two am all eight of them, all at once, got to their feet, stumbled out the door, lurched down the front steps of the bar, and meandered off into the dark, groping and weaving like name sakes of the establishment they had just left. It was a peculiar phenomenon of the drink that it made those who imbibed it search for a resting place in the lower branches of a tree. Even though they were pie-eyed drunk, somehow, and no one knew why, they'd manage to shimmy up a trunk and settle themselves down across a few choice branches. It was a law that if you tried to stop them or disturb them it would be cause for arrest. So when the drinkers of the Night Whiskey left the bar, no one followed. The next day, they'd be found fast asleep in mid-air, only a few precarious branches between them and gravity. That's where old man Witzer and I came in. At first light, we were to make our rounds in his truck with the poles bungeed on top, partaking of what was known as The Drunk Harvest.

Dangerous? You bet, but there was a reason for it. I told you about the weird part, but even though this next part gives a justification of sorts, it's even weirder. When the natives gave the berry and the recipe for the Night Whiskey to our forefathers, they considered it a gift of a most divine nature, because after the dark drink was ingested and the drinker had climbed aloft, sleep would invariably bring him or her to some realm between that of dream and the sweet hereafter. In this limbo they'd come face to face with their relatives and loved ones who'd passed on. That's right. It never failed. As best as I can remember him having told it, here's my own father's recollection of the experience from the year he won the lottery:

"I found myself out in the swamp at night with no memory of how I'd gotten there or what reason I had for being there. I tried to find a marker—a fallen tree or a certain turn in the path, to find my way back to town. The moon was bright, and as I stepped into a clearing, I saw a single figure standing there stark naked. I drew closer and said hello, even though I wanted to run. I saw it was an old fellow, and when he heard me approaching, he looked up and right there I knew it was my uncle Fic. 'What are you doing out here without your clothes,' I said to him as I approached. 'Don't you remember, Joe,' he said, smiling. 'I'm passed on.' And then it struck me and made my hair stand on end. But uncle Fic, who'd died at the age of ninety-eight when I was only fourteen, told me not to be afraid. He told me a good many things, explained a good many things, told me not to fear death. I asked him about my ma and pa, and he said they were together as always and having a good time. I bid him to say hello to them for me, and he said he would. Then he turned and started to walk away but stepped on a twig, and that sound brought me awake, and I was lying in the back of Witzer's pickup, staring into the jowly, pitted face of Bo Elliott."

My father was no liar, and to prove to my mother and me that he was telling the truth, he told us that uncle Fic had told him where to find a tie pin he'd been given as a commemoration of his twenty-fifth year at the feed store but had subsequently lost. He then walked right over to a tea pot shaped like an orange that my mother kept on a shelf in our living room, opened it, reached in and pulled out the pin. The only question my father was left with about the whole strange episode was, "Out of all my dead relations, why Uncle Fic?"

Stories like the one my father told my mother and me abound. Early on, back in the 1700's, they were written down by those who could write. These rotting manuscripts were kept for a long time in the Gatchfield library—an old shoe repair store with book shelves—in a glass case. Sometimes the dead who showed up in the Night Whiskey dreams offered premonitions, sometimes they told who a thief was when something had gone missing. And supposedly it was the way Jolle had solved the Latchey murder, on a tip given to Mrs. Windom by her great aunt, dead 10 years. Knowing that our ancestors were keeping an eye on things and didn't mind singing out about the untoward once a year usually convinced the citizens of Gatchfield to walk the straight and narrow. We kept it to ourselves, though, and never breathed a word of it to outsiders as if their rightful skepticism would ruin the power of the ceremony. As for those who'd left town, it was never a worry that they'd tell anyone, because, seriously, who'd have believed them?

On a Wednesday evening, the second week in September, while sitting in the pickup truck, drinking a beer, old man Witzer said, "I think you got it, boy. No more practice now. Too much and we'll overdo it." I simply nodded, but in the following weeks leading up to the end of the month celebration, I was a wreck, envisioning the body of one of my friends or neighbors sprawled broken on the ground next to the bed of the truck. At night I'd have a recurring dream of prodding a body out of an oak, seeing it fall in slow motion, and then all would go black and I'd just hear this dull crack, what I assumed to be the drunk's head slamming the side of the pickup bed. I'd wake and sit up straight, shivering. Each time this happened, I tried to remember to see who it was in my dream, because it always seemed to be the same person. Two nights before the celebration, I saw a tattoo of a coiled cobra on the fellow's bicep as he fell and knew it was Henry Grass. I thought of telling Witzer, but I didn't want to seem a scared kid.

The night of the celebration came and after sundown my mother and father and I left the house and strolled down the street to The Blind Ghost. People were already starting to arrive and from inside I could hear the band tuning up fiddles and banjos. Samantha Ocean had made the place up for the event—black crepe paper draped here and there and wrapped around the support beams. Hanging from the ceiling on various lengths of fishing line were the skulls of all manner of local animals; coyote, deer, beaver, squirrel, and a giant black bear skull suspended over the center table where the lottery winners were to sit and take their drink. I was standing on the threshold, taking all this in, feeling the same kind of enchantment as when a kid and Mrs. Musfin would do up the three classrooms of the school house for Christmas, when my father leaned over to me and whispered, "You're on your own tonight, Ernest. You want to drink, drink. You want to dance, dance." I looked at him and he smiled, nodded and winked. I then looked to my mother and she merely shrugged, as if to say, "That's the nature of the beast."

Old man Witzer was there at the bar, and he called me over and handed me a cold beer. Two other of the town's oldest men were with him, his chess playing buddies, and he put his arm around my shoulders and introduced them to me. "This is a good boy," he said, patting my back. "He's doing Bo Elliott proud out there under the trees." The two friends of his nodded and smiled at me, the most notice I'd gotten from either of them my entire life. And then the band launched into a reel, and everyone turned to watch them play. Two choruses went by and I saw my mother and father and some of the other couples move out onto the small dance floor. I had another beer and looked around.

About four songs later, Sheriff Jolle appeared in the doorway to the bar and the music stopped mid-tune.

"OK," he said, hitching his pants up over his gut and removing his black, wide brimmed hat, "time to get the lottery started." He moved to the center of the bar where the Night Whiskey drinkers table was set up and took a seat. "Everybody drop your lottery tickets into the hat and make it snappy." I'd guessed that this year it was Samantha Ocean who was going to drink her own concoction since Reed stayed behind the bar and she moved over and took a seat across from Jolle. After the last of the tickets had been deposited into the hat, the sheriff pushed it away from him into the middle of the table. He then called for a whiskey neat, and Reed was there with it in a flash. In one swift gulp, he drained the glass, banged it onto the table top and said, "I'm ready." My girlfriend Darlene's step-mom came up from behind him with a black scarf and tied it around his eyes for a blind fold. Reaching into the hat, he ran his fingers through the lottery tickets, mixing them around, and then started drawing them out one by one and stacking them in a neat pile in front of him on the table. When he had the seven, he stopped and pulled off the blind fold. He then read the names in a loud voice and everyone kept quiet till he was finished—Becca Staney, Stan Joss, Pete Hesiant, Berta Hull, Moses T. Remarque, Ronald White, and Henry Grass. The room exploded with applause and screams. The winners smiled, dazed by having won, as their friends and family gathered round them and slapped them on the back, hugged them, shoved drinks into their hands. I was overwhelmed by the moment, caught up in it and grinning, until I looked over at Witzer and saw him jotting the names down in a little notebook he'd refer to tomorrow when we made our rounds. Only then did it come to me that one of the names was none other than *Henry Grass*, and I felt my stomach tighten in a knot.

Each of the winners eventually sat down at the center table. Jolle got up and gave his seat to Reed Ocean, who brought with him from behind the bar the bottle of Night Whiskey and a tray of eight shot glasses. Like the true barman he was, he poured all eight without lifting the bottle once, all to the exact same level. One by one they were handed around the table. When each of the winners had one before him or her, the barkeep smiled and said, "Drink up." Some went for it like it was a draught from the fountain of youth, some snuck up on it with trembling hand. Berta Hull, a middle–aged mother of five with horse teeth and short red hair, took a sip and declared, "Oh my, it's so lovely." Ronald White, the brother of one of the men I worked with at the gas station, took his up and dashed it off in one shot. He wiped his mouth on his sleeve and laughed like a maniac, drunk already. Reed went back to the bar. The band started up again and the celebration came to life like a wild animal in too small a cage.

I wandered around the bar, nodding to the folks I knew, half taken by my new celebrity as a participant in the Drunk Harvest and half preoccupied watching Henry Grass. He was a young guy, only twenty-five, with a crew cut and a square jaw, dressed in the camouflage sleeveless T-shirt he wore in my recurring dream. With the way he stared at the shot glass in front of him through his little circular glasses, you'd have thought he was staring into the eyes of a king cobra. He had a reputation as a gentle, studious soul, although he was most likely the strongest man in town—the rare instance of an outsider who'd made a place for himself in Gatchfield. The books he read were all about UFOs and The Bermuda Triangle, Chariots of the Gods; stuff my father proclaimed to be "dyed in the wool hooey." He worked with the horses over at the Haber family farm, and lived in a trailer out by the old Civil War shot tower, across the meadow and through the woods. I stopped for a moment to talk to Lester II, who mumbled to me around the hard boiled eggs he was shoving into his mouth one after another, and when I looked back to Henry, he'd finished off the shot glass and left the table.

I overheard snatches of conversation, and much of it was commentary on why it was a lucky thing that so and so had won the lottery this year. Someone mentioned the fact that poor Pete Hesiant's beautiful young wife, Lonette, had passed away from leukemia just at the end of the spring, and another mentioned that Moses had always wanted a shot at the Night Whiskey but had never gotten the chance, and how he'd soon be too old to participate as his arthritis had recently given him the devil of a time. Everybody was pulling for Berta Hull, who was raising those five children on her own, and Becca was a favorite because she was the town mid-wife. The same such stuff was said about Ron White and Stan Joss.

In addition to the well-wishes for the lottery winners, I stood for a long time next to a table where Sheriff Jolle, my father and mother, and Dr. Kvench sat and listened to the doctor, a spry little man with a gray goatee, who was by then fairly well along in his cups, as were his listeners, myself included, spout his theory as to why the drinkers took to the trees. He explained it, amidst a barrage of hiccups, as a product of evolution. His theory was that the deathberry plant had at one time grown everywhere on earth, and that early man partook of some form of the Night Whiskey at the dawn of time. Because the world was teeming with night predators then, and because early man was just recently descended from the tree tops, those who became drunk automatically knew, as a means of self-preservation, to climb up into the trees and sleep so as not to become a repast for a saber-toothed tiger or some other onerous creature. Dr. Kvench, citing Carl Jung, believed that the imperative to get off the ground after drinking the Night Whiskey had remained in the collective unconscious and was passed down through the ages. "Everybody in the world probably still has the unconscious command that would kick in if they were to drink the dark stuff, but since the berry doesn't grow anywhere but here now, we're the only ones that see this effect." The doctor nodded, hiccupped twice, and then got up to fetch a glass of water. When he left the table Jolle looked over at my mother, and she and he and my father broke up laughing. "I'm glad he's better at pushing pills than concocting theories," said the Sheriff, drying his eyes with his thumbs.

At about midnight, I was reaching for yet another beer, which Reed had placed on the bar, when my grasp was interrupted by a vise like grip on my wrist. I looked up and saw that it was Witzer. He said nothing to me but simply shook his head, and I knew he was telling me to lay off so as to be fresh for the harvest in the morning. I nodded. He smiled, patted my shoulder, and turned away. Somewhere around two am, the lottery winners, so incredibly drunk that even in my intoxicated state it seemed impossible they could still walk, stopped dancing, drinking, whatever, and headed for the door. The music abruptly ceased. It suddenly became so silent we could hear the wind blowing out on the street. The sounds of them stumbling across the wooden porch of the bar and then the steps creaking, the screen door banging shut, filled me with a sense of awe and visions of them groping through the night. I tried to picture Berta Hull climbing a tree, but I just couldn't get there, and the doctor's theory seemed to make some sense to me.

I left before my parents did. Witzer drove me home and before I got out of the cab, he handed me a small bottle.

"Take three good chugs," he said.

"What is it?" I asked.

"An herb mix," he said. "It'll clear your head and have you ready for the morning."

I took the first sip of it and the taste was bitter as could be. "Good god," I said, grimacing.

Witzer wheezed. "Two more," he said.

I did as I was told, got out of the truck and bid him good night. I didn't remember undressing or getting into bed, and luckily I was too drunk to dream. It seemed as if I'd only closed my eyes when my father's voice woke me, saying, "The old man's out in the truck, waiting on you." I leaped out of bed and dressed, and when I finally knew what was going on, I was surprised I felt as well and refreshed as I did. "Do good, Ernest," said my father from the kitchen. "Wait," my mother called. A moment later she came out of their bedroom, wrapping a robe around her. She gave me a hug and a kiss, and then said, "Hurry." It was brisk outside, and the early morning light gave proof that the day would be a clear one. The truck sat at the curb, the prods strapped to the top. Witzer sat in the cab, drinking a cup of coffee from the delicatessen. When I got in beside him, he handed me a cup and an egg sandwich on a hard roll wrapped in white paper. "We're off," he said. I cleared the sleep out of my eyes as he pulled away from the curb.

Our journey took us down the main street of town and then through the alley next to the Sheriff's office. This gave way to another small tree lined street we turned right on. As we headed away from the center of town, we passed Darlene's house, and I wondered what she'd done the previous night while I'd been at the celebration. I had a memory of her last time we were together. She was sitting naked against the wall of the abandoned barn by the edge of the swamp. Her blonde hair and face were aglow, illuminated by a beam of light that shone through a hole in the roof. She had the longest legs and her skin was pale and smooth. Taking a drag from her cigarette, she said, "Ernest, we gotta get out this town." She'd laid out for me her plan of escape, her desire to go to some city where civilization was in full swing. I just nodded, reluctant to be too enthusiastic. She was adventurous and I was a homebody, but I did care deeply for her. She tossed her cigarette, put out her arms and opened her legs, and then Witzer said, "Keep your eyes peeled now, boy," and her image melted away.

We were moving slowly along a dirt road, both of us looking up at the lower branches of the trees. The old man saw the first one. I didn't see her till he applied the brakes. He took a little notebook and stub of a pencil out of his shirt pocket. "Samantha Bocean," he whispered and put a check next to her name. We got out of the cab, and I helped him unlatch the prods and lay them on the ground beside the truck. She was resting across three branches in a magnolia tree, not too far from the ground. One arm and her long gray hair hung down, and she was turned so I could see her sleeping face.

"Get the ten," said Witzer, as he walked over to stand directly beneath her.

I did as I was told and then joined him.

"What d'ya say?" he asked. "Looks like this one's gonna be a peach."

"Well, I'm thinking if I get it on her left thigh and push her forward fast enough she'll flip as she falls and land perfectly."

Witzer said nothing but left me standing there and went and got in the truck. He started it up and drove it around to park so that the bed was precisely where we hoped she would land. He put it in park and left it running, and then got out and came and stood beside me. "Take a few deep breaths," he said. "And then let her fly."

I thought I'd be more nervous, but the training the old man had given me took hold and I knew exactly what to do. I aimed the prod and rested it gently on the top of her leg. Just as he'd told me, a real body was going to offer a little more resistance than one of the dummies, and I was ready for that. I took three big breaths and then shoved. She rolled slightly, and then tumbled forward, ass over head, landing with a thump on the mattresses, facing the morning sky. Witzer wheezed to beat the band, and said, "That's a solid ten." I was ecstatic.

The old man broke a twig next to Samantha's left ear and instantly her eyelids fluttered. Eventually she opened her eyes and smiled.

"How was your visit?" asked Witzer.

"I'll never get tired of that," she said. "It was wonderful."

We chatted with her for a few minutes, filling her in on how the party had gone at The Blind Ghost after she'd left. She didn't divulge to us what passed relative she'd met with, and we didn't ask. As my mentor had told me when I started, "There's a kind of etiquette to this. When in doubt, Silence is your best friend."

Samantha started walking back toward the center of town, and we loaded the prods onto the truck again. In no time, we were on our way, searching for the next sleeper. Luck was with us, for we found four in a row, fairly close by each other, Stan Joss, Moses T. Remarque, Berta Hull, and Becca Staney. All of them had chosen easy to get to perches in the lower branches of ancient oaks, and we dropped them, one, two, three, four, easy as could be. I never had to reach for anything longer than the 10, and the old man proved a genius at placing the truck just so. When each came around at the insistence of the snapping twig, they were cordial and seemed pleased with their experience. Moses even gave us a ten dollar tip for dropping him into the truck. Becca told us that she'd spoken to her mother, whom she'd missed terribly since the woman's death two years earlier. Even though they'd been blind drunk the night before, amazingly none of them appeared to be hung over, and each walked away with a perceptible spring in his or her step, even Moses, though he was still slightly bent at the waist by the arthritis.

Witzer said, "Knock on wood, of course, but this is the easiest year I can remember. The year your daddy won, we had to ride around for four solid hours before we found him out by the swamp." We found Ron White only a short piece up the road from where we'd found the cluster of four, and he was an easy job. I didn't get him to land on his back. He fell face first, not a desirable drop, but he came to none the worse for wear. After Ron, we had to ride for quite a while, heading out toward the edge of the swamp. I knew the only two left were Pete Hesiant and Henry Grass, and the thought of Henry started to get me nervous again. I was reluctant to show my fear, not wanting the old man to lose faith in me, but as we drove slowly along, I finally told Witzer about my recurring dream.

When I was done recounting what I thought was a premonition, Witzer sat in silence for a few moments and then said, "I'm glad you told me."

"I'll bet it's really nothing," I said.

"Henry's a big fellow," he said. "Why should you have all the fun. I'll drop him." And with this, the matter was settled. I realized I should have told him weeks ago when I first started having the dreams.

"Easy, boy," said Witzer with a wheeze and waved his hand as if wiping away my cares. "You've got years of this to go. You can't manage everything on the first harvest."

We searched everywhere for Pete and Henry—all along the road to the swamp, on the trails that ran through the woods, out along the meadow by the shot tower and Henry's own trailer. With the dilapidated wooden structure of the tower still in sight, we finally found Henry.

"Thar she blows," said Witzer, and he stopped the truck.

"Where?" I said, getting out of the truck, and the old man pointed straight up.

Over our heads, in a tall pine, Henry lay face down, his arms and legs spread so that they kept him up while the rest of his body was suspended over nothing. His head hung down as if in shame or utter defeat. He looked in a way like he was crucified, and I didn't like the look of that at all.

"Get me the 20," said Witzer, "and then pull the truck up."

I undid the prods from the roof, laid the other two on the ground by the side of the path, and ran the 20 over to the old man. By the time I went back to the truck, got it going, and turned it toward the drop spot, Witzer had the long pole in two hands and was sizing up the situation. As I pulled closer, he let the pole down and then waved me forward while eyeing back and forth, Henry and then the bed. He directed me to cut the wheel this way and that, reverse two feet, and then he gave me the thumbs up. I turned off the truck and got out.

"OK," he said. "This is gonna be a tricky one." He lifted the prod up and up and rested the soft end against Henry's chest. "You're gonna have to help me here. We're gonna push straight up on his chest so that his arms flop down and clear the branches, and then as we let him down we're gonna slide the pole, catch him at the belt buckle and give him a good nudge there to flip him as he falls."

I looked up at where Henry was, and then I just stared at Witzer.

"Wake up, boy!" he shouted.

I came to and grabbed the prod where his hands weren't.

"On three," he said. He counted off and then we pushed. Henry was heavy as ten sacks of rocks. "We got him," cried Witzer, "now slide it." I did and only then did I look up. "Push," the old man said. We gave it one more shove and Henry went into a swan dive, flipping like an Olympic athlete off the high board. When I saw him in mid-fall, my knees went weak and the air left me. He landed on his back with a loud thud directly in the middle of the mattresses, dust from the old cushions roiling up around him.

We woke Henry easily enough, sent him on his way to town, and were back in the truck. For the first time that morning I breathed a sigh of relief. "Easiest harvest I've ever been part of," said Witzer. We headed further down the path toward the swamp, scanning the branches for Pete Hesiant. Sure enough, in the same right manner with which everything else had fallen into place we found him curled up on his side in the branches of an enormous maple tree. With the first cursory glance at him, the old man determined that Pete would require no more than a 10. After we got the prods off the truck and positioned it under our last drop, Witzer insisted that I take him down. "One more to keep your skill up through the rest of the year," he said.

It was a simple job. Pete had found a nice perch with three thick branches beneath him. As I said, he was curled up on his side, and I couldn't see him all too well, so I just nudged his upper back and he rolled over like a small boulder. The drop was precise, and he hit the center of the mattresses, but the instant he was in the bed of the pickup, I knew something was wrong. He'd fallen too quickly for me to register it sooner, but as he lay there, I now noticed that there was someone else with him. Witzer literally jumped to the side of the truck bed and stared in.

"What in fuck's name," said the old man. "Is that a kid he's got with him?"

I saw the other body there, naked, in Pete's arms. There was long blond hair, that much was sure. It could have been a kid, but I thought I saw in the jumble, a full size female breast.

Witzer reached into the truck bed, grabbed Pete by the shoulder and rolled him away from the other form. Then the two of us stood there in stunned silence. The thing that lay there wasn't a woman or a child but both and neither. The body was twisted and deformed, the size of an eight year old but with all the characteristics of maturity, if you know what I mean. And that face . . . lumpen and distorted, brow bulging and from the left temple to the chin erupted in a range of discolored ridges.

"Is that Lonette?" I whispered, afraid the thing would awaken.

"She's dead, ain't she?" said Witzer in as low a voice, and his Adam's apple bobbed.

We both knew she was, but there she or some twisted copy of her lay. The old man took a handkerchief from his back pocket and brought it up to his mouth. He closed his eyes and leaned against the side of the truck. A bird flew by low overhead. The sun shone and leaves fell in the woods on both sides of the path.

Needless to say, when we moved again, we weren't breaking any twigs. Witzer told me to leave the prods and get in the truck. He started it up, and we drove slowly, like about fifteen miles an hour, into the center of town. We drove in complete silence. The place was quiet as a ghost town, no doubt everyone sleeping off the celebration, but we saw that Sheriff Jolle's cruiser was in front of the bunker-like concrete building that was the police station. The old man parked and went in. As he and the sheriff appeared at the door, I got out of the truck cab and joined them.

"What are you talking about?" Jolle said as they passed me and headed for the truck bed. I followed behind them.

"Shhh," said Witzer. When they finally were looking down at the sleeping couple, Pete and whatever that Lonette thing was, he added, "That's what I'm fucking talking about." He pointed his crooked old finger and his hand was obviously trembling.

Jolle's jaw dropped open after the second or two it took to sink in. "I never . . . ," said the Sheriff, and that's all he said for a long while.

Witzer whispered, "Pete brought her back with him."

"What kind of crazy shit is this?" asked Jolle and he turned quickly and looked at me as if I had an answer. Then he looked back at Witzer. "What the hell happened? Did he dig her up?"

"She's alive," said the old man. "You can see her breathing, but she got bunched up or something in the transfer from there to here."

"Bunched up," said Jolle. "There to here? What in Christ's name . . . " He shook his head and removed his shades. Then he turned to me again and said, "Boy, go get Doc Kvench."

In calling the doctor, I didn't know what to tell him, so I just said there was an emergency over at the Sheriff's office and that he was needed. I didn't stick around and wait for him, because I had to keep moving. To stop would mean I'd have to think too deeply about the return of Lonette Hesiant. By the time I got back to the truck, Henry Grass had also joined Jolle and Witzer, having walked into town to get something to eat after his dream ordeal of the night before. As I drew close to them, I heard Henry saying, "She's come from another dimension. I've read about things like this. And from what I experienced last night, talking to my dead brother, I can tell you that place seems real enough for this to happen."

Jolle looked away from Henry at me as I approached, and then his gaze shifted over my head and he must have caught sight of the doctor. "God job," said the Sheriff and put his hand on my shoulder as I leaned forward to catch my breath.

"Hey, doc," he said as Kvench drew close, "you got a theory about this?"

The doctor stepped up to the truck bed and, clearing the sleep from his eyes, looked down at where the sheriff was pointing. Doctor Kvench had seen it all in his years in Gatchfield—birth, death, blood, body rot, but the instant he laid his eyes on the new Lonette, the color drained out of him, and he grimaced like he'd just taken a big swig of Witzer's herb mix. The effect on him was dramatic, and Henry stepped up next to him and held him up with one big tattooed arm across his back. Kvench brushed Henry off and turned away from the truck. I thought for a second that he was going to puke.

We waited for his diagnosis. Finally he turned back and said, "Where did it come from?"

"It fell out of the tree with Pete this morning," said Witzer.

"I signed the death certificate for that girl five months ago," said the doctor.

"She's come from another dimension . . . " said Henry, launching into one of his Bermuda Triangle explanations, but Jolle held a hand up to silence him. Nobody spoke then and the Sheriff started pacing back and forth, looking into the sky and then at the ground. It was obvious that he was having some kind of silent argument with himself, cause every few seconds he'd either nod or shake his head. Finally, he put his open palms to his face for a moment, rubbed his forehead and cleared his eyes. Then he turned to us.

"Look, here's what we're gonna do. I decided. We're going to get Pete out of that truck without waking him and put him on the cot in the station. Will he stay asleep if we move him?" he asked Witzer.

The old man nodded. "As long as you don't shout his name or break a twig near his ear, he should keep sleeping till we wake him."

"OK," continued Jolle. "We get Pete out of the truck, and then we drive that thing out into the woods, we shoot it and bury it."

Everybody looked around at everybody else. The doctor said, "I don't know if I can be part of that."

"You're gonna be part of it," said Jolle, "or right this second you're taking full responsibility for its care. And I mean full responsibility."

"It's alive, though," said Kvench.

"But it's a mistake," said the sheriff, "either of nature or God or whatever."

"Doc, I agree with Jolle," said Witzer, "I never seen anything that felt so wrong to me than what I'm looking at in the back of that truck."

"You want to nurse that thing until it dies on its own?" Jolle said to the doctor. "Think of what it'll do to Pete to have to deal with it."

Kvench looked down and shook his head. Eventually he whispered, "You're right."

"Boy?" Jolle said to me.

My mouth was dry and my head was swimming a little. I nodded.

"Good," said the sheriff. Henry added that he was in. It was decided that we all participate and share in the act of disposing of it. Henry and the sheriff gently lifted Pete out of the truck and took him into the station house. When they appeared back outside, Jolle told Witzer and me to drive out to the woods in the truck and that he and Henry and Kvench would follow in his cruiser.

For the first few minutes of the drive out, Witzer said nothing. We passed Pete Hesiant's small yellow house and upon seeing it I immediately started thinking about Lonette, and how beautiful she'd been. She and Pete had only been in their early thirties, a very handsome couple. He was thin and gangly and had been a star basketball player for Gatchfield, but never tall enough to turn his skill into a college scholarship. They'd been high school sweethearts. He finally found work as a municipal handy man, and had that good natured youth-going-to-seed personality of the washed up, once lauded athlete.

Lonette had worked the cash register at the grocery. I remembered her passing by our front porch on the way to work the evening shift one afternoon, and I overheard her talking to my mother about how she and Pete had decided to try to start a family. I'm sure I wasn't supposed to be privy to this conversation, but whenever she passed in front of our house, I tried to make it a point of being near a window. I heard every word through the screen. The very next week, though, I learned that she had some kind of disease. That was three years ago. She slowly grew more haggard through the following seasons. Pete tried to take care of her on his own, but I don't think it had gone all too well. At her funeral, Henry had to hold him back from climbing into the grave after her.

"Is this murder?" I asked Witzer after he'd turned onto the dirt path and headed out toward the woods.

He looked over at me and said nothing for a second. "I don't know, Ernest," he said. "Can you murder someone who's already dead? Can you murder a dream? What would you have us do?" He didn't ask the last question angrily but as if he was really looking for another plan than Jolle's.

I shook my head.

"I'll never see things the same again," he said. "I keep thinking I'm gonna wake up any minute now."

We drove on for another half mile and then he pulled the truck off the path and under a cluster of oak. As we got out of the cab, the Sheriff parked next to us. Henry, the doctor, and Jolle got out of the cruiser, and all five of us gathered at the back of the pickup. It fell to Witzer and me to get her out of the truck and lay her on the ground some feet away. "Careful," whispered the old man, as he leaned over the wall of the bed and slipped his arms under her. I took the legs, and when I touched her skin a shiver went through me. Her body was heavier than I thought, and her sex was staring me right in the face, covered with short hair thick as twine. She was breathing lightly, obviously sleeping, and her pupils moved rapidly beneath her closed lids like she was dreaming. She had a powerful aroma, flowers and candy, sweet to the point of sickening.

We got her on the ground without waking her, and the instant I let go of her legs, I stepped outside the circle of men. "Stand back," said Jolle. The others moved away. He pulled his gun out of its holster with his left hand and made the sign of the cross with his right. Leaning down, he put the gun near her left temple, and then cocked the hammer back. The hammer clicked into place with the sound of a breaking twig and right then her eyes shot open. Four grown men jumped backward in unison. "Good lord," said Witzer. "Do it," said Kvench. I looked to Jolle and he was staring down at her as if in a trance. Her eyes had no color. They were wide and shifting back and forth. She started taking deep raspy breaths and then sat straight up. A low mewing noise came from her chest, the sound of a cat or a scared child. Then she started talking backwards talk, some foreign language never heard on earth before, babbling frantically and drooling.

Jolle fired. The bullet caught her in the side of the head and threw her onto her right shoulder. The side of her face, including her ear, blew off, and this black stuff, not blood, splattered all over, flecks of it staining Jolle's pants and shirt and face. The side of her head was smoking. She lay there writhing in what looked like a pool of oil, and he shot her again and again, emptying the gun into her. The sight of it brought me to my knees, and I puked. When I looked up, she'd stopped moving. Tears were streaming down Witzer's face. Kvench was shaking. Henry looked as if he'd been turned to stone. Jolle's finger kept pulling the trigger, but there were no rounds left.

After Henry tamped down the last shovel full of dirt on her grave, Jolle made us swear never to say a word to anyone about what had happened. I pledged that oath as did the others. Witzer took me home, no doubt having silently decided I shouldn't be there when they woke Pete. When I got to the house, I went straight to bed and slept for an entire day, only getting up in time to get to the gas station for work the next morning. The only dream I had was an infuriating and frustrating one of Lester II, eating hard boiled eggs and explaining it all to me but in backwards talk and gibberish so I couldn't make out any of it. Carrying the memory of that Drunk Harvest miracle around with me was like constantly having a big black bubble of night afloat in the middle of my waking thoughts. As autumn came on and passed and then winter bore down on Gatchfield, the insidious strength of it never diminished. It made me quiet and moody, and my relationship with Darlene suffered.

I kept my distance from the other four conspirators. It went so far as we tried not to even recognize each others' presence when we passed on the street. Only Witzer still waved at me from his pick up when he'd drive by, and if I was the attendant when he came into the station for gas, he'd say, "How are you, boy?" I'd nod and that would be it. Around Christmas time I'd heard from my father that Pete Hesiant had lost his mind, and was unable to go to work, would break down crying at a moment's notice, couldn't sleep, and was being treated by Kvench with all manner of pills.

Things didn't get any better come spring. Pete shot the side of his head off with a pistol. Mrs. Marfish, who'd gone to bring him a pie she'd baked to cheer him up, discovered him lying dead in a pool of blood on the back porch of the little yellow house. Then Sheriff Jolle took ill and was so bad off with whatever he had, he couldn't get out of bed. He deputized Reed Bocean, the barkeep and the most sensible man in town, to look after Gatchfield in his absence. Reed did a good job as Sheriff and Samantha double timed it at The Blind Ghost—both solid citizens.

In the early days of May, I burned my hand badly at work on a hot car engine and my boss drove me over to Kvench's office to get it looked after. While I was in his treatment room with him, and he was wrapping my hand in gauze, he leaned close to me and whispered, "I think I know what happened." I didn't even make a face, but stared ahead at the eye chart on the wall, not really wanting to hear anything about the incident. "Gatchfield's so isolated that change couldn't get in from the outside, so Nature sent it from within," he said. "Mutation. From the dream." I looked at him. He was nodding, but I saw that his goatee had gone squirrely, there was this over-eager gleam in his eyes, and his breath smelled like medicine. I knew right then he'd been more than sampling his own pills. I couldn't get out of there fast enough.

June came, and it was a week away from the day that Witzer and I were to begin practicing for the Drunk Harvest again. I dreaded the thought of it to the point where I was having a hard time eating or sleeping. After work one evening, as I was walking home, the old man pulled up next to me in his pick-up truck. He stopped and opened the window. I was going to keep walking, but he called, "Boy, get in. Take a ride with me."

I made the mistake of looking over at him. "It's important," he said. I got in the cab and we drove slowly off down the street.

I blurted out that I didn't think I'd be able to manage the Harvest and how screwed up the thought of it was making me, but he held his hand up and said, "Shh, shh, I know." I quieted down and waited for him to talk. A few seconds passed and then he said, "I've been to see Jolle. You haven't seen him have you?"

I shook my head.

"He's a gonner for sure. He's got some kind of belly rot, and, I swear to you he's got a deathberry bush growing out of his insides . . . while he's still alive, no less. Doc Kvench just keeps feeding him pills, but he'd be better off taking a hedge clipper to him."

"Are you serious?" I said.

"Boy, I'm dead serious." Before I could respond, he said, "Now look, when the time for the celebration comes around, we're all going to have to participate in it as if nothing had happened. We made our oath to the Sheriff. That's bad enough, but what happens when somebody's dead relative tells them in a Night Whiskey dream what we did, what happened with Lonette?"

I was trembling and couldn't bring myself to speak.

"Tomorrow night—are you listening to me?—tomorrow night I'm leaving my truck unlocked with the keys in the ignition. You come to my place and take it and get the fuck out of Gatchfield."

I hadn't noticed but we were now parked in front of my house. He leaned across me and opened my door. "Get as far away as you can, boy," he said. The next day, I called in sick to work, withdrew all my savings from the bank, and talked to Darlene. That night, good to his word, the keys were in the old pick up. I noticed there was a new used truck parked next to the old one on his lot to cover when the one we took went missing. I'd left my parents a letter about how Darlene and I had decided to elope, and that they weren't to worry. I'd call them.

We fled to the biggest brightest city we could find, and the rush and maddening business of the place, the distance from home, our combined struggle to survive at first and then make our way was a curative better than any pill the doctor could have prescribed. Every day there was change and progress and crazy news on the television, and these things served to shrink the black bubble in my thoughts.

Still to this day, though, so many years later, there's always an evening near the end of September when I sit down to a Night Whiskey, so to speak, and Gatchfield comes back to me in my dreams like some lost relative I'm both terrified to behold and want nothing more than to put my arms around and never let go.

A FINE MAGIC

—

Margo Lanagan

Well, in the town where these two beautiful daughters lived there was a fascinator, name of Gallantine. He was neither young nor hand-some, but he had no wife and he was as interested as any of the young men were in getting one of the girls—if not the rich elder girl, the more beautiful younger one. Whichever he won, he would be an object of other men's envy—and even magic-men are not immune to wanting that.

Gallantine did all the things that those young men were trying. First he put himself regularly in the young women's way, happening by outside their house just as they crossed from door to carriage, or arriving at the edge of the path as they made their daily park promenade. Tall and thin in his dark suit, he lifted his dark hat and lowered his gaze to their lovely feet as they passed.

On one of these occasions, seeing that the mamma's carry-dog was suffering some kind of skin affliction, he struck up a conversation with her, professing more interest than he truly felt in the care of such animals. Afterwards he sent her a pot of a cream to apply to the dog's skin. He had magicked the cream both to cure the lesions and to engender tenderness towards himself in any person who touched it. Which ended with my lady's chambermaid developing quite a crush on him, while Mamma herself, who almost always wore gloves when carrying the dog, came no closer than being able to abide having Gallantine near, where before she had felt a natural repugnance towards his self-conscious bearing, his funereal clothes and his conspicuous lack of associates or friends. The two beautiful daughters, who thoroughly disliked the dog, no more noticed him than they noticed iron fenceposts or singular grass blades among the many.

Gallantine was thus driven to exert his powers more forcefully to impress himself upon the young ladies. By various subtle hand-wavings he managed an invitation to one of the mamma's afternoons, and to hold the girls' admirers at bay long enough to engage first the older then the younger in several minutes' 'conversation', during which each responded most politely to his observations on the weather, the present company, and the pleasantness of walking in parks.

He came away satisfied that he had fixed himself in their memories as an intriguing man of the world. He read interest into the smiles he had collected, quickenings of the heart into the girls' casting their glances downward or away from him. He was very hopeful of his chances with either of the lovelies.

He next engineered his attendance at a ball at which the daughters were to be present. He went to great pains and some expense to prepare himself, travelling up to the port city to have himself outfitted by a good tailor. Once he was dressed he put what he felt must be an irresistible glamour all around himself, and he was rewarded at the ball by many glances, dances and fan-flutterings from the older women, as well as a dance with each of the daughters. He was light on his feet, you can imagine, which left the girls free to concentrate on words, and words they had in plenty, buoyed up by their excitement at being out in society and by far the most marriageable persons in the room, indeed in the town. Gallantine read their happy chatter entirely as regard for himself. Watching them in exactly the same play with others on the dance floor, he thought the girls very kind for their patience with lesser men when their hearts were so clearly leaning and yearning towards his own.

When he felt that enough such meetings had taken place, Gallantine made his feelings known, first to the older daughter and then, on being rejected by her repeatedly, to the younger. At first made gentle by her own surprise and by the strong glamours he had carried to the meeting, this lovely girl did not utterly reject him, but soon, with her sister's and her mother's horrified exclamations ringing in her ears, she found sufficient will, reinforced by true and natural feelings of revulsion, to be definite enough in her refusal of him that he could hold no further hopes of a match with her.

Well, it's never a good idea to get on the wrong side of a fascinator, is it? For he's unlikely just to retire and lick his wounds. Gallantine went off to his house—which was not small and not large, and not in a good part of town nor yet in a bad, but which of course bore no womanly touches barring some lace at the windows put there by his late mother that, if touched (which it never was), would have crumbled from age and poor quality—and he brewed himself a fine magic. It was so powerful that to all intents and purposes Gallantine did not exist for a while, except as instrument or agent of his own urge to revenge. And so at this point in the story it behoves us to leave Gallantine in his formless obsession and join the two daughters, through whose eyes the working-out of that obsession is much clearer.

So here is the younger girl, alone in her room, sitting up in bed writing a breathless account of that evening's events in her day-journal.

And here is the older, sitting more solemnly in front of her mirror, having just accepted (her father is to be consulted tomorrow) an offer of marriage to a most suitable gentleman: young, fine-looking, and possessed of a solid fortune, and of a character to which her heart can genuinely warm.

Under each girl's door, with a small but significant sound, is slipped a white envelope. Each starts up, and crosses her room; each takes the envelope up and listens for—but does not hear—receding footsteps outside. The seal on the envelope is unfamiliar, marvellous; breaking it releases a clean, pine-y, adventurous scent onto the bed-room air, and each girl breathes this scent in.

Step through the door, says the card inside. Each girl hesitates, then reaches to take the doorknob. But the doorknob won't be taken, will it? The hands—the younger tentative, the older more resolute—close to fists on nothing.

Step through the door. Two hands touch two doors, and find the timber to be, in fact, a stable brown smoke. The hands sink into the surface, the smoke curls above the pale skin like stirred-up silt. The moment passes when they might choose whether to stay or go, and they step through.

And they are in a wood, a dim, cold, motionless wood. The trees are poles of indigo with maybe foliage, maybe cloud, on high; the light is blue, the ground is covered with drifts of snow.

They see each other, the one in her white nightgown and wrap, the other in her dance-dress, the hothouse orchid still in her hair. Each gives a cry of relief, and they run together.

"I'm so glad you're here, sister!"

"Where are we? In a dream?"

"I've never known a dream so cold!"

They clutch arms and look around.

"There, look! Is that a fire?" For warm yellow lights move, far off among the trees.

"It must be! Let us go and warm ourselves!"

They set off. Bare or in thin embroidered slippers, their feet are soon numb with cold. But the ground under the snow is even, and the strange trees are smooth and sprout no projections to catch their clothing or otherwise hinder them. Music floats to meet them, music such as they've never danced to, beguiling, rhythmical, minor-keyed. Their minds don't know what to make of it. It seems ugly, yet it attracts them. It is clumsily, grossly appropriate. It is a puzzle, and to solve it they must move closer and hear it more clearly.

Apart from this music the wood is like a large and silent room. No bird flies through it; no wind disturbs the air. The chill rises like a blue fume from the snow; it showers with the grey light from above.

The music deepens and brightens as they stumble on: various hummings as of rubbed wet crystal, and many different pitches of tinkling, or jingling, adorn its upper reaches. It grows other sounds that are nearly voices, uttering nearly words, words the two daughters want to hear, are convinced they must hear, if they are to understand this adventure. A deep, slow, sliding groan travels to them through the ground.

"It is!" says the older girl, peering around a tree. "It's a carousel! An enormous one! Beautiful!"

"Oh, I'm so cold!"

They hurry now, and soon are in the clearing where the magnificent creation revolves. The music is rosy-fleshed arms gathering them up in a dance; the horses rise and fall with the rhythm, the foxes too, the carriages and sleighs, the swans and cats and elephants. The lightbulbs are golden; the mirrors shed sunlight, the carven faces laughter; the revolving makes a breeze that flows warmly spring-like out into the daughters' faces, that lifts the manes and tails and furs and feathers of the carved animals, that brightens the horses' flanks until the older girl is convinced she sees galloping muscles move, until the younger would vow on a bible that she saw a fly land on that bay's shoulder, and be shaken off by a flesh-tremor.

And they would swear that, for a moment, each creature, each sleigh, carried a figure: pretty girls in their detailed fashions, fine-figured young men waving their hats, all with such joyful expressions, all with such eagerness in their bodies and gestures, that the daughters' single impulse is to join them, to be in among the throng, so warm in colour and mood, to be swept up and a part of that strange heavy-lively crystalline music—

Which winds, with a spirited suddenness, to a triumphant flour-ish and stop. There is no one on the carousel. Only the creatures stand in the golden light, a hoof raised here, a head lowered there. Then the hoof strikes the wooden floor, the head lifts and the lips whiffle; an ostrich turns and blinks at the daughters down its beak. Life, minor life, entrances each girl's eye.

"Look, the eagle! His wings are like fire!"

"So beautiful! So warm! I wish that music would start again."

They stand in the snow, clutching each other.

"Do you suppose we are meant to ride it? In this dream?"

"Look, there are steps up to it—of course we are, sister! Come! Which mount will you choose?"

"Oh, are you sure?" But she climbs the stairs after her sister.

And there follows delight—the last delight of their lives. They run about, in the warmth, with no mammas or chaperones to restrain them, choosing now the lion for his sumptuous warm mane and wise eye; now the cat for its flexibility and fur and for the fish, flashing rainbows, it holds in its jaws; now the sleigh for its quilts and candles; now the eagle again for the grandeur of his red-gold wings.

Finally the older daughter chooses the black stallion with the bejewelled harness and the saddle of warm bronze leather. The younger finds a strawberry roan nearby with an improbably frothing cream mane, all its harness a supple blood red. She climbs astride and it tosses its head, showering her with tiny white blossoms, sweetly scented, that melt like snowflakes on her skin. Delighted, she turns to her sister, in time to see her glister with tiny melting gems, shaken from the coal-black's mane.

"What bewitching animals!" she cries—then, "Oh!" as the beautiful machine creeps into motion around them. The music bursts out from the central fantasia of mirrors and organ pipes and glossy coloured figures and gold-painted arabesques.

All is beautiful and wonderful, warm and alive while the carousel gathers speed. Everywhere they look something catches the eye: the deft paintwork that makes that cherub look so cunning, the glitter of eagle feathers as the lights pass over, the way the giraffe runs beside them, clumsy and elegant at the same time, the lozenges of *trompel'oeil* that offer whole worlds in a glance, brine-plashy seascapes, folly-bedecked parks, city squares thronged with characters and statuary, alpine vistas where one might as easily spring up into the sky as tumble to the crags below.

And their ears and their hearts are too full of the weighty rhythms of the music to allow proper thought. And the beasts below them are just alive enough to intrigue them, and to respond to the supple reins. The carousel reaches its full speed, and they gallop there awhile, calling to each other, perfectly happy.

And then it spins just a little faster.

The music accelerates, veers upward in pitch, sounds a little mad, a little wild. There is a jerk as of slipping gear-wheels, and the roan plunges.

"Sister!" The younger girl grasps the gold-and-white-striped pole to which the horse is fixed.

But her sister is wrestling with the reins of her own bounding stallion. Now, half-tossed from the saddle, she clings to the horse's pole, struggles to regain her seat.

So frightened are they, so dizzied by the machine's whirling, so busy with their desperate cries for each other's aid, that they do not see the shiny paintwork of the poles fade to a glassy blue in their grasp, the warmer colours drain down, down out of the poles entirely. They do not discover until too late that—

"Sister, my hands! They are frozen fast!"

The machine and the music spin on, but the horses' movements slow and cease. Their painted coats—glossy black, pink-brown—fade to blue where the pole strikes through them, and the blueness spreads across the saddles under the folds of nightgown and dance-dress. The girls' fine cotton drawers are no protection against the terrible coldness. It locks their thighs to the saddles; it locks their seats; it strikes up into their women's parts, fast as flame, clear as glass, cold as ice.

"Sister!"

"Sister, help me!"

They gaze aghast at each other. The animals between and around them fade to blue, freeze to stillness, beaks agape, teeth points of icy light, manes and tails carven ice. The music raves, high-pitched and hurrying. The golden lights become ice-bulbs gathering only the blue snow-light below, the grey cloud-light above. The forest spins around the carousel, a mad, icy blur.

The park promenade. It is early spring and still quite cold.

Gallantine, raising his hat to every muffled personage who passes, is older now; his figure is fuller, almost imposing in the well-cut dark coat. His new wife, upon his arm, is slender, dark-haired, and has more than a touch of magic about her.

She glances over her shoulder, back along the path. "If I'm not mistaken," she says, removing her hand from his arm and placing it in her ermine muff, "one of those ladies once had a place in your affections."

"The Leblanc sisters? Well, they were beauties in their time, though you may find that hard to credit now."

"Did they always clutch each other so?" she says, glancing back again. 'Did they always carry themselves in that strange way?"

"On the contrary, they were very fine dancers, once," says Gallantine mildly.

His wife is silent until he will look at her, and then for a while of looking.

She laughs a very little, through her beautiful nose. "How very gauche," she murmurs, narrowing her eyes at him. "How very crude of you." Her mouth is lovely, too. It is the only spot of colour in the whole wintry park. She hisses at him, almost inaudibly. "There are so many things for which to *punish* you."

"Madam." His voice cracks with gratification. He offers her his arm.

She reattaches herself to him, and they walk on.

NATURALLY

––––––

Daniel Handler

It was the sort of day when people walk in the park and solve problems. "We'll simply call the taxi company, David, and request a large one, like one of those vans" is the sort of thing you would overhear if you were overhearing in the park. Hank was. He heard that one, and "Let's tell them six and then they'll show up at six-thirty" and "America just needs to get the hell out of there and not look back." Hank lay on an obscure corner of the grass, eyes closed, not moving, getting cold even in the nice day, and he overheard "Maybe we shouldn't move in together at all" and "If taxi companies don't take requests the company will rent you a car probably" and "The guests can gather out on the porch and then come in when dinner's ready" and "Oh my fucking Christ! Don't look, honey, don't look! The man is dead, honey, that's a dead man, oh God somebody call the police."

It was not a mistake. It was perfectly natural, although it ruined the whole day in the park for everyone who was there. Certainly for Hank. It made all the other problems recede for a little bit, although soon they returned, which is as natural as the park itself. Grass, trees, flowers trampled by the paramedics, a few people sticking around to watch with the small wisdom that reaches us in such moments: It is all natural. Someday we will all be dead people but in the meantime we have these problems to solve.

The police asked bystanders who did not see it happen, but there weren't any details. Only a body, what seemed like the end of a story to anyone who spoke to the police. "I found him, officer, but I don't know anything else and I must walk around the park and talk with my girlfriend about myself because after all I did not see it happen and I did not know him."

Hank was all packed up, like a song about a man leaving a woman. A zipper closed across his dead face like he had never been there, only a duffel bag. Hank's life was over. He kept his eyes closed, slowly figuring it out and wondering how it would go—a bright light or what—surprised that, given that we all wonder it, you would have to wait to find out like anything else.

An interval here, nearly indescribable.

It happened. Hank got up while the morgue guy was signing a piece of paper. He saw his own body lying on the thing but to tell you the truth that wasn't what he was most interested in looking at. He had seen himself naked and so had quite a few other people, although some of them do not remember. Hank was more curious that he could walk through the rooms of the place, but even this faded almost immediately. Hank moved through this time and did not know what to do with it, those first few blank days at a new job. Where do I go? What do I do? What time do we meet and where do we go for lunch and where are the people who are nicer? He sat on benches and tried to get in a spooky mood. But all the things he could see were all the things you see anyway. People having sex, sure, a couple of times. But Hank had seen movies in which people had sex, and those people did not know he was in the room either. We do not want to be in a room and people not to know. Alive or dead this begins to hurt our feelings. We want to be seen. We want to haunt people, if they'll have us, and if they won't have us we feel as sad as we do in life.

And yet it was nothing like life, this thing he was living through. It was as far from life as pizza served on an airplane is from Italy, even if the plane is flying over Italy at the time. People did not see him and so he grew hungry. He did not need to eat, but who does not go into the place anyway sometimes, and order a snack something, just for something to do and because you are not a ghost? The girl at the counter stood and looked at the mouth of a honey bear. It was a clear plastic thing, shaped in the shape of a real bear, somewhat, with honey instead of blood and organs and bones. The girl at the counter was young and named Lila unless the nametag was a joke too, and she was peering into a hole in the fake bear's head to see what the problem was. "It keeps sticking!" she called behind her. Hank overheard her call it as he stood there dimly hoping she would look up and give him a donut if he asked. The donuts sat there under a clear dome, covered in icing and sprinkles, waiting to be chosen and picked up by the pretty girl's tongs. But Hank felt the thin weight of ignored and left the place without his snack. Woe filled him at least halfway. He had missed his funeral because no one had told him when it was, and always this feeling of *What if this is heaven and I'm screwing it up? What if I'm also screwing this up?*

Hank kicked a few things around in the street and floated through the door of a private home. A man was opening his mail, who cares. Down the block was the neighbor, an older woman who had sent the letter. There Hank found he could pick up pens, which is where they go when you can't find them. The cat saw him do it. "Mr. Mittens, what's that?" she said. "What do you see, Mr. Mittens, that you behave like that?" Hank gave Mr. Mittens the finger, not for the first time. He walked out holding the pens like a dozen skinny roses for no one he could think of who would see him.

But it turns out someone did. Back at the park, Hank was revisiting the scene of the crime in the hopes of haunting maybe. He walked down to the stables where the girls look at the horses and the boys wonder if it's time to go home. Hank steered fairly clear because you never know with horses. He stood on the lawn and cast a shadow over a woman eating cookies on a blanket. The cookies are a favorite of my wife's, dull biscuits with a chocolate picture on top, of a boy eating one of the cookies. The boy on the cookie sees the cookie on the cookie, so why wouldn't the woman see Hank? And she did and said, "Hey."

"Hey yourself," Hank said, very happy.

"You're in the light is what I mean," said the woman, but she was smiling. "Do you want to sit down so you're not blocking my light?"

Hank got on the blanket and the sun shone on both of them. "Do I get a cookie?" he asked.

"I don't think so," the woman said. "For years my husband ate more than his share of cookies. This is the first time I'm in the park without him. I told myself I'm going to eat all these cookies myself and Joe won't have a single one."

"You'll get sick," Hank said.

"That is the trouble," the woman agreed. "When the marriage is over there's no one to hold your head when you're sick in the toilet. But there were other reasons, you know. It wasn't just all the cookies."

"Of course not," Hank said.

The woman sighed. The joking part with the cookies relented a little, and she stared out at where the horses were living in individual pens. "It was sad, actually," she said, "and it's sad that I'm talking to a stranger in the park about it."

"I guess you don't remember me," Hank said. "I'm Hank Hayride."

"Hank Hayride?" the woman said. "That's your name, or are you the king of a hayride company?"

"I'm no king," Hank said. "We went to high school together. You're Eddie Terhune."

"High school?" the woman said.

"Go Magpies!" Hank said. "You were in Ms. Wylie's class."

"Hank *Hayride*?" she said. Eddie looked up for a moment like Hank was still blocking her light. "*Hank* Hayride? That can't be right."

"It's right all right," Hank said. "I had a crush on you the whole time."

"In Wylie?" Eddie said. "It was her with the chivalry, right? And old poems about love?"

"You didn't even know I existed," Hank said.

"That much is clear," Eddie said. "What was I doing in that class while you were crushing on me?"

Hank looked over at the horses too and watched a bird land on the fence and then drop to the ground, dead or clumsy. "Fiddling with your hair," he said. "You would take this pen you had that was red with the gold type of a company across one side. The cap was a strange shape like the edge of a pier. I could draw it for you now from the memory of it. You would chew on this thing like a bone and then reed it through your hair, and your hair would curl over it in sort of a waterfall way and you never even noticed."

"Tell me," Eddie said. "Tell me you haven't loved me ever since and followed me here or something scary."

"No no no," Hank said. "I used to look at you and think of that song where it says it's not the way that you smile or the way you do your hair, even though it was probably both those things."

"You're not putting me at ease," Eddie said, "in terms of are you in creepy love with me since high school?"

"The answer is no," Hank said, "because the point is I don't like that song anymore. It's stupid, the song, and anyway I graduated high school, you know."

"And?" Eddie said.

"And," Hank said, "I've been in other kinds of love. My life has been hard though, I guess you'd say. But I didn't come to the park to find you. I haven't been here in a while because I got beat up here real bad, like with a knife."

"Oh my God," Eddie said, "but you look fine. You look okay. I guess you didn't die."

Now was not the time to tell her. It never is, right when you meet someone, slap them with a big secret when they're trying to enjoy themselves. It is natural to let the worst parts of ourselves hide in the shade, while the sun shines down on our features like shimmering hair. "I guess not," Hank said. "I guess you brought me back to life." There is an interval here too, and it is also nearly impossible to write about. A short version would be, Eddie Terhune gave him a cookie. But this is not the description I mean. Something closer is, my wife and I once were in an automobile. We were not married but had moved to New York and were driving someplace where inexpensive furniture might live. We were very quiet in the car, for no reason, and the land outside the car window bobbed by us, flat, unnoticed except for the landmarks that told us where to turn. We were quiet, quiet, quiet, just the engine humming us toward a sofa we might afford, or lamps, and in the quiet my wife spoke up and said something suddenly.

"Cookies," she said.

Why did she say this? We did not care. We laughed the rest of the way, because the point of this story is, it is not the cookies. It is the love. My wife could eat all the cookies and it would not change the love, and if she ate all those cookies I would hold her head while she threw them up, and this too is part of the love. It does not matter if Eddie gave Hank a cookie or not. The cookies do not matter. It is not the cookies that matter, or the donuts suffering under the dome, or the horses in the pasture or the honey in the bear or the duffel bag that will close around us when our day in the park is over. There is only the laughing across the land as the car moves you along, on your way someplace with love in the car. It is not the things; it is the way the things are done, and Eddie and Hank fell in love in the way it is done. Naturally they went to restaurants and naturally they went to bed, and they were comfortable in the bed at the end of the evening. Eddie even stood up from the bed without a sheet around her body to get a glass of water. She was thirsty, but what mattered was her body, not shy, in the doorway of the bathroom as they looked each other over again.

"You have a handsome face," she said, "and you haven't let yourself go in the ass department, Hank Hayride."

"No," Hank said. "You're thinking of another guy. Remember Keith, from the swim team? He even had a handsome name."

"Your name is handsome enough," said Eddie. "Are you hungry? Do you want to go out someplace? It's past lunchtime now, or an early dinner. Around the same corner I live on is a magic Chinese restaurant. The Lantern something. Something Lantern. I haven't been there since Joe, when we had a fight. It was a big fat fight, but I feel like I lost that weight, so we could go and have the fried dumplings."

"Sounds good to me," Hank said, "and maybe a sesame something. Chicken."

"Did you really go to high school with me?" Eddie said. "Because I still don't remember you from then, and I could check around."

Hank stared at the ceiling and sang the song:

> *We're the Monteverdi Magpies,*
> *And we're here to win the game,*
> *From coast to coast we win the most,*
> *And you'll go down the same.*

> *Ev'ry team is beaten,*
> *And ev'ry player dies,*
> *You stupid geeks will feel the beaks*
> *Of the pow-er-ful Magpies!*

By now Eddie had joined in and flopped down on top of Hank in his sheet. "It's a terrible verse," she said to his cotton stomach. "That second verse with every player dies. I can't believe they allowed it like that, yet we all sang it with glee. I was even in the glee club."

Hank remembered her in the sweater they made you wear. Back then her lips were all with the singing and now they were kissing him like a miracle. The miracle was, she could see him, Hank, after all this time. "I know," he said.

"I guess death was nothing then," she said quietly. "When I married Joe it was, you know, until we part. But we parted in a Chinese restaurant."

"I'm not sure we should go there," Hank said.

Eddie lifted up the sheet and let it fall parachuted over her like a ghost costume. "Sorry," she said. "Here I am trying with you like a fresh start, and I keep bringing in the ghost of Joe. It's a good restaurant. I won't mope when I'm there."

"It's okay," Hank said, and he knew this was maybe the time to tell her about himself and that day in the park. But he did not want to, which was natural. He could picture the heartbroken scene if he admitted what was known only by Mr. Mittens. Why do this? Why behave this way? There are so many of these ghostly scenes already, the trails of things that did not happen quite. I was in the building days before it collapsed, I walked across that street hours before the accident. I almost married him and now look. I dumped her and look what happened. I'd be rich now, dead, married, happy, run over, covered in lava. I have a dream of what would have happened if what happened instead hadn't. Hank looked at Eddie and dreamed up what would happen if she learned how he was, that instead of blood inside his heart he was only a ghost, slain on the lawn like a dead bird. She would think less of him once she knew there was less of him. Instead he suggested a diner, but Eddie was asleep, her face thick with a nap of dreams. He floated away from her and looked through her stuff. It is natural to do this and natural to stop yourself so the person will not be angry when they awake. Hank did not stop himself.

"Dear Joe," the letter said.

The window rattles without you, you bastard. The trees are the cause, rattling in the wind, you jerk, the wind scraping those leaves and twigs against my window. They'll keep doing this, you terrible husband, and slowly wear away our entire apartment building. I know all these facts about you and there is no longer any use for them. What will I do with your license plate number, and where you hid the key outside so we'd never get locked out of this shaky building? What good does it do me, your pants size and the blue cheese preference for dressing? Who opens the door in the morning now, and takes the newspaper out of the plastic bag when it rains? I'll never get back all the hours I was nice to your parents. I nudge my cherry tomatoes to the side of the plate, bastard, but no one is waiting there with a fork to eat them. I miss you and love you, bastard bastard bastard, come and clean the onion skins out of the crisper and trim back the tree so I can sleep at night.

I met a man, Joe, but he is a ghost of a boyfriend compared with you. He will not treat me well, you bastard, and he is already made of lies. He says he went to my high school. He says he's Hank Hayride when I say I could check. But I don't need to check, Joe. I know Hank Hayride died like they say in the paper, like I know how to mix that drink you like, with the gin and brandy and lime and sugar and bitters and you fill it with ginger ale and you slice a cucumber if you have one in the crisper. It's a Suffering Bastard, you bastard. I must have made up my new boyfriend so I wouldn't be alone in this room. I must be desperate sad, all without you. Come back to me, you prick. You took all the pens except this one and you left me all the cookies and none of it matters without my Joe. God I hope I never send this letter. I'm going to go to bed now and lose a lot of sleep over you.

Love,
Eddie

Hank shut the drawer and reset things the best he could so that he'd be undetected. He leaned his forehead against the creaky window and watched people walk by without noticing him. A damp policeman. Two girls returning from someplace, rolling suitcases in a hurry. A guy looking for a newspaper that could work as an umbrella if you were desperate enough. No one.

"Cookies," Eddie said, and opened her eyes. She could still see him, and for a minute they were both still happy.

"I had a dream," she said, as if there aren't enough supernatural elements in here, "that I had another boyfriend who I think filmed things with a camera. We were making love in the woods," but something happens when you die. You are no longer interested in other people's dreams. "And so the other guy reached in his backpack and I thought it was a weapon, but then I saw it was the same kind of cookies . . ." Her voice evaporated into Hank's disinterest. He stood in the doorway and wrapped the sheet tighter around him like an angry king.

"How long have you known?" he said.

"You bastard, you read the letter," Eddie sighed, and dabbed a fingerprint swipe underneath her eyes like she might cry later. "It was in a *drawer*," she said. "It was a secret for a reason."

"How long," Hank said again, "have you known?"

"As long as you haven't told me," Eddie said. "You think I don't read the paper, Hank Hayride?"

"There are five newspapers sitting on your stoop still in plastic bags," he said.

"And," Eddie said, "you were holding my pen in the park. It was part of the whole handful of pens you were holding, a red pen with gold letters, and you put it in that story you made up. How could you do that, when I said *first thing* that I was already sad, and with a broken heart? You took me for a ride, Hank. I thought we were going someplace and all the time I knew we were going someplace else, to answer your question."

"Don't look at me, please," Hank said, "like I'm in your light. I know a place with fancy drinks. Let me buy you one, Eddie, and we can sit together."

"A drink won't matter," she said.

"Then have one," he said. "We learned things about each other, Eddie, but couldn't we go out anyway?"

"You weren't what you said you were," Eddie said. "Story of my life, it wasn't what you said." She ran her hand down the wall sadly, like it was the last of the house. "I suppose it never is," she said, "and I'm hungry."

"They have food there too," Hank said. "Great music and food and fancy drinks."

"No no no," she said. "It's raining. Let's break up at the diner, Hank. It's around the same corner. Put your shoes on, baby."

She looked at his shoes and this is when she cried. Hank floated toward her. He knew this must be what she had said to her husband, about the shoes, yet what else could he do but put them on? Her gentle blouse was on the chair with her tossed keys, and they went out under an umbrella Eddie had bought yesterday so her hair would survive the season. Outside people hurried. A newspaper came in handy, but not as handy as the guy would have liked, and a little boy was crying on the corner with the wailing you can never console. It is natural, this heartbreak, which arrives first when you are young and never leaves your house no matter where you move, but still everyone wants the kid to stop the fussing and shut up. Inside at least it was dry, although ugly. Hank and Eddie walked past a thirsty-looking woman they did not know and a lonely boy at the jukebox and sat down as far as possible from the windows, where old Christmas paintings waited to be scraped away. It was not a good day to eat at the diner, dead or alive. Nothing on the menu was tempting, and a neglected chalkboard in the corner suggested that today's soups were nothing. No soups. They unfolded their napkins and, I'm sad to say, they bickered in the back.

"I'm sorry I didn't tell you earlier," Hank said. "We met in the park and talked immediately, and I guess I didn't want to. I never meant, you know, to hurt you."

"*That*," Eddie said, "is the oldest line in this book."

"Lines get old because people say them over and over," Hank said. "It's the same story—we all lose our charms in the end. I knew when we met with the cookies. I want to love you and take you pretty places. Yes, I have things wrong, but also I can walk through walls if you'll let me show you. Don't abandon this here. Don't find some other boyfriend and leave me alone with only the cats for company." He looked at her and there it was, the panic of screwing up heaven and earth if you say the wrong thing and seal the envelope. Someone can break your heart, leave you dead on the lawn, and still you never learn what to say to stop it all over again.

"I don't think so," Eddie said, and this wasn't it either. "I thought you were nice and I wouldn't be alone, but I must have been dreaming. I should have my head examined, wishing you into my life. Someone should peer into my head for letting you into my house."

"You could have told me you knew," Hank said. "If you think you can find a man who doesn't have secrets, then you're *still* dreaming."

"You're a *ghost!*" Eddie cried. "You're *empty* and you have *nothing* inside you. I'm tired of men I have to shape into something."

"I'm tired too," Hank said, and he said no more. He thought she knew what he meant, but the biggest mistake you can make is thinking they know what you mean. If you mean that you are also exhausted and feel dead in the park, and that you ache for a love to pull you to your feet and make you human again, then you must say so. If you have soup to sell, you must write it on the chalkboard or no one will buy your homemade soup. Otherwise they think you mean, "I'm tired of arguing and I give up on you." Naturally they will think this, and naturally they will give up on you, and you will give each other up in a grimy diner. Hank was tired and Eddie was tired, and if they were both tired they should have gone to bed, but instead Eddie said nothing too, just sat and watched her boyfriend vanish from her eyes.

So, the same old story, they decided not to see each other anymore. Hank felt himself fall away as the decision was served up on a sticky plate. He could see through his own body barely, the curl of a napkin through his hand on the table, and the sticky floor through his legs like he was a clear shell, something shaped in the shape of Hank, as Eddie looked up at him and slayed him all over again. He felt the last of him slip away. He would not reappear, Hank Hayride. He was dead to the woman in the diner. He was dead to her.

But there was more, as there always is when the love goes. She was haunted, naturally. Otherwise what is the point, why leave your rickety house, and why this yo-yo world giving us things and yanking them back? Hank Hayride haunted her. Naturally he haunted her and he should haunt her, for what good are the dead if they do not haunt us, what is the point of these lives? Read instead the names of people who died before I dreamed they would: Amanda Davis, Jacques Hymans, Phil Snyder, Samy-Leigh Webster-Woog, with his odd and agile dancing like a very bad figure skater on the ice; read the names you think of when you are in bed losing your own sleep, for the names don't matter. What matters is how they haunt us, when the love has floated away and we're alone in the diner. Over by the windows, the lonesome boy and the thirsty woman were all in a commotion in another story, and Eddie would have another one too. Perhaps she would drive a taxi, or pilot a plane, and once again feel the land shaking happy beneath her. But now Eddie just sat in the back, all the fight drained out of her, and she felt the haunting, and she sipped the bad coffee, and at last in the roar of the rain she gave up the ghost.

MOON VIEWING AT SHIJO BRIDGE

Richard Parks

In the early evening a tiny moth-demon was trying to batter its way into my room through a tear in the paper screen, no doubt attracted by the scent of poverty. I was debating whether to frighten the silly thing away or simply crush it, when the Widow Tamahara's delightful voice sent the poor creature fluttering away as fast as its little wings could carry it.

"Yamada-san, you have a visitor!"

Tamahara kneeled by the shoji screen that was the only door to my rooms. Besides the volume, there was an edge of excitement in the formidable old woman's voice that worried me just a little. The fact that aristocracy impressed her had worked to my advantage more than once when the rent was late, but her deference meant that just about anyone could get closer to me than might be healthy. That is, if they were of the right station in life. Anyone else giving a hint of trouble in her establishment she would throw out on their ear, if they were lucky.

"Who is it, Tamahara-san?"

"A messenger and that is all I know. She's waiting in the courtyard with her escort."

She?

Well, that explained why Widow Tamahara had not simply brought the person to my rooms. That would not have been proper, and the Widow Tamahara always did the right thing, to the degree that she understood what "the right thing" was.

"Just a moment," I said.

After some thought I tucked a long dagger into my sleeve but left my *tachi* where it was. I wasn't wearing my best clothes, but my best would have been equally unimpressive. At least everything was clean. I followed Tamahara out into the courtyard. The sun had set but there was light enough still.

The woman kneeled near a small pine tree, flanked on either side by her escorts. No rough provincial warriors these; the two men were polite, impassive, well-dressed and well-armed. The younger man wore the red and black clothing and bore the butterfly *mon* of the Taira Clan, the other wore plain black and bore no family crest or identification at all. I judged them as best I could. The escort wearing Taira livery I think I could have bested, if absolutely necessary and with a bit of luck. But the other . . . well, let's just say I didn't want any trouble. I also could not escape the feeling that we had met before.

I bowed formally and then kneeled in front of the woman. I noted the rightmost warrior's quick glance at my sleeve and how he inched almost imperceptibly closer, all the while not appearing to have noticed or moved at all. The man was even more formidable than I had suspected, but now my attention was on the woman.

Her *kimono* was very simple, as befitted a servant. Two shades of blue at most, though impeccably appropriate for the time of year. She wore a *boshi* with a long veil that circled the brim and hid her features. Naturally, she did not remove it. She merely bowed again from her seated position and held out a scroll resting on the palms of her small hands.

I took the offered scroll, all the while careful to make no sudden movements, and unrolled it to read:

The Peony bows
to no avail; the March wind
is fierce, unceasing.

Caught like a rabbit in a snare. And so damn easily. Just the first three lines of a *tanka*. The poem was not yet complete, of course; the rest was up to me.

I looked at the shadow of the woman's face, hidden behind the veil. "Are you instructed to await my reply?"

Again she bowed without speaking. The escort on her right produced a pen case and ink. I considered for a few moments, then added the following two lines:

The donkey kneels down to rest.
In his shadow, flowers grow.

My poetic skills—never more than adequate—were a little rusty and the result wasn't better than passable. Yet the form was correct and the meaning, like that of the first segment, more than clear to the one who would read it. The woman took the message from me, bowed again, then rose as one with her escort and withdrew quickly without further ceremony. The Widow Tamahara watched all this from the discreet distance of the veranda encircling the courtyard.

"Is this work?" she asked when I passed her on the way back to my room. "Will you be paid?"

"'Yes' seems the likely answer to both," I said, though that was mostly to placate the old woman. I was fairly certain that I would be the one paying, one way or the other.

Later that evening I didn't bother to prepare my bedding. I waited, fully clothed and in the darkness of my room, for my inevitable visitor. The summons was clear and urgent, but I couldn't simply answer it. The matter was much more complicated than that.

The full moon cast the man's shadow across the thin screen that was my doorway. It wasn't a mistake; he wanted me to know he was there. I pulled the screen aside, but I was pretty sure I knew who would be waiting.

He kneeled on the veranda, the hilt of his sword clearly visible. "Lord Yamada? My name is Kanemore."

"Lord" was technically correct but a little jarring to hear applied to me again. Especially coming from a man who was the son of an emperor. I finally realized who he was. "Prince Kanemore. You were named after the poet, Taira no Kanemore, weren't you?" I asked.

He smiled then, or perhaps it was a trick of the moonlight. "My mother thought that having a famous poet for a namesake might gentle my nature. In that I fear she was mistaken. So, you remember me."

"I do. Even when you were not at Court, your sister Princess Teiko always spoke highly of you."

He smiled faintly. "And so back to the matter at hand: Lord Yamada, I am charged to bring you safely to the Imperial compound."

The light was poor, but I used what there was to study the man a little more closely than I'd had time to do at our meeting earlier in the day. He was somewhat younger than I, perhaps thirty or so, and quite handsome except for a fresh scar that began on his left cheek and reached his jawline. He studied me just as intently; I didn't want to speculate on what his conclusions might be. Whether caused by my involvement or the situation itself—and I still didn't have any idea what that was—Kanemore was not happy. His face betrayed nothing, but his entire being was as tense as a bow at full draw.

"I am ready, Prince Kanemore."

"Just 'Kanemore,' please. With the Emperor's permission, I will renounce my title and found a new clan, since it is neither my destiny nor wish to ascend the throne."

"I am Goji. Lead on then."

The streets were dark and poorly lit. I saw the flare of an *onibi* down an alleyway and knew the ghosts were about. At this time of evening demons were a possibility too, but one of the beauties of Kyoto was that the multitude of temples and shrines tended to make the atmosphere uncomfortable for most of the fiercer demons and monsters. The rest, like that moth-demon, were used to skulking about the niches and small spaces of the city, unnoticed and deliberately so—being vulnerable to both exorcism and common steel.

We reached the Kamo River without incident and crossed at the Shijo Bridge. The full moon was high now, reflecting off the water. Farther downstream I saw an entire procession of ghost lights floating above the water. I'm not sure that Kanemore saw the *onibi* at all.

His attention was focused on the moon's reflection as he paused for a second or two to admire it. I found this oddly reassuring. A man who did not pause to view a full moon at opportunity had no soul. But the fact that his moon-viewing amounted to little *more* than a hesitation on Shijo Bridge showed his attention to duty. I already knew I did not want Kanemore as my enemy. Now I wondered if we could be friends.

"Do you know what this is about?" I asked.

"Explanations are best left to my sister," he said. "My understanding is far from complete."

"At this point I would be glad of scraps. I only know that Princess Teiko is in difficulty—"

He corrected me instantly. "It is her son Takahito that concerns my sister most. She always thinks of him first."

I didn't like the direction this conversation was taking. "Is Takahito unwell?"

"He is healthy," Kanemore said. "And still his half-brother's heir, at present."

That was far too ominous. "Kanemore-san, it was my understanding that the late Emperor only allowed the current Emperor to ascend on the condition that Takahito be named heir after him, and that Takahito in turn take his royal grandfather's nickname, Sanjo, upon his eventual ascent. Is Emperor Reizei thinking of defying his father's wishes?"

Kanemore looked uncomfortable. "There have been complications. Plus, the Fujiwara favor another candidate, Prince Norihira. He is considered more agreeable. I will say no more at present."

More agreeable because, unlike Princess Teiko, Norihira's mother was Fujiwara. I considered this. If the Fujiwara Clan supported another candidate, then this was bad news for Teiko's son. As the Taira and Minamoto and other military families were the might of the Emperor, so were the Fujiwara his administration. Court ministers and minor officials alike were drawn primarily from their ranks. All power was the Emperor's in theory, but in practice his role was mostly ceremonial. It was the Fujiwara who kept the government in motion.

Still, the politics of the Imperial Court and the machinations of the Fujiwara were both subjects I had happily abandoned years ago. Now it appeared that I needed to renew my understanding, and quickly. Despite my desire to question him further, I knew that Kanemore had said all he was going to say on the matter for now. I changed the subject.

"Did you see much fighting while you were in the north?"

"A bit," he admitted. "The Abe Clan is contained, but not yet defeated . . . " he trailed off, then stopped and turned toward me. "Goji-san, are you a seer in addition to your other rumored talents? How did you know I had been in the north?"

I tried to keep from smiling. "That scar on your jaw is from a blade and fairly new. Even if you were inclined to brawling—which I seriously doubt—I don't believe the average drunken *samuru* could so much as touch you. That leaves the northern campaigns as the only reasonable conclusion. It was an educated guess. No more."

He rubbed his scar, thoughtfully. "Impressive, even so. But the hour grows late and I think we should be on our way."

We had taken no more than a few steps when two *bushi* staggered out of a nearby drinking establishment. One collided with me and muttered a slurred curse and reached for his sword. I didn't give the fool time to draw it. I struck him with my open palm square on the chin and his head snapped back and collided with a very hard lintel post. Fortunately for him, since Kanemore's *tachi* was already clear of its scabbard and poised for the blow swordsmen liked to call "the pear splitter," because that's what the victim's bisected head would resemble once the blow was completed. I have no doubt that Kanemore would have demonstrated this classic technique on that drunken lout had I not been in the path of his sword. The drunk's equally inebriated companion had his own sword half-drawn, but took a long look at Kanemore and thought better of it. He sheathed his sword, bowed in a rather grudging apology, and helped his addled friend to his feet. Together they staggered off into the night.

Kanemore watched them disappear before he put his sword away. "That, too, was impressive. But pointless. You should have let me kill him. One less provincial thug swaggering about the city. Who would miss him?"

I sighed. "His lord, for a start. Who would demand an explanation, and the man's companion would say one thing and we would say another and justice ministers would become involved and there would be time spent away from the matter at hand that I don't think we can afford. Or am I mistaken?"

Kanemore smiled. "I must again concede that you are not. I'm beginning to see why my honored sister has summoned you. May your lack of error continue, for all our sakes."

The South Gate to the Imperial compound was closest, but Kanemore led me to the East Gate, which was guarded by *bushi* in the red and black Taira colors, one of whom I recognized as the messenger's other escort. They stood aside for Kanemore and no questions were asked.

We weren't going to the Palace proper. The Imperial Compound covered a large area in the city and there were many smaller buildings of various function spread out through the grounds, including houses for the Emperor's wives and favorites. Considering our destination, it was clear we needed to attract as little attention as possible; Kanemore led me through some of the more obscure garden paths. At least, they had been obscure to other people. I remembered most of them from my time at Court. Losing access to the gardens was one of two regrets I had about leaving the Court.

Princess Teiko was the other.

Kanemore escorted me to a fine large house. A small palace, actually, and quite suitable for the widow of an Emperor. A group of very well-dressed and important-looking visitors was leaving as we arrived, and we stepped aside on the walkway to let them pass. There was only one I recognized in the lamplight before I kneeled as courtesy demanded: Fujiwara no Sentaro. It seemed only fitting— my one visit to the compound in close to fifteen years and I *would* encounter my least-favorite person at the Imperial Court. The coldness of Kanemore's demeanor as they walked by wasn't exactly lost on me either.

If Sentaro recognized me, he gave no sign. Possibly he'd have forgotten me by now, but then a good politician did not forget an enemy while the enemy still drew breath.

"I gather Lord Sentaro is not in your favor?" I asked after they had gone.

"To call him a pig would be an insult to pigs," Kanemore said bluntly. "But he is the Minister of Justice, a skilled administrator, and has our Emperor's confidence. The gods may decree that he becomes Chancellor after Lord Yorimichi, as luck seems to favor the man. My sister, for some reason I cannot fathom, bears his company from time to time."

I started to say something about the realities of court life, but thought better of it. While the saints teach us that life is an illusion, Sentaro's presence indicated that, sadly, some aspects of life did not change, illusion or not. We climbed the steps to the veranda.

"Teiko-hime is expecting us," Kanemore said to the *bushi* flanking the doorway, but clearly they already knew that and stepped back as we approached. A servant-girl pulled the screen aside, and we stepped into a large open room, impeccably furnished with bright silk cushions and flowers in artful arrangements and lit by several paper lanterns. There was a dais on the far wall, curtained-off, and doubtless a sliding screen behind it that would allow someone to enter the room without being seen. I had hoped to at least get a glimpse of Teiko, but of course that wasn't proper. I knew the rules, even if I didn't always follow them. Kanemore kneeled on a cushion near the dais, and I followed his example.

"My sister has been informed—" he started to say, but didn't get to finish.

"Your older sister is here, Kanemore-kun."

Two more maids impeccably dressed in layered yellow and blue *kimono* entered the room and pulled back the curtain. A veil remained in front of the dais, translucent but not fully transparent. I could see the ghostly form of a woman kneeling there, her long black hair down loose and flowing over her shoulders. I didn't need to see her clearly to know it was the same woman who had brought the message to me in the courtyard and whose face I had not seen then, either. No need—

the way she moved, the elegance of a gesture, both betrayed her. Now I heard Teiko's voice again, and that was more than enough.

Kanemore and I both bowed low.

There was silence, and then that beautiful voice again, chiding me. "A *donkey*, Lord Yamada? Honestly . . . "

I tried not to smile, but it was hard. "My poetry is somewhat . . . untrained, Teiko-hime."

"Teiko. Please. We are old friends."

At this Kanemore gave me a hard glance, but I ignored him. He was no longer the most dangerous person in my vicinity, and I needed all my attention for the one who was.

"I think there is something you wish to discuss with me," I said. "Is this possible?" It was the most polite way I knew to phrase the question, but Teiko waved it aside.

"There is no one within hearing," she said, "who has not already heard. You may speak plainly, Lord Yamada. I will do the same—I need your help."

"You have read my answer," I said.

"True, but you have not heard my trouble," Teiko said, softly. "Listen, and then tell me what you will or will not do. Now then—do you remember a young Fujiwara named Kiyoshi?"

That was a name I had not heard in a long time. Kiyoshi was about my age when I came to the Court as a very minor official of the household. Since he was handsome, bright, and a Fujiwara, his destiny seemed fixed. Like Kanemore he chose the *bushi* path instead and died fighting the northern barbarians. He was one of the few of that clan I could tolerate, and I sincerely mourned his death.

"I do remember him," I said.

"There is a rumor going around the Court that Kiyoshi was my lover, and that my son Takahito is his issue, not my late husband's."

For a moment I could not speak. This matter was beyond serious. Gossip was close to the rule of law at Court. If this particular gossip was not silenced, both Takahito's and Teiko's positions at court were in peril, and that was just for a start.

"Do you know who is responsible for the slander?"

"No. While it's true that Kiyoshi was very dear to me, we grew up together at court and our affections to each other were as brother and sister, as was well understood at the time. You know this to be true."

I did. If I knew anything. "And you wish for me to discover the culprit? That will be . . . difficult."

She laughed softly then, decorously covering her face with her fan even through the veils prevented me from seeing her face clearly. "Lord Yamada, even if I knew who started the rumors it would do little good. People repeat the gossip without even knowing who they heard it from. What I require now is tangible and very public proof that the rumors are false."

I considered. "I think that will be difficult as well. The only one who could swear to your innocence died fifteen years ago. Or am I to pursue his ghost?"

She laughed again. The sound was enchanting, but then everything about her was enchanting to me. There was a reason Princess Teiko was the most dangerous person in that room. I found myself feeling grateful that the screen was in place as I forced myself to concentrate on the business at hand.

"Nothing so distasteful," she said. "Besides, Kiyoshi died in loving service to my husband the late Emperor, and on the path he himself chose. If he left a ghost behind I would be quite surprised. No, Lord Yamada, Kiyoshi left something far more reliable—a letter. He sent it to me when he was in the north, just before . . . his final battle. It was intended for his favorite and was accompanied by a second letter for me."

I frowned. "Why didn't he send this letter to the lady directly?"

She sighed then. "Lord Yamada, are you a donkey after all? He couldn't very well do so without compromising her. My friendship with Kiyoshi was well-known; no one would think twice if I received a letter from him, in those days. In his favorite's case the situation was quite different. You know the penalty for a Lady of the Court who takes a lover openly."

I bowed again. I did know, and vividly. Banishment, or worse. Yet for someone born for the Court and knowing no other life, there probably *was* nothing worse. "Then clearly we need to acquire this letter. If it still exists, I imagine the lady in question will be reluctant to part with it."

"The letter was never delivered to her." Teiko raised her hand to silence me before I even began. "Do not think so ill of me, Lord Yamada. News of Kiyoshi's death reached us months before his letter did. By then my husband had given the wretched girl in marriage to the *daimyo* of a western province as reward for some service or other, so her romantic history is no longer at issue. Since Kiyoshi's letter was not intended for me I never opened it. I should have destroyed it, I know, but I could not."

"Perhaps foolish, but potentially fortunate. Yet I presume there is a problem still or I would not be here."

"The letter is missing, Lord Yamada. Without it I have no hope of saving my reputation and my son's future from the crush of gossip."

I let out a breath. "When did you notice the letter was stolen?"

"Lord Sentaro says it disappeared three days ago."

Now I really didn't understand and, judging from the grunt to my immediate right, neither did Kanemore. "What has Lord Sentaro to do with this?"

"He is the Emperor's Minister of Justice. In order to clear my reputation, I had to let him know of the letter's existence and arrange a time for the letter to be read and witnessed. He asked that it be given to him for safekeeping. Since he is also Kiyoshi's uncle I couldn't very well refuse."

She said it so calmly, and yet she had just admitted cutting her own throat. "Teiko-hime, as much as this pains me to say, the letter has surely been destroyed."

There was nothing but silence on the other side of the veil for several seconds, then she simply asked, "Oh? What makes you think so?"

I glanced at Kanemore, but there was no help from that direction. He looked as confused as I felt.

"Your pardon, Highness, but it's my understanding that the Fujiwara have their own candidate for the throne. As a member of that family, it is in Lord Sentaro's interest that the letter never resurface."

"Lord Sentaro is perhaps overly ambitious," Teiko said, and there was a more than hint of winter ice in her voice. "But he is also an honorable man. He was just here to acquaint me with the progress of the search. I believe him when he says the letter was stolen; I have less confidence in his ability to recover it. Lord Yamada, Will you help me or not?"

I bowed again and made the only answer I could. "If it lies within my power, I will find that letter for you."

"That," said Kanemore later after we passed through the eastern gate, "was very strange."

The man, besides his martial prowess, had quite a gift for understatement. "You didn't know about the letter?"

"Teiko never mentioned it before, though it doesn't surprise me. Yet . . . "

"The business with the Minister of Justice does surprise you, yes?"

He looked at me. "Since my sister trusts you I will speak plainly —Lord Sentaro is Chancellor Yorimichi's primary agent in the Fujiwara opposition to Takahito. If I had been in Lord Sentaro's place I would have destroyed that letter the moment it fell into my hands and danced a tribute to the gods of luck while it burned."

I rubbed my chin. "Yet Teiko-hime is convinced that the letter was not destroyed."

Kanemore grunted again. "Over the years I've gone where my Emperor and his government have required. My sister, on the other hand, knows no world other than the Imperial Court. If Teiko were a *koi*, the Court would be her pond, if you take my meaning. So why would something that is immediately obvious to us both be so unclear to her?"

"Perhaps we're the ones who aren't clear," I said. "Let's assume for the moment that your sister is right and that the letter was simply stolen. That would mean that Lord Sentaro had a good reason for not destroying it in the first place."

"That makes sense. Yet I'm having some difficulty imagining that reason," Kanemore admitted.

"As am I."

I looked around. Our path paralleled the river Kamo for a time, then turned south-west. Despite the lateness of the hour there were a few people on the road, apparently all in a hurry to reach their destinations. Demons were about at this time of night, and everyone's hurry and wariness was understandable. Kanemore and I were the only ones walking at a normal pace by the light of the setting moon.

"Your escort duties must be over by now and, as I'm sure you know, I'm used to moving about the city on my own," I said.

Kanemore looked a little uncomfortable. "It was Teiko's request. I know you can take care of yourself under most circumstances," Kanemore said, and it almost sounded like a compliment, "But if someone *did* steal the letter, they obviously would not want it found, and your audience with my sister will not be a secret. Sentaro himself saw you, for one."

"I didn't think he recognized me."

"I would not depend on that," Kanemore said drily. "The man forgets nothing. His enemies, doubly so."

"You flatter me. I was no threat to him, no matter how I might have wished otherwise."

"Why did you resign your position and leave the Court? If I may be so impolite as to ask. It could not have been easy to secure the appointment in the first place."

I had no doubt he'd already heard the story from Teiko, but I didn't mind repeating events as I remembered them.

"Your sister was kind to me, in those early days. Of course there would be those at Court who chose to misinterpret her interest. I had become a potential embarrassment to Princess Teiko, as Lord Sentaro delighted in making known to me."

"Meaning he would have made certain of it," Kanemore said. "I wondered."

I shrugged. "I made my choice. Destiny is neither cruel nor kind. So. Kanemore-san, I've answered a personal question of yours. Now I must ask one of you: what are you afraid of?"

"Death," he said immediately, "I've never let that fear prevent me from doing what I must, but the fear remains."

"That just means you're not a fool, which I already knew. So, you fear death. Do you fear things that are already dead?"

"No . . . well, not especially," he said, though he didn't sound completely convincing or convinced. "Why do you ask?"

"Because I'm going to need help. If the letter is in the Imperial Compound, it's beyond even your reach. Searching would be both dangerous and time-consuming."

"Certainly," Kanemore agreed. "Yet, what's the alternative?"

"The 'help' I spoke of. We're going to need several measures of uncooked rice."

He frowned. "I know where such can be had. Are you hungry?"

"No. But I can assure you that my informant is."

About an hour later we passed through Rashamon, the south-west gate. There was no one about at this hour. The south-west exit of the city, like the north-east, was not a fortunate direction, as the priests often said these were the directions from which both demons and trouble in general could enter the city. I sometimes wondered why anyone bothered to build gates at such places, since it seemed to be asking for trouble, yet I supposed the demands of roads and travelers outweighed the risks. Even so, the most hardened *bushi* would not accept a night watch at the Rasha Gate.

The bridge I sought was part of a ruined family compound just outside the city proper, now marked by a broken-down wall and the remnants of a garden. In another place I would have thought this the aftermath of a war, but not here. Still, death often led to the abandonment of a home; no doubt this family had transferred their fortunes elsewhere and allowed this place to go to ruin. Wasteful, but not unusual.

The compound was still in darkness, but there was a glow in the east; dawn was coming. I hurried through the ruins while Kanemore kept pace with me, his hand on his sword. There were vines growing on the stone bridge on the far side of the garden, but it was still intact and passable, giving an easy path over the wide stream beneath it. Not that crossing the stream was the issue. I pulled out one of the small bags of uncooked rice that Kanemore had supplied and opened it to let the scent drift freely on the night breezes.

The red lantern appeared almost instantly. It floated over the curve of the bridge as if carried by someone invisible, but that wasn't really the case—the lantern carried itself. Its one glowing eye opened, and then its mouth.

I hadn't spoken to the ghost in some time, and perhaps I was misremembering, but it seemed much bigger than it had been on our first meeting. Still, that wasn't what caught my immediate attention: it was the long, pointed teeth.

Seita did not have teeth—

"Lord Yamada, drop!"

I didn't question or hesitate but threw myself flat on the ground just as the lantern surged forward and its mouth changed into a gaping maw. A shadow loomed over me and then there was a flash of silver in the poor light. The lantern shrieked and then dissolved in a flare of light as if burning to ashes from within. I looked up to see the neatly sliced-open corpse of a *youkai* lying a few feet away from me. The thing was ugly, even for a monster. A full eight feet tall and most of that consisting of mouth. The thing already stank like a cesspit, and in another moment it dissolved into black sludge and then vanished. I saw what looked like a scrap of paper fluttering on a weed before it blew away into the darkness.

Where did the creature go?

I didn't have time to ponder; another lantern appeared on the bridge and Kanemore made ready, but I got to my feet quickly. "Stop. It's all right."

And so it was. Seita came gliding over the bridge, with his one eye cautiously watching the pair of us. Now I recognized the tear in the paper near his base and his generally tatty appearance, things that had been missing from the imposter's disguise.

"Thank you for ridding me of that unpleasant fellow," he said, "but don't think for a moment that will warrant a discount."

Kanemore just stared at the ghost for a moment, then glanced at me, but I indicated silence. "Seita-san, you at least owe me an explanation for allowing your patron to walk into an ambush. How long has that thing been here?"

I think Seita tried to shrug, but that's hard to do when your usual manifestation is a red paper lantern with one eye and one mouth and no arms, legs, or shoulders. "A day or so. Damned impertinent of it to usurp my bridge, but it was strong and I couldn't make it leave. I think it was waiting on someone. You, perhaps?"

"Perhaps? Almost certainly, yet that doesn't concern me now. I need your services."

"So I assumed," said the lantern. "What do you want to know?"

"A letter was stolen from the Imperial Compound three days ago. I need to know who took it and where that letter is now. It bears the scent of Fujiwara no Kiyoshi, among others."

Kanemore could remain silent no more. He leaned close and whispered, "Can this thing be trusted?"

"That 'thing' remark raises the price," Seita said. "Four bowls."

"I apologize on behalf of my companion. Two now," I countered. "Two more when the information is delivered. Bring the answer by tomorrow night and I'll add an extra bowl."

The lantern grinned very broadly. "Then you can produce five bowls of uncooked rice right now. I have your answer."

That surprised me. I'd expected at least a day's delay. "Seita-san, I know you're good or I wouldn't have come to you first, but how could you possibly know about the letter already? Were the *rei* involved?"

He looked a little insulted. "Lord Yamada, we ghosts have higher concerns than petty theft. This was the work of *shikigami*. The fact that they were about in the first place caught my attention, but I do not know who sent them. That is a separate question and won't be answered so quickly or easily."

"Time is short. I'll settle for the location of the letter."

Seita gave us directions to where the letter was hidden. We left the rice in small bags, with chopsticks thrust upright through the openings as proper for an offering to the dead. I offered a quick prayer for Seita's soul, but we didn't stay to watch; I'd seen the ghost consume an offering before and it was . . . unsettling.

"Can that thing be trusted?" Kanemore repeated when we were out of earshot of the bridge, "and what is this *shikigami* it was referring to?"

"As for trusting Seita, we shall soon know. That thing you killed at the bridge was a *shikigami*, and it's very strange to encounter one here. Thank you, by the way. I owe you my life."

Kanemore grunted. "My duty served, though you are quite welcome. Still, you make deals with ghosts, and encountering a simple monster is strange?"

"A *shikigami* is not a monster, simple or otherwise. A *youkai* is its own creature and has its own volition, nasty and evil though that may be. A *shikigami* is a created thing; it has no will of its own, only that of the one who created it."

He frowned. "Are you speaking of sorcery?"

"Yes," I said. "And of a high order. I should have realized when the thing disappeared. A monster or demon is a physical creature and, when slain, leaves a corpse like you or I would. A *shikigami* almost literally has no separate existence. When its purpose is served or its physical form too badly damaged, it simply disappears. At most it might leave a scrap of paper or some element of what was used to create it."

"So one of these artificial servants acquired the letter and hid it in the Rasha Gate. Fortunate, since that's on our way back into the city."

"Very fortunate."

Kanemore glanced at me. "You seem troubled. Do you doubt the ghost's information?"

"Say rather I'm pondering something I don't understand. There were rumors that Lord Sentaro dabbled in Chinese magic, even when I was at Court. Yet why would he choose *shikigami* to spirit the letter away? It was in his possession to begin with; removing it and making that removal seem like theft would be simple enough to arrange without resorting to such means."

Kanemore shrugged. "I've heard these rumors as well, but I gave them no credence. Even so, it is the letter that concerns me, not the workings of Lord Sentaro's twisted mind."

Concentrating on the matter at hand seemed a very sensible

suggestion, and I abandoned my musings as we approached the deserted Rasha Gate. At least, it had seemed deserted when we passed through it earlier that evening. I was not so certain of that now. I rather regretted having to leave my sword behind for my audience with Teiko-hime, but I still had my dagger, and I made certain it was loose in its sheath.

The gate structure loomed above us. We checked around the base as far as we could but found no obvious hiding places. Now and then I heard a faint rustle, like someone winding and unwinding a scroll. Kanemore was testing the looseness of a stone on the west side of the gate. I motioned him to be still and listened more closely. After a few moments the sound came again.

From above.

This time Kanemore heard it, too. He put his sword aside in favor of his own long dagger, which he clenched in his teeth like a Chinese pirate as he climbed the wooden beams and cross-bars that supported the gate. I quickly followed his example, or as quickly as I could manage. Kanemore climbed like a monkey, whereas I was not quite so nimble. Still, I was only a few seconds behind him when he reached the gap between the gate frame and the elaborate roof.

"Goji-san, they are here!"

I didn't have to ask who "they" were. The first of the *shikigami* plummeted past, missing me by inches before it dissolved. If the body survived long enough to strike the flagstones, I never heard it, but then I wasn't listening. I hauled myself over the top beam and landed in a crouch.

I needn't have bothered; the gap under the roof was quite tall enough for me to stand. Kanemore had two other lumbering *shiki-gami* at bay, but a third moved to attack him from the rear. It was different from the other two. Snakelike, it slithered across the floor, fangs bared and its one yellow eye fixed on Kanemore's naked heel.

I was too far away.

"Behind you!"

I threw myself forward and buried my dagger in the creature near the tip of its tail, which was all I could reach. Even there the thing was as thick as my arm, but I felt the dagger pierce the tail completely and bury its tip in the wood beneath it. My attack barely slowed the creature; there was a sound like the tearing of paper as it ripped itself loose from my blade to get at Kanemore.

Kanemore glanced behind him and to my surprise took one step backward. Just as the creature's fangs reached for him he very swiftly lifted his left foot, pointed the heel, and thrust it down on the creature's neck just behind the head. There was a snap! like the breaking of a green twig and the serpent began to dissolve. In that instant the other two *shikigami* seized the chance and attacked, like their companion, in utter silence.

"Look out!"

I could have saved my breath. Kanemore's dagger blade was already a blur of motion, criss-crossing the space in front of him like a swarm of wasps. Even if the other two creatures intended to scream they had no time before they, too, dissolved into the oblivion from whence they came. Kanemore was barely breathing hard.

"Remind me to never fight on any side of a battle opposite yourself," I said as I got back off the floor.

"One doesn't always get to choose one's battles," Kanemore said drily, "In any case it seems you've returned the favor for my earlier rescue, so we my call our accounts settled in that regard."

I picked up a ragged bit of mulberry-paper, apparently all that remained of our recent foes. There were a few carefully printed *kanji*, but they were faded and impossible to read. "Fine quality. These servitors were expensive."

"And futile, if we assume they were guarding something of value."

It didn't take long to find what we were searching for; I located a small pottery jar hidden in a mortise on one of the beams and broke it open with my dagger hilt. A scroll lay within. It was tied with silk strings and the strings' ends in turn were pressed together and sealed with beeswax impressed with the Fujiwara *mon*. I examined it closely as Kanemore looked on.

"Your sister will have to confirm this," I said at last, "but this does appear to be the missing letter."

The relief on the man's face was almost painful to see. "And now I am in your debt again, Lord Yamada. It has been a long night and we are both weary, yet I do not think that this can wait. Let us return to the Palace now; it will be stirring by the time we arrive."

The lack of sleep plus the sudden stress of the fight, now relieved, had left me feeling as wrung out as a washerwoman's towel. I knew Kanemore must have been nearly as bad off, even though from his stoic demeanor I'd have thought he could take on another half-dozen *shikigami* without breaking a sweat.

"We'll go directly," I said, "but I'm going to need a breath or two before I try that climb again. You could do with some rest yourself."

He nodded and only then allowed himself to sit down in that now empty place. "I am too tired to argue, so you must be right."

We greeted the dawn like two roof-dragons from the top of the Rasha Gate and then made our way back into the city. The Imperial Compound was already alive with activity by then, but Kanemore didn't bother with circuitous routes. We proceeded directly to Teiko-hime's manor and at the fastest speed decorum allowed. We probably attracted more attention than we wanted to, but Kanemore was in no mood for more delays.

Neither was I, truth to tell, but Teiko-hime had not yet risen, and I had to wait on the veranda while Kanemore acquainted his sister with the news. I waited. And I waited. I was starting to feel a little insulted by the time Kanemore finally reappeared. But he did not come from the house; he came hurrying through the garden path, and his face . . . well, I hope I never see that expression again on a human being.

"I am truly sorry . . . to have kept you waiting, Lord Yamada. This . . . I was to give you this . . . "

"This" was a heavy pouch of quilted silk. Inside were half a dozen small cylinders of pure gold. I take pride in the fact that I only stared at them for a moment or two.

"Kanemore-san, what has happened?"

"I cannot . . . "

"I think you can. I think I will have to insist."

His eyes did recover a little of their old fire then, but it quickly died away. "My sister was adamant that we deal with the matter at once. I escorted her to the Ministry of Justice as she insisted. I guess the burden of waiting had been too much; she did not even give me time to fetch you . . . oh, how could she be so reckless?"

I felt my spirit grow cold, and my own voice sounded lifeless in my ears. "The letter was read at the Ministry? Without knowing its contents?"

"Normally these matters take weeks, but considering what had happened to the letter under his care, Lord Sentaro couldn't very well refuse Teiko's demand for an audience. I must say in his favor that he tried to dissuade her, but she insisted he read it before the court. We all heard, we all saw . . . "

I put my hands on his shoulders, but I'm not even sure he noticed. "Kanemore?"

He did look at me then, and he recited a poem:

"The Wisteria pines
alone in desolation,
without the bright Peony."

I could hardly believe what I was hearing. Three lines of an incomplete *tanka*. Like the three that Teiko had used to draw me back to court, these three in turn had damned her. Wisteria was of course a reference to the Fujiwara family crest, and "Peony" had been Teiko's nickname at Court since the age of seven. Clearly the poem had been hers to complete, and return to Kiyoshi. The imagery and tone were clear, too. There was no one who could hear those words and doubt that Kiyoshi and Teiko had been lovers. For any woman at court it would have been indiscreet; for an Imperial Wife it amounted to treason.

"What is to be done?" I asked.

"My sister is stripped of her titles and all Court honors. She will be confined and then banished . . . " and here Kanemore's strength failed him, and it was several heartbeats before he could finish. "Exiled. To the northern coast at Suma."

Say, rather, to the ends of the earth. It was little short of an execution.

"Surely there is—"

"Nothing, Goji-san. In our ignorance we have done more than enough. The writ is sealed."

He left me there to find my own way out of the compound. It was a long time before I bothered to try.

It took longer to settle my affairs in Kyoto than I'd hoped, but the gold meant that the matter would be merely difficult, not impossible. The Widow Tamahara was, perhaps, one of the very few people genuinely sorry to see me leave. I sold what remained of my belongings and kept only what I could carry, along with my new traveling clothes, my sword, and the balance of the gold which was still quite substantial.

On the appointed day, I was ready. Teiko's party emerged from the eastern gate of the compound through the entrance still guarded by the Taira. Yet b*ushi* of the Minamoto Clan formed the bulk of her escort. Kanemore was with them, as I knew he would be. His eyes were sad but he held his head high.

Normally a lady of Teiko's birth would have traveled in a covered ox-cart, hidden from curious eyes, but now she walked, wearing the plain traveling clothes that she'd used to bring that first message in disguise, completing her disgrace. Still, I'd recognized her then as I did now. When the somber procession had moved a discreet distance down the road, I fell in behind, just another traveler on the northern road.

I was a little surprised when the party took the northeast road toward Lake Biwa, but I was able to learn from an attendant that Teiko wished to make a pilgrimage to the sacred lake before beginning her new life at Suma. Since it was only slightly out of the way, her escort had seen no reason to object. Neither did I, for that matter, since I was determined to follow regardless. The mountains surrounding the lake slowed the procession's progress and it took three days to get there. When the party made camp on the evening of the third day, I did the same nearby.

I wasn't terribly surprised to find Kanemore looming over me and my small fire within a very short time.

"I was just making tea, Kanemore-san. Would you care for some?"

He didn't meet my gaze. "My sister has instructed me to tell you to go home."

"I have no home."

"In which case I am instructed to tell you to go someplace else. I should warn you that, should you reply that where you are now *is* 'someplace else,' she has requested that I beat you senseless, but with affection."

I nodded. "Anticipated my response. That's the Teiko I always knew. So. Are you also instructed to kill me if I refuse your sister's order?"

Now he did look me squarely in the eye. "If killing you would atone for my own foolishness," Kanemore said, "I'd do it in a heartbeat. Yet I cannot blame you for what happened, try as I might. You only did as my sister bid—"

"As did you," I pointed out.

He managed a weak smile. "Even so, we still share some of the responsibility for what happened. I could not prevent her disgrace, so I am determined to share it."

"That is my wish as well," I said.

"You have no—" he began but did not finish.

"Exactly. My failure gives me that right, if nothing else does. Now consider: what about Prince Takahito? Your nephew? Where is he?"

"At Court. Takahito of course asked to accompany his mother, but permission was refused."

"Indeed. And now he remains at Court surrounded by his enemies. Who will look after him?"

"Do not lecture me on my duties! Who then, shall look after my sister? These men are to escort her to Suma. They will not remain and protect her afterward."

I waved that aside. "I well understand the burden of conflicting obligations. Your instinct for love and loyalty is to protect both your sister and her son. How will you accomplish this when they are practically on opposite ends of the earth? Which path would Teiko choose for you?"

His face reddened slightly; I could tell that the subject had already come up. Repeatedly, if I knew Teiko.

"We've spoken our minds plainly to each other in the past, Kanemore-san, and I will do the same now: your sister is going to a place where life is harsh and she will be forced to make her own way. Despite her great gifts, neither she nor her two charming and loyal attendants have the vaguest idea of how to survive outside the shelter of the Imperial Court. I do."

Kanemore didn't say anything for several long moments. "My sister is the daughter of an Emperor. She was born to be the mother of an Emperor," he said finally.

"If that were the case, then it would still be so," I said. "Life does not always meet our expectations, but that should not prevent us from seeking what happiness we can."

"You are unworthy of Princess Teiko," Kanemore said, expressionless, "and I say that as someone who holds you in high regard. Yet you are also right. For what little it may be worth, I will speak to my sister."

"When I finish my tea," I said, "and with your sister's permission, so will I."

Teiko agreed to see me, perhaps because she saw no good way to prevent it. After fifteen years I did not care what her reasons might be. The fact that she did agree was enough.

I found her sitting by herself in a small clearing. She gazed out at a lovely view of Lake Biwa beyond her. The sun had dipped just below the mountains ringing the lake and the water had turned a deep azure. Teiko's escort was present but out of earshot, as were both of her attendants. She held an empty teacup; the rice cakes beside her looked hardly touched. She still wore her *boshi*, but the veil was pulled back now to reveal her face. It was a gift, I knew, and I was grateful.

I can't say that she hadn't changed at all in fifteen years: there might have been one or two gray strands among the glossy black of her hair, perhaps a line or two on her face. I can say that the changes didn't matter. She was and remained beautiful. She looked up and smiled at me a little wistfully as I kneeled not quite in front of her but a little to the side, so as not to spoil her view.

"So. Have you come to lecture me on my recklessness as well? Please yourself, but be warned—my brother has worried the topic to exhaustion."

"Your brother thinks only of you. Yet what's done cannot be undone."

"Life is uncertain in all regards," Teiko said very seriously, then she managed a smile and waved a hand at the vast stretch of water nearby. "An appropriate setting, don't you think? I must look like a fisherman's wife now. What shall I do at Suma, Lord Yamada? Go bare-breasted like the abalone maidens and dive for shells? Learn to gather seaweed to make salt, like those two lovers of the exiled poet? Can you imagine me, hair loose and legs bared, gleaning the shore?"

"I can easily so imagine," I said.

She sighed. "Then your imagination is better than mine. I am a worthless creature now."

"That is not possible."

She smiled at me. There were dimples in her cheeks. "You are kind, Goji-san. I'm glad that the years have not changed this about you."

She offered me a cup of tea from the small pot nearby, but I declined. She poured herself another while I pondered yet again the best way to frame one of the questions that had been troubling me. I finally decided that there simply was no good way, if I chose to ask.

"No lectures, Teiko-hime, but I must ask about the letter."

Her expression was unreadable. "Just 'Teiko,' please. Especially now. So. You're curious about Kiyoshi's letter, of course. That poem was unexpected."

"You weren't Kiyoshi's lover," I said.

Teiko smiled a little wistfully. "You know I was not," she said. "But at the moment there is no explanation I can offer you."

"I'm not asking for one. What's done is done."

She sipped her tea. "Many things have been done, Goji-san. There is more to come, whatever our place in the order of events may be. Speaking of which, my brother in his own delicate way hints that there is another matter you wish to speak to me about."

"I am going to Suma," I said.

"That is noble, but pointless. Your life is in Kyoto."

"My life is as and where it is fated to be, but still I am going to Suma," I repeated. "Do you require me to say why?"

She actually blushed then, but it did not last. "You say that what's done cannot be undone. Perhaps that is true, but you do not yet know all that has been done. As at our last meeting, I must ask you to listen to me, and then decide what you will or will not do. Please?"

"I am listening."

"You left Court because people were starting to talk about us."

"Yes. When the Emperor bestowed his favor on you, Lord Sentaro—"

"Did no more or less than what I asked him to do."

For a little while I forgot to breathe. I idly wondered, somewhere above the roar in my ears, whether I ever would again. "What you . . . ?"

"It's unforgivable, I know, but I was not much more than a child, and both foolish and afraid. Once I had been chosen by the former Emperor there could be nothing between us nor even the rumor of such. I knew that you would do what you did, to protect my reputation."

"I would have done anything," I said, "if you had asked me."

"That is the true shame I have born these past fifteen years," Teiko said softly. "I let this person you detest be the one to break your heart because I lacked the courage to do it myself. I heard later that he took undue pleasure in this. I must bear the blame for that also."

Fifteen years. I could feel the weight of every single one of them on my shoulders. "Why are you telling me this now?"

"Because I needed to tell you," she said. "More importantly, you needed to hear it, and know just how unworthy I am of your regard before you choose to throw your life away after mine. Or do you still wish to speak to me of things that cannot be undone?"

Perhaps it was a test. Perhaps it was a challenge. Perhaps it was the simple truth. I only knew what remained true for me. "My decision is not altered," I said. "I would like to know yours."

There were tears in her dark eyes now. "There are things we may not speak of, even now. If it is our fate to reach Suma together, speak to me then and I will answer you."

The demons were teasing me in my dreams. At least, so I believe. In a vision I saw myself and Teiko on the beach at Suma. The land was desolate but the sea was beautiful and it met most of our needs. We walked on its shore. Teiko was laughing. It was the most exquisite of sounds, at least until she started laughing at me, and it wasn't Teiko at all but some ogress with Teiko's smile.

"What have you done with Teiko?" I demanded, but the demon just mocked me. I drew my sword but the blade was rusted and useless; it would not cut. I looked around frantically at the sea but there was nothing but gigantic waves, one after another racing toward the beach. Sailing against them was one small boat. I could see Teiko there, her back turned to me, sailing away. I ignored the demon and chased after her, but the sea drove me back again and again until her boat was swallowed by the attacking sea.

"—amada!"

Someone was calling me. The ogress? I did not care. Teiko was gone.

"Lord Yamada!"

I was shaken violently awake. Kanemore kneeled beside my blankets, looking frantic.

"What—what's happened?" I said, trying to shake off the nightmare.

"My sister is missing! Help us search!"

I was awake now. "But . . . how? Her guards worked in paired shifts!"

Kanemore looked disgusted as I scrambled to my feet. "The fools swear they never took their eyes off of her, that Teiko and her maids were sleeping peacefully, and then suddenly Teiko wasn't there! Nonsense. They must have been playing *Go* or some such rot. I'll have their heads for this!"

"We'll need their heads to help us search. She could not have gotten far. Go ahead. I will catch up."

Kanemore ran through the camp with me not far behind, but when I came to the place where I knew Teiko and her ladies had been sleeping, I paused. The two maidservants were huddled together looking confused and frightened, but I ignored them. There was a small screen for some privacy, but no way that Teiko could have left the spot without one of the guards seeing her. I looked in and found her bedding undisturbed, but empty. I pulled her coverlet aside and found a crumpled piece of paper.

"She's up there!"

I heard Kanemore call to me from the shore of the lake and I raced to join him. Just a little further down the shoreline was a place where the mountains dropped sheer to the water. On the very edge of that high promontory stood a small figure dressed in flowing white, as for a funeral.

"Teiko, no!"

I started to shout a warning to Kanemore, but he was already sprinting ahead looking for the quickest route up the slope and I followed hot on his heels, but it was far too late. In full sight of both of us, Teiko calmly stepped off the edge.

With her broad sleeves fluttering like the wings of a butterfly, one could almost imagine her fall would be softened, but the sound of her body striking the water carried across the lake like the crack of ice breaking on the Kamo River in spring.

One could also imagine, first hope having failed, that there would be nothing in the water to find except, perhaps, a few scraps of paper. One tried very hard to hold on to this hope and only relented when the fishermen from a nearby village helped us locate and remove the cold, broken body of former Princess Teiko from the deep dark waters of the sacred lake.

The moon was high again and cast its reflection on the river. The modest funeral rites for Teiko were well under way, and once more I stood on the Shijo bridge, staring down at the moon and the dark water beneath it. Again I saw the *onibi* flare out on the water. I knew that, if I waited long enough, the ghost lights would be followed by the graceful spirits of women who had drowned themselves for love.

I had seen them before; they would soon appear just above the water in solemn procession, drifting a bit as if with the currents below. The legend was that men unfortunate enough to stare at them too closely would drown themselves out of love as well. I wondered if I, too, before I drowned myself in turn, might see one small figure with the face of Princess Teiko.

I didn't know what Kanemore intended when he appeared beside me on the bridge. At that moment I did not care. I simply gazed at the moon's reflection and waited for whatever might come.

He placed a small scroll on the railing in front of me. "This is for you, Lord Yamada," he said formally.

I frowned. "What is it?"

"A letter," he said. "From my sister. I have already opened and read the one intended for me."

I didn't move or touch the letter. "Meticulous. She had this planned before we even left the capitol. She never intended to go to Suma."

"The shame of her disgrace was too much to bear," he said. He sounded about as convinced as I was.

"I rather doubt," I said, "that there was anything your sister could not bear, at need."

"Then why did she do it?" he asked softly.

A simple question that covered so much, and yet at the moment I didn't have a clear answer. I think I understood more of what had happened than Kanemore did, but the "why" of it all was as big a mystery to me as it was to him. I shared the one thing I thought I knew for certain.

"I've only been able to think of one clear reason. I have been drinking for the past day or so to see if I could perhaps forget that reason."

"Have you succeeded?"

"No."

He leaned against the rail with me. Out on the water, the mists were forming into the likenesses of young women. Kanemore glanced at them nervously. "Then share that reason with me. Preferably someplace else."

I smiled. "You must drink with me then."

"If needs must then let's get to it."

I picked up Teiko's letter and we left the ghostly women behind. From there we went to the Widow Tamahara's establishment, as it was the closest. Usually it was filled with drinking *samuru*, but for the moment all was quiet. We found an unused table, and Kanemore ordered saké, which the smiling Widow Tamahara delivered personally. Kanemore poured out two generous measures, and we drank in companionable silence until Kanemore could stand it no longer. "So. What is the answer you drink to forget?" he asked, as he topped off his cup and my own. "Why did Teiko kill herself?"

"The only obvious and immediate answer is that, upon her death, you would be free to return to the capital and look after Takahito."

He frowned. "But you were going to be with her."

I sighed deeply. "Which did not alter her plans in the slightest, as apparently I was not an acceptable alternative."

"That is a very sad thing to bear," he said after a while, "and also very odd. I know my sister was fond of you."

"Maybe. And yet . . . "

"Yet what?"

I took a deep breath and then an even deeper drink. "And yet there is a voice deep in my brain that keeps shouting that I am a complete and utter ass, that I do not understand anything, and the reason Teiko killed herself had nothing to do with me. Try as I might, *drink* as I might, that troublesome fellow only shouts louder."

"You have suffered greatly because of my family," Kanemore

said. "And I know that I have no right to ask more of you. Yet it was my sister's wish that you read her letter. Will you grant her last request?"

I didn't answer right away. "I once asked what you were afraid of, Kanemore-san. I think it only fair to tell you what *I* am afraid of. I am very afraid of what Princess Teiko will say to me now."

Yet there was never really any question of refusing. I took out the letter. After hesitating as long as I dared I broke the seal. In doing so I discovered that, when I feared the very worst, I had shown entirely too little imagination.

And, yes, I was in fact a complete and utter ass.

The letter was very short, and this is most of what it said:

"The crane flies above
The lake's clear shining surface.
White feathers glisten,
Made pure by sacred water,
As the poet's book was cleansed."

At the end of the poem she had simply written: "Forgive me—Teiko."

I thought, perhaps, if one day I was able to forgive myself, maybe then I would find the strength to forgive Teiko. Not this day, but that didn't matter. I had other business. I put the letter away.

"*Kampai*, Kanemore-san. Let us finish this jar of fine saké."

I knew Kanemore was deeply curious about the letter but too polite to ask, for which I was grateful. He hefted the container and frowned. "It is almost empty. I'll order another."

"No, my friend, for this is all we will drink tonight. From here we will visit the baths, and then go to sleep, for tomorrow our heads must be clear."

"Why? What happens tomorrow?"

"Tomorrow we restore your sister's honor."

The Imperial Court was composed more of tradition and ritual than people. Everything in its time, everything done precisely so. Yet it was astonishing to me how quickly matters could unfold, given the right impetus.

Kanemore kneeled beside me in the hall where justice, or at least Fujiwara no Sentaro's version of it, was dispensed. The Minister had not yet taken his place on the dais, but my attention was on a curtained alcove on the far side of the dais. I knew I had seen that curtain move. I leaned over and whispered to Kanemore.

"His Majesty Reizei is present, I hope?"

"I believe so, accompanied by Chancellor Yorimichi I expect. He will not show himself, of course."

Of course. The acknowledged presence of the Emperor in these proceedings was against form, but that didn't matter. He was here, and everyone knew it. I was almost certain he would be, once word reached him. Kanemore, through another relative in close attendance on His Majesty, made sure that word did so reach him. I think Lord Sentaro convened in such haste as a way to prevent that eventuality, but in this he was disappointed. He entered now, looking both grave and more than a little puzzled.

Kanemore leaned close, "I've sent a servant for a bucket of water, as you requested. I hope you know what you're doing."

Kanemore was obviously apprehensive. Under the circumstances I did not blame him. Yet I was perfectly calm. I claimed no measure of courage greater than Kanemore's; I simply had the distinct advantage that I no longer cared what happened to me.

"What is this matter you have brought before the Imperial Ministry?" Lord Sentaro demanded from the dais.

"I am here to remove the unjust stain on the honor of the late Princess Teiko, daughter of the Emperor Sanjo, Imperial Consort to the late Emperor Suzaku II," I said, clearly and with more than enough volume to carry my words throughout the room.

There was an immediate murmur of voices from the clerks, minor judges, members of the Court, and attendants present. Lord Sentaro glared for silence until the voices subsided.

"This unfortunate matter has already been settled. Lady Teiko was identified by my nephew, who died a hero's death in Mutsu province. Consider your words carefully, Lord Yamada."

"I choose my words with utmost care, Your Excellency. Your nephew was indeed a hero and brought honor to the Fujiwara family. He did not, however, name Princess Teiko as his lover. This I will prove."

Lord Sentaro motioned me closer, and when he leaned down his words were for me alone. "Shall I have cause to embarrass you a second time, Lord Yamada?"

Up until that point I almost felt sorry for the man, but no longer. Now my blade, so to speak, was drawn. "We shall soon see, Lord Minister of Justice. May I examine the letter?"

He indicated assent and I returned to my place as Lord Sentaro's stentorian voice boomed across the room. "Produce my nephew's letter so that Lord Yamada may examine it and see what everyone knows is plainly written there."

A few snickers blossomed like weeds here and there in the courtroom despite the seriousness of the proceedings, but I ignored them. A waiting clerk hurried up, bowed low, and handed me the letter in question. I unrolled it and then signaled Kanemore who in turn signaled someone waiting at the back of the room. A young man in Taira livery came hurrying up with a bucket of clear water, placed it beside me, and then withdrew.

Lord Sentaro frowned. "Lord Yamada, did you neglect to wash your face this morning?"

More laughter. I was examining the poem closely and did not bother to look up. "The water is indeed to wash away a stain, Lord Sentaro. Not, however, one of mine."

The letter was not very long, and mostly spoke of the things Kiyoshi had seen and the hardships of the camp. The poem actually came after his personal seal. I unrolled the letter in its entirety, no more than the length of my forearm, and carefully dipped the paper into the water.

There was consternation in the court. Two guards rushed forward, but one glare from Prince Kanemore made them hesitate, looking to Lord Sentaro for instruction.

"Lady Teiko's sin dishonors us all," Lord Sentaro said, and his voice was pure sweet reason, "but the letter has been witnessed by hundreds. Destroying it will change nothing."

"I am not destroying the letter, Lord Sentaro. I am merely cleansing it. As the poet Ono no Komachi did in our great-grandsires' time."

Too late the fool understood. A hundred years before, a Lady of the Court had been accused by an enemy of copying a poem from an old book and presenting the piece as her own work. She faced her accuser and washed the book in question in clear water, just as I was doing now, and with the same result. I held the letter up high for all to see. Kiyoshi's letter was, of course, perfectly intact.

Except for the poem. That was gone.

More consternation. Lord Sentaro looked as if someone had struck him between the eyes with a very large hammer. I didn't wait for him to recover.

"It is a sad thing," I said, again making certain my voice carried to every corner—and alcove—of the court, "that a mere hundred years after the honored poet Ono no Komachi exposed this simple trick we should be deceived again. The ink in Fujiwara no Kiyoshi's letter is of course untouched, for it has been wedded to this paper for the past fifteen years. Clearly, the poem slandering Princess Teiko was added within the month."

"Are you accusing me—" Lord Sentaro stopped, but it was too late. He himself had made the association; I needed to do little else.

"I accuse no one. I merely state two self-evident facts: That Teiko-hime was innocent, and that whoever wrote the poem accusing her had both access to the letter," and here I paused for emphasis, "and access to a Fujiwara seal. These conclusions are beyond dispute, Excellency. At the present time the identity of the person responsible is of lesser concern."

The man was practically sputtering. "But . . . but she was here! Why did Princess Teiko not speak up? She said nothing!"

I bowed low. "How should innocence answer a lie?"

The murmuring of the witnesses was nearly deafening for a time. It had only just begun to subside when a servant appeared from behind the alcove, hurried up to the dais, and whispered briefly in Lord Sentaro's ear. His face, before this slowly turning a bright pink, now turned ashen gray. Kanemore and I bowed to the court as the official part of the proceedings were hastily declared closed. The proceedings that mattered most, I knew, had just begun.

That evening Kanemore found me once more on Shijo Bridge. The moon was beginning to wane, now past its full beauty, but I still watched its reflection in the water as I waited for the ghosts to appear. Kanemore approached and then leaned against the rail next to me.

"Well?" I asked.

"Teiko's honors and titles are to be posthumously restored," he said. "Lord Sentaro is, at his own expense and at Chancellor Yorimichi's insistence, arranging prayers for her soul at every single temple in Kyoto."

"If you'll pardon my saying so, Kanemore-san, you don't sound happy about it."

"For the memory of my sister, I am," he said. "Yet one could also wish we had discovered this deception soon enough to save her. Still, I will have satisfaction against Lord Sentaro over this, Minister of Justice or no."

I laughed. "No need. Even assuming that the expense of the prayers doesn't ruin him, Lord Sentaro will be digging clams at the beach at Suma or Akashi within a month, or I will be astonished," I said. "It's enough."

"Enough? It was *his* slander that killed my sister! Though I must ask, while we're on the subject—how did you know?"

I had hoped to spare us both this additional pain, but clearly Kanemore wasn't going to be content with what he had. There was that much of his sister in him.

"Lord Sentaro did not kill your sister, Kanemore-san. We did."

One can never reliably predict a man's reaction to the truth. I thought it quite possible that Kanemore would take my head then and there. I'm not sure what was stopping him, but while he was still staring at me in shock, I recited the poem from his sister's letter. "I trust you get the allusion," I said when I was done.

From the stunned look on the poor man's face it was obvious that he did. "Teiko *knew* the poem was a forgery? Why didn't she—"

At that moment Kanemore's expression bore a striking resemblance to Lord Sentaro's earlier in the day. I nodded.

"You understand now. Teiko knew the poem was forged for the obvious reason that she did it herself. She used a carefully chosen ink that matched the original for color but was of poorer quality. I don't know how she acquired the proper seal, but I have no doubt that she did so. It's likely she started the original rumors as well, probably through her maids. We can confirm this, but I see no need."

Kanemore grasped for something, anything. "If Lord Sentaro thought the letter was genuine, that does explain why he didn't destroy it, but it does *not* explain why he didn't use it himself! Why didn't he accuse Teiko openly?"

"I have no doubt he meant to confront her in private if he'd had the chance, but in court? Why should he? If Takahito was Kiyoshi's son, then the Emperor's heir was a Fujiwara after all, and with Teiko the Dowager Empress under Sentaro's thumb, thanks to that letter. Until that day came he could continue to champion Prince Norihira, but he won no matter who took the throne, or so the fool thought. Teiko was not mistaken when she said Sentaro was searching for the letter—he wanted it back as much as she did."

Kanemore, warrior that he was, continued to fight a lost battle. "Rubbish! Why would Teiko go to such lengths to deliberately dishonor herself?"

I met his gaze. "To make her son Emperor."

Despite my sympathy for Kanemore, I had come too far alone. Now he was going to share my burden whether he liked it or not. I gave him the rest.

"Consider this—so long as the Fujiwara preferred Prince Norihira, Takahito's position remained uncertain. Would the Teiko you knew resign herself to that if there was an alternative? *Any* alternative?"

Kanemore looked grim. "No. She would not."

I nodded. "Just so. Teiko gave Sentaro possession of the letter solely to show that he *could* have altered it. Then she likewise arranged for the letter to disappear and for us to find it again. In hindsight I realize that it had all been a little too easy, though not so easy as to arouse immediate suspicion. Those *shikigami* might very well have killed me if I'd been alone, but Teiko sent you to make certain that did not happen. Her attention to detail was really astounding."

Kanemore tried again. "But . . . if this was her plan, then it worked perfectly! Lord Sentaro was humiliated before the Emperor, the Chancellor, the entire Court! His power is diminished! She didn't have to kill herself."

I almost laughed again. "Humiliated? *Diminished*? Why should Teiko risk so much and settle for so little? With the responsibility for her death laid solely at his feet, Lord Sentaro's power at Court has been *broken*. The entire Fujiwara clan has taken a blow that will be a long time healing. No one will oppose Prince Takahito's claim to the Throne now, or dare speak ill of your sister in or out of the Imperial Presence. It was Teiko's game, Kanemore-san. She chose the stakes."

Kanemore finally accepted defeat. "Even the *shikigami* . . . Goji-san, I swear I did not know."

"I believe you. Teiko understood full well what would have happened if she'd confided in either of us. Yet we can both take comfort in this much—we did not fail your sister. We both performed exactly as she hoped."

Kanemore was silent for a time. When he spoke again he looked at me intently. "I thought my sister's payment was in gold. I was wrong. She paid in revenge."

I grunted. "Lord Sentaro? That was . . . satisfying, I admit, but I'd compose a poem praising the beauty of the man's hindquarters and recite it in front of the entire Court tomorrow if that would bring your sister back."

He managed a brief smile then, but his expression quickly turned serious again. "Not Sentaro. I mean you could have simply ignored

Teiko's final poem, and her death would have been for nothing and my nephew's ruin complete and final. She offered this to you."

I smiled. "She knew . . . Well, say in all fairness that she left the choice to me. Was that a choice at all, Kanemore-san?"

He didn't answer, but then I didn't think there was one. I stood gazing out at the moon's reflection. The charming ghosts were in their procession. I think my neck was extended at the proper angle. The rest, so far as I knew or cared, was up to Kanemore.

I felt his hand on my shoulder. I'm not sure if that was intended to reassure me or steady himself.

"You must drink with me, Goji-san," he said. It wasn't a suggestion.

"I must drink," I said. "With or without you."

We returned to the Widow Tamahara's establishment. I wondered if we would drink to the point of despair and allow ourselves to be swallowed up by the darkness. Or would we survive and go on, as if I had said nothing at all on Shijo Bridge? While we waited for our saké, I think I received an answer of sorts as Kanemore's attention wandered elsewhere in the room. He watched the *samuru* laughing and drinking at the other low tables, and his distaste was obvious.

"A sorry lot. Always drinking and whoring and gambling, when they're not killing each other." Kanemore sighed deeply and continued, "And yet they are the future."

I frowned. "These louts? What makes you think so?"

Our saké arrived and Kanemore poured. "Think? No, Goji-san—I know. Year by year the power and wealth of the provincial *daimyos* increases, and their private armies are filled with these *samurai*," he said, now using the more common corrupted word, "whose loyalties are to their lords and not the Emperor. They are the reason upstarts like the Abe Clan are able to create so much trouble in the first place."

"Dark days are ahead if you are correct."

Kanemore raised his cup. "Dark days are behind as well."

So. It seemed we had chosen to live, and in my heart I hoped that, at least for a while, things might get better. To that end I drank, and as the evening progressed I used the saké to convince myself that all the things I needed desperately to believe were really true.

I told myself that Teiko was right to do as she did. That it wasn't just family scheming or royal ambition. That Kanemore and I, though mostly unaware, had helped her to accomplish a good thing, a noble thing, and time would prove it so. First, in the continued decline of the power and influence of the Fujiwara. Second, in the glory to come under the reign of Crown Prince Takahito, soon to be known to history as His Imperial Majesty, Sanjo II.

My son.

CITRINE: A FABLE

Elise Moser

Citrine was her husband's most prized possession. He had paid more for her than anything else he owned, and he covered her in gorgeous robes, and jewels, and imported slippers. She was very beautiful, and docile, and she had strangely luminous eyes which watched him from across a room like orbs of deep golden amber—but pulsingly alive. Her hair shone; her skin was soft; her bones lay under her skin as if designed by a brilliant yet subtle artist, to form the most perfect architecture for her features.

It had taken Citrine's husband, a minor nobleman who preferred to be known as the Lord, years of quiet negotiation with Citrine's father to close the deal. The price was enormous; from the time of her engagement at the age of twelve until her marriage to the Lord six years later, Citrine's father gradually became a landowner of substance, which gave him great satisfaction as he drank his ale of an evening, a tankard in his grasping hand and a wink in his avid eye.

From the time of her engagement, Citrine was never allowed to leave the stone house and walled gardens of her father's estate, even to walk with her little dog to the riverbank. She was no longer allowed to run through the fragrant rich soil of newly turned fields in bare feet, or push her younger sister into the snow and be pushed herself, rising damp and flushed with laughter, her strong legs kicking the cold, pure whiteness in all directions. She was no longer allowed to hang over the gate to talk to the peddlers who passed. The Lord did not want a wife with experience of the world.

Citrine's mother, from whom she had inherited her unusual eyes, wept and stormed and agitated on her daughter's behalf, but she had little influence. Citrine's father did not believe in listening to women's talk. His wife, too, was kept inside the walls of her home, and although she worked during every waking moment for the benefit of her family, kneading bread, mending stockings, and, when necessary, turning her own striking eyes and full-lipped smile on visitors—traders, men of the cloth, or, from time to time, the governor—even so, her husband disregarded her opinion. He considered it a stroke of good fortune that their countryman the Lord showed such a vivid interest in his daughter, and he was intent on exploiting it to his best advantage. He knew little and cared less about Citrine's preferences, or for that matter her capacities for lively curiosity, sly wit and warm affection, which made her popular among the servants. Even the animals appeared to love her—the muscular dog who guarded the front door, the ill-tempered donkey whose back bore bundles of firewood, the geese who hissed and nipped at anyone who dared to enter the fowl yard—from all of these, Citrine could call forth gentleness with a glance, or a touch of her graceful fingertips. The walls of the house and the fences around the yard were the limits of her existence.

Citrine neither knew nor expected any other life. There were women in the household besides her mother and herself; a woman who did the laundry, her arms chapped red up to the elbows. There were servants who prepared food, sweating red-faced over the fire; a girl who brought Citrine water for washing in the mornings, removing the chamber pot on her way out.

Their lives were just as circumscribed, if differently so. And Citrine knew there were other tasks required of women which neither her mother nor the lowest servant could escape. She was prepared for it. She only desired to be occupied, and useful.

But the Lord did not want his decorative bride to mend stockings, or thread dried apples, or sweep mud from the doorstep. He did not want his glittering plaything to stretch her strong legs running through the corridors with a white dog at her heels, or apply the vigor of her arms to transform cows' milk into butter, or add up the grocer's bill. In fact he did not want her to do anything at all that required exertion of the body or the mind, unless it was he who was doing the exerting. He considered that the donning of perfumes and fine stockings, the dressing of hair and arrangement of jewelry, were all the activity Citrine ought to require. So after their marriage, when she moved to his estate, her close confinement without any kind of useful occupation continued. And thus, both before and after the lavish wedding which completed the transfer of property between Citrine's father and the Lord, she was kept in enforced idleness—for her, a state of misery.

It was this extreme restriction of her activities, this weakening of her body and enforced lethargy of her mind, this boredom and lone-liness, that dulled Citrine's sparkle, oppressed her warm heart. She walked the small dog, her devoted companion, in the kitchen garden, but that was much too little activity for Citrine. She had been pre-pared to work hard, to endure, to give herself into the hands of a man she barely knew. But she had not been prepared to be denied even the meager satisfaction of ordinary labor. And gradually, she wilted. So much so that in spite of the expensive adornments that helped disguise her fading, eventually even the Lord saw that suffering was erasing the glow that had made Citrine so valuable. She became dull in her chair during the day, limp beneath him at night. His anger did not affect her, except that it made her cry; neither coddling nor physical punishment restored her. When he crushed the skull of her little white dog with his walking stick, meaning to persuade her, she became instead so pale and weak and listless that he sent for the doc-tor, who bled Citrine twice, with no useful result. So when the strange old woman came to his enormous carved doors and offered to paint the Lady's portrait, the Lord agreed. He thought it would look well next to the picture he had had made of his favorite horse, a sleek half-Arabian that had died of the bloat two winters before. And he thought it might amuse Citrine, rouse her back into the state of vibrant beauty he had paid for.

The old woman was of a singular appearance. Her eyes were an infinite shining black within her weathered face, her hair matted and twisted, her clothing unlike any the Lord had ever seen before, a bizarre mixture of stripes and blocked patterns, colors thrown together, unusual angles; the whole was almost shabby, and yet not faded or frayed. He nearly changed his mind when she stepped past him, pulling her great bag over the stone threshold, and he caught a whiff of some exotic, almost fetid odor—like cloves in sour wine, or cinnamon stick broken over milk left out in the heat—but just then she turned and pierced him with a glance. He felt his heart squirm within his breast, and he waved her on—in spite of this twinge of fear, which he would not acknowledge, even to himself. And he was glad of it when Citrine, desperate for any diversion, raised grateful amber eyes to him, and he saw, just for a moment, a glimmer there.

So the old woman was installed in a disused room in the back of the house. She was given bread and milk by the kitchen fire in the mornings while Citrine dressed in the violet gown the Lord had chosen for the portrait, with gold links around her neck and green stones at her throat, golden lace at her wrists. The old woman posed Citrine holding a green velvet purse filled with gold in one hand, and a deep red apple with tawny spots in the other; the Lord thought to object to these oddities, but once again the hag pinned him with her gaze, and his lips closed, the words unspoken. There was a tall vase filled with an armload of goldenrod behind Citrine; it was as if the light from her eyes had shattered and re-formed itself in an exuberant spray; the effect was not diminished as the days passed and the tiny petals dried and darkened, scattering themselves around the base of the vase and snowing themselves delicately onto the floor.

The old woman painted slowly. From her great bag she had pulled a folding easel and pots of paint; she had oilcloth-wrapped parcels filled with red-handled brushes of different sizes and color-encrusted palettes. When the easel and canvas and brushes were laid out, she reached into the bag again and carefully brought out a parcel wrapped in bright satin cloths and silken cushions as if it were a great treasure, although it was only a squat glass jar, segmented like a pumpkin, the divisions reinforced with shining bands of worked metal. It was filled with clear water and, prying the cork from its wide mouth, she used

319

it to dip her brushes clean between colors. It hardly seemed so much could fit inside the peculiar sack, and yet, somehow, it did. Over her curious clothing the woman fastened an equally odd billowing cloak. It was made of some iridescent material the Lord had never seen before; when the old dame moved it rustled. He had the sensation that he could see shards of yellow light from Citrine's eyes dance along its threads, but when he shook his head and looked again he saw nothing.

As time passed the Lord questioned himself: had he done the right thing? Day after day, working with excruciating slowness, the old woman applied thin layers of color to her canvas, building an image which, unfinished, shimmered strangely in the light. At first Citrine seemed to brighten; she ate well for the first time in months, and moved beneath her husband in bed, rather than lying like a corpse among the imported linens. Her cheeks regained their blush, her eyes their sparkle, her hair its luster. Yet he couldn't shake a gnawing feeling that Citrine was nevertheless becoming thinner, less substantial—he felt that if he peered hard enough he might be able to see through her. But standing behind the painter, mesmerized by the slow strokes of her brush, the fibers clotted with color and then, as she dipped them, releasing their threads of pigment into the clean water of her strange squat jar, the Lord felt the old woman was gazing at him even through the back of her head, and he could not make himself stay long enough to see what he thought was there.

He assigned a servant to attend the old woman while she worked, thinking to please her while making the work go faster; he was eager to have his brilliant Citrine restored to him as soon as possible. He instructed the boy to lay a generous fire in the room if it became chilly, to clean the woman's brushes for her; to carry away her water jar and wash it, and refill it with clear water from the spring. But the boy came fearfully to him that evening when the Lord returned from his rounds; the old woman had declined his service, in fact had forbidden him to enter the room at all. He showed the Lord the reddened welt that ran the length of his coarse hand and forearm. The old woman had done that to him when he'd reached out to touch the water jar.

The boy flushed, embarrassed. He didn't know how she'd done it, the boy whispered, she hadn't seemed to touch him. Only, it burned like a whip of lightning. (Afterward, the Lord would think to himself that although he had seen her dip her brushes into the jar many times, he had never seen the water become cloudy. There was something wrong with that water, something eerily, glisteningly alive about it. But how do you explain that to a magistrate? Or a girl's father?)

The Lord was in the habit of going out every morning on a fine steed to inspect some part of his extensive properties. Now he adopted the variation of stopping in to observe the progress of Citrine's portrait before taking to his horse. One morning, after several weeks of painting, he stepped into the corridor leading to the chamber where the old woman was painting Citrine. As he approached, he heard the low murmur of voices, although it stopped as soon as his hand touched the knob of the heavy wooden door; when he stepped in their faces were calm, set with concentration. There was sunlight coming in through the leaded-glass window and it seemed to flow right through Citrine's skin, making her glow from the inside. The Lord suddenly had the thought that Citrine was finally going to give him an heir, and he silently congratulated himself for being clever enough to have this portrait made—it seemed clear that it was this which had opened Citrine to him, and made her shine again. As he stood behind her, watching the old woman mix a dollop of russet paint on her palette, he suddenly became aware that she was speaking to him. "The portrait is almost finished, my Lord," she said in a low voice, without taking her eyes off her dabbing brush. "By the time you return this evening it shall be completed."

The Lord glanced up at Citrine and saw that she was gazing at him, a radiant smile of contentment on her face. His heart leapt within him; now he was sure that she was carrying his child. "You have pleased me well; you shall have that bag of gold as your reward, Madame," he cried, pointing at the green velvet prop in Citrine's graceful hand. Still without turning to look at him, the old woman inclined her head by way of reply. The Lord strode from the room and nearly danced through the corridor. As he set off upon his mount along the rutted track to his orchard, his mind's eye was so preoccupied with visions of the golden son he would soon have the pleasure of beholding, that he failed to notice a pulsing glow that emanated from the window of the room where the strange old woman had just finished painting his wife.

When he returned that evening, thrilling with anticipation, the Lord called for Citrine and her portrait to be brought to him at table. Timidly, the servant informed him that his wife was not to be found anywhere on the estate, although no-one could remember seeing her leave. Thinking to find a clue to her whereabouts, the Lord crashed into the room where the old woman had been working these last weeks, but he found the chamber empty save for the painting in its frame, leaning against a window. It looked dull somehow, lifeless.

Before the moon had risen he had destroyed it in his rage.

The light in the quaint little building was bright and glimmering, strangely alive, as if seen through pure water. There was a fragrance like freshly cut hay, or new herbs, on the breeze; the air was sweet and warm here, with a caressing mildness. The queerly segmented, domed ceiling of the hut hung with colored cloths and shining bits of mirrored glass; the only furniture was an intricately carved table, its legs in the forms of wild-looking mythical creatures, strange faces with polished eyes of inlaid stone adorning the table's edge. Here sat the squat glass jar into which the woman dipped her red-handled brush.

She stood before her easel, patiently applying colors to a fresh canvas.

Although the water in the jar seemed clear, every time the tip of the clean brush touched the water a tiny thread of color seemed to spark from it, and as the brush was applied to the canvas, the image of a young woman slowly became visible, as if it was being drawn from the plain water and made manifest by the mere action of stroking with the brush. The image was of a beautiful woman, dressed in a violet gown. The painter stayed at her slow work until the sun was high on the horizon, brushing in her subject's golden eyes last of all.

As soon as the last drop of golden paint had completed the woman's eyes, the painter stood back and laid down her brush. And then the canvas glowed briefly and the woman in the picture stood forth and stepped onto the floor, pulling herself through the canvas and into the air with a slight distortion of her features, as a child comes through from the womb with its head pulled long by its journey.

"Welcome, Citrine," said the painter, and Citrine lifted her head and looked around at the unfamiliar room. Then she fell to her knees and, with tears in her eyes, offered the velvet bag of gold in her hand to her savior. The old woman smiled and accepted her payment. Then she helped Citrine to her feet. "You need not kneel here," she said. Then she took her palette knife and, holding Citrine's hand over the instrument, directed her to cut the apple in half. They went outside together. They walked to the small orchard, a beautiful place where the trees were not in rows but rather grew anywhere and everywhere, plum trees clinging to a little hillside, pears espaliering themselves along an outcropping of rock, green apples overshadowing cherry trees and a single, thick-trunked quince lifting its arms to the sun. Citrine looked around until she found a lovely spot, a grassy slope where a golden-winged butterfly hovered, and there she planted the seeds of her apple. "Now you belong here," said the old woman, and Citrine twirled in an exuberant circle, stretching her legs and arms as hard as she could. Then she noticed, at the edge of the yard, all the other women; strong, healthy, beautiful women. Smiling at her.

A SIEGE OF CRANES

Benjamin Rosenbaum

The land around Marish was full of the green stalks of sunflowers: tall as men, with bold yellow faces. Their broad leaves were stained black with blood.

The rustling came again, and Marish squatted down on aching legs to watch. A hedgehog pushed its nose through the stalks. It sniffed in both directions.

Hunger dug at Marish's stomach like the point of a stick. He hadn't eaten for three days, not since returning to the crushed and blackened ruins of his house.

The hedgehog bustled through the stalks onto the trail, across the ash, across the trampled corpses of flowers. Marish waited until it was well clear of the stalks before he jumped. He landed with one foot before its nose and one foot behind its tail. The hedgehog, as hedgehogs will, rolled itself into a ball, spines out.

His house: crushed like an egg, smoking, the straw floor soaked with blood. He'd stood there with a trapped rabbit in his hand, alone in the awful silence. Forced himself to call for his wife Temur and his daughter Asza, his voice too loud and too flat. He'd dropped the rabbit somewhere in his haste, running to follow the blackened trail of devastation.

Running for three days, drinking from puddles, sleeping in the sunflowers when he couldn't stay awake.

Marish held his knifepoint above the hedgehog. They gave wishes, sometimes, in tales. "Speak, if you can," he said, "and bid me don't kill you. Grant me a wish! Elsewise, I'll have you for a dinner."

Nothing from the hedgehog, or perhaps a twitch.

Marish drove his knife through it and it thrashed, spraying more blood on the bloodstained flowers.

Too tired to light a fire, he ate it raw.

On that trail of tortured earth, wide enough for twenty horses, among the burnt and flattened flowers, Marish found a little doll of rags, the size of a child's hand.

It was one of the ones Maghd the mad girl made, and offered up, begging for stew meat, or wheedling for old bread behind Lezur's bakery. He'd given her a coin for one, once.

"Wherecome you're giving that sow our good coins?" Temur had cried, her bright eyes flashing, her soft lips pulled into a sneer. None in Ilmak Dale would let a mad girl come near a hearth, and some spit when they passed her. "Bag-Maghd's good for holding one thing only," Fazt would call out and they'd laugh their way into the alehouse. Marish laughing too, stopping only when he looked back at her.

Temur had softened, when she saw how Asza took to the doll, holding it, and singing to it, and smearing gruel on its rag-mouth with her fingers to feed it. They called her "little life-light," and heard her saying it to the doll, "il-ife-ight," rocking it in her arms.

He pressed his nose into the doll, trying to smell Asza's baby smell on it, like milk and forest soil and some sweet spice. But he only smelled the acrid stench of burnt cloth.

When he forced his wet eyes open, he saw a blurry figure coming toward him. Cursing himself for a fool, he tossed the doll away and pulled out his knife, holding it at his side. He wiped his face on his sleeve, and stood up straight, to show the man coming down the trail that the folk of Ilmak Dale did no obeisance. Then his mouth went dry and his hair stood up, for the man coming down the trail was no man at all.

It was a little taller than a man, and had the body of a man, though covered with a dark gray fur; but its head was the head of a jackal. It wore armor of bronze and leather, all straps and discs with curious engravings, and carried a great black spear with a vicious point at each end.

Marish had heard that there were all sorts of strange folk in the world, but he had never seen anything like this.

"May you die with great suffering," the creature said in what seemed to be a calm, friendly tone.

"May *you* die as soon as may be!" Marish cried, not liking to be threatened.

The creature nodded solemnly. "I am Kadath-Naan of the Empty City," it announced. "I wonder if I might ask your assistance in a small matter."

Marish didn't know what to say to this. The creature waited.

Marish said, "You can ask."

"I must speak with . . . " it frowned. "I am not sure how to put this. I do not wish to offend."

"Then why," Marish asked before he could stop himself, "did you menace me on a painful death?"

"Menace?" the creature said. "I only greeted you."

"You said, 'may you die with great suffering.' That like to be a threat or a curse, and I truly don't thank you for it."

The creature frowned. "No, it is a blessing. Or it is from a blessing: 'May you die with great suffering, and come to know holy dread and divine terror, stripping away your vain thoughts and fancies until you are fit to meet the Bone-White Fathers face to face; and may you be buried in honor and your name sung until it is forgotten.' That is the whole passage."

"Oh," said Marish. "Well, that sound a bit better, I reckon."

"We learn that blessing as pups," said the creature in a wondering tone. "Have you never heard it?"

"No, indeed," said Marish, and put his knife away. "Now, what do you need? I can't think to be much help to you—I don't know this land here."

"Excuse my bluntness, but I must speak with an embalmer, or a sepulchrist, or someone of that sort."

"I've no notion what those are," said Marish.

The creature's eyes widened. It looked, as much as the face of a jackal could, like someone whose darkest suspicions were in the process of being confirmed.

"What do your people do with the dead?" it said.

"We put them in the ground."

"With what preparation? With what rites and monuments?" said the thing.

"In a wood box for them as can afford it, and a piece of linen for them as can't; and we say a prayer to the west wind. We put the stone in with them, what has their soul kept in it." Marish thought a bit, though he didn't much like the topic. He rubbed his nose on his sleeve. "Sometime we'll put a pile of stones on the grave, if it were someone famous."

The jackal-headed man sat heavily on the ground. It put its head in its hands. After a long moment it said, "Perhaps I should kill you now, that I might bury you properly."

"Now you just try that," said Marish, taking out his knife again.

"Would you like me to?" said the creature, looking up.

Its face was serene. Marish found he had to look away, and his eyes fell upon the scorched rags of the doll, twisted up in the stalks.

"Forgive me," said Kadath-Naan of the Empty City. "I should not be so rude as to tempt you. I see that you have duties to fulfill, just as I do, before you are permitted the descent into emptiness. Tell me which way your village lies, and I will see for myself what is done."

"My village—" Marish felt a heavy pressure behind his eyes, in his throat, wanting to push through into a sob. He held it back. "My village is gone. Something come and crushed it. I were off hunting, and when I come back, it were all burning, and full of the stink of blood. Whatever did it made this trail through the flowers. I think it went quick; I don't think I'll likely catch it. But I hope to." He knew he sounded absurd: a peasant chasing a demon. He gritted his teeth against it.

"I see," said the monster. "And where did this something come from? Did the trail come from the North?"

"It didn't come from nowhere. Just the village torn to pieces and this trail leading out."

"And the bodies of the dead," said Kadath-Naan carefully. "You buried them in—wooden boxes?"

"There weren't no bodies," Marish said. "Not of people. Just blood, and a few pieces of bone and gristle, and pigs' and horses' bodies all charred up. That's why I'm following." He looked down. "I mean to find them if I can."

Kadath-Naan frowned. "Does this happen often?"

Despite himself, Marish laughed. "Not that I ever heard before."

The jackal-headed creature seemed agitated. "Then you do not know if the bodies received . . . even what you would consider proper burial."

"I have a feeling they ain't received it," Marish said.

Kadath-Naan looked off in the distance towards Marish's village, then in the direction Marish was heading. It seemed to come to a decision. "I wonder if you would accept my company in your travels," it said. "I was on a different errand, but this matter seems to . . . outweigh it."

Marish looked at the creature's spear and said, "You'd be welcome." He held out the fingers of his hand. "Marish of Ilmak Dale."

The trail ran through the blackened devastation of another village, drenched with blood but empty of human bodies. The timbers of the houses were crushed to kindling; Marish saw a blacksmith's anvil twisted like a lock of hair, and plows that had been melted by enormous heat into a pool of iron. They camped beyond the village, in the shade of a twisted hawthorn tree. A wild autumn wind stroked the meadows around them, carrying dandelion seeds and wisps of smoke and the stink of putrefying cattle.

The following evening they reached a hill overlooking a great town curled around a river. Marish had never seen so many houses—almost too many to count. Most were timber and mud like those of his village, but some were great structures of stone, towering three or four stories into the air. House built upon house, with ladders reaching up to the doors of the ones on top. Around the town, fields full of wheat rustled gold in the evening light. Men and women were reaping in the fields, singing work songs as they swung their scythes.

The path of destruction curved around the town, as if avoiding it.

"Perhaps it was too well defended," said Kadath-Naan.

"May be," said Marish, but he remembered the pool of iron and the crushed timbers, and doubted. "I think that like to be Nabuz. I never come this far south before, but traders heading this way from the fair at Halde were always going to Nabuz to buy."

"They will know more of our adversary," said Kadath-Naan.

"I'll go," said Marish. "You might cause a stir; I don't reckon many of your sort visit Nabuz. You keep to the path."

"Perhaps I might ask of you . . . "

"If they are friendly there, I'll ask how they bury their dead," Marish said.

Kadath-Naan nodded somberly. "Go to duty and to death," he said.

Marish thought it must be a blessing, but he shivered all the same.

The light was dimming in the sky. The reapers heaped the sheaves high on the wagon, their songs slow and low, and the city gates swung open for them.

The city wall was stone, mud, and timber, twice as tall as a man, and great gates were iron. But the wall was not well kept. Marish crept among the stalks to a place where the wall was lower and trash and rubble were heaped high against it.

He heard the creak of the wagon rolling through the gates, the last work song fading away, the men of Nabuz calling out to each other as they made their way home. Then all was still.

Marish scrambled out of the field into a dead run, scrambled up the rubble, leapt atop the wall and lay on its broad top. He peeked over, hoping he had not been seen.

The cobbled street was empty. More than that, the town itself was silent. Even in Ilmak Dale, the evenings had been full of dogs barking, swine grunting, men arguing in the streets and women gossiping and calling the children in. Nabuz was supposed to be a great capital of whoring, drinking and fighting; the traders at Halde had always moaned over the delights that awaited them in the south if they could cheat the villagers well enough. But Marish heard no donkey braying, no baby crying, no cough, no whisper: nothing pierced the night silence.

He dropped over, landed on his feet quiet as he could, and crept along the street's edge. Before he had gone ten steps, he noticed the lights.

The windows of the houses flickered, but not with candlelight or the light of fires. The light was cold and blue.

He dragged a crate under the high window of the nearest house and clambered up to see.

There was a portly man with a rough beard, perhaps a potter after his day's work; there was his stout young wife, and a skinny boy of nine or ten. They sat on their low wooden bench, their dinner finished and put to the side (Marish could smell the fresh bread and his stomach cursed him). They were breathing, but their faces were slack, their eyes wide and staring, their lips gently moving. They were bathed in blue light. The potter's wife was rocking her arms gently as if she were cradling a newborn babe—but the swaddling blankets she held were empty.

And now Marish could hear a low inhuman voice, just at the edge of hearing, like a thought of his own. It whispered in time to the flicker of the blue light, and Marish felt himself drawn by its caress. Why not sit with the potter's family on the bench? They would take him in. He could stay here, the whispering promised: forget his village, forget his grief. Fresh bread on the hearth, a warm bed next to the coals of the fire. Work the clay, mix the slip for the potter, eat a dinner of bread and cheese, then listen to the blue light and do what it told him. Forget the mud roads of Ilmak Dale, the laughing roar of Perdan and Thin Deri and Chibar and the others in its alehouse, the harsh cough and crow of its roosters at dawn. Forget willowy Temur, her hair smooth as a river and bright as a sheaf of wheat, her proud shoulders and her slender waist, Temur turning her satin cheek away when he tried to kiss it. Forget the creak and splash of the mill, and the soft rushes on the floor of Maghd's hovel. The potter of Nabuz had a young and willing neice who needed a husband, and the blue light held laughter and love enough for all. Forget the heat and clanging of Fat Deri's smithy; forget the green stone that held Pa's soul, that he'd laid upon his shroud. Forget Asza, little Asza whose tiny body he'd held to his heart . . .

Marish thought of Asza and he saw the potter's wife's empty arms and with one flex of his legs, he kicked himself away from the wall, knocking over the crate and landing sprawled among rolling apples.

He sprang to his feet. There was no sound around him. He stuffed five apples in his pack, and hurried towards the center of Nabuz.

The sun had set, and the moon washed the streets in silver. From every window streamed the cold blue light.

Out of the corner of his eye he thought he saw a shadow dart behind him, and he turned and took out his knife. But he saw nothing, and though his good sense told him five apples and no answers was as much as he should expect from Nabuz, he kept on.

He came to a great square full of shadows, and at first he thought of trees. But it was tall iron frames, and men and women bolted to them upside down. The bolts went through their bodies, crusty with dried blood.

One man nearby was live enough to moan. Marish poured a little water into the man's mouth, and held his head up, but the man could not swallow; he coughed and spluttered, and the water ran down his face and over the bloody holes where his eyes had been.

"But the babies," the man rasped, "how could you let her have the babies?"

"Let who?" said Marish.

"The White Witch!" the man roared in a whisper. "The White Witch, you bastards! If you'd but let us fight her—"

"Why . . . " Marish began.

"Lie again, say the babies will live forever—lie again, you cowardly blue-blood maggots in the corpse of Nabuz . . . " He coughed and blood ran over his face.

The bolts were fast into the frame. "I'll get a tool," Marish said, "you won't—"

From behind him came an awful scream.

He turned and saw the shadow that had followed him: it was a white cat with fine soft fur and green eyes that blazed in the darkness. It shrieked, its fur standing on end, its tail high, staring at him, and his good sense told him it was raising an alarm.

Marish ran, and the cat ran after him, shrieking. Nabuz was a vast pile of looming shadows. As he passed through the empty city gates he heard a grinding sound and a whinny As he raced into the moonlit dusk of open land, down the road to where Kadath-Naan's shadow crossed the demon's path, he heard hoofbeats galloping behind him.

Kadath-Naan had just reached a field of tall barley. He turned to look back at the sound of the hoofbeats and the shrieking of the devil cat. "Into the grain!" Marish yelled. "Hide in the grain!" He passed Kadath-Naan and dived into the barley, the cat racing behind him.

Suddenly he spun and dropped and grabbed the white cat, meaning to get one hand on it and get his knife with the other and shut it up by killing it. But the cat fought like a devil and it was all he could do to hold onto it with both hands. And he saw, behind him on the trail, Kadath-Naan standing calmly, his hand on his spear, facing three knights armored every inch in white, galloping towards them on great chargers.

"You damned dog-man," Marish screamed. "I know you want to die, but get into the grain!"

Kadath-Naan stood perfectly still. The first knight bore down on him, and the moon flashed from the knight's sword. The blade was no more than a handsbreadth from Kadath-Naan's neck when he sprang to the side of it, into the path of the second charger.

As the first knight's charge carried him past, Kadath-Naan knelt, and drove the base of his great spear into the ground. Too late, the second knight made a desperate yank on the horse's reins, but the great beast's momentum carried him into the pike. It tore through the neck of the horse and through the armored chest of the knight riding him, and the two of them reared up and thrashed once like a dying centaur, then crashed to the ground.

The first knight wheeled around. The third met Kadath-Naan. The beast-man stood barehanded, the muscles of his shoulders and chest relaxed. He cocked his jackal head to one side, as if wondering: *is it here at last? The moment when I am granted release?*

But Marish finally had the cat by its tail, and flung that wild white thing, that frenzy of claws and spit and hissing, into the face of the third knight's steed.

The horse reared and threw its rider; the knight let go of his sword as he crashed to the ground. Quick as a hummingbird, Kadath-Naan leapt and caught it in midair. He spun to face the last rider.

Marish drew his knife and charged through the barley. He was on the fallen knight just as he got to his knees.

The crash against armor took Marish's wind away. The man was twice as strong as Marish was, and his arm went around Marish's chest like a crushing band of iron. But Marish had both hands free, and with a twist of the knight's helmet he exposed a bit of neck, and in Marish's knife went, and then the man's hot blood was spurting out.

The knight convulsed as he died and grabbed Marish in a desperate embrace, coating him with blood, and sobbing once: and Marish held him, for the voice of his heart told him it was a shame to have to die such a way. Marish was shocked at this, for the man was a murderous slave of the White Witch: but still he held the quaking body in his arms, until it moved no more.

Then Marish, soaked with salty blood, staggered to his feet and remembered the last knight with a start: but of course Kadath-Naan had killed him in the meantime. Three knights' bodies lay on the ruined ground, and two living horses snorted and pawed the dirt like awkward mourners. Kadath-Naan freed his spear with a great yank from the horse and man it had transfixed. The devil cat was a sodden blur of white fur and blood: a falling horse had crushed it.

Marish caught the reins of the nearest steed, a huge fine creature, and gentled it with a hand behind its ears. When he had his breath again, Marish said, "we got horses now. Can you ride?"

Kadath-Naan nodded.

"Let's go then; there like to be more coming."

Kadath-Naan frowned a deep frown. He gestured to the bodies.

"What?" said Marish.

"We have no embalmer or sepulchrist, it is true; yet I am trained in the funereal rites for military expeditions and emergencies. I have the necessary tools; in a matter of a day I can raise small monuments. At least they died aware and with suffering; this must compensate for the rudimentary nature of the rites."

"You can't be in earnest," said Marish. "And what of the White Witch?"

"Who is the White Witch?" Kadath-Naan asked.

"The demon; turns out she's somebody what's called the White Witch. She spared Nabuz, for they said they'd serve her, and give her their babies."

"We will follow her afterwards," said Kadath-Naan.

"She's ahead of us as it is! We leave now on horseback, we might have a chance. There be whole lot more bodies with her unburied or buried wrong, less I mistake."

Kadath-Naan leaned on his spear. "Marish of Ilmak Dale," he said, "here we must part ways. I cannot steel myself to follow such logic as you declare, abandoning these three burials before me now for the chance of others elsewhere, if we can catch and defeat a witch. My duty does not lie that way." He searched Marish's face. "You do not have the words for it, but if these men are left unburied, they are *tanzadi*. If I bury them with what little honor I can provide, they are *tazrash*. They spent only a little while alive, but they will be *tanzadi* or *tazrash* forever."

"And if more slaves of the White Witch come along to pay you back for killing these?"

But try as he might, Marish could not dissuade him, and at last he mounted one of the chargers and rode onwards, towards the cold white moon, away from the whispering city.

The flowers were gone, the fields were gone. The ashy light of the horizon framed the ferns and stunted trees of a black fen full of buzzing flies. The trail was wider: thirty horses could have passed side by side over the blasted ground. But the marshy ground was treacherous, and Marish's mount sank to its fetlocks with each careful step.

A siege of cranes launched themselves from the marsh into the moon-abandoned sky. Marish had never seen so many. Bone-white, fragile, soundless, they ascended like snowflakes seeking the cold womb of heaven. Or a river of souls. None looked back at him. The voice of doubt told him: *You will never know what became of Asza and Temur.*

The apples were long gone, and Marish was growing light-headed from hunger. He reined the horse in and dismounted; he would have to hunt off the trail. In the bracken, he tied the charger to a great black fern as tall as a house. In a drier spot near its base was the footprint of a rabbit. He felt the indentation: it was fresh. He followed the rabbit deeper into the fen.

He was thinking of Temur and her caresses. The nights she'd turn away from him, back straight as a spear, and the space of rushes between them would be like a frozen desert, and he'd huddle unsleeping beneath skins and woolen blankets, stiff from cold, arguing silently with her in his spirit; and the nights when she'd turn to him, her soft skin hot and alive against his, seeking him silently, almost vengefully, as if showing him—see? This is what you can have. This is what I am.

And then the image of those rushes charred and brown with blood and covered with chips of broken stone and mortar came to him, and he forced himself to think of nothing: breathing his thoughts out to the west wind, forcing his mind clear as a spring stream. And he stepped forward in the marsh.

And stood in a street of blue and purple tile, in a fantastic city.

He stood for a moment wondering, and then he carefully took a step back.

And he was in a black swamp with croaking toads and nothing to eat.

The voice of doubt told him he was mad from hunger; the voice of hope told him he would find the White Witch here and kill her; and thinking a thousand things, he stepped forward again and found himself still in the swamp.

Marish thought for a while, and then he stepped back, and, thinking of nothing, stepped forward.

The tiles of the street were a wild mosaic—some had glittering jewels; some had writing in a strange flowing script; some seemed to have tiny windows into tiny rooms. Houses, tiled with the same profusion, towered like columns, bulged like mushrooms, melted like wax. Some danced. He heard soft murmurs of conversation, footfalls, and the rush of a river.

In the street, dressed in feathers or gold plates or swirls of shadow, blue-skinned people passed. One such creature, dressed in fine silk, was just passing Marish.

"Your pardon," said Marish, "what place be this here?"

The man looked at Marish slowly. He had a red jewel in the center of his forehead, and it flickered as he talked. "That depends on how you enter it," he said, "and who you are, but for you, catarrhine, its name is Zimzarkanthitrugenia-fenstok, not least because that is easy for you to pronounce. And now I have given you one thing free, as you are a guest of the city."

"How many free things do I get?" said Marish.

"Three. And now I have given you two."

Marish thought about this for a moment. "I'd favor something to eat," he said.

The man looked surprised. He led Marish into a building that looked like a blur of spinning triangles, through a dark room lit by candles, to a table piled with capon and custard and razor-thin slices of ham and lamb's foot jelly and candied apricots and goatsmilk yogurt and hard cheese and yams and turnips and olives and fish cured in strange spices; and those were just the things Marish recognized.

"I don't reckon I ought to eat fairy food," said Marish, though he could hardly speak from all the spit that was suddenly in his mouth.

"That is true, but from the food of the djinn you have nothing to fear. And now I have given you three things," said the djinn, and he bowed and made as if to leave.

"Hold on," said Marish (as he followed some candied apricots down his gullet with a fistful of cured fish). "That be all the free things, but say I got something to sell?"

The djinn was silent.

"I need to kill the White Witch," Marish said, eating an olive. The voice of doubt asked him why he was telling the truth, if this city might also serve her; but he told it to hush up. "Have you got aught to help me?"

The djinn still said nothing, but he cocked an eyebrow.

"I've got a horse, a real fighting horse," Marish said, around a piece of cheese.

"What is its name?" said the djinn. "You cannot sell anything to a djinn unless you know its name."

Marish wanted to lie about the name, but he found he could not. He swallowed. "I don't know its name," he admitted.

"Well then," said the djinn.

"I killed the fellow what was on it," Marish said, by way of explanation.

"Who," said the djinn.

"Who what?" said Marish.

"Who was on it," said the djinn.

"I don't know his name either," said Marish, picking up a yam.

"No, I am not asking that," said the djinn crossly, "I am telling you to say, 'I killed the fellow who was on it.'"

Marish set the yam back on the table. "Now that's enough," Marish said. "I thank you for the fine food and I thank you for the three free things, but I do not thank you for telling me how to talk. How I talk is how we talk in Ilmak Dale, or how we did talk when there were an Ilmak Dale, and just because the White Witch blasted Ilmak Dale to splinters don't mean I am going to talk like folk do in some magic city."

"I will buy that from you," said the djinn.

"What?" said Marish, and wondered so much at this that he forgot to pick up another thing to eat.

"The way you talked in Ilmak Dale," the djinn said.

"All right," Marish said, "and for it, I crave to know the thing what will help me mostways, for killing the White Witch."

"I have a carpet that flies faster than the wind," said the djinn. "I think it is the only way you can catch the Witch, and unless you catch her, you cannot kill her."

"Wonderful," Marish cried with glee. "And you'll trade me that carpet for how we talk in Ilmak Dale?"

"No," said the djinn, "I told you which thing would help you most, and in return for that, I took the way you talked in Ilmak Dale and put it in the Great Library."

Marish frowned. "All right, what do you want for the carpet?"

The djinn was silent.

"I'll give you the White Witch for it," Marish said.

"You must possess the thing you sell," the djinn said.

"Oh, I'll get her," Marish said. "You can be sure of that." His hand had found a boiled egg, and the shell crunched in his palm as he said it.

The djinn looked at Marish carefully, and then he said, "The use of the carpet, for three days, in return for the White Witch, if you can conquer her."

"Agreed," said Marish.

They had to bind the horse's eyes; otherwise it would rear and kick, when the carpet rose into the air. Horse, man, djinn: all perched on a span of cloth. As they sped back to Nabuz like a mad wind, Marish tried not to watch the solid fields flying beneath, and regretted the candied apricots.

The voice of doubt told him that his companion must be slain by now, but his heart wanted to see Kadath-Naan again: but for the jackal-man, Marish was friendless.

Among the barley stalks, three man-high plinths of black stone, painted with white glyphs, marked three graves. Kadath-Naan had only traveled a little ways beyond them before the ambush. How long the emissary of the Empty City had been fighting, Marish could not tell; but he staggered and weaved like a man drunk with wine or exhaustion. His gray fur was matted with blood and sweat.

An army of children in white armor surrounded Kadath-Naan. As the carpet swung closer, Marish could see their gray faces and blank eyes. Some crawled, some tottered: none seemed to have lived more than six years of mortal life. They held daggers. One clung to the jackal-man's back, digging canals of blood.

Two of the babies were impaled on the point of the great black spear. Hand over hand, daggers held in their mouths, they dragged themselves down the shaft towards Kadath-Naan's hands. Hundreds more surrounded him, closing in.

Kadath-Naan swung his spear, knocking the slack-eyed creatures back. He struck with enough force to shatter human skulls, but the horrors only rolled, and scampered giggling back to stab his legs. With each swing, the spear was slower. Kadath-Naan's eyes rolled back into their sockets. His great frame shuddered from weariness and pain.

The carpet swung low over the battle, and Marish lay on his belly, dangling his arms down to the jackal-headed warrior. He shouted: "Jump! Kadath-Naan, jump!"

Kadath-Naan looked up and, gripping his spear in both hands, he tensed his legs to jump. But the pause gave the tiny servitors of the White Witch their chance; they swarmed over his body, stabbing with their daggers, and he collapsed under the writhing mass of his enemies.

"Down further! We can haul him aboard!" yelled Marish.

"I sold you the use of my carpet, not the destruction of it," said the djinn.

With a snarl of rage, and before the voice of his good sense could speak, Marish leapt from the carpet. He landed amidst the fray, and began tearing the small bodies from Kadath-Naan and flinging them into the fields. Then daggers found his calves, and small bodies crashed into his sides, and he tumbled, covered with the white-armored hell-children. The carpet sailed up lazily into the summer sky.

Marish thrashed, but soon he was pinned under a mass of small bodies. Their daggers probed his sides, drawing blood, and he gritted his teeth against a scream; they pulled at his hair and ears and pulled open his mouth to look inside. As if they were playing. One gray-skinned suckling child, its scalp peeled half away to reveal the white bone of its skull, nuzzled at his neck, seeking the nipple it would never find again.

So had Asza nuzzled against him. So had been her heft, then, light and snug as five apples in a bag. But her live eyes saw the world, took it in and made it better than it was. In those eyes he was a hero, a giant to lift her, honest and gentle and brave. When Temur looked into those otter-brown, mischievous eyes, her mouth softened from its hard line, and she sang fairy songs.

A dagger split the skin of his forehead, bathing him in blood. Another dug between his ribs, another popped the skin of his thigh. Another pushed against his gut, but hadn't broken through. He closed his eyes. They weighed heavier on him now; his throat tensed to scream, but he could not catch his breath.

Marish's arms ached for Asza and Temur—ached that he would die here, without them. Wasn't it right, though, that they be taken from him? The little girl who ran to him across the fields of an evening, a funny hopping run, her arms flung wide, waving that rag doll; no trace of doubt in her. And the beautiful wife who stiffened when she saw him, but smiled one-edged, despite herself, as he lifted apple-smelling Asza in his arms. He had not deserved them.

His face, his skin were hot and slick with salty blood. He saw, not felt, the daggers digging deeper—arcs of light across a great darkness. He wished he could comfort Asza one last time, across that darkness. As when she would awaken in the night, afraid of witches: now a witch had come.

He found breath, he forced his mouth open, and he sang through sobs to Asza, his song to lull her back to sleep:

"Now sleep, my love, now sleep—
The moon is in the sky—
The clouds have fled like sheep—
You're in your papa's eye.
Sleep now, my love, sleep now—
The bitter wind is gone—
The calf sleeps with the cow—
Now sleep my love 'til dawn."

He freed his left hand from the press of bodies. He wiped blood and tears from his eyes. He pushed his head up, dizzy, flowers of light still exploding across his vision. The small bodies were still. Carefully, he eased them to the ground.

The carpet descended, and Marish hauled Kadath-Naan onto it. Then he forced himself to turn, swaying, and look at each of the gray-skinned babies sleeping peacefully on the ground. None of them was Asza.

He took one of the smallest and swaddled it with rags and bridle leather. His blood made his fingers slick, and the noon sun seemed as gray as a stone. When he was sure the creature could not move, he put it in his pack and slung the pack upon his back. Then he fell onto the carpet. He felt it lift up under him, and like a cradled child, he slept.

He awoke to se clouds sailing above him. The pain was gone. He sat up and looked at his arms: they were whole and unscarred. Even the old scar from Thin Deri's careless scythe was gone.

"You taught us how to defeat the Children of Despair," said the djinn. "That required recompense. I have treated your wounds and those of your companion. Is the debt clear?"

"Answer me one question," Marish said.

"And the debt will be clear?" said the djinn.

"Yes, may the west wind take you, it'll be clear!"

The djinn blinked in assent.

"Can they be brought back?" Marish asked. "Can they be made into living children again?"

"They cannot," said the djinn. "They can neither live nor die, nor be harmed at all unless they will it. Their hearts have been replaced with sand."

They flew in silence, and Marish's pack seemed heavier.

The land flew by beneath them as fast as a cracking whip; Marish stared as green fields gave way to swamp, swamp to marsh, marsh to rough pastureland. The devastation left by the White Witch seemed gradually newer; the trail here was still smoking, and Marish thought it might be too hot to walk on. They passed many a blasted village, and each time Marish looked away.

At last they began to hear a sound on the wind, a sound that chilled Marish's heart. It was not a wail, it was not a grinding, it was not a shriek of pain, nor the wet crunch of breaking bones, nor was it an obscene grunting; but it had something of all of these. The jackal-man's ears were perked, and his gray fur stood on end.

The path was now truly still burning; they flew high above it, and the rolling smoke underneath was like a fog over the land. But there ahead they saw the monstrous thing that was leaving the trail; and Marish could hardly think any thought at all as they approached, but only stare, bile burning his throat.

It was a great chariot, perhaps eight times the height of a man, as wide as the trail, constructed of parts of living human bodies welded together in an obscene tangle. A thousand legs and arms pawed the ground; a thousand more beat the trail with whips and scythes, or clawed the air. A thick skein of hearts, livers, and stomachs pulsed through the center of the thing, and a great assemblage of lungs breathed at its core. Heads rolled like wheels at the bottom of the chariot, or were stuck here and there along the surface of the thing as slack-eyed, gibbering ornaments. A thousand spines and torsos built a great chamber at the top of the chariot, shielded with webs of skin and hair; there perhaps hid the White Witch. From the pinnacle of the monstrous thing flew a great flag made of writhing tongues. Before the awful chariot rode a company of ten knights in white armor, with visored helms.

At the very peak sat a great headless hulking beast, larger than a bear, with the skin of a lizard, great yellow globes of eyes set on its shoulders and a wide mouth in its belly. As they watched, it vomited a gout of flame that set the path behind the chariot ablaze. Then it noticed them, and lifted the great plume of flame in their direction. At a swift word from the djinn, the carpet veered, but it was a close enough thing that Marish felt an oven's blast of heat on his skin. He grabbed the horse by its reins as it made to rear, and whispered soothing sounds in its ear.

"Abomination!" cried Kadath-Naan. "Djinn, will you send word to the Empty City? You will be well rewarded."

The djinn nodded.

"It is Kadath-Naan, lesser scout of the Endless Inquiry, who speaks. Let Bars-Kardereth, Commander of the Silent Legion, be told to hasten here. Here is an obscenity beyond compass, far more horrible than the innocent errors of savages; here Chaos blocks the descent into the Darkness entirely, and a whole land may fall to corruption."

The jewel in the djinn's forehead flashed once. "It is done," he said.

Kadath-Naan turned to Marish. "From the Empty City to this place is four days' travel for a Ghomlu Legion; let us find a place in their path where we can wait to join them."

Marish forced himself to close his eyes. But still he saw it—hands, tongues, guts, skin, woven into a moving mountain. He still heard the squelching, grinding, snapping sounds, the sea-roar of the thousand lungs. What had he imagined? Asza and Temur in a prison somewhere, waiting to be freed? Fool. "All right," he said.

Then he opened his eyes, and saw something that made him say, "No."

Before them, not ten minutes' ride from the awful chariot of the White Witch, was a whitewashed village, peaceful in the afternoon sun. Arrayed before it were a score of its men and young women. A few had proper swords or spears; one of the women carried a bow. The others had hoes, scythes, and staves. One woman sat astride a horse; the rest were on foot. From their perch in the air, Marish could see distant figures—families, stooped grandmothers, children in their mothers' arms—crawling like beetles up the faces of hills.

"Down," said Marish, and they landed before the village's defenders, who raised their weapons.

"You've got to run," he said, "you can make it to the hills. You haven't seen that thing—you haven't any chance against it."

A dark man spat on the ground. "We tried that in Gravenge."

"It splits up," said a black-bearded man. "Sends littler horrors, and they tear folks up and make them part of it, and you see your fellow's limbs, come after you as part of the thing. And they're fast. Too fast for us."

"We just busy it a while," another man said, "our folk can get far enough away." But he had a wild look in his eye: the voice of doubt was in him.

"We stop it here," said the woman on horseback.

Marish led the horse off the carpet, took its blinders off and mounted it. "I'll stand with you," he said.

"And welcome," said the woman on horseback, and her plain face broke into a nervous smile. It was almost pretty that way.

Kadath-Naan stepped off the carpet, and the villagers shied back, readying their weapons.

"This is Kadath-Naan, and you'll be damned glad you have him," said Marish.

"Where's your manners?" snapped the woman on horseback to her people. "I'm Asza," she said.

No, Marish thought, staring at her. No, but you could have been. He looked away, and after a while they left him alone.

The carpet rose silently off into the air, and soon there was smoke on the horizon, and the knights rode at them, and the chariot rose behind.

"Here we are," said Asza of the rocky lands, "now make a good accounting of yourselves."

An arrow sang; a white knight's horse collapsed. Marish cried "Ha!" and his mount surged forward. The villagers charged, but Kadath-Naan outpaced them all, springing between a pair of knights.

He shattered the forelegs of one horse with his spear's shaft, drove its point through the side of the other rider. Villagers fell on the fallen knight with their scythes.

It was a heady wild thing for Marish, to be galloping on such a horse, a far finer horse than ever Redlegs had been, for all Pa's proud and vain attention to her. The warmth of its flanks, the rhythm of posting into its stride. Marish of Ilmak Dale, riding into a charge of knights: miserable addle-witted fool.

Asza flicked her whip at the eyes of a knight's horse, veering away. The knight wheeled to follow her, and Marish came on after him. He heard the hooves of another knight pounding the plain behind him in turn.

Ahead the first knight gained on Asza of the rocky plains. Marish took his knife in one hand, and bent his head to his horse's ear, and whispered to it in wordless murmurs: *Fine creature, give me everything.* And his horse pulled even with Asza's knight.

Marish swung down, hanging from his pommel—the ground flew by beneath him. He reached across and slipped his knife under the girth that held the knight's saddle. The knight swiveled, raising his blade to strike—then the girth parted, and he flew from his mount.

Marish struggled up into the saddle, and the second knight was there, armor blazing in the sun. This time Marish was on the sword-arm's side, and his horse had slowed, and that blade swung up and it could strike Marish's head from his neck like snapping off a sun-flower; time for the peasant to die.

Asza's whip lashed around the knight's sword-arm. The knight seized the whip in his other hand. Marish sprang from the saddle. He struck a wall of chainmail and fell with the knight.

The ground was an anvil, the knight a hammer, Marish a rag doll sewn by a poor mad girl and mistaken for a horseshoe. He couldn't breathe; the world was a ringing blur. The knight found his throat with one mailed glove, and hissed with rage, and pulling himself up drew a dagger from his belt. Marish tried to lift his arms.

Then he saw Asza's hands fitting a leather noose around the

knight's neck. The knight turned his visored head to see, and Asza yelled, "Yah!" An armored knee cracked against Marish's head, and then the knight was gone, dragged off over the rocky plains behind Asza's galloping mare.

Asza of the rocky lands helped Marish to his feet. She had a wild smile, and she hugged him to her breast; pain shot through him, as did the shock of her soft body. Then she pulled away, grinning, and looked over his shoulder back towards the village. And then the grin was gone.

Marish turned. He saw the man with the beard torn apart by a hundred grasping arms and legs. Two bending arms covered with eyes watched carefully as his organs were woven into the chariot. The village burned. A knight leaned from his saddle to cut a fleeing woman down, harvesting her like a stalk of wheat.

"No!" shrieked Asza, and ran towards the village.

Marish tried to run, but he could only hobble, gasping, pain tearing through his side. Asza snatched a spear from the ground and swung up onto a horse. Her hair was like Temur's, flowing gold. My Asza, my Temur, he thought. I must protect her.

Marish fell; he hit the ground and held onto it like a lover, as if he might fall into the sky. Fool, fool, said the voice of his good sense. That is not your Asza, or your Temur either. She is not yours at all.

He heaved himself up again and lurched on, as Asza of the rocky plains reached the chariot. From above, a lazy plume of flame expanded. The horse reared. The cloud of fire enveloped the woman, the horse, and then was sucked away; the blackened corpses fell to the ground steaming.

Marish stopped running.

The headless creature of fire fell from the chariot—Kadath-Naan was there at the summit of the horror, his spear sunk in the its flesh as a lever. But the fire-beast turned as it toppled, and a pillar of fire engulfed the jackal-man. The molten iron of his spear and armor coated his body, and he fell into the grasping arms of the chariot.

Marish lay down on his belly in the grass.

Maybe they will not find me here, said the voice of hope. But it was like listening to idiot words spoken by the wind blowing through a forest. Marish lay on the ground and he hurt. The hurt was a song, and it sang him. Everything was lost and far away. No Asza, no Temur, no Maghd; no quest, no hero, no trickster, no hunter, no father, no groom. The wind came down from the mountains and stirred the grass beside Marish's nose, where beetles walked.

There was a rustling in the short grass, and a hedgehog came out of it and stood nose to nose with Marish.

"Speak if you can," Marish whispered, "and grant me a wish."

The hedgehog snorted. "I'll not do *you* any favors, after what you did to Teodor!"

Marish swallowed. "The hedgehog in the sunflowers?"

"Obviously. Murderer."

"I'm sorry! I didn't know he was magic! I thought he was just a hedgehog!"

"Just a hedgehog! Just a hedgehog!" It narrowed its eyes, and its prickers stood on end. "Be careful what you call things, Marish of Ilmak Dale. When you name a thing, you say what it is in the world. Names mean more than you know."

Marish was silent.

"Teodor didn't like threats, that's all . . . the stubborn old idiot."

"I'm sorry about Teodor," said Marish.

"Yes, well," said the hedgehog. "I'll help you, but it will cost you dear."

"What do you want?"

"How about your soul?" said the hedgehog.

"I'd do that, sure," said Marish. "It's not like I need it. But I don't have it."

The hedgehog narrowed its eyes again. From the village, a few thin screams and the soft crackle of flames. It smelled like autumn, and butchering hogs.

"It's true," said Marish. "The priest of Ilmak Dale took all our souls and put them in little stones, and hid them. He didn't want us making bargains like these."

"Wise man," said the hedgehog. "But I'll have to have something. What have you got in you, besides a soul?"

"What do you mean, like, my wits? But I'll need those."

"Yes, you will," said the hedgehog.

"Hope? Not much of that left, though."

"Not to my taste anyway," said the hedgehog. "*Hope is foolish, doubts are wise.*"

"Doubts?" said Marish.

"That'll do," said the hedgehog. "But I want them all."

"All . . . all right," said Marish. "And now you're going to help me against the White Witch?"

"I already have," said the hedgehog.

"You have? Have I got some magic power or other now?" asked Marish. He sat up. The screaming was over: he heard nothing but the fire, and the crunching and squelching and slithering and grinding of the chariot.

"Certainly not," said the hedgehog. "I haven't done anything you didn't see or didn't hear. But perhaps you weren't listening." And it waddled off into the green blades of the grass.

Marish stood and looked after it. He picked at his teeth with a thumbnail, and thought, but he had no idea what the hedgehog meant. But he had no doubts, either, so he started toward the village.

Halfway there, he noticed the dead baby in his pack wriggling, so he took it out and held it in his arms.

As he came into the burning village, he found himself just behind the great fire-spouting lizard-skinned headless thing. It turned and took a breath to burn him alive, and he tossed the baby down its throat. There was a choking sound, and the huge thing shuddered and twitched, and Marish walked on by it.

The great chariot saw him and it swung toward him, a vast mountain of writhing, humming, stinking flesh, a hundred arms reaching. Fists grabbed his shirt, his hair, his trousers, and they lifted him into the air.

He looked at the hand closed around his collar. It was a woman's hand, fine and fair, and it was wearing the copper ring he'd bought at Halde.

"Temur!" he said in shock.

The arm twitched and slackened; it went white. It reached out: the fingers spread wide; it caressed his cheek gently. And then it dropped from the chariot and lay on the ground beneath.

He knew the hands pulling him aloft. "Lezur the baker!" he whispered, and a pair of doughy hands dropped from the chariot. "Silbon and Felbon!" he cried. "Ter the blind! Sela the blue-eyed!" Marish's lips trembled to say the names, and the hands slackened and fell to the ground, and away on other parts of the chariot the other parts fell off too; he saw a blue eye roll down from above him and fall to the ground.

"Perdan! Mardid! Pilg and his old mother! Fazt—oh Fazt, you'll tell no more jokes! Chibar and his wife, the pretty foreign one!" His face was wet; with every name, a bubble popped open in Marish's chest, and his throat was thick with some strange feeling. "Pizdar the priest! Fat Deri, far from your smithy! Thin Deri!" When all the hands and arms of Ilmak Dale had fallen off, he was left standing free. He looked at the strange hands coming toward him. "You were a potter," he said to hands with clay under the nails, and they fell off the chariot. "And you were a butcher," he said to bloody ones, and they fell too. "A fat farmer, a beautiful young girl, a grandmother, a harlot, a brawler," he said, and enough hands and feet and heads and organs had slid off the chariot now that it sagged in the middle and pieces of it strove with each other blindly. "Men and women of Eckdale," Marish said, "men and women of Halde, of Gravenge, of the fields and the swamps and the rocky plains."

The chariot fell to pieces; some lay silent and still, others which Marish had not named had lost their purchase and thrashed on the ground.

The skin of the great chamber atop the chariot peeled away and the White Witch leapt into the sky. She was three times as tall as any woman; her skin was bone white; one eye was blood red and the other emerald green; her mouth was full of black fangs, and her hair of snakes and lizards. Her hands were full of lightning, and she sailed onto Marish with her fangs wide open.

And around her neck, on a leather thong, she wore a little doll of rags, the size of a child's hand.

"Maghd of Ilmak Dale," Marish said, and she was also a young woman with muddy hair and an uncertain smile, and that's how she landed before Marish.

"Well done, Marish," said Maghd, and pulled at a muddy lock of her hair, and laughed, and looked at the ground. "Well done! Oh, I'm glad. I'm glad you've come."

"Why did you do it, Maghd?" Marish said. "Oh, why?"

She looked up and her lips twitched and her jaw set. "Can you ask me that? You, Marish?"

She reached across, slowly, and took his hand. She pulled him, and he took a step towards her. She put the back of his hand against her cheek.

"You'd gone out hunting," she said. "And that Temur of yours"—she said the name as if it tasted of vinegar—"she seen me back of Lezur's, and for one time I didn't look down. I looked at her eyes, and she named me a foul witch. And then they were all crowding round—" She shrugged. "And I don't like that. Fussing and crowding and one against the other." She let go his hand and stooped to pick up a clot of earth, and she crumbled it in her hands. "So I knit them all together. All one thing. They did like it. And they were so fine and great and happy, I forgave them. Even Temur."

The limbs lay unmoving on the ground; the guts were piled in soft unbreathing hills, like drifts of snow. Maghd's hands were coated with black crumbs of dirt.

"I reckon they're done of playing now," Maghd said, and sighed.

"How?" Marish said. "How'd you do it? Maghd, what *are* you?"

"Don't fool so! I'm Maghd, same as ever. I found the souls, that's all. Dug them up from Pizdar's garden, sold them to the Spirit of Unwinding Things." She brushed the dirt from her hands.

"And . . . the children, then? Maghd, the babes?"

She took his hand again, but she didn't look at him. She lay her cheek against her shoulder and watched the ground. "Babes shouldn't grow," she said. "No call to be big and hateful." She swallowed. "I made them perfect. That's all."

Marish's chest tightened. "And what now?"

She looked at him, and a slow grin crept across her face. "Well now," she said. "That's on you, ain't it, Marish? I got plenty of tricks yet, if you want to keep fighting." She stepped close to him, and rested her cheek on his chest. Her hair smelled like home: rushes and fire smoke, cold mornings and sheep's milk. "Or we can gather close. No one to shame us now." She wrapped her arms around his waist. "It's all new, Marish, but it ain't all bad."

A shadow drifted over them, and Marish looked up to see the djinn on his carpet, peering down. Marish cleared his throat. "Well . . . I suppose we're all we have left, aren't we?"

"That's so," Maghd breathed softly.

He took her hands in his, and drew back to look at her. "Will you be mine, Maghd?" he said.

"Oh yes," said Maghd, and smiled the biggest smile of her life.

"Very good," Marish said, and looked up. "You can take her now."

The djinn opened the little bottle that was in his hand and Maghd the White Witch flew into it, and he put the cap on. He bowed to Marish, and then he flew away.

Behind Marish the fire beast exploded with a dull boom.

Marish walked out of the village a little ways and sat, and after sitting a while he slept. And then he woke and sat, and then he slept some more. Perhaps he ate as well; he wasn't sure what. Mostly he looked at his hands; they were rough and callused, with dirt under the nails. He watched the wind painting waves in the short grass, around the rocks and bodies lying there.

One morning he woke, and the ruined village was full of jackal-headed men in armor made of discs who were mounted on great red cats with pointed ears, and jackal-headed men in black robes who were measuring for monuments, and jackal-headed men dressed only in loincloths who were digging in the ground.

Marish went to the ones in loincloths and said, "I want to help bury them," and they gave him a shovel.

CONTRIBUTORS

————

MARY RICKERT was eighteen she moved to California, where she worked at Disneyland. She still has fond memories of selling balloons there. After many years (and through the sort of "odd series of events" that describe much of her life), she got a job as a kindergarten teacher in a small private school for gifted children. She worked there for almost a decade, then left to pursue her life as a writer. She has had many stories published by *The Magazine of Fantasy & Science Fiction*, Her most recent book is collection, *Map of Dreams*.

DAVID J. SCHWARTZ's short fiction has appeared in such venues as the anthologies *Twenty Epics* and *Polyphony* and the magazine *Strange Horizons*. His first novel, *Superpowers*, will appear in 2008 from Three Rivers Press and Vintage UK Originals. He keeps a blog at http://snurri.blogspot.com.

GEOFF RYMAN is the author of *The Warrior Who Carried Life*, novella "The Unconquered Country," *The Child Garden, Was, Lust*, and *Air*. His work *253, or Tube Theatre* was first published as hypertext fiction. A print version was published in 1998 and won the Philip K. Dick Memorial Award. He has also won the World Fantasy Award, Campbell Memorial Award, Clarke, British SF, Sunburst, and Gaylactic Spectrum awards. His most recent novel, *The King's Last Song*, is set in Cambodia, both at the time of Angkorean emperor Jayavarman VII, and in the present period. He currently lectures in Creative Writing for University of Manchester's English Department.

GREG VAN EEKHOUT'S stories have appeared in *Asimov's, Magazine of Fantasy and Science Fiction, Realms of Fantasy*, and a number of other magazines and anthologies. He lives corporeally in Tempe, Arizona, and electronically at www.sff.net/people.

PETER S. BEAGLE was born in 1939 and raised in the Bronx, just a few blocks from Woodlawn Cemetery, the inspiration for his first novel, A Fine And Private Place. He originally proclaimed he would be a writer when ten-years-old: subsequent events have proven him either prescient or even more stubborn than hitherto suspected. Today, thanks to classic works such as *The Last Unicorn, Tamsin*, and *The Innkeeper's Song*, he is acknowledged as America's greatest living fantasy author; and his dazzling abilities with language, characters, and magical storytelling have earned him many millions of fans around the world.

In addition to stories and novels he has written numerous teleplays and screenplays, including the animated versions of *The Lord of the Rings* and *The Last Unicorn*, plus the fan-favorite "Sarek" episode of *Star Trek: The Next Generation*. He is also a gifted poet, lyricist, and singer/songwriter. Fans of Peter's work are about to be very happy, because there are lots of new projects and reissues in the pipeline: new books, new stories, new essays, even his first CD of recorded songs!

For more on Peter and his work, see: <www.peterbeagle.com> or www.conlanpress.com.

PETER HIGGINS lives in a small town on the south coast of Wales. His stories have appeared in *Revelation* and *Zahir*.

YSABEAU S. WILCE is a new writer whose first story, "Metal More Attractive," was published in *The Magazine of Fantasy and Science Fiction* in 2004. Like all of her work to date, it was set in 'Alta Califa', an alternate California, and is heavily influenced by Wilce's military history studies. A second story, "The Biography of a Bouncing Boy Terror," appeared in 2005 and "The Lineaments of Gratified Desire" appeared in 2006. Wilce's first novel, a young adult fantasy with a preposterously long title, *Flora Segunda: Being the Magickal Mishaps of a Girl of Spirit, Her Glass-Gazing Sidekick, Two Ominous Butlers (One Blue), a House with Eleven Thousand Rooms, and a Red Dog*, was published to considerable acclaim earlier this year. She currently lives with her husband, a dog, and a large number of well-folded paper-towels in Chicago, Illinois.

MATTHEW CORRADI is the production manager for the multimedia department of the local PBS affiliate in Tucson, Arizona.

By day he scuffles with the lesser gods of the video industry and by night he enjoys the greater enchantments of the domestic realm with his wife and three magical children. Every once in a blue moon he manages to spin a "tall" tale such as "Journey to Gantica."

MATTHEW JOHNSON lives in Ottawa with his wife Megan. Recent and forthcoming stories of his can be found in places such as *Asimov's Science Fiction, Strange Horizons, Fantasy Magazine* and anthologies like *Tesseracts Ten* and *North of Infinity III*. More about him and his work can be found at his website, www.zatrikion. blogspot.com.

SARAH TOTTON'S short fiction has appeared in *Realms of Fantasy, Polyphony* 5, *The Nine Muses, Tesseracts* 9 & 10, and will shortly be appearing in *Text: UR – The New Book of Masks*. She is a third place winner in the L. Ron Hubbard's Writers of the Future Contest.

JEFFREY FORD was born in West Islip, New York in 1955. He worked as a machinist and as a clammer, before studying English with John Gardner at the State University of New York. He is the author of six novels, including World Fantasy Award winner *The Physiognomy, The Portrait of Mrs. Charbuque,* and Edgar Allan Poe Award winner *The Girl in the Glass.* His short fiction is collected in World Fantasy Award winning collection *The Fantasy Writer's Assistant and Other Stories* and in *The Empire of Ice Cream.* His short fiction has won the World Fantasy, Nebula Awards, and Fountain Awards. He is currently working on a new novel, *The Shadow Year,* which will be published next year. Ford lives in southern New Jersey where he teaches writing and literature.

MARGO LANAGAN has written poetry, novels and short stories for adult, young adult and junior readers. Her second collection of speculative fiction short stories, *Black Juice,* was widely acclaimed, won two World Fantasy Awards, two Ditmars and two Aurealis Awards, and was shortlisted for the *Los Angeles Times* Book Prize and made an Honor Book in the American Library Association's Michael L. Printz Award. The story "Wooden Bride"was shortlisted for the James Tiptree Jr Award, and "Singing My Sister Down" was nominated for many other awards, including a Nebula and a Hugo. Her third collection, *Red Spikes*, will be published in the US in October 2007. Margo lives in Sydney, Australia.

DANIEL HANDLER is the author of the books *The Basic Eight*, *Watch Your Mouth*, and *Adverbs*. He is also, as Lemony Snicket, the author of a sequence of novels for children collectively entitled *A Series of Unfortunate Events*. He lives in San Francisco with his wife and child.

RICHARD PARKS lives in Mississippi with one wife and a varying number of cats. His fiction has appeared in *Asimov's SF*, *Realms of Fantasy*, *Lady Churchill's Rosebud Wristlet*, *Fantasy Magazine*, *Weird Tales*, and numerous anthologies. His first story collection, *The Ogre's Wife*, was a World Fantasy Award finalist. A stand-alone novella, *Hereafter and After*, is scheduled for early 2007 from PS Publishing (UK) as a signed, limited edition. His second story collection, *Worshipping Small Gods* (Prime Books), is scheduled for early 2007 and should be out even as you read this.

ELISE MOSER has published short stories in a variety of periodicals, including *Flytrap*, and anthologies, including *Witpunk* and *Island Dreams*. Several of her stories received Honorable Mentions in *Year's Best Fantasy and Horror* 2004 and 2006. With Claude Lalumière, she co-edited *Lust for Life: Tales of Sex and Love*.

BENJAMIN ROSENBAUM lives in Virginia with his wife Esther, his son Noah, and his daughter Aviva, who describes him thusly: "he is grat.he likes being jumpt on.and loves kids." His stories have appeared in *F&SF*, *Asimov's*, *Strange Horizons*, *Nature*, *Harper's*, and *McSweeney's*, and been nominated for a Nebula, a Hugo, a Sturgeon and a BSFA award. Despite Noah's insistence, he does not want to turn into a pig. See his website at http://www.benjaminrosenbaum.com

RICH HORTON is a software engineer in St. Louis. He is a contributing editor to *Locus*, for which he does short fiction reviews and occasional book reviews; and to *Black Gate*, for which he does a continuing series of essays about SF history. He also contributes book reviews to *Fantasy Magazine*, and to many other publications.

PUBLICATION HISTORY

PUBLICATION HISTORY